INSPIRED BY

THE ANCESTRAL RING OF HOPE

A high price for freedom in war torn Hungary

S. E. O'CONNOR

O'Connor, S. E. (author)
The Ancestral Ring of Hope
ISBN: 978-1-922890-45-0
Fiction / Historical / War

Georgia Regular 10pt/15pt

Cover and book design by Green Hill Publishing

DEDICATION

To my mother, Katalin.

A truly inspiring and courageous woman.

MAPS OF HUNGARY

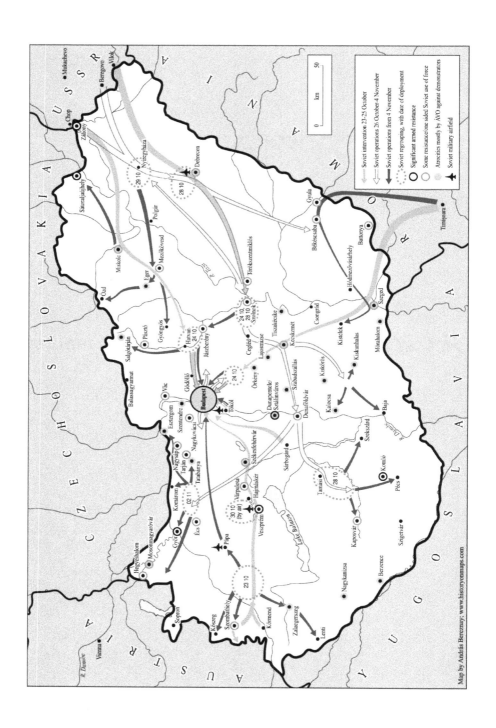

Map by András Bereznay: www.historyonmaps.com

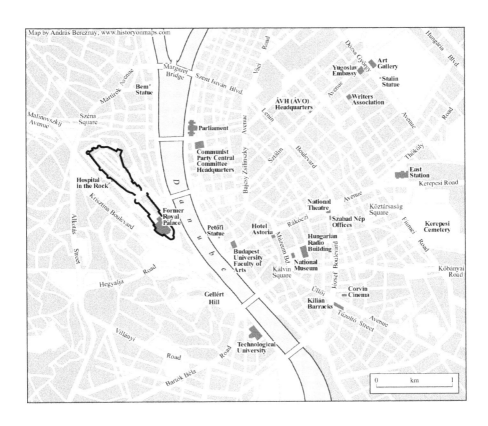

Map by András Bereznay, www.historyonmaps.com

Margaret
Bridge

Mártírok Avenue

Bem
Statue

Szent István Blvd.

Váci Road

Dózsa György

Yugoslav
Embassy

Art
Gallery

Stalin
Statue

Hungária Blvd.

Malinovszkij
Avenue

Széna
Square

ÁVH (ÁVO)
Headquarters

Avenue

Writers
Association

Lenin

Avenue

Road

Parliament

Avenue

Communist
Party Central
Committee
Headquarters

Bajcsy Zsilinszky

Sztálin

Boulevard

Thököly

Hospital
in the Rock

Danube

East
Station

Krisztina Boulevard

Kerepesi Road

Former
Royal
Palace

National
Theatre

Avenue

Köztársaság
Square

Petőfi
Statue

Hotel
Astoria

Rákóczi

Szabad Nép
Offices

Fiumei

Kerepesi
Cemetery

Alkotás
Street

Hegyalja

Road

Budapest
University
Faculty of
Arts

Múzeum Bd.

Hungarian
Radio
Building

Road

Kálvin
Square

National
Museum

József Boulevard

Kőbányai
Road

Üllői

Corvin
Cinema

Villányi

Gellért
Hill

Kilián
Barracks

Tűzoltó Street

Avenue

Road

Road

Technological
University

Bartók Béla

0   km   1

KEY POLITICAL FIGURES

Joseph Stalin (1878 – 1953)
General Secretary of the Communist Party of the Soviet Union
(April 1922 – October 1952)

Nikita Khrushchev (1894 – 1971)
First Secretary of the Communist Party of the Soviet Union
(September 1953 – October 1964)

Mátyás Rákosi (1892 – 1971)
First Secretary of the Hungarian Working People's Party
(June 1948 – July 1956)
Prime Minister and Chairman of the Council of Ministers of the People's Republic
of Hungary
(August 1952 – July 1953)

Imre Nagy (1896 – 1958)
Chairman of the Council of Ministers of the Hungarian People's Republic
(July 1953 – April 1955 and again between 24 October 1956 – 4 November 1956)
Minister of Foreign Affairs (2 November 1956 – 4 November 1956)

Anastas Mikoyan (1895 – 1978)
First Deputy Chairman of the Council of Ministers of the Soviet Union
(February 1955 – July 1964)

Ernő Gerő (1898 – 1980)
First Secretary of the Hungarian Working People's Party
(July 1956 – October 1956)
Minister of the Interior (July 1953 – June 1954)

János Kádár (1912 – 1989)
General Secretary of the Hungarian Socialist Worker's Party
(October 1956 – May 1988)

PROLOGUE

Puffing on his favourite cherry root pipe, Stalin patiently waited for Churchill to conclude his deliberations regarding Eastern Europe. The room was warmed and scented by the huge pine wood fire. Stalin found himself sweating under his heavy uniform. The others didn't seem particularly affected. Dabbing the sweat from the back of his neck with his worn handkerchief he feigned interest in the conversation.

World War II was ending. Japan needed to be crushed, and the German allies punished for their decision to support the Nazi regime. Of course, he would assist Churchill and Roosevelt in defeating Japan in the Pacific as was promised at the Yalta Conference. Nonetheless, Stalin had no intention of complying with the demands of the Western Allies in forming a democratic government. It was obvious that the war had taken a great toll on everyone, and the political will to further debate the issue around sovereignty of Eastern Bloc nations was dissipating.

"How feeble they really are", he mused, peering at Churchill and Roosevelt, scratching the stubble on his chin, dabbing the moisture from his brow. Words have no meaning without action, and it was clear that no action would be taken by the weakened democracies of the bourgeois. Whilst Stalin appeared to listen intently to the tired, old men before him, he chuckled to himself.

***

Hungary was an independent country prior to the Second World War. Its borders constantly shifted after generations of skirmishes. The Mongols invaded twice. Their first successful campaign was launched in 1241 under Batu Khan, decimating the Hungarian population and reducing the kingdom to ashes. The second invasion in 1285 was thwarted by the stone castles and fortifications that were constructed under their sovereign, King Béla. A long period of stability, expansion, and prosperity followed in Hungary.

Dark forces were gathering once again, yet the Hungarians—too consumed by their own internal power struggles—failed to notice the looming threat. By the late 15th and early 16th centuries another power was on the rise, the Ottoman Empire, the second most populous political state in the world. Their military activities in the region went largely unnoticed by the feudal lords and wealthy merchants, who were too busy bickering over land rights and expanding their holdings at the expense of the Hungarian Treasury. With finances heavily depleted, the country's defences swiftly declined. Guards went unpaid, fortresses fell into disrepair, and efforts to increase taxes to build the coffers failed. Hungary was vulnerable to attack once more.

Hungary looked to the Habsburg Monarchy as a defence against the ongoing Ottoman expansion. The remainder of the Hungarian Kingdom came under the rule of the Habsburgs. The Turks suffered a significant defeat in the Great Turkish Wars of 1683-1699, and large amounts of territory were reclaimed by the Hungarians. War continued between the Habsburgs and the Ottomans for many more years, until the final onslaught in 1787-1791, when Habsburg-Austria allied with Russia and defeated the Ottomans.

Whilst peace was restored for a time, an unease swept the people of Hungary, who demanded independence from Austria. The failed uprising of 1848 was a huge disappointment for the Hungarians—particularly the intellectuals. They paid a heavy price for their insurrection by being placed under Martial Law, with a military dictatorship controlling the nation. Continued military campaigns by Austria against Prussia led to a complete defeat in 1866. The Habsburg Empire was close to bankruptcy and on the brink of collapse. To save their dynasty, the Habsburgs were forced to reconcile with Hungary. In 1867, an alliance with the Habsburgs resulted in the establishment of the Austrian-Hungarian Monarchy, and peace once again descended upon the land.

By 1914, the Austro-Hungarian Empire was one of the great powers of Europe. Of the fifty-two million people governed by the empire, Hungarians represented forty percent of the total population, and Hungary comprised forty-eight percent of the territory. When the First World War broke out, Hungary and Austria joined forces with Germany. After the United States entered the war against the Germans in 1917, Hungary soon realised that it had backed the wrong side.

World War I ended for Austria and Hungary with a comprehensive military defeat which spelt the collapse of the Austro-Hungarian Empire. At the Treaty of Trianon, signed on the 4th of June 1920, Hungary suffered a devastating blow by losing two-thirds of its territory and sixty percent of its population. Independent nation states were created. Under the leadership of Miklós Horthy, the Kingdom of Hungary rose from the ashes.

In 1934, Hungary entered a trade agreement with Germany to stimulate the Hungarian economy. The deal meant that in exchange for a favourable price for Hungary's wheat, the funds were retained in a German bank account, whereby Hungary would purchase German industrial goods. This provided Germany with economic domination over Hungary, making the smaller nation inextricably tied to their neighbour during the years leading up to World War II.

During the latter stages of the Second World War, when the United States joined the fray, it was apparent that Hungary had backed the wrong side once again. Hitler's suicide on the 30th of April 1945 led to Germany's unconditional surrender on the 7th of May 1945, thereby sealing Hungary's fate. War reparations devastated the economy for decades.

Many intellectuals fled Hungary after the Second World War, as fears of a Russian occupation rose. The Hungarian elite understood the impact of communist dogma on Russia, and few remained in the country to live through the effects of the occupation that were destined to grip Hungary. The unsuspecting populace was in for a rude awakening with the advent of Soviet annexation.

Down through the centuries, hostile neighbours and constant battles resulting in the continuous shifting of borders had made it difficult for the Hungarian economy to flourish. Its people, however, were free thinking, creative, and enterprising—taking credit for inventions such as the safety match and the biro. From farming to movies, the economy was based upon a variety of industries, many of which were privately owned. Innovation and entrepreneurship were a way of life in Hungary, with opportunities for all to prosper.

Education, particularly in the arts and sciences, was extremely valued. The country produced highly acclaimed and distinguished academics. Several Nobel Prize winners emanated from Hungary, for innovations in physics, medicine, and chemistry. Albert Szent-Gyorgyi, a biochemist, won the Nobel Prize in Physiology in 1937 for first isolating vitamin C and discovering the components and reactions of the citric acid cycle. Georg Von Hevesy, a radiochemist, won the Nobel Prize in Chemistry in 1943 for his key role in the development of radioactive tracers to study chemical processes such as the metabolism of animals.

The cultural, intellectual, and spiritual fabric of Hungarian society was completely at odds with the doctrines of the communist Soviets, who, in turn, underestimated the spirit and determination of the Hungarian people.

***

As the trio sat around the conference table debating the future of post-war Europe, Stalin was already formulating his own plan for world domination. The Soviet Union hosted the meeting at the Livadia Palace in the resort town of Yalta, located on the south coast of the Crimean Peninsula. The stunning palace of one hundred and sixteen rooms, constructed from local limestone as white as alabaster, was the summer retreat of the last Russian Tsar, Nichols II.

From a position of strength on home ground, Stalin played the part of the perfect host. Silver trays with an array of his favourite sweets were placed in the centre of the table. Coffee and English teas were offered as refreshments. Selecting a walnut, honey, and cinnamon pastry, he savoured the burst of flavour as he popped it into his mouth, sighing with pleasure. Smiling amicably at Churchill and Roosevelt, demonstrating a cooperative spirit of compromise, the Yalta Agreement was signed in February 1945. One of the conditions of the agreement was to conduct a democratic election in Hungary. Stalin allowed the farce to play out, to demonstrate compliance with the agreement.

The Smallholders Party, an anti-fascist group that represented the interests of landed peasants and the urban middle class, advocated for land reform and democratisation. They won a landslide victory at the election on the 4th of November 1945, much to the surprise of the Communists. Whilst the Hungarian Communist Party, under the leadership of Mátyás Rákosi and Ernő Gerő, secured only seventeen percent of the vote, Stalin refused to allow the Smallholders Party to take full control of parliament. A coalition was formed, with members of the Communist Party holding key positions in government—including finance, the interior ministry, transport, social welfare, and the post of Deputy Prime Minister.

Soviet influence was carefully camouflaged during this early phase of reconstruction. They controlled the secret police, and covertly infiltrated the shaky post-war government. By 1949, the Communists completed the takeover by establishing the People's Republic of Hungary. The war was over in Europe, yet the ideological conflict that was to overwhelm the citizens of Hungary was just beginning.

The sweeping changes that occurred post-World War II took the masses by surprise. The Russian Red Army targeted their perceived political enemies, together with various ethnic groups, with violent consequences. Land holdings were confiscated and redistributed according to the ideology of collectivism. Local communists quickly took control of the media and radio network to ensure all Hungarians received the exact messages Stalin wanted to embed into the psyche of the population. Religions and independent community groups, such as the Boy Scouts and Girl Scouts, were closely scrutinised and eventually banned. Priests were persecuted as traitors. A desire to create ethnically homogeneous nation states led to the mass expulsion of Germans living in Hungary.

Communist propaganda seeped through every inch of society. The rise of the working class at the expense of the middle class was applauded. Free thinking was not only forbidden, but it was also deemed to be duplicitous. Private businesses were nationalised. Creativity was quashed. Education was completely censored. No-one knew who could be trusted. Family members and friends betrayed each other to the Red Army as a self-preservation tool, claiming disloyalty and other anti-establishment behaviour. Fear permeated throughout the nation. It was only a matter of time before the fabric of this new society would unravel, birthing a rebellion.

PART ONE

1953: THE DECLINE OF STALINISM

CHAPTER ONE

Perspiration snaked down his spine at the sound of footsteps rever-berating along the corridor. Cold beads of salty sweat made his skin itch profusely under the filthy rag that barely covered his body. The echo of boots smacking the concrete floor became louder and louder, a sure purpose in their stride. Panic gripped him. Bile welled up in his throat in anticipation of what was to come. Suppressing the urge to vomit was futile, but only a thin, red-tinged spittle dribbled down his chin from his raspy throat, his stomach churning from the lack of sustenance, not having eaten since the previous morning. He held his breath as the key was inserted into the lock, trembling uncontrollably—not just from the bitter cold but from fear of the dreaded pain that would soon be inflicted upon him. Shutting his eyes tightly he screamed silently over and over in his mind, *"Leave me be"*.

Years of decay seeped through the fabric of the building, mixing with the stale, metallic odour of dried blood and urine that encrusted the damp, crumbling walls and bare concrete floor of his cell, filling his nostrils with an unrelenting stench that made him constantly gag, even though he had been confined there for months. He would not allow himself to become accustomed to the sounds and smells of this place. Determined to retain his humanity, he gloried in his disgust of his surroundings and the monsters he faced each day. His blood mingled with the blood of others who had inhabited this space over decades. How many had died here before him? The ghosts were a constant torment as he wondered if this would be the day he joined them.

"Please, please, not me," he whimpered.

Sentenced to three years in a Gulag prison for having the nerve to question his superiors, and demand better working conditions and fairer production quotas, István feared he would rot in his cell. No one knew where he was. No one cared for his safety, save perhaps the men he had tried to protect. But they were powerless to help him, frightened for their own lives and families. In fact, he wasn't altogether sure which prison he had been taken to. Knocked senseless by his interrogators in Budapest, he'd been bound, gagged, and thrown into a windowless truck with a dozen other men, before awaking to his new reality.

Many of the guards took pleasure in the different forms of torture they inflicted upon the inmates. It was a game to them. In recent months they had been acting in a conciliatory manner, asking the prisoners which punishment they preferred, from a selection of choices including tearing out fingernails, administering electric shocks, beatings, or having their heads submerged in a bucket of icy water for several minutes at a time, not knowing if they would drown that day. Some days the guards would draw straws as to which of them would conduct the torture while the other watched, laughing with each muffled scream that escaped from the bruised lips of the defiant prisoners. Shame consumed István whenever he heard others screaming in the adjacent cells, knowing that he would be spared that day. Yet he still felt the pain, almost as if it had been inflicted upon him, further punishment for his shameful thoughts. Humanity was left outside the gates of the stone fortress. Prisoners were treated worse than stray dogs, deemed traitors to the Communist Party, lucky to be incarcerated and not executed, as was the fate of so many others.

The footsteps suddenly stopped. There was a clink of keys and he held his breath, his heart pounding in his emaciated chest. *"At least it's still beating,"* he thought.

"Today's your lucky day," the guard said nonchalantly, wrenching open the steel door.

István closed his eyes, unable to speak.

"Hey, I'm speaking to you," the guard barked, kicking him in the ribs. "Where's your respect? Look at me when I address you."

Cowering in a foetal position, István screamed as a bolt of pain pierced his side, his cracked ribs surely now broken. Nevertheless, he opened his right eye and glared at the guard. His left eye was still swollen shut and encrusted with blood.

"I've got news for you. There'll be no punishment today. In fact, it's over for you. Stalin is dead. We have a new leader—Nikita Khrushchev—and he's decreed that prisoners like you are to be released. You are free to go." And then, the guard raised his right fist to his heart as a sign of allegiance and pronounced in a loud voice, "Long live Khrushchev!"

István's head was reeling as the guard strode away down the corridor. *Free to go? Was this a joke?* Shaking his head to clear the cobwebs from his clouded and exhausted mind he became aware of the sounds of people running and shouting. Unable to believe what the guard had said, he listened intently for the sound of gun shots. Was this a trap to lure everyone outside to be killed? Disbelieving the notion of freedom, István strained to hear above the clamour in the corridor but couldn't hear gunfire. Clutching his left side where his broken ribs repeatedly stabbed him with the most excruciating pain with each breath, he gingerly stood and hobbled to the entrance of his cell. Tentatively peering out, he was astonished to see prisoners scurrying in all directions. Some of them were supporting those too weak to stand on their own. *Was it true then? Were they free to leave?* As he gathered his wits to digest this revelation, István staggered into the corridor and grabbed the arm of a prisoner passing his cell, "Hey, is it true, we're free?" he wheezed through his cracked lips, his vocal cords unused to speaking.

"That's what they said," the man replied. "So, I'm getting the hell out of here before they change their mind."

István stared at him through his one good eye. "Can you help me? I don't know the way."

The other prisoner looked him over, and taking pity on the broken man clutching his arm with surprising force, replied, "Hell, you're in a bad way. Here, lean on me. I'll get you out of here. But we've got to hurry. As I said, we don't want the guards to change their minds."

István did his best to keep up with his new friend, who was in much better shape than he, as the man walked briskly, half dragging him along. They shuffled to the infirmary in search of medical supplies and warm clothing but in the chaos of escaping prisoners, soon became separated, the corridors filled with men pushing and shoving each other out of the way. István lost sight of his friend amongst the crowd of desperate men. Unfamiliar with the layout of the prison, it took István precious minutes to finally locate the entrance to the infirmary. The room was quite large, with a row of single beds along one wall. Then, in the far corner of the room, he spotted a tall glass cabinet where several men were congregating. He noticed that the glass doors had been smashed, and broken glass was scattered on the floor. Tiptoeing around the jostling men, careful not to cut the soles of his bare feet, he edged his way forward until he reached the cabinet. Fossicking through the remnants of the supplies that were strewn around the cabinet, he found an array of bandages and picked up the largest pieces he could find, before moving out of the way to the furthest corner of the room, where he carefully bound his torso to restrict his upper body movement. Sharp pain sliced through every sinew of his being with each twist and turn, yet he persevered, knowing it would allow him to walk more easily. Despite the cold, fresh beads of sweat trickled down his face, such was the effort to bind his ribs. Returning to the cabinet in the hope of finding pain killers he rummaged around until he found a bottle of pills. The Russian word for pain, боль, was the only word István could decipher, so he swallowed a couple of tablets then pocketed the bottle, chastising himself for failing to learn Russian beyond rudimentary conversation.

Odd pieces of clothing lay about an adjacent room, so he sifted through the piles and changed into a crumpled pair of trousers, a baggy grey shirt and a heavy, black, woollen coat that reached his ankles. Finding a few pairs of old boots that had been abandoned in a cupboard, he slid his feet into a slightly oversized pair. They would have to do. Scanning the room for anything else that might be useful, he grabbed a blanket and a pillow slip to use as a rucksack, then followed a few of the other prisoners towards the kitchen in the hope of finding food for the journey. Thankfully, there was plenty of bread and cheese left in the larder but no other fresh food that he could find. Unsure how long it would take to reach Budapest, he took as much as he thought was needed for a few days travel, then shuffled his way outside in search of his new-found friend. Surprisingly, the guards left the prisoners unmolested, allowing the men to take whatever they wanted for their arduous journey.

The sky was a brilliant, cobalt blue. The air was crisp and still. A light snowfall the night before had blanketed the landscape with a thin carpet of white crystals that sparkled like diamonds. Once he stepped outside, István instinctively shut his eyes. Having spent many months in his dark, windowless cell, the glare from the late morning sun stabbed viciously at his good eye. So, for the moment, he stood still, revelling in the clear, fresh air, cautiously filling his lungs with every breath, which meant tolerating the pain from his damaged ribs. Though the sun's rays were weak, he felt the healing power of the warmth that caressed his upturned face. Smiling for the first time in over a year and glad to be alive he searched the crowd. A trail of dishevelled men was already making its way through the gates of the prison, to freedom. Sentries lined the path, their demeanour relaxed, rifles by their sides, non-threatening. Another sign that they were free to leave. Reaching into his rucksack, he pulled out a small piece of rye bread and began to hungrily devour it, when a hand clapped him on the shoulder.

"So, there you are. Got everything?" the man asked.

István nodded, pleased that his new friend had sought him out. Completely disoriented, he had no clue where he was in relation to Budapest and could only hope his fellow Hungarian was familiar with their whereabouts.

"I'm truly grateful for your help. My name's István and I come from Budapest but I've no idea how to get there."

"As it happens, that's where I'm headed," the man replied. "Sándor's my name." Glancing down at István's filthy hands, he thought better of sealing their introduction with the usual greeting of a handshake. "The nearest railroad is only about five kilometres west of here. Freight trains pass through this area regularly. We can hitch a ride to Moscow and make our way to Budapest from there. You look a bit sturdier than when I lost you near the infirmary. Are you able to walk on your own?"

István nodded, "I think so. I've taken some pain killers and bandaged my chest as best I could. It should see me through."

"Good. Let's go then."

Avoiding probing questions as to how this man knew so much, an overwhelming sense of hope clutched István's heart. It was the first hint of compassion he had experienced in a long time. Too weak to think clearly, he was grateful that someone else was taking control and that he needed only to follow. A few tears of joy filled the corner of his eyes, but he blinked them away, steeling himself for the journey ahead. Imprisoned for almost a year, and having endured horrendous acts of torture, he was dangerously thin and battered compared to some of the other prisoners, including Sándor. Deciding that they must have been new arrivals, István noticed that Sándor looked relatively unscathed. The only hint of abuse was the dark rings that circled his eyes, and he carried not an ounce of fat. Regardless, István happily followed Sándor, hoping he'd be home soon.

A handful of grey clouds that dotted the sky, staining the otherwise clear day, were not particularly threatening. A good omen for their journey home. Off they marched in the direction of the railroad, a motley collection of several dozen souls. Occasionally, one of them would steal a glance behind to see if the guards were lurking nearby with rifles aimed at their backs. None were visible. Only when the prison was nothing more than a speck in the distance did István and the others relax. Someone started humming the Hungarian anthem, and before long more voices joined in. Another group was singing in Polish. Freedom was a whisper in the chilly air which each and every one of them greedily breathed in.

Five kilometres did not sound that far, yet the railroad was still not in sight after four hours of travelling. The going was slow given the physical state of the men, and whilst the snow was not deep, the crystals were slippery underfoot, further hindering their progress. Sándor remained with István, as promised, and despite his best efforts to walk on his own István struggled to stay upright after the first three hours. Without hesitation, Sándor grabbed István's left arm and slung it over his neck in support. They stopped once to rest, ate some bread and cheese, then pushed on. Snow was scooped up and sucked insatiably from the palms of their hands, heedless of the icy coldness that left their mouths burning. István swallowed another couple of the pills stashed in the deep pocket of his heavy coat whenever the pain intensified. Twice they encountered a farmhouse hoping to seek shelter, a little warmth, or perhaps a nip of vodka. It was not to be. Doors remained locked and curtains drawn. The locals feared the prisoners. No one wanted to invite trouble. The group trudged on, a long line of men winding their way home.

Up ahead, some of the men seemed agitated, waving their arms, and pointing to the sky. Word passed down the line that the rumbling of a train was just audible. A faint trace of what appeared to be black smoke was billowing into the air. A surge of energy pulsed through the group as they hurried towards their salvation, cheering, and whistling excitedly. István was at the end of the pack with the other severely battered men, and though his injuries hampered his progress, he too managed to pick up the pace, adrenalin pumping through his veins. The slow-moving train seemed to go on for ever, with some thirty or more carriages crawling along behind the steam engine. By the time István reached the railroad most of the others had already jumped into the open carriages. Sándor easily climbed aboard, and with the help of another man grabbed István's arms and hoisted him in. With a thump and another agonising stab in his chest he collapsed onto the wooden floor. Remnants of straw and large pats of cow dung lay scattered around them. The rural smells were a comforting change from the damp stench of death in his cell. Exhaustion and agony from the difficult trek through the slippery snow, combined with sheer elation that he had survived the first leg of the journey, assaulted his frailty. With his head in his hands, István succumbed to his emotions and wept, alleviating some of the pent-up tension in his stiff body. Sándor lifted a hand to pat István's shoulder, then thought better of it and left him in peace.

Growling stomachs cut through the subdued atmosphere. Laughing, the newfound friends shared their provisions. Sándor's presence of mind led to his kitchen raid being more fruitful that István's meagre bread and cheese stash. A paring knife, a mug, and a flask had been taken. Filling the flask with water, it served as an emergency supply once the snow was no longer accessible. Further snooping led him to another room, where he located the commercial fridges. Few items were transportable, save for two twenty-centimetre-long pieces of salami. Pulling one of these from his rucksack, Sándor proudly displayed it to István—a prize worth more than gold. István whooped with delight at the sight of the delicacy as Sándor cut a few thick slices, handing him a piece. Between bites they chatted amicably about what awaited them in Budapest. Despite the easy banter, Sándor saw István's pain clearly etched on his furrowed brow. The pills he'd ingested had obviously worn off.

"We should get some sleep. It's a long way to Moscow, so we have plenty of time," Sándor suggested as he shuffled away from the door and settled himself on a patch of straw.

Reaching into his coat pocket, István pulled out the bottle of pills, popped another couple into his mouth, then tossed his head back to force them down his throat. He curled up in the corner of the carriage, draped his blanket over his shoulders and instantly fell into a deep sleep. It was the first time in more than twelve months that he was able to sleep peacefully, without the usual nightmares of being tortured or killed.

***

"Good of you to join us again. Here, have a drink!" Sándor said, pushing a mug of water to István's parched lips as he stirred, half awake.

He drank deeply and wiped his mouth on the sleeve of his coat. Rubbing a hand over his face to rouse himself he asked, "How long have I slept?"

"Quite a few hours, although I'm not too sure, as I dozed off for a while as well. At one point I thought you were dead; your breathing was that shallow. Glad you're still with us," Sándor remarked, smiling broadly.

"I'm not done yet," István replied, smiling back, his mood lifting after the much-needed rest.

"We'll be changing trains soon so you should eat something. Get a little of your strength back."

Reaching into his rucksack, István pulled out a small piece of cheese and tore off a chunk of bread which he hastily consumed before instinctively reaching for another couple of painkillers. Checking the contents of the bottle, he hoped they would last until they reached Budapest.

"Do you know why we were released, Sándor? The guard didn't explain anything, other than that Stalin is dead and the new leader ordered us to be freed. I didn't even know that Stalin had died."

István chewed the stale bread, his words muffled as he contemptuously added, "The prison guards hardly kept me abreast of news from the outside world. I was transported here in January after about a fortnight in custody when I was arrested in Budapest, and Stalin was still alive then."

"I didn't realise you were imprisoned for so long. No wonder you look a wreck. Well, Stalin died in March. Khrushchev's the new leader, but it took a few months before he was installed as First Secretary of the Communist Party. As for why we were released, I'm not too sure, although most of the men I've spoken to are political prisoners who were incarcerated for less than five years. I received a four-year sentence three months ago for advocating freedom of speech across the university where I work. My superiors had me arrested for contradicting communist principles and inciting unrest amongst the students. I suppose I should have expected it. Still, I managed to avoid the beatings that so many of you suffered. Being a university professor, and fluent in Russian, the prison warden had me translating some documents from Hungarian to Russian. It's how I managed to get snippets of news. But it was exhausting work, forcing me to sit at a desk for sixteen hours a day with only two twenty-minute breaks during that time. I often dozed off, but a guard would check on me from time to time and smack the back of my head, yelling at me to keep writing. I never anticipated that my university degree would save my life." Sándor chuckled.

"Lucky you. Only three months in that hell hole. I was arrested for my big mouth," István said, then went on the explain the circumstances of his arrest.

Peering through the gaps in the wooden slats of the carriage walls, István saw that they were now passing through larger towns. The drab rundown dwellings were crammed closer together. The streets were silent, with only the occasional truck rumbling down the road, providing a contrast to the otherwise desolate landscape. Just a few solitary people were spotted going about their business. The scenes were depressing. If this was the Soviet ideal that the Hungarians were forced to embrace, then the future looked bleak. Shaking the gloom from his thoughts, István reminded himself that he was on his way home, free from prison, with an opportunity for a second chance at life.

CHAPTER 2

Ruby droplets of blood spilled onto the white lace. The scissors clattered to the ground and Natália instinctively sucked her thumb like a petulant child. She pushed the chair back and ran to fetch a wet towel to gently sponge off the blood before it permanently stained the delicate bodice of the gown. Her daily quota of tasks had increased over the past two weeks and she struggled to keep up, hence the small mistakes that had begun creeping into her work. She silently cursed herself as she dabbed away the evidence of her inattention. Errors were not part of her meticulous nature and it upset her terribly.

Treated as a slave by her Godmother and employer, Mrs Kalmár, Natália's spirit and passion for her craft was waning. The team of six dressmakers worked from 8am to 6.30pm for five days of the week, and half a day every second Saturday on a rotational shift. Only one thirty-minute break was permitted. The girls ate their lunch outside in the courtyard, savouring the small opportunity for the warmth and brightness of the sunshine. Three of the girls smoked cigarettes. Their wages were docked for each minute they stopped working when they stepped outside for a cigarette break, such were the strict conditions wielded by Mrs Kalmár.

The workshop was a small, low-ceilinged room with a large window facing north, maximising the natural light needed for the delicate needlework. It was painted white to reflect the light streaming in. Only two feet separated each wooden trestle table, each housing garments at various stages of completion. Each corner of the room was cluttered with a variety of fabrics: summer weight, winter woollens, satins and silks for evening wear, wedding chiffons and lace, linings—every conceivable cloth required for the current fashions. Shelves lined two of the walls with containers bursting with beads, buttons, braids, faux pearls, cottons, zippers, and a multitude of other haberdashery, all meticulously labelled. Thick dust from the materials constantly hung in the air causing sneezing fits throughout the day. A large jug of water and six tumblers were left on a table near the door of the workroom each morning to wash away the grime from their dry throats.

In contrast, at the front of the premises, the reception room in which the clients were received was elegantly furnished. The timber parquetry floor gleamed like a mirror. Three antique sofas and four chairs covered in royal blue damask were positioned in the centre of the room, together with two large antique burr walnut coffee tables. The seating could accommodate up to a dozen visitors—a necessity as ladies frequently brought an entourage of friends and children, to assist with choosing styles or to have their own miniature creations fitted. Fabric samples hung from a rail at one end of the room, from the most delicate of laces to the heaviest winter woollens. Patrons were encouraged to sit, partake in refreshments, and peruse the salon's portfolio of designs for inspiration whilst they waited to be attended. Off to the right of the entrance were three fitting rooms, also elegantly furnished, with large, cushioned antique chairs and an enormous rectangular mirror on each wall to maximise the reflection from all angles. Mrs Kalmár ran the most exclusive dressmaking salon in the district, and her clientele was the who's who of Szarvas and the neighbouring towns, including Szolnok and Kecskemét. A small handful of her regular customers even ventured from Budapest; such was her reputation. Over three decades of changing fashions, the salon had continued to burgeon through word of mouth to become a thriving and well-respected enterprise.

The best quality materials and other accessories were sourced from Budapest. General haberdashery and stock standard fabrics were easily obtained in Szarvas, but the wealthier clients—particularly the wives of senior government officials—demanded exclusivity in design. Mrs Kalmár would venture to Budapest, often spending two or three days seeking out the more exquisite cloths and trimmings, haggling with her regular suppliers on quantity and price. Natália's ambition was to design and create the dresses, suits, and evening wear the younger women wore to church on Sundays, on more formal occasions such as weddings and christenings, and even to the nightclubs. Travelling to the wholesale fabric houses and selecting the most up to date styles and colours for her designs was something she yearned to do, yet her Godmother refused to allow Natália to accompany her. "You don't need to know how to run the salon. Just stick to the tasks I give you," would be the usual offhand response whenever Natália begged her Godmother to let her go on the buying trips.

A bright nineteen-year-old, Natália Kardos was the most talented graduate from her recently completed four-year dressmaking apprenticeship, and her Godmother knew it. For years she hand-stitched delicate beads, sequence and faux pearls of all shapes and sizes onto the white organza and silk wedding dresses. Beautiful floral patterns with leaves and stems tightly packed upon the bodice, gradually dissipating down the length of the gown. Some had long trains which were as intricately beaded as the bodice, whilst others were shorter and simpler. It often took many days to draft the designs and transpose them onto the fabrics before the beading could commence. The other girls were not as accomplished nor did they have the patience for such delicate work.

Natália had a flair for sketching from nature, and this was one of her most pleasurable tasks. Her inspiration was taken from the garden and adjacent fields on her grandmother's property where she was a frequent visitor. Delicate red poppies swayed in the spring breeze like a romantic waltz. Ancient rose bushes in a variety of colours, some highly perfumed, overwhelmed the senses. Bees buzzed in and out of the lavender shrubs that framed the rose garden, catching her attention, as did the wheat stalks at various stages of growth. Spending time outdoors with her sketch pad and charcoal pencils was a pastime she relished when the weather permitted. The warmth of the sun on her face, a cup of lavender tea on the table beside her, and the larks chirping in the nearby oak trees fed her soul and sustained her through the days that followed, spent indoors, sewing. Visiting her grandmother, whom Natália loved dearly, provided an escape from the arduous life at home, where there was a constant list of chores awaiting her each day, and a scolding from her mother if something was left unattended. By contrast, her grandmother made no demands on her time;

affection and home-baked cakes were the only things that awaited her on each visit.

Supervising the fittings and making the necessary adjustments to the bodice, sleeves or hemlines was another favourite aspect of dressmaking, although Natália wasn't often allowed to interact directly with the clients. Her Godmother refused to acknowledge her worth, insisting that she was still too young and inexperienced for such a crucial job for the more important clients, which, as it happened, seemed to be most of them. The monotonous jobs were assigned each morning with strict deadlines for completion. The tasks were piecemeal. Overlocking cut sections one day, making shoulder pads and sewing buttons onto jackets the next, then laying the patterns onto the fabric and cutting out the pieces the next. The only constant in amongst it all was the beading. The beading was endless. Recognising it was work that needed to be done, Natália still found it dreary and repetitious. She yearned to create a garment from start to finish and then see how beautiful the client looked as she twirled around in the fitting room, admiring the gown from all angles, the gratifying result after hours of labour. Mostly, she was relegated to the back room with the others. Completing her apprenticeship had made no difference to her position at the salon. She was still just one of the workers. The situation became more intolerable with each passing day. Not one to give up too easily, Natália was determined to progress within the salon, and to force her Godmother to take her ambition seriously.

***

Weekends were the girls' only free time to spend socialising with friends, although they were expected to attend mass on Sunday mornings at the Szent Klára Catholic Church. It seemed everyone in the town was a practising Catholic; the church brimmed with parishioners every week. Occasionally, Natália skipped mass and caught the train to Budapest to spend the day in one of the many famous museums and galleries. She loved the city, with its history and art and fabulous cafés. Strolling down the avenues of the Sixth District, particularly the fashion hub along Andrássy Avenue and Váci Street, she would call into boutiques and check out the latest styles, always thinking about how she could adapt her own designs to those she spied in Budapest. The last indulgence of the day would be to sip coffee at one of the chic cafés before boarding the train home. Natália thoroughly loved immersing herself in the most fashionable part of town, even fantasising about the possibility of meeting a handsome man who would sweep her off her feet. These excursions, however, were met with absolute fury by her mother, who was a very strict Catholic and saw no reason to visit the city; a wasteful, futile exercise. Skipping mass was totally unacceptable. Good girls went to church with the family and did their parents' bidding. Natália was strong willed and was often at odds with her mother. They were two very different souls with completely disparate expectations in life. For this reason, Natália could never confide in her mother about her hopes and dreams of living a more elegant, fulfilled life in the city. Yet the verbal abuse Natália endured at home never deterred her from the wonderful outings in Budapest, one of her few joys in life.

Over several weeks, Natália laboured in the evenings on her own dress designs, her imagination spilling onto the page with ideas she'd picked up whilst browsing the upmarket boutiques in Budapest. With the changing seasons, winter was on the horizon. Her initial designs focused on the woollens and heavier materials needed for the harsher climate. Before leaving work, she would rifle through the fabric samples, selecting the appropriate materials and colour palate to match each of her designs. It was a thrill to envisage how each completed piece would look on one of her own, younger clients. Once her portfolio contained sketches of a variety of day and evening wear, she was ready to present her work and build a case for promotion. This would be her final attempt to convince Mrs Kalmár to allow her the opportunity to shine.

Six months after her graduation, Natália drummed up the courage to confront her Godmother.

It was a day like any other, except this day Natália had a steely resolve to advance her career. Rising early, just before the birds heralded the new dawn, she skipped breakfast, arriving at work forty minutes early, stomach churning with fear in anticipation of the impending discussion with her Godmother. Sleep had eluded her for most of the previous night, as she rehearsed over and over in her mind the best way to approach the topic. After a brief preamble about her ambition to cultivate her own clients, Natália would reveal the sketches and fabric swatches of the two suits with complementing blouses, followed by the four, casual dresses, before ending with the two evening gowns, simple in structure, yet elegant. Applying more makeup than usual to cover the dark circles under her eyes from lack of sleep and pent-up anxiety, Natália wore one of her favourite dresses and her best woollen coat in the hope of making a good impression.

"What brings you into work so early, my dear?" Mrs Kalmár quizzed her Goddaughter, eyebrows raised curiously at the compendium that Natália placed upon the table in front of her, noting that the girl's attire was more in line with a trip to the city than a day in the workroom. Natália smiled warmly at the cranky-looking woman sitting before her. Shrugging off her coat and placing it on the coat rack, Natália ignored the sharp edge to her Godmother's tone, and proceeded with her proposal.

"I've been working on new designs in the latest fashion trends that I believe will lure some of the younger women to our salon," Natália replied confidently as she opened the compendium, sliding the first two sketches out from the file and placing them alongside each other on the table.

"These two suits, whilst both double breasted, differ by the size and shape of the lapels and the number of buttons on the jackets. The skirts are similar, pencil thin, cut just below the knee. Navy blue wool, one plain the other checked, with plain cream satin blouses to complement each suit, as shown by the samples I've pinned to the sketches. These outfits would be suitable for church services or ceremonies, dining with friends or trips to the city."

Natália met her Godmother's unreadable gaze and quickly pushed on. Next, she presented the four casual dresses with a similar explanation of the styles, together with the occasions at which they could be worn and ended with the jewel in her crown: the evening gowns. Throughout Natália's presentation, Mrs Kalmár sat silently, bristling, her back as straight as a rod, patiently waiting for her young charge to finish describing each of her designs. Staring intently at the drawings in front of her, eyes finally resting on the evening gowns with heightened interest, Mrs Kalmár sniffed—the only reaction from the old woman. Taking silence from her tutor as a positive sign, Natália seized the moment and pressed her advantage.

"If you allow me to manage a small handful of new clients, I know I can produce outfits and gowns that will delight them, such as these I've already created," she said, waving a hand across her work in emphasis. "Word of mouth will generate more clients and repeat custom. I just need a chance to showcase my designs to them. This would be a great opportunity for me to utilise my creativity but also good for you to grow the number of customers and increase profits."

Butterflies fluttered around her stomach with trepidation, yet Natália remained composed as she endured standing in front of her Godmother, awaiting her response. The hair on the back of her neck was damp with sweat and she wiped her clammy palms on the sides of her dress, all the while trying to look self-assured, despite the opposite being true. Several silent minutes passed before Mrs Kalmár glanced up from the sketches and scoffed between clenched teeth, "As I have told you on previous occasions, you're too inexperienced to manage *my* clients. What do you know about design, customers, and profits? You have no idea of the cost associated with making garments. I've spent a lifetime building this establishment. Women come from all over the district seeking *my* advice on the new fashion trends. You've been sewing for what, a few short years, and you think you know everything, wanting to take over. Well, it doesn't work like that. I'll decide if we need to expand and if you're ready to manage your own clientele. Now get to work."

By the time she had finished admonishing Natália she was practically shouting at her. Anger welled up inside Natália, shocked at her Godmother's outright rejection. For a moment she just stood motionless, her lips pressed together tightly to stifle the fury that was threatening to burst through. How could she be so mean spirited, shunning new talent instead of helping the next generation? Her face bright red with fury, tears glistened in her eyes but she refused to allow the drops to slide down her cheeks. It took all her strength to let the moment pass without further comment. She hastily gathered up the sheets of paper from the table, shoved them back into her compendium and walked across to the workroom. She flung the compen-dium onto the nearest table, ran to the bathroom, locked herself in the toilet and burst into tears. Sobbing with rage, hurt, disappointment and humil-iation Natália cried until there were no tears left to shed. Wiping her face with her hanky she strode back to the workroom, picked up a piece of fabric and started sewing, without acknowledging her workmates as they slowly drifted in. Sensing her disquiet, they left her alone. As the day progressed, Natália's thoughts turned to her future. Realising that her prospects at the salon were shattered, she decided it was time to leave and make a fresh start elsewhere. Budapest had been tugging at her heart for well over a year. Could she leave all her friends and family and move to the city? The longer she dwelled on the notion the more appealing it became.

***

During the evening meal, Natália aimlessly pushed the noodles around her plate, deep in thought. Her mother glanced up at her a few times then looked around the table. The room was silent. The rest of the family ate with gusto—particularly her brother, as was his way—not allowing anything or anyone to interrupt their sole purpose of satisfying their bellies.

"Anything you wish to share with us, Natália?" her mother probed, noticing something amiss with her eldest daughter.

"Hmm? Sorry, what was that?"

"You seem a bit moody today. Something bothering you? Not boy troubles, I hope."

Natália rolled her eyes at her mother and replied, "You know I don't have a boyfriend so why jump to that conclusion?"

"How would I know if you have a boyfriend or not? You never tell me anything about what's going on with you or your friends. Really, Natália I don't know you at all anymore," the mother rebuked the daughter she was secretly jealous of, born too soon after she wed, resentful that her youth had been robbed from her and replaced with nursing the whining child now sitting opposite her, scowling.

Natália's father sat patiently, observing the heated exchange, saddened once again by the lack of empathy his wife showed their first born, the light of his life. Glancing up at Natália, noticing how rattled she seemed to be this night, he spoke in a soft calm voice and asked, "What's wrong, kicsim? Your mother's right, you seem quite distracted tonight. Are you upset about something?"

Natália took a deep breath and looked at the expectant faces peering at her from around the worn dining table, her gaze resting on her mother's stern face, the face that often frightened her into submission. Pausing, she garnered her strength, then blurted out the thoughts that had been simmering in the back of her mind for weeks, culminating in her recent decision to leave the salon, spewing her words out like a rapid-fire machine gun.

"Everything's wrong! This town, my job, my vile Godmother, the constant chores here at home. I hate my life here in Szarvas. I don't feel I belong here anymore, and I want to leave and make a fresh start in Budapest."

The truth she couldn't reveal is that she was also desperate to leave the shadow of her harsh, hardhearted mother. No matter how hard she tried to please her, her efforts were never appreciated, only criticised. It was exhausting. She wanted to give up trying and move away from the ever-present disapproval.

The usually peaceful room with its faded lace curtains and scuffed timber floorboards erupted in a cacophony of sound like gaggling geese. Everyone was talking over each other. All Natália could decipher was a string of negative words: inexperience, young, danger, duty, loyalty. Her father tried to calm everyone down, without affect. Natália tried to block out the racket, but it was useless and she ran from the room. Her youngest sibling started howling, not understanding what the fuss was about but sensing the tension and anger in the room. The noise followed her down the corridor until Natália slammed her bedroom door shut. Sliding to the floor with her back to the door, she wrapped her arms around her knees and allowed the tears to spill freely down her cheeks, giving way to her emotions. The response was everything she expected. How can they possibly understand the feeling of being trapped in a small town with little opportunity? "I'm an adult now," she mumbled to herself "and they can't stop me." A steely resolve extinguished the tears. Hurt was replaced with anger, a rage that sat in the pit of her stomach. No one was going to dictate how she should live her life, least of all her mother, a woman who rarely ventured further than the edge of town to the local market garden. For the next hour or so a plan was hatched as to when she would leave and whom she would commandeer to go with her. Courage to leave Szarvas was in short supply. Whilst Natália felt grown up, she was a little frightened to move to Budapest on her own. Moving to the city with a companion was far more appealing. Two young women exploring all that a big city has to offer was a much safer proposition. "Julia is a good friend. A bit older and wiser than me," she mused. Yes, Julia often boasted about her trips to Budapest, threatening never to return.

"Perhaps we can support one another to find good jobs and then, well, who knows?" Pleased with her decision she got up from the floor, undressed, and crawled into bed. Sleep came quickly. It was the most restful sleep she'd had in months.

Natália was the eldest of three children. Ten years separated her from her brother Lajos, whilst her little sister, Éva, was two years younger still. Her parents relied on Natália to manage certain chores around the property, feeding the pigs, chickens, and geese, and babysitting her siblings. It was too much to expect given that she was working full time as a dressmaker. Her brother was the apple of her mother's eye. Lajos could do no wrong and he knew it. Taking advantage of that, he was always getting into the kinds of mischief typical of a nine-year-old. When things went wrong or if he was caught in the act of terrorising the animals he would run to Mamma, crying, calling Natália a bully and blaming her for any mishaps. And, as always, Natália was chastised for being too hard on her brother.

It was no wonder the relationship with her mother was strained, at best. Love seemed to be reserved only for the boy-child and Natália felt this keenly. Even before her brother was born, her mother never showed much affection towards her. No cuddles, no kiss goodnight. Yet the opposite was true for Lajos. Natália knew that her father noticed the favouritism shown by her mother. How could he not? It was blatantly obvious to everyone. Yet he seemed powerless to affect any change.

Over the years, he tried discussing the matter, looking for the causes of his wife's cold-hearted behaviour, but she refused to acknowledge there was a problem. She was a complex woman and he needed to pick his battles. The strained relationship between mother and daughter not one of them. So, he stopped questioning his wife, instead giving Natália as much love and attention he could. They shared a relaxed and jovial relationship, which inadvertently fuelled his wife's hostility toward Natália, jealous of the close bond he had nurtured with their first-born daughter. He always had time for Natália, no matter how busy or tired he was. It was he who had secured her apprenticeship at the salon, and he who came to her defence whenever there was a family argument. He knew his wife resented the devotion he lavished on Natália, but it was his way of balancing the scales. It was a vicious cycle that was never going to end well.

Despite the soft spot he held for Natália, her father was a hard man with strict rules, particularly as she blossomed into womanhood. No staying out late at night. Curfew was 11.00pm. No boyfriends. Not too much make-up. In spite of this, they were like-minded in many ways and shared a strong bond. Often, they would play cards after dinner while he puffed on his favourite old pipe or talk about places he had visited in his youth, before he had married Natália's mother. A cousin of his had moved to America and they speculated on what it would be like living there. Were the customs very different? Natália was obsessed with foreign places and longed to travel the world. Her father shared the same sense of adventure and had lost opportunities to fulfil his desire to explore, with a wife who saw no purpose in venturing beyond the town walls of Szarvas.

Breakfast the next morning was a sullen affair, until Natália's mother appeared. Everyone avoided eye contact with Natália. Even Lajos was quiet for a change. But when Natália's mother took her place at the table, the venom that erupted from her mouth was shocking, shaming her daughter as an ungrateful girl who thought too highly of herself.

"So, this town isn't good enough for you? Your family no longer good enough for you? Get off your high horse. You're not royalty. What do you know about life in Budapest? You're just an inexperienced and ungrateful child!" her mother spat.

Natália struggled to keep her emotions under control, but her bottom lip quivered, too afraid to speak, fearing she would regret the words that sprung to the surface of her lips. Her mother took Natália's silence as an opportunity to keep on haranguing, "You think you can just throw away your job at the salon? Is that how you repay your Godmother for all she's done for you? You're no daughter of mine."

"Enough!"

The room was suddenly as still and silent as the local cemetery at midnight. All eyes were now focused on the head of the household. Slight in build, with mousey brown hair, Natália's father nevertheless maintained a commanding presence. Although her mother thought she had the power over everyone under the Kardos' roof, it was Natália's father who had the final say on any important matters. And this morning was one of those moments.

"Let her go," he said. "She's a grown woman now. Let her find her place in the world."

His tone softened a little when he continued, imploring,

"Mamma, we knew we'd have to let her leave sometime, and that time has come. That's the end of the matter." He then turned to Natália, smiled, and said, "You have my blessing to leave home. But know that if things don't work out, you can always come back to us."

Natália's mother fell silent, staring furiously at her husband. She got up to leave the room, glaring at Natália, keeping her voice even behind her clenched teeth.

"Go then. The sooner the better."

The following Sunday, Natália met a couple of her girlfriends at a café after the morning church service. The Spritz Café and Bar was a favourite spot in town for the young crowd. It was in the centre of the main thoroughfare. Guys hung out with their buddies, drinking vodka and beer, acting older than they really were, and eyeing off the girls who strode in. The girls, for the most part, ignored their stares. The boys leered at Natália wherever she went, always dressed impeccably in frocks she'd made herself. Her auburn, shoulder length wavy hair was quaffed in the latest styles with just enough make-up not to offend her father but to give a hint of sophistication. Piercing emerald, green eyes sparkled mischievously as she glanced around the room. Keeping her distance from those she believed inferior to her—well, all the local boys—she walked up to the counter and ordered a round of coffees. The counter was crafted from a rich rosewood timber that was magnificent once but now showed the years of neglect. Stained with a variety of spilled drinks and cigarette burns, the timber was as faded, scratched, and timeless as the rest of the town. The girls had found a quiet corner table away from the bar. As Natália approached her friends she heard them chatting about their future hopes and dreams. It was a weekly ritual. When Natália sat down, she told them of her plans to make her dreams a reality.

"I'm leaving!" she declared, smiling broadly, proud of her decision. "I've had enough of Szarvas. It's time to head to the city and get a real job instead of being treated like a servant by my Godmother. I'm sick and tired of Mamma telling me what I can and can't do with my life. It's my life and they're my choices. I'm out of here."

After a few seconds of stunned silence Kati said, "Gee Natália, you're sounding a bit too serious this time."

"I'm deadly serious," Natália replied. "I've saved some money and have enough to make a fresh start. There are great opportunities in Budapest. It's where the action is and I'm going. Besides, Pappa has given me his blessing."

She then softened her tone and added, "Of course, I expect you all to visit me once I'm settled."

Silence descended upon the group as they finished their coffees. Kati got up and walked to the counter to order another round when another one of their friends, Julia, walked in.

"Hi ladies, what's new? Any gossip for me this week?"

All heads turned to Natália, who was grinning from ear to ear. When she relayed her plan to Julia her friend squealed with delight and said, "That's brilliant news. I've been vacillating for ages about moving to the city but always chickened out when it came to the crunch."

The girls spent another couple of hours at the café, lunching on pickles and salami sandwiches whilst devising their plan to leave town for the big smoke. Julia was more than ready to take the plunge, often having thought about a permanent move. With the company of Natália, well, what a dynamic duo they would make! Plans were crystallised and timings agreed. Natália would give two weeks' notice of her resignation, and then they'd be off.

For the next fortnight Natália's mother hardly spoke to her. In fact, she ignored her completely aside from setting a place at the dinner table for her. In contrast, her father quizzed her about where she planned to stay, her expected work opportunities, how much money she would need to get settled, and offered any assistance she needed from him. He even went as far as writing a letter of introduction to two past business associates, vouching for her honesty and integrity, seeking their assistance in providing his eldest daughter a safe start in the capital. Natália's siblings were equally excited about her adventure and animatedly joined in on the conversation, neither of them really grasping the fact that her move to Budapest would be permanent. This infuriated Natália's mother even more. She sulked her way through every mealtime, her sullenness increasing as the rest of the family studiously ignored her selfish behaviour.

One evening, when Natália and her father sat together in the living room playing cards, just a few days before she was scheduled to leave for Budapest, she leant over, reached for her father's hand, and kissed his knuckles gently. Looking into his kind face she thanked him profusely for supporting her decision to leave and for paving the way for her to get settled through his contacts. Patting her cheek, he rose from the chair and disappeared out the door, returning a few minutes later with an envelope that he pressed into her hands then whispered, "A little extra to help you get established, until you secure a new job. A secret between us." He winked at her conspiratorially. Peeking into the envelope she spied a wad of cash.

Hugging him fiercely, Natália said through a choked sob, "I'll miss you terribly."

Natália's dreams were finally becoming a reality. Excitement was tinged with the regret of leaving her father and some of her girlfriends, yet she knew it was the right decision. She and Julia would take Budapest by storm. Sleep was once again elusive as her excitement mounted, as the day of departure drew closer.

CHAPTER 3

For the first time in months István could breathe easily. The stabbing pain in his ribs had subsided considerably, with little evidence of the trauma he had endured. He was on the mend. When they finally reached Budapest, Sándor had taken him straight to the Szent Rókus Hospital, and the four weeks since then had been filled with a mixture of warm baths, which he greatly enjoyed; having his open wounds thoroughly cleaned, disinfected, and bandaged, which he detested; being administered countless bags of saline for rehydration, which was neither here nor there; but also, most delightfully of all, being fed extremely well. The first week in the ward was a complete blur, and István slept like the dead for most of it. He couldn't even remember saying goodbye to Sándor, but hoped he'd been lucid enough to thank him again for his unconditional kindness.

Critically observing his reflection in the mirror as he dabbed on the shaving cream, István saw a normal face peering back. The swelling around his cheeks and eyes had gone and only a hint of yellow remained, remnants of the bruising he suffered during the beatings. It would take longer for his gaunt frame to resume its robust, peak physical condition, but the doctors agreed that he was well enough to be discharged from hospital. A faint smile crept across his face. He could finally go home. Frowning at the image looking back at him, he appeared much older than his thirty years, the experience in prison forever etched on his features and his soul.

István was not particularly handsome. Even prior to his recent ordeal he was no Mr Universe but was attractive in other ways. Tall and lean with an angular face, his receding hairline made him look quite severe, even aloof, but added to the air of sophistication and style that somehow made him stand apart from other men in a crowd. Intense hazel eyes sparkled with mischief or hinted at secrets he chose not to share. What he lacked in looks, he made up for in charisma. He possessed a quick wit and humour that endeared him to those around him—even to the stuffy hospital matron, who was not easily amused. A few compliments here or there produced an extra spoonful of stew or an additional baked potato. István had a knack for charming women of all ages. The hospital food was the equivalent of a five-star restaurant compared to the scraps he had been fed at the prison, and it didn't take long for a few kilos to be added to his skeletal frame and for the dark hollows under his eyes to disappear.

Most of the nursing staff, young and old, fussed over István. Whilst they all suspected his injuries were sustained from a stint in prison, having seen many similar patients over the years since the Soviet occupation, no questions were asked. Their job was to patch him up as best they could and send him on his way. One nurse spent a great deal more time with István than with any other patient. Anna was a lovely young girl, competent and extremely attentive. Quite pretty, with clear pale skin, her high cheekbones were flushed with a faint rosiness that deepened whenever she approached István's bed. As he gained in strength each week, she became more flirtatious. Fluffing up his pillow each time she attended him, leaning over his shoulder so that her breasts were inches from his face, and taking twice as long to complete his daily sponge bath than the time she gave to other patients. Her actions didn't go unnoticed. Anna's ministrations were a welcome change from the visits he received from the prison guards only a few short weeks before. István encouraged Anna with kind words and a warm smile. He would often wave her over, asking for more pain killers just to have some company in the otherwise boring days confined to his bed.

The hospital housed a store of second-hand clothing. Many patients arrived wearing nothing but rags. The staff ensured everyone left in better shape than when they arrived, including what they wore. Patients were discharged in clean clothes and with a full stomach. Anna presented István with trousers, shirt, and undergarments on his last day. The staff retained his battered shoes. Anna scrubbed them clean and left them under his bed. The rags he arrived in were thrown into the incinerator, apart from his heavy woollen coat that was cleaned and laid out on his bed. Before he had a chance to get dressed, Anna produced a pair of scissors from her pocket, sat him down, draped a small towel over his shoulders and trimmed his hair. István hadn't realised how long it had grown until it was trimmed nice and short, thanking his dutiful nurse for the third time that morning. Pausing in front of the mirror one last time, István sighed as thoughts of his father popped into his mind.

Before the war, István's father had owned a prosperous establishment as a tailor to the Budapest aristocracy. That had all changed once Hungary was corralled into the Eastern Bloc States under Soviet Communist control. The family had been reasonably well off, and were always dressed in good quality, handmade garments of the latest fashion. In the years since Soviet occupation, much of the aristocracy had fled Hungary or had been executed, and so orders for new clothing had virtually dried up. Besides, his father's services as a tailor were demanded elsewhere. The Soviets seized the family home and closed the shop. István's parents, including his younger brother, were transported to a large clothing factory located in a provincial town several kilometres east from Budapest, close to the Russian border, to make uniforms for the Red Army.

One of the lucky few to have survived active duty in the Budapest Infantry, István had managed to avoid falling prey to the new Communist masters. Choosing not to return to his family home when the war ended, he remained in Sopron for a while, recuperating from the trauma of the fighting and reassessing his future. The garment trade was not a profession he was interested in pursuing, despite his father's ambition for István to be his successor once he retired. Instead, István secured work in one of the biggest steel factories in Budapest. Once he was settled into his new life, he attempted to contact his family. After a week of discreet enquiries, he eventually located a former neighbour who advised István of their fate. Ties with his family were not to be reinstated, and István was destined to become a loner.

Walking through the ward, saying his goodbyes to the other patients and the nurses, István spotted Anna alone by his bed. She seemed a little anxious.

"I can't thank you enough for what you've done for me in my convalescence, Anna," he said sincerely and then laughed, "I think that's now the fourth time I've thanked you this morning."

"Oh, don't mention it. It's my job to care for you and all the other patients," she replied, her cheeks flushing pink, trying to sound dismissive, yet gazed deeply into his alluring hazel eyes, breath caught in her throat. She hesitated for a moment then reached up onto her toes and kissed his cheek.

"Take care of yourself and keep out of trouble," she said, and quickly thrust a piece of paper into the top pocket of his coat. "Perhaps we can catch up for a drink sometime?"

Her face was flushed, and she looked awkwardly around to see if anyone noticed. István winked at her, smiled one of his dazzling smiles, turned, and strode toward the exit. It was late November and the cold air pinched his cheeks as he made his way to the bus stop. Realising that he'd completely missed the warm summer months, having been incarcerated the previous winter and released from his ordeal just as autumn was ending, István shivered. This chapter of his life was one he was keen to forget. It was time to rethink his future. The future, however, could involve pretty Anna, who seemed rather keen to see him again. He felt himself harden at the thought of her naked body pressed against him. Too long had passed since he'd been with a young, eager woman, and the thought made him amorous.

***

István's room in the small, two-bedroom flat he had shared with his best friend, János Vadas, was now occupied by another fellow, Péter. Not surprising. János could not afford to pay the monthly rental on his meagre wage. He needed another housemate to share the cost once István was arrested. No matter. János was thrilled to see his friend again, despite being taken by surprise. Once someone was arrested, they often disappeared, never to be heard from again. So, when István turned up unannounced, János was both delighted and relieved that his friend was still alive. They made room for him in the flat, allowing him to sleep on the worn, brown velvet sofa until he could find a job and somewhere else to live. István felt comforted to be back amongst friends in familiar surroundings. They enjoyed a celebratory dinner that first night, polishing off a bottle of red wine, an indulgence that István had keenly missed. After the initial barrage of questions about what became of him when he was arrested, István was eager to change the subject and leave the past behind. The humiliation, pain, and fear were still too vivid, and he desperately needed to erase that time from his mind.

István had previously been employed at the nearby steelworks, which is where he had met János. Starting out as a general labourer, István had quickly advanced to the position of leading hand for the rail component division. Smart and hardworking, he soon gained the respect of the other men. He was a natural leader. The hours were long, but the pay that came with his new position was much better than when he'd first started as a labourer. The increase in pay made no difference to the level of danger, though. There were many hazards to contend with. The raw steel slabs, blooms, and billets needed to be reheated in a high temperature furnace before being fashioned into various extruded profiles. The processing lines were high speed but antiquated, leaving workers vulnerable to injury. Most of the machinery lacked protective guards, and those that did have some form of guard were slower. The output from these machines was therefore considerably less, and competitive pressures from more advanced technologies in Western domains exacerbated the disregard of safety by the management, so that the men were encouraged to remove the guards in order to increase productivity, causing the injury rate to rise. On top of which, ventilation was inadequate and the overalls the men wore were made from thick hessian, adding to the heat and discomfort. They were constantly bathed in sweat and grime. István found the working conditions intolerable. He constantly raised the dangers with the management committee, suggesting changes to improve ventilation and protective equipment, fighting for the welfare of the men under his charge. As time wore on, he realised that he was fighting a futile battle. Productivity targets were to be achieved regardless of the cost to the workers. No one was brave enough to question the targets. The few that did, found themselves ostracised. Rumours would circulate around the factory that there were traitors in their midst. Before long, arrests were made and the troublemakers were taken away, never to be heard from again. That was István's fate almost a year before. Only Khrushchev's decree to free political prisoners ensured that he made it home.

Whilst the work available at the factory was gruelling, István's experience and knowledge of the steel manufacturing processes gave him the confidence to approach his old boss again, and so the following Monday he accompanied János to the factory, walked straight to the office, and asked for an appointment with the manager of the rail division. The receptionist, Mária, recognised him instantly. With a huge smile she welcomed him back and squeezed him in for an interview, even though the manager's schedule was tight. The next day at 10.00am he was sitting opposite his old boss, Béla Németh, explaining why he should be given another chance. Luck was on his side that day, as he wielded his charm and convinced Béla that he would not cause any trouble. With a conciliatory tone he said that time in prison had taught him not to question the authorities or his superiors. Béla, a balding, rotund man nearing retirement, was entrenched in the communist mandate. He searched István's face, seeking the sincerity he hoped was there, and relented—mainly because István was a reliable worker and the men respected him. If he'd survived prison, then maybe he was owed another chance.

"You can't have your old position as leading hand. I have another capable man who has replaced you in that role. You can re-join the team as a labourer. If you toe the line then there may be opportunities for promotion—but I'm not making any promises. It's up to you to show your loyalty to the regime. You can start next Monday, comrade."

István thanked his boss, shook his hand, and said, "You won't regret this Mr Németh. I won't let you down."

"Be sure that you don't."

István winked at Mária, smiling cheekily as he walked past her desk, "Thanks for squeezing me in to see the old man. I start back next week," he said.

Mária returned the smile and congratulated him. It did not go unnoticed that she had freshened up her lipstick during his interview with the boss. István chuckled, his self-assurance returning.

As he walked out of the building, István wondered if the conditions at the factory had improved since he last worked there or whether the same dodgy practices and unachievable quotas persisted. Were there any traces of the resistance remaining at the factory, or had the communists succeeded in culling everyone that opposed the working conditions and caused trouble? János was a trusted friend, and while he chose not to become embroiled in politics and management issues, he was not deaf to the word on the ground. István knew he could speak candidly with his best friend and uncover any information before he began snooping around. He needed to tread very carefully this time, appearing to be a loyal communist whilst ferreting out anyone who was actively working against the regime. Living conditions would only improve with a change of government and, more importantly, with purging the Russians. István was determined to play his part, but for now he would take things slowly, knowing he would not survive another stint in prison. Buoyed by his good fortune in securing a job at the factory, his life back on the path to normality, István's thoughts turned to Anna. Perhaps they could celebrate his new beginning together.

***

Humming the tune to a favourite waltz, Anna was scrubbing the concrete floor of the tiny bedsitter apartment she shared with another nurse from the hospital. The two rugs that provided some warmth underfoot were draped over the clothesline outside to air until she'd finished cleaning the apartment, at which time she would beat the dust from them with her broom handle. It was a while since she'd thoroughly cleaned her home, and she wanted to make a good impression on István. *"Men appreciate women who not only excel at cooking but are also good at housekeeping,"* her mother's words echoed in her head. Arrangements had been made for her flatmate to visit friends for a couple of days, so that Anna could entertain István unimpeded. She was thrilled when István called her, inviting her out to dinner to celebrate his success in returning to work. Instead of dinner out, Anna suggested that she prepare him a home cooked meal at her place, to which he happily agreed, not having much money until his weekly pay cheques started to flow again.

There were a few dishes that Anna made frequently which were always popular with her friends— well-practiced recipes her mother had handed down to her. Stuffed cabbage rolls with smoked pork ribs and sour cream, slow cooked chicken casserole with homemade noodles served with dill cucumbers, and pork schnitzel with creamy lentils. Of course, she needed to improvise these days, as certain food items were increasingly in short supply and therefore rationed. Meat was the hardest to come by. Often, she would queue for twenty minutes or more to buy bread, meat, or vegetables, only to find that there was little left by the time it was her turn to purchase. Not this time. Anna was determined that her romantic dinner with István would be perfect. Szent Rókus Hospital was afforded a constant supply of provisions for the patients. Anna knew how to bribe the inventory manager and succeeded in obtaining half a chicken in exchange for six of her food coupons. Costly, but worth it. Chicken Paprikás with homemade noodles and a side of dill cucumbers was the dish that Anna knew would impress her guest. Her mother's words of wisdom sounded in her head, *"A way to a man's heart is through his stomach."* Anna smiled to herself, keen to weave a little magic with her cooking and ingratiate herself with István. Her pulse quickened and she blushed at the thought of him.

The floors done, the rugs back in place, she turned her attention to brightening up the flat with fresh flowers cut from the rose bushes at the rear of her building. They were the last blooms of the season, a dark pink variety that filled the small space with their heady fragrance. The two-seater dining table was set with a traditionally embroidered tablecloth that she'd made in school for her craft project. The floral motif around the edge of the cloth complimented the bouquet that was placed in the centre of the table. Wine glasses, cutlery, two candles and cloth napkins that matched the tablecloth were carefully arranged. Anna stepped back to admire the setting. Perfect! The candles added a little romance to the scene, which she hoped would not be lost on István. Lastly, she changed the sheets on the bed to her best cotton set. The pillowslips were embroidered with blue birds, another one of her handy crafts. She wondered whether the night would end with István making love to her, secretly hoping that he would want her in that way. With two hours to go before István was scheduled to arrive, Anna opened her scrapbook of recipes and began preparing the meal.

Both István and Anna were nervous throughout the dinner, István because it was such a long time since he'd been alone with a woman and Anna because she was eager to impress. István arrived with a bottle of red wine, most of which was consumed during the dinner. Anna was not accustomed to drinking alcohol. Gulping rather than sipping the wine she became tipsy very quickly, hoping to calm her nerves. István tried to engage in conversation with Anna, but it was hard work.

"Tell me about yourself, Anna. Apart from being a very capable nurse, for which I can truly testify, what are your interests in life?"

Anna blushed and replied, "Oh well, not much, really. I'm very busy at the hospital but I do enjoy sewing and cooking when I have the time."

"Have you always lived in Budapest? Do you have family nearby?"

"No. I moved here to study nursing a few years ago and then stayed when I secured a job. My family live in Tatabánya."

"You must miss them."

Anna just nodded and gulped another mouthful of wine.

A further pregnant pause in the conversation left István at a loss to know what else to say, and so he complimented Anna on the meal again just to break the silence in the room. There was very little in common to talk about and nothing else to do other than refill their glasses and comment on the meal. The matter of why István was imprisoned was an awkward moment, Anna naively probing his past. Not wanting to dredge things up, István coolly stated that a co-worker accused him of faking his production quotas and, despite his protests, the management believed it to be true, so he was arrested. It was not an uncommon occurrence; people fabricating lies against colleagues to curry favour with the superiors. Anna gasped, reached for his hand, stating how cruel people had become. It was the first time she'd touched him in such an intimate way that evening. Realising this, she made to pull her hand away, but István wouldn't release her for a few moments. Squeezing her hand, he raised it to his lips and kissed it gently, saying how kind-hearted she was. Anna felt she would melt right there. She couldn't help staring at him for the rest of the evening. He made an extremely dashing figure in his steel grey suit and highly polished leather shoes, with his hair slicked back from his forehead, highlighting his angular features and beautiful eyes. She had never met anyone as dashing, nor as attentive to her meaningless prattle.

The candles burned low and the wine bottle was empty. Anna rose from her chair to clear the plates away when István grabbed her wrist and slowly pulled her to him, murmuring in a husky voice, "The dishes can wait."

He kissed her gently on the mouth, looked into her surprised blue eyes, then kissed her more fiercely. Tongue probing her mouth he found Anna responding with equal fervour. Sweeping her into his arms he carried her to the bed. Sitting up, Anna's face flushed bright red when she said, "I, I've never done this before."

"Do you want to? I can leave now if you want."

"No, please don't leave. It's just, well, I'm not sure what to expect."

István smiled warmly, stroked Anna's upturned face and said, "Then leave everything to me. I promise I won't hurt you."

István slowly undid the buttons of her blouse, cupping her large, firm left breast while stroking her nipple with his thumb. The nipple hardened instantly. Anna squealed then relaxed a little, allowing the wondrous sensations to overtake her. Reaching for his hand, she placed it between her thighs and was surprised at how quickly she became wet with desire. Within moments, Anna was undressed. Slipping off her panties, she spread her legs apart, inviting her lover to take her. Continuing to fondle her breasts he slid his middle finger inside her. Anna couldn't stop writhing on the bed, groaning with absolute pleasure. Before she climaxed, he released her and stripped off his clothing. Anna gazed, wide eyed, at István's erect nakedness and shuddered as he gently slid inside her. Gentleness was replaced with an acute desire to climax, thrusting only a few times before it was over for him. István continued to caress Anna, apologising for his swift climax. They lay together, entwined for an hour or so, kissing and stroking one another before István found himself hardening again, taking Anna more slowly, wanting to please her more the second time. Anna shrieked as she climaxed, indifferent to what her neighbours might think. Sated for now, they fell asleep in each other's arms, waking with the first rays of the new dawn.

The following morning after a light breakfast, Anna insisted that István stay another night as her flatmate was not due to return until the following day. Cheekily, she called the hospital and told the matron she was ill and wouldn't be at work that day. Instead, the couple spent the day and evening in each other's arms, exploring one another's bodies.

Life was looking up. A second chance given to him at the steel factory, a steady income, and the lovely Anna who couldn't seem to get enough of their lovemaking. What more could a man want? A routine soon developed that allowed István to stay with Anna when her flatmate was on a late shift at the hospital. Dinner followed by sex became a pleasant ritual that suited him for the time being. Anna was falling in love, yet love was far from István's mind. Re-establishing himself at the factory and infiltrating the underground forces conspiring to defeat the Communist regime were the only thoughts occupying his mind.

CHAPTER 4

Most days, the heady scent of the oils, waxes, fragrances, pigments, alcohol, solvents, and other chemicals used in the manufacture of cosmetics gave Natália a headache. Poor ventilation throughout the factory, together with the heat generated from melting the large vats of wax, compounded her discomfort. Ten-hour shifts standing in one spot as the lipstick moulds came down the production line caused her legs to cramp and her lower back to ache. She was not accustomed to this type of labour but refused to complain. It was her decision, after all. Her tasks were to take the lipsticks from the steel moulds, shape the ends over an open flame, and when sufficiently cooled, place twelve of the completed lipsticks into the pre-folded cardboard boxes. These were then placed onto the adjacent conveyer belt where another worker would seal the boxes and label them according to the customers' order requirements—largely for export. There were many colours produced in large quantities, a different colour each day. Quality control was strict. Products that failed to meet the required standards were set aside and the quantity added to the daily production quota. The workers could purchase these substandard lipsticks and other cosmetic products that were referred to as 'seconds' at a discounted price. They queued for the duration of their lunch break just to buy a tub of moisturiser or one lipstick, the women, and the men—the latter purchasing items for their wives or girl-friends to win their hearts. Lipsticks, facial creams, and fragrant soaps were luxuries that were unaffordable for most working-class women. It was a profitable sideline for the factory, ensuring that very little went to waste.

Whilst the days were gruelling, Natália took great pride in maintaining the company's quality control standards and meeting her daily quota. The factory management praised and rewarded those employees who exceeded their production targets, and Natália liked seeing her name on the 'Recognition Board' that hung in the cafeteria. It was testament to her positive attitude and outlook on life and being respected and acknowledged for a job well done was a welcome change from what she was accustomed to in Szarvas.

The only reprieve during the long hours was the half hour lunch break in the communal cafeteria. There were several large, wooden trestle tables and bench chairs that filled the space. A counter was located at one end of the room containing pre-prepared sandwiches with a variety of fillings, bread, cheeses, hot stews and soups, and an assortment of cakes, all of which could be purchased for a reasonable price, as the factory subsidised the cafeteria, making the meals affordable. For some workers this was their main meal of the day. A small, rectangle window, high up near the ceiling, was always left open for fresh air to circulate, despite the weather. During the winter months, snowflakes drifted in and melted quickly on the concrete floor. No one seemed to notice. The cold air was a welcome reprieve from hours spent in the stifling factory. Here, Natália would slip off her shoes and rub her tired feet for a few minutes whilst devouring her salami and cheese sandwich, followed by two walnut cookies and a cup of tea.

Most of the workers at the factory were women. Many girls had a similar background to Natália, having moved to Budapest from the rural towns, seeking a better life and the excitement of the city. Some of the longer serving women were promoted to supervisory roles. The men held the more senior positions. Natália grew her circle of friends in no time. She was popular with management as she worked diligently, often exceeding her daily quota, and equally popular with her workmates with her bright personality and warm smile. It was a steady job with a reasonable income for a girl with only rudimentary schooling. Everyone who knew Natália puzzled over why she would turn her back on her dressmaking skills and seek work in a cosmetic factory. It was as if she intended to leave all aspects of her life in Szarvas behind and start afresh. The answer was rather straightforward. Natália chose a job that was readily available, close to her new home, required no skill other than diligence and hard work, and where Julia could also gain employment. The girls would travel to work together, settling into their new life in the safety of each other's company. Once established, Natália planned to cultivate a few clients, pursuing her dream of creating her own dress designs. What she refused to contemplate was a return to a labouring position with an established dressmaking salon, subjected to the same tedium as she had experienced in Szarvas.

***

Natália and Julia had arrived in Budapest during the last week in November. They each carried one suitcase crammed with the essentials needed to sustain them until they found work. The night before their departure, Natália vacillated over what to take and what to leave behind. Her one suitcase, the largest in the household, was unable to hold as much as she originally chose to take. The heavier garments needed for the upcoming winter months were bulky and used up precious room in the bag. But it was only a minor issue. She could return home and collect more of her things when needed. Still, Natália planned to quickly gain independence from home, not wanting to run back regularly for any reason and give her mother the satisfaction of saying that she was not coping on her own.

Establishing a routine was easier than expected, thanks to Natália's father. One of his business associates knew of a women's boarding house located on Barát Street, near the East Railway Station. It was run by Mrs Hajdu, a middle-aged no-nonsense war widow who kept a clean and tidy establishment with strict rules about allowing visitors —meaning men — beyond the communal living room. After much scrutiny, the girls were offered a small room on the first floor with two single beds and a small set of timber draws sandwiched between the beds. Perched on top of the draws was a brass reading lamp. An old walnut timber wardrobe, heavily carved with a floral motif and smelling of moth balls, stood against the wall opposite the beds. In the centre of the wardrobe was an oval full-length mirror, a must for all young ladies. A single sash window above the beds was covered with a thin, white lace curtain. Natália parted the curtain, peered out the window and noticed it faced the street. The bus stop was conveniently located around the corner on Dohány Street. It was a bright, sunny day and light flooded the room. No need for alarm clocks here.

"This is perfect!" she said to Julia excitedly, as they scanned their room. "Come on, let's explore the rest of the place. We can unpack later." Grabbing Julia's hand, she dragged her friend out of their room like a puppy, Julia laughing the whole time, equally thrilled to have finally moved to the city.

The compact bathroom at the end of the corridor, which the girls were told was to be shared with four other lodgers on their floor, was bright and airy. Ceramic blue and white tiles adorned the walls, spotlessly clean. A large oval mirror hung above the sink, essential for hair styling. Under the sink was a set of draws, one draw for each room, numbered accordingly, where the girls could store their toiletries. Natália squealed with delight when she spied the large, claw-footed enamel bathtub along the far wall with a variety of soaps stacked on the shelf at one end of it. Luxuriating in a steaming bath at the end of a long day was one of her absolute plea-sures. Only two of the other girls were home at the time, Edit and Lili. They made their introductions, and whilst they were friendly enough the new arrivals were told quite firmly that there was a hierarchy to using the bathroom. Those who had boarded the longest had the first time slot. It didn't bother Natália, as she preferred to bathe after a long day at work and looked forward to dressing up to explore the city's nightlife with her friends.

Natália would ideally have liked a room to herself, but she couldn't afford it. Whilst the rent was quite reasonable, sharing meant that their weekly pay stretched further. This was integral, given that the girls loved to socialise frequently, even after a long shift. Sometimes it was just sipping coffee at the nearby café and watching the passers-by, but mostly the girls enjoyed dancing at the nightclubs around town and attending the local picture theatre. The film stars provided inspiration for new frocks and hair-styles, which Natália practiced on herself. The cosmetic factory was a short bus ride from their new home, so all in all it was a very convenient arrange-ment. Natália was truly happy with her new life: making her own decisions, choosing how she spent her free time without criticism, and being treated as an adult. She'd never had so much fun. It was a complete contrast to the drudgery of her life in Szarvas—and it was all possible because Julia had agreed to escape to the city with her. The girls became inseparable. As time passed, Natália's trips back home to visit the family became less frequent, much to her mother's disapproval.

Shortly after being inducted and trained on the production line, Natália noticed a couple of young men hanging around her section on a regular basis. They would smile and wink at her when she looked up from her tasks and caught their eye. She would smile back and resume working. This went on for over a week. Natália ignored them for the most part, but they persisted in seeking her attention.

"Do you know who these boys are and why they're loitering here?" she asked Angela, who was standing on the opposite side of the conveyer belt.

"Oh, that's Robi and Lukács, two of the mechanics. They're part of the crew that maintain and repair the machinery here. They're harmless enough, just checking out the new talent. News travels fast around here. Don't be surprised if one of them finally plucks up the courage to ask you out," Angela replied.

Natália smiled to herself, deciding that the boys were rather cute, then resumed working. Talking only slowed her down. She was determined to meet her daily quota, so she rarely chatted at her workstation.

The next time Lukács appeared he caught her attention and smiled warmly. Natália felt herself blush and was instantly annoyed by her lack of emotional control. She had wanted to maintain a look of indifference but failed miserably. When the bell sounded at 12.30pm, indicating the first lunch shift, Lukács followed Natália to the lunchroom and sat opposite her. While he appeared bold when he introduced himself, he also seemed a little nervous, as he kept sweeping his long black fringe away from his face with his right hand and fidgeting in his seat. The black grease under his finger-nails seemed to be a permanent fixture, since she had seen him wash his hands at the sink before sitting down. Natália frowned at his hands, but decided it was a hazard of being a mechanic.

"It wouldn't be such a nuisance if you just had that fringe cut short," Natália said in an offhand way as she glanced at him, noticing that he was staring at her. Lukács was a little taken aback by the comment and sat silently for a moment, mesmerised by Natália's emerald eyes. She smiled coyly at him then continued, "My name is Natália. I'm pleased to finally meet you." Lukács grinned broadly. He was enthralled by the way her eyes twinkled at him. All nervousness seemed to vanish as he spent the next few minutes asking where she was from and why she had moved to Budapest, before prattling on about himself. Natália answered his questions and then listened politely, until Lukács finally built up the courage to invite her to his favourite nightclub for a drink and supper. They agreed to meet on the following Friday evening at 9.00pm, but only if her friend Julia chose to accompany her.

"I'll bring Robi along for a foursome," Lukács said, quite pleased with himself.

Over the next couple of days Lukács made a point of passing the packaging line as often as he dared. His supervisor didn't tolerate slack behaviour, so he was careful to appear busy, but he would smile at Natália and remind her of their upcoming date.

Finally, Friday arrived. On her way home after her shift ended, Natália mentally perused her wardrobe, trying to decide what to wear on her first date since arriving in Budapest. Skipping up the stairs to her floor she dashed into the vacant bathroom, drew a hot bath, and soaked in it for as long as she dared before her skin became too wrinkly. Her weary bones revitalised, she washed and dried her hair, then dabbed a little of her favourite perfume behind each ear, an essential oil made from rose petals. Natália owned four dresses, two suits, and a good woollen coat, all of which she had made herself. Not many girls her age were as lucky. The choice of which outfit to wear was perplexing. She wanted to look attractive but not too eager, elegant but not too severe, pretty but not childish. After an hour of deliberating, trying on each of the dresses twice, she selected a bottle green, fitted, woollen dress with a wide, cream lace neckline, cut just above her cleavage. Not too daring but revealing a little flesh. Returning to the bathroom her next task was makeup and hair. A little rouge to accentuate her high cheekbones and a ruby coloured lipstick. Her hair was pinned up in a French roll leaving her neck exposed, resulting in an overall look of sophistication. Admiring her image in the mirror, Natália was satisfied that Lukács would be impressed.

"Come on Natália. The club will be closed by the time you're ready to leave." Julia yelled, pounding on the bathroom door, encouraging Natália to get moving. She had agreed to tag along, thinking it would be fun dancing the night away with two new fellows. Julia was not as concerned with how she looked so was ready in half the time it took Natália to finally announce she was set to leave.

They had arranged to meet the boys at the club. Julia suggested that they should be fashionably late to keep them guessing as to whether they'd turn up at all. The girls donned their woollen coats and tied their scarves around their necks to keep out the chilly air. Finally, before heading out the door, Julia skipped down the corridor in search of Mrs Hajdu to let her know they'd be late home—one of the house rules.

The nightclub was called Cat's Eyes, and was located on Klauzál Street, roughly twenty minutes' walk from their home. The girls were in high spirits, the adrenalin pumping with excitement. They arrived at 9.15pm. Searching the crowded bar, Natália spotted Lukács—although for some reason he looked different. As she approached him, she laughed out loud and remarked,

"You cut that fringe. I barely recognised you!"

Lukács grinned, kissed her on the cheek and, while she was taking her coat off, said, "You look gorgeous. I'm glad you decided to come."

Natália smiled back and replied, "I was looking forward to it."

Introductions were made all round before Robi shuffled through the crowd to the bar and ordered a round of drinks, while Lukács located a booth where they settled in for the evening. The band played a combination of folk songs, slow waltzes, and livelier dance music for about forty minutes before taking a twenty-minute break. During the first break Lukács ordered a platter of cold meats, cheese, and an assortment of condiments. They all tucked in heartily. Drinks flowed throughout the night, beer for the boys and Tokaji wine for the girls. Julia and Robi hit it off instantly. They spent most of the evening in each other's arms swaying and writhing to the music. Natália felt a little uncomfortable during the slow numbers. Lukács pulled her close, his left hand sliding down her back and resting on her bottom while kissing her neck. She wasn't ready for anything too serious with Lukács, or any other boy for that matter, so when another slow number started, she ducked off to the bathroom to powder her nose. The foursome stayed for three sets before Natália—the most sensible and the least inebriated of the group—declared it was time to head home. The other three protested, albeit a little weakly as it was undeniably late, at 1.00 am. Natália slid out of the booth, wrapped her coat around her shoulders, and headed for the exit. She quickly turned back to the booth, kissed Lukács on the cheek, and thanked him for a wonderful evening, before making her way through the crowd and out the front door. She was a hundred metres past the club when Julia caught up with her, panting from running.

"What a great night!" Julia declared. "I had the best time. Isn't Robi cute? He's such a great dancer."

"Yes, it was fun." Natália said casually. After a few minutes, deep in thought, she continued, "Lukács was a little too fresh with me, though. His hands kept wandering all over me, resting on my bottom. I didn't really like that. Not on our first date."

"Oh, don't be such a prude. You need to lighten up. Isn't this what we came to Budapest for? Some excitement!" Julia retorted.

The girls walked home, arm in arm, Julia continuing to extol Robi's virtues. Despite the late hour, Natália struggled to fall asleep, adrenalin still coursing through her veins, recapping the wonderful evening in her mind, affirming her decision to move to Budapest—the city full of promise. And how sweet it was for Lukács to have cut his hair as she had suggested. Grinning to herself, she pictured his handsome face and ready smile, the last things she remembered before dozing off.

For the next few months, a routine was established. Natália, Julia, and their two boyfriends went out together two or three times a week to one of their favourite clubs or to the movies. They all worked hard, saved hard, and spent their free time having fun. Over time, Natália and Lukács became closer, at times going out for dinner, just the two of them, Natália no longer needing a chaperone. She was forever probing him about his plans and expectations of life, hoping to find something she could latch onto as a common goal. Lukács' sexual advances persisted, despite Natália clearly stating that she was saving herself for her marriage bed. Lukács was not too keen on the idea of marriage, even though he was besotted with Natália. The carefree life he enjoyed was far more appealing than the responsibilities that marriage brought. His parents and other married couples he knew seemed too serious and not that happy. That didn't stop him from trying to persuade Natália to take their kissing a little further as he fondled her breasts and slid his hand up the inside of her thighs in encouragement.

Gradually, Natália conceded that she had very little in common with Lukács. He had no political views, nor any interest in world affairs, the theatre, or art—such as it was in a repressed, communist society. Conversation was dull. He was just an uneducated country boy who lacked ambition. Natália had moved to Budapest to grow and expand her view of the world and to improve her position in life. Unlike Lukács, she was ambitious, with dreams of establishing her own salon still tugging at her heart. Her thirst for knowledge was immense. Reading the daily news-papers—though everyone knew the news was censored by the regime— was one tool for broadening her understanding of the affairs of the state and the country's priorities. Frequently tuning into the radio broadcasts was another. She often visited the city's museums and galleries on her own—Lukács, Julia, and her other friends were disinterested in the arts— feasting on the visual treasures and their historical context. On many occasions, when the two were alone together, sitting in front of a roaring log fire, sipping Pálinka in the drawing room of her boarding house to take the chill out of their bones, she would try to engage Lukács in more serious conversation. She would ask what he thought about the current way of life, the daily hardships everyone faced, the difficulty in getting ahead, and whether he thought life was the same everywhere else in the world. Lukács often became frustrated, saying she was too serious and obsessed with these ideas, steering her to other less controversial topics. Mostly, he just wanted to fondle her and convince her to move in with him to the flat he shared with Robi.

Natália persevered with the relationship, despite her misgivings. Certain that Lukács loved her, she reciprocated his love and tried to find a depth to the essence of his being, hoping to eventually pique his interest in subjects and aspects of life that were important to her. He was handsome and kind and would do just about anything for her. But the seed of doubt flourished as time passed. She loved him, but in her quiet moments she was unsure if she was truly *in love* with him.

Over a year passed in this rhythm of life, until finally the liaison with Lukács gradually cooled. Dating became less frequent. Natália found excuses for being unavailable to see him, seeking solitude to search her heart for the right path. When they did meet, she no longer felt the tingling of her skin nor the flutter of her heart at the sight of him. Lukács sensed something amiss but presumed it was family issues—Natália's obligatory yet infrequent visits to Szarvas and more particularly time spent with her mother always left her in a depressed state. Julia, on the other hand, suspected there was more to her excuses than family troubles. Knowing her friend very well, she confronted Natália on numerous occasions, needling her about why she had stopped going out as much with the boys, and the cause of her sadness that had become a constant companion. Not knowing how to answer her friend, Natália brushed aside the concern, perked up, and carried on with a happy façade for a while, before slipping back into her sombre mood.

After much soul searching and countless sleepless nights, Natália decided that her relationship with Lukács was untenable and arranged to meet him at a café close to the cosmetic factory to break the news. The café was quiet during the late afternoon. Although they had worked the same shift, Lukács arrived a few minutes late, and kissed Natália on the cheek before ordering the coffee for both of them. Sitting opposite her, he nattered about an accident at the roller mill that grinds the pigment before it is added to the wax, which had resulted in a worker being carted off to hospital, pausing now and then to sip his coffee. Natália battled to concentrate, anxiously awaiting the right moment to break her news. Lukács was oblivious to the reason for the meeting but noticed that Natália was preoccupied. Placing his empty cup on the saucer he searched Natália's face, noticing her frown and worried expression, and asked, "What did you want to talk about, Natália? Is everything alright?"

Natália glanced up at her boyfriend, her first true love, concern etched on his brow, took a deep breath, then replied, "You know that I care for you very much Lukács," Her emerald eyes were glistening with tears, supressing the urge to cry, focusing on the speech she had rehearsed over and over earlier that day, before pushing on, "and we've had a wonderful time together. I've been thinking a lot these past few weeks about the future. You and I have very different dreams and desires, important things that I can't see being reconciled. I'm sorry, Lukács, but I believe it's best we go our separate ways."

A few patrons drifted in, the buzz of their chatter creating a distraction, yet Natália's gaze remained steadfastly fixed on Lukács's face, awaiting his reaction. The rejection completely caught him by surprise. Stunned by Natália's pronouncement he just sat, staring, digesting the words that called an end to their fifteen-month relationship.

"But I love you, Natália, and I know you love me. We have our differences, all couples do, but that's what makes the spark between us so electric. If it's about marriage, well we can talk about that, make plans if that's what you want."

"I do have strong feelings for you, Lukács, but I'm not in love with you. I'm sorry."

The words stung as if she had slapped him hard across the face. Lukács' shock and wounded pride were soon replaced with scorn. Whispering through clenched teeth he uttered, "You just think you're superior to everyone else, but you're not. You, with your fancy ideas, pretending to be an intellectual. You're just the same as the rest of us peasants from the villages."

Lukács stood abruptly, knocked over his chair, and stormed out of the café, leaving Natália weeping into her hands. His words reverberated in her head, cutting deeply, mirroring those of her mother. She pictured her mother, hands on hips, laughing at her. Wiping her tear-streaked face with the napkin, Natália sighed, relieved that she had succeeded in severing the relationship but at the same time distraught about the hurt she had caused Lukács. She felt dreadful, but it was not yet over. The next challenge was to let Julia know of her decision. Walking slowly home, Natália knew she must break the news to Julia as soon as she saw her, rather than risking her friend hearing about the breakup from someone else.

Unsurprisingly, Julia was terribly upset by the breakup. She thought the foursome made a great team and really enjoyed their escapades. She couldn't understand why Natália had broken up with the handsome, funny, easy-going Lukács. Everyone loved him. Natália tried to explain her feelings, but Julia was deaf to her reasons.

"You've spoiled everything. Lukács will be devastated. How could you be so cruel?" Julia yelled at her friend. After this unjust outburst, she avoided Natália for days, refusing to communicate with her unless absolutely necessary. Natália was heartbroken that Julia was drifting away. They had been such firm friends. Julia continued to see Robi at every opportunity, and Natália guessed that Julia and Robi's relationship had blossomed into something quite serious. Julia often failed to return home, sometimes for three days at a time, choosing to stay over at Robi's place. Whilst the two girls continued to share a room, Julia's manner changed irrevocably. She was abrupt, cool, and less inclusive. It seemed everyone thought Natália was mad to leave Lukács. No one really understood her and didn't know why she had ended the relationship with the dashingly handsome Lukács. Only Mrs Hajdu didn't question her decision.

"Affairs of the heart are complex. Who am I to probe or interfere?" she shrugged.

Natália took comfort from those words, and her landlady became a new confidante whenever she needed independent council.

After the breakup, life at the cosmetic factory became tense. Natália sensed people talking behind her back. Everyone had thought that Lukács and Natália made a handsome couple, and they were all sure that wedding bells were in the air. People often asked when they were planning on tying the knot, who would be invited, and how many bridesmaids she would choose. This presumptuous banter irritated Natália, but she understood their questions. One minute the couple looked happy, and the next, they split up for no apparent reason. Some of her friends at the factory shunned her. Lukács was popular with all the girls, and they believed that Natália was the cause for his misery. Lukács avoided her section and took his lunch break at a different time slot to her, taking all precautions not to inadvertently bump into her. Occasionally, Natália spotted him chatting with someone, but he looked straight through her and walked off. Natália had hoped that she could remain friends with Lukács once he had recovered from the initial blow but knew now that this would be impossible. She had never felt so alone and so rejected. After two weeks of self-pity and shame for 'ruining Lukács' life', as Julia had summed it up one day, Natália's attitude changed. She no longer accepted the burden of Lukács' unhappiness. Defiantly, she stuck her chin out, got on with the job, and hoped that over time people would forget the matter.

A few weeks after the split, the tension at the factory began to ease. It dawned on Natália that she hadn't seen Lukács at all for a while, and she sensed it wasn't simply that he was still avoiding her. She dared not ask Julia, who had become more distant over time, but discreet enquiries with other co-workers revealed that Lukács left the company to take a mechanics position with a shoe factory on the other side of the city. Whilst she felt some remorse for the pain she knew she had caused Lukács, Natália was pleased he was gone. It made her circumstances at work a little easier. With Lukács now completely out of her life, Natália believed she could truly move on. Her independence had come at a high price—abandoned by her friends, she felt lonelier than ever.

***

With so much free time on her hands, few friends, and a non-existent social life, Natália decided it was the opportune time to rekindle her dress designing ambition. The bedroom she shared with Julia was too small to include a workspace. It was time she had a chat with Mrs Hajdu.

"What's for dinner tonight, Mrs Hajdu? Something smells fabulous," Natália asked as she walked into the kitchen. Natália frequently chose to have dinner with her landlady since her split from Lukács. Occasionally a few of the other boarders chose to stay home and pay the extra fee for an evening meal, so that they formed a family of sorts, which Natália was happy to be a part of.

"Bean soup followed by prune dumplings," Mrs Hajdu replied as she stirred the pot, remaining intent on her endeavour.

"Delicious!" Natália smiled, before continuing, "I have a proposition for you, if you have the time to discuss it?"

"Oh, and what would that be, young lady?" Mrs Hajdu asked as she turned to see Natália seated at the table, hands clasped over a compendium, grinning from ear to ear, such was the excitement that sparkled from her eyes.

"Come and sit beside me and I'll explain what I have in mind."

Turning the stove down to its lowest setting, Mrs Hajdu complied and listened intently as Natália proceeded to reveal her plan and present her sketches. In exchange for a small room, preferably on the ground floor, which Natália would commandeer as a dressmaking workshop, she would make Mrs Hajdu some new clothes free of charge, the details of which would be agreed on later. Once Natália established a few paying clients she would be able to pay rent on the room—the fee to be negotiated when the time came.

"That's a marvellous idea! I haven't bought any clothes in years. I do have a small vacant room off the living room, which none of the girls want to rent because it's too far from the bathrooms. I'd be happy to let you use that. Would you like to take a look?"

Natália had never seen her landlady so animated. Before she had a chance to gather the sketches and return them to the folder, Mrs Hajdu was down the corridor and heading for the living room, muttering about new dresses, Natália in hot pursuit. As the door swung open Mrs Hajdu waved a hand over the boxes and miscellaneous items that dotted the floor, claiming she would find somewhere else to store the stuff. A large window provided natural light, and the space was ample. All she needed was to retrieve her sewing machine and incidental tools from the cellar at home, buy a couple of tables and chairs, a full-length mirror, and a sturdy, bright lamp, and she would be set. Making the initial garments for Mrs Hajdu would also provide much needed practice before Natália sought paying clients, thereby building her confidence to deal with strangers. Once she was ready, she would create advertising fliers and pin them to the noticeboard at the factory and around the local cafés. Everything had been thoroughly considered, and Natália was the happiest she'd been in months. She clapped her hands in delight and said, "This is perfect, Mrs Hajdu. So, do we have a deal?"

"Of course, my dear. Now, let's talk about the dresses."

Natália hugged the woman and thanked her profusely—a virtual stranger who had offered more kindness and support in the last year than her own mother had in a lifetime.

CHAPTER 5

István was dismayed to discover that life after prison had become quite sombre in Budapest, with food scarcer and more expensive, and wages stagnating. Communist propaganda permeated all aspects of life. Socialist realism continued to expand, glorifying communism and its values through depictions of powerful, just leaders and hard-working, happy people. István's team mates certainly worked hard, but they were not very happy. The communist mantra, of equal rights and a prosperous life for all had proved to be nothing more than hollow words.

The Hungarian economy declined disastrously in a relatively short period of time. Human rights continued to be trampled. Manufacturing quotas rose without extra pay. City workers whose relatives farmed the land reported that if production targets were not achieved, regardless of the reasons, their families were rounded up and forced to work as prison labourers in factories or on construction projects. Removing the farmers from the land exacerbated the food shortages. In addition, anyone thought to be associated with one of the outlawed opposition parties was arrested. Beliefs in any ideology other than communism were forbidden, and religious leaders were persecuted. Art and literature could only support the Soviet Communist doctrine. The once creative and successful movie industry was forced to produce films illustrating the political leaders as heroes of the nation. The education system dramatically changed its curriculum to embed the theories and principals of communism. The media was totally controlled by the regime. Those that dared to speak out against the worsening, oppressive conditions were intimidated, threatened, arrested, beaten, imprisoned, or simply disappeared. The loss of national independence, the disregard for local traditions, heritage and religious freedoms, and the enforced glorification of Soviet Communism was a bitter pill not easily or readily swallowed by István and his fellow Hungarians, and István's urge to derail the tyrant only grew stronger within him as more and more stories of suffering emerged.

István had already been imprisoned and tortured for speaking up for workers' rights. Safety in the steelworks had been compromised for higher outputs—an unacceptable situation that he had refused to tolerate, both before his arrest and since his release. Though the pain inflicted upon him whilst in prison was still fresh in his mind, he could not be a passive bystander. He was determined to find a way to fight back. But he needed to be smarter this time.

One of the supervisors of the furnace at the factory, a man by the name of Ferenc Kertesz, was a former member of the Smallholders Party, which gained 57% of the national vote of 1945, outstripping the communist vote threefold. The so-called democratic election did not stop the Soviet Communists from utilising other methods to achieve ultimate power, which they successfully realised in 1949. The destruction of the Smallholders Party gave rise to a tightknit band of freedom fighters who conspired to disrupt Soviet ambitions, however minor, and find ways to let Western countries know of their deteriorating plight, hoping for salvation. István was aware of this. His stint in prison for defending the rights of his fellow workers was well known, and he assumed the status of a folk hero when he returned to the factory. Careful not to draw attention to himself by seeking information about the state of play while at the factory, István made a point of calling into the local pub, where many of the workers socialised over a couple of pints before heading home. One by one, colleagues would sidle up to him at a quiet booth, where István was known to sit alone, filling him in on their antics in derailing production quotas, and faking illnesses to disrupt shifts. It soon became apparent who the key schemers were. Ferenc Kertesz's name cropped up on more than one occasion. István planned to join their cause, albeit more cautiously than before his arrest, as he had no intention of returning to prison or of facing execution.

***

Within a few short months, István had settled into a rhythm with his renewed, second chance of life. He had restored relationships with his co-workers and demonstrated to management that he was a solid, competent worker who was not about to cause trouble. He performed his tasks by the book, with no argument. With his knowledge and natural leadership qualities he soon rose once again to a supervisory position. Together with his team of labourers he modified some of the machine guards, to create an element of protection for the men whilst maintaining the production quotas. He was invited to monthly management meetings where he outlined the process improvements he was developing, emphasising that the changes would increase production, regardless if that were actually true. It was important to build trust with the establishment and his co-workers before he felt safe to covertly approach anyone about his true views. As his reputation within the factory grew, so too did his confidence.

It soon became apparent that the factory management was not interested in his process improvement plans. Production statistics were closely monitored. His boss argued that there was no evidence of increased outputs, in fact the reverse was true in some departments—including István's. In light of this, István was tasked with correcting the problem quickly, if he wanted to retain his supervisory position. The week following the management meeting where István was chastised for decreased outputs, one of his men suffered a fatal injury. Rather than stop the rolling mill to clean the rollers as needed to remove grit that damaged the steel coils, the worker had wiped the rollers whilst they were still in motion, as he had been instructed to do by the factory's management. Unfortunately, this day, the right-hand sleeve of his shirt was quickly snatched through the roller, dragging the poor fellow along, badly crushing his arm and upper torso. He died on his way to hospital. István was devastated. The incident was the catalyst that spurred István into action. It was time he stopped talking about fighting back and did something. The time had come to seek out his colleague, Ferenc, to arrange a meeting. The ex-politician was reputed to be intelligent and trustworthy. István hoped his reputation was justified.

One afternoon, after a long and harrowing shift, with attendance low since the death of their colleague, István strolled over to the furnace where Ferenc was giving instructions to a worker and waited quietly until the former politician was free to talk. Wiping his sweaty face with his grubby handkerchief, to look a little more presentable, he opened the conversation.

"Hello, Ferenc. I may have the advantage. Your reputation precedes you, whereas there is no reason for you to know of me. My name is István Szabó."

Ferenc turned around to look at the man covered in soot, paused for a moment, steadied his gaze on István's face and replied, "Yes, I've heard of you. I thought you'd been imprisoned for speaking out against the management?" His gaze shifted, and he yelled over István's shoulder, "Hey, you two," A couple of men resting on their shovels straightened up and followed the line of Ferenc's finger as he pointed towards a huge iron bin. "You can empty that bin into the oven. Get moving."

István waited patiently until Ferenc turned his attention back to him, then responded to the query, "You thought correctly. I was indeed arrested, but Khrushchev's clemency saw me released. I got myself back in shape and here I am again, right back where I started." Lowering his voice, he went on, "Perhaps we can get together for a drink sometime. We could discuss the joys of the Russian prison system and, more to the point, how not to get arrested. I could use the wisdom of a veteran with a history of survival, and I hear that you're the man. I know a good bar with private booths on Dohány Street. It's called The Fox. What do you say? My shout."

Ferenc turned his attention back to his team of men, barked more orders at them, then turned to face István, his gaze steady and unflinching.

"I must watch these men every minute of the day. As soon as I turn my back they slacken off. I can't say I blame them, though. They don't earn much for the hours they put in. Anyway, I know The Fox. Seeing as you're paying, how can I refuse?"

"Let's make it tomorrow evening, then. 6.00pm, if that suits you?"

"Sure, I'll see you there." Ferenc said, then turned away and continued yelling at the men to pick up their pace. He surreptitiously watched István leave, trying to get the measure of the man.

István was relieved that his initial contact with Ferenc had gone well. The man appeared approachable; he could have brushed István off but didn't. Should that be concerning? István was glad he had some time to get his thoughts together before their meeting the following evening.

He wanted to be sure he could trust Ferenc and not be betrayed. The intelligence he had gathered from his mates at the pub suggested Ferenc was a solid Hungarian and completely anti-communist. But he needed to convince Ferenc that he too was the genuine article. Ideas floated in and out of his mind, as he sought to determine the best possible way to casually broach the subject of helping 'the cause'. István was generally very direct with people, and more often than not it was this lack of diplomacy that got him into strife. He didn't want to scare Ferenc off with a blunt manner but needed to let him know he was completely trustworthy and not a spy for the secret police. The fear instilled in the populace by the brutal, inhumane AVO led to a culture of self-preservation. People would name neighbours or even family members as traitors when interrogated, just to save their own skins and show allegiance to the Party. István had to convince Ferenc that they were on the same side.

Sleep was elusive that night, as István tossed and turned, contemplating how the meeting would play out the following evening. Eventually he drifted off, before his rest was shattered by a vivid nightmare in which he was being interrogated by two hooded men who then pulled a sack over his head and began flogging him to death. Before they struck the fatal blows, he awoke, sat bolt upright, dripping with sweat, the image of his back covered in blood and his skin flayed vivid in his mind.

Nerves overcame him. He retched several times the following day, his innards churning uncontrollably. Thoughts whizzed through his head about how to approach the subject of being anti-communist. Trust was difficult to win, but even more difficult to recognise. He needed to keep a cool head and not speak too directly, whilst also taking a gamble on Ferenc's willingness to take him at his word.

He purposefully arrived at the bar thirty minutes before the scheduled meeting, scanned the room, and then took a seat away from the main crowd gathered at the counter. Rehearsing his opening lines in his head, he was halfway through his second glass of beer when Ferenc walked in. His weathered face etched even more deeply as he furrowed his brow in search of the younger man. István stood and waved him over to the corner booth at the rear of the bar.

"Glad you made it, Ferenc. What can I get you?" István asked.

"What you're having looks good. I'll have one of those, thanks."

István downed his drink in two gulps. Making his way through the crowd gathered at the counter, he waited for a few minutes, trying to get the barmaid's attention. Angela was a young girl, rather easy on the eye with bleached blonde, wavy hair down to her shoulders and large breasts that stood out proudly without the help of a bra. He noticed that because he could easily see her nipples pressed against the flimsy fabric of her blouse. Playfully flirting with her when he first arrived, she was a pleasant distraction from his otherwise serious thoughts. She smiled when she noticed István at the counter again, and blushed when he paid her another compliment, suggesting she should be a movie star instead of pulling beer.

"What can I get you? I mean, what would you like to drink?" Angela giggled.

"Ah, pity it's only the drink on offer. Two more pints of beer, thanks Angela," he replied, winking.

"Sure," Angela said, expertly pulling two beers with only a little froth on top. "Here you go".

"Thanks, and keep the change," he said as he placed some coins on the counter.

Once he was seated back at the booth, Ferenc asked, "So what is it you want to talk about?"

István drank deeply from his beer, set the glass on the table, and looked around the room to feel sure that no one was paying them any attention. He then gazed directly into Ferenc's eyes and said in a hushed tone, "I was imprisoned and tortured for no reason other than speaking out for workers' rights—for trying to improve safety standards at the factory where I worked, for men whose wellbeing was my responsibility. Too many men were getting injured, purely because machine guards were removed. And for what? To increase outputs. I think I can trust you when I say that this ridiculous pretence that we are all living under must stop. The promises made by the Soviets and their Hungarian lackey, Rákosi, of higher living standards, good jobs with good pay and an economy that would outstrip Western democracies have proven to be falsehoods. The exact opposite is true. There must be a way to expel the occupier and take back control of our destiny. We need to restore our heritage, our independence, and our religious liberties. I can't stand by and accept that this level of poverty and oppression is here to stay for generations to come. I can't imagine bringing children into this miserable world."

His voice was rising in pitch. He quickly glanced around again to ensure no one was looking their way. István was clearly emotional. So much for a measured approach. As it was now impossible to retract his pronouncement, István decided that he would run with his instinct and trust the man sitting opposite him. Leaning back in his chair, he sighed, ran his hand over his face and quickly got his emotions under control. He took another swig of his beer and went on, "I've heard that there are secret organisations plotting to undermine the regime. I hoped you would know someone who could introduce me to one of these groups. I want to become involved in the demise of the current leadership and see Rákosi hang for the crimes he has perpetrated against his own people."

Ferenc looked intently at István, searching for any sign of deceit. All he saw was a passionate young man, yearning for a better life. After a long pause, Ferenc whispered, "Well, that's a very dangerous sentiment, particularly expressed out loud in a public place. You never know where the spies are lurking. Anyway, what makes you think I can help you rather than betray you?"

István lowered his voice and replied, "I know you were a member of the Smallholders' Party. It's common knowledge that the Soviets undermined the democratic process to gain control. I can't image you acquiesced easily when your party was outlawed. I also heard that some former members of your party have formed a resistance group. A few colleagues suggested you were a man to be trusted with links to this group. I hoped that you could help me gain entry. I'm willing to work in any capacity to restore our freedoms and rid our country of the Russian oppressor."

There was a long pause as both men drank their beer in contemplation.

"I'm not sure that I can help you," Ferenc replied. With that, he downed his beer and left.

István sat quietly for a few minutes, watching the man walk away, trying to make sense of Ferenc's reaction. He then walked back to the counter to order another beer, his mind racing. Returning to his booth he slowly drank his beer, digesting the conversation with his colleague. István wasn't sure if the meeting went well. The man was very guarded. The realisation that Ferenc hardly spoke at all sent a chill up his spine. Why hadn't he asked Ferenc any questions? What a fool to have spoken so candidly with someone he hardly knew without getting a sense of the man's views. A big mistake. Perhaps he was not so easily convinced by István's motives. Maybe he had been too direct. He didn't intend on speaking so frankly, but as usual his emotions got the better of him. Too many maybes ran through his head. He finished his beer and left the bar. He would not sleep easily until Ferenc showed his hand. Was he friend or foe? Stepping outside, the chill air slashed at his cheeks, snapping his mind out of his reverie. The deed was done. It was now a waiting game.

Putting the conversation with Ferenc aside, his thoughts turned back to the bar maid, Angela. What a flirtatious creature she was, wearing nothing under her blouse, blushing with every compliment, and teasing him. Guilty that his lust had strayed from his girlfriend, István lit a cigarette, took two long puffs then started making his way home when he remembered that he was having dinner with Anna that night. Stopping at a bottle shop on the way to her flat, he purchased a red wine that he knew Anna liked. Yielding to his caresses when she was a little tipsy, her inhibitions dissolving with each glass of alcohol. The thought of her naked body eager for his touch aroused him.

***

Four weeks had passed since his meeting with Ferenc, and still no word. István was edgy and wondered what, if anything, Ferenc's silence meant. Luckily, the AVO hadn't come knocking on his door. Obviously, Ferenc hadn't reported him to the authorities—yet. It was a waiting game that made István increasingly worried with each passing day. Anna noticed that his mood had recently changed, but monosyllabic answers were all she got to her probing. Her lover was distracted, inattentive, and often snapped at her. Then, in the next breath, István would apologise profusely for his behaviour and show signs of his old self. She suspected he was having an affair and questioned him many times about his lack of interest in her and the irregularity of his visits. István could not confide in Anna about his political views nor why he was so on edge. Keeping Anna ignorant of his activities kept her safe, but he also knew that she wouldn't understand his motives. She yearned for marriage and children, a desire far from his own at this point in his life. He brushed off her jealous notions, claiming his promotion at work came with added responsibilities which consumed him, but she wasn't so easily convinced.

Two more weeks passed when, out of the blue, Ferenc sat down beside István in the factory lunchroom and casually ate his sandwich without a word. When he got up to leave, he calmly slid an envelope that was concealed under his hand across to István. István quickly pocketed the envelope before anyone noticed, dying to get home that night to read the letter. The rest of his shift dragged on interminably. He was so distracted that a few workmates asked if he was feeling under the weather. Quickly snapping out of his pensiveness, he tried to laugh it off, saying he had women troubles. Everyone around him chuckled at the all too familiar problem men faced with their womenfolk. Finally, the siren sounded and the shift was over. István raced towards the shower block, quickly washed the grime from his tired body, hurriedly dressed, and made for the exit. Some of the men hooted at him as he ran out the door. Once outside, he waited for what seemed an age for the tram home. There were no seats left, so he stood near the door, jammed in tightly with the other weary travellers; but it was anxiety, not the close proximity of his travelling companions, that caused the perspiration to soak through his shirt.

There were no elevators in the prefabricated apartment blocks that had popped up like ugly concrete mushrooms across the city, designed and built to Russian specifications. Khrushchev outlawed the architectural excesses of the Stalin era, claiming that in a socialist society everything should be functional, with no funds wasted on elaborate ornamentation. Row upon row of concrete boxes with small, square windows now lined the streets. They were built quickly and cheaply, often without insulation, to house the workers. There was nothing appealing or welcoming about their appearance. As with every other aspect of life under the Soviets, they were filled with grey drabness.

Taking the stairs two at a time, he reached the flat that he still shared with his friend János. István hadn't bothered finding a place of his own, given that he spent a few nights each week at Anna's. The arrangement suited him perfectly. Saving a good portion of his weekly pay was a high priority given the wasted time in prison with no income. No sooner had he opened the door than István yanked the envelope from his pocket and opened it with trembling hands. He read the single sheet of paper three times before he finally understood that it was merely a dinner invitation to Ferenc's house for the following Saturday night at 7.00pm. That was it, nothing more. Tapping the invitation against his palm, he stood in the middle of the flat wondering who else had been invited, if anyone. Of course, Ferenc couldn't divulge anything in writing in case the letter fell into the wrong hands. He was clearly being careful. Should this raise alarm bells? István wasn't sure but knew all too well that secrecy was critical for everyone's survival.

The next few days dragged. István was completely preoccupied with the forthcoming dinner, and anxious about what awaited him. When Saturday night finally arrived, he dressed in his steel grey suit, white shirt, and thin, black tie, as was the custom when attending someone's home for dinner. He bought a bottle of wine on his way to the tram stop. Thoughts churned around in his mind. Was it a trap? Would the AVO be waiting for him? Had he placed his trust in the wrong man? Feeling it was too late to back out now, István resigned himself to his fate.

The timing was perfect. Hopping off the tram and walking the two blocks to Ferenc's address, he arrived precisely five minutes before 7.00pm. Being punctual was good. It revealed discipline and reliability; solid traits that he hoped would impress his host. István climbed the stairs to the fourth floor of Ferenc's apartment block, braced himself, and then rapped three times on the wooden door. The door slowly opened and Ferenc peered around the frame, before ushering István into the living room. Three other men were already seated, drinking beer, and chatting quietly. They stood when István entered the room.

"Gentlemen, I'd like to introduce István Szabó, the colleague I mentioned who was imprisoned for arguing for his workers' rights. He was beaten and tortured for months, accused of being a traitor to the government, and now wants to fight back in a more proactive way to disrupt the regime." The others nodded in unison. "He took a great risk in approaching me, so I believe we can trust him."

Ferenc had not simply taken István's impassioned speech in the pub as proof of his trustworthiness; he had gone to great lengths to discreetly enquire about the credentials of his fellow worker before inviting him to his home. He was satisfied that the man was genuine.

István shook hands with each of the men as they introduced themselves to him. Albert had been a minor minister in the defunct Smallholders Party and was now a labourer in another steel factory. He was a close friend of Ferenc. Tomás and Iván had previously been upper middle-class citizens with significant land holdings and prosperous farms before the occupation, when they had been stripped of their assets—including their ancestral family homes—and were both now employed as low-ranking civil servants. They were all equally aggrieved by the communist ideology. Formal introductions aside, the men were just about to sit down again when Kati, Ferenc's wife, suddenly appeared, announcing that dinner was ready. She ushered them over to the small timber dining table at the other end of the room. Once they were seated, István produced the wine he had brought along as a contribution to the evening and Ferenc filled the glasses as Kati served the meal. Everyone commented on the wonderful aroma and Kati beamed with pride. It was not easy finding meat at affordable prices, especially to feed five men, herself, and the two children. She thanked them for their compliments and promptly left the room, leaving the men to discuss their business. Albert started the dialogue in between mouthfuls of the delicious smoked pork ribs and sauerkraut,

"A cousin of mine lives in Sopron. He came to visit two weeks ago, looking for better employment in the city. He brought with him a handful of pamphlets which he claims were delivered by air. Not airplanes, but balloons!"

Everyone laughed, shaking their heads at the preposterous notion of 'balloon mail'.

"What do you mean balloons?" Ferenc asked.

"Exactly that," Albert said as he pulled a large envelope from his jacket pocket and distributed the contents. A hush came over the room as they each read one of the propaganda leaflets before passing it onto the next man.

"Apparently, they were huge balloons that floated across parts of Hungary, particularly around the western districts, that eventually burst high up in the sky, spilling their contents. Thousands of leaflets rained down on the towns and in fields. Those who saw this, including my cousin, quickly collected the papers and secretly distributed them amongst their friends. As you can see, there are a variety of themes: pictures of life in

America; a caricature of the villain, Rákosi; and, most potent of all, the pamphlet of the 'Twelve Points' from the 1848 revolution. It's a reminder to us all of the rights that were commanded against the leaders of the country at the time, demanding equality, liberty, and brotherhood. It's as relevant now as it was back then. Reading it made the hairs on the back of my neck rise," Albert said, then read out loud to the group.

"What the Hungarian People want"
1. *We demand the freedom of the press, the abolition of censorship.*
2. *Independent Hungarian government in Buda-Pest.*
3. *Annual national assembly in Pest.*
4. *Civil and religious equality before the law.*
5. *National army.*
6. *Universal and equal taxation.*
7. *The abolition of socage, feudalism and serfdom.*
8. *Juries and courts based on an equal legal representation.*
9. *A national bank.*
10. *The army must take an oath on the Constitution, our soldiers must not be sent abroad, foreign soldiers must be sent away.*
11. *Free all political prisoners.*
12. *Union with Transylvania."*

"Much of this is what we are aiming for now. Radio Free Europe is responsible for some of this, as you can see from the top of these papers. Rumour has it that they have enlisted the Americans to increase the effective opposition to the Communists. The Americans have an interest in restoring democracies around the world, reinstating self-government, and individual liberties. Regrettably, we believe they have no appetite for another war, so military intervention is probably out of the question, but they seem to be helping in this passive way."

Tomás piped up and added, "It suggests that our Western neighbours have not abandoned us entirely to our fate. Maybe we have allies after all."

Albert nodded, then continued, "My cousin reported that the people who were caught distributing this anti-communist material were whisked away to prison. Or that's what he thinks. No one really knows what happened to them. It's rumoured that a few are in hiding or trying their luck at crossing the border into Austria."

"Good luck to them, I say," Ferenc nodded.

Iván sat quietly, listening intently, before remarking, "Can you imagine how furious the Communists are with this Western propaganda? How many balloons have successfully scattered thousands of copies of this caricature of Rákosi, and more especially sent up a call to arms by reminding us of the 1848 Twelve Points? Ridiculing our Soviet dictators and stirring up patriotism won't be tolerated by them; I can assure you of that."

***

Anna was distraught. István was slipping away from her. His excuses for not being able to spend much time with her these last few weeks were feeble and her instincts told her that something was amiss. István had changed, and the only reason she could think of was that there must be another woman. She decided to stake out his apartment, and so on Saturday afternoon she positioned herself across the road from István's apartment block. Hours passed and fatigue crept into Anna's bones. She was just about to give up when István left the building, dressed in a dark suit and tie. To be going out for the evening dressed so smartly could only mean one thing. Anna followed at a safe distance as István made his way to the nearby bottle shop and, after a few minutes, exited with a bottle wrapped in a brown paper bag. He then made his way to the tram stop. Tears instantly sprung into Anna's wide eyes as she witnessed the betrayal. Her worst fear was realised. The love of her life was meeting someone else for dinner. Slowly, she walked away from the scene, berating herself for not being enough of a woman to keep István faithful. As she made her way home, Anna brushed away the tears, resolving to confront him at the next opportunity, in the hope of saving their future.

CHAPTER 6

"I'm moving out!" Julia declared one Friday evening after work as she swept into the bedroom she shared with Natália. "Robi finally asked me to move in with him, and I agreed. It was my suggestion, but I made it sound like it was his idea. You know what men are like. They need to feel in control of everything." Julia was laughing as she changed out of her uniform.

"Oh, that's wonderful, Julia. I know how much you love Robi. I'm truly happy for you. Of course, I'll miss you. I don't know how I'll manage without you," Natália replied kindly.

"Don't worry, we'll stay in touch," Julia said dismissively, not meeting Natália's eyes.

"Have you told Mrs Hajdu?" Natália asked.

"Not yet. I'll pop down now and let her know. I'll be gone by the end of next week."

With that pronouncement, Julia flew out the door, leaving Natália alone, sitting on the edge of her bed, saddened by the realisation that Julia was probably lost to her forever. Julia and Robi hadn't forgiven Natália for dumping Lukács, no longer including her in any of their social outings, which hurt her deeply. The girls rarely even saw each other at work, since Julia had been transferred to a different wing of the factory, making men's shaving cream, and always chose to take her lunchbreaks with Robi. Despite Natália's best efforts to patch things up with her friend, even offering to make her a dress as a practice run for her new venture, the girls continued to drift further apart. Most weeknights Julia was out partying or staying at Robi's, and on the nights she chose to sleep at the guesthouse, she crept into their room well after Natália had already gone to sleep. Perhaps Julia's decision to leave was for the best. The air between them was still tense and uneasy, without any attempt by Julia at reconciling. None the less, Natália was still devastated about losing her friend.

Searching for a glimmer of optimism amid the choking misery, the notion of having the bedroom to herself was quite appealing, although she doubted her sanctuary would remain hers alone for long. Knowing Mrs Hajdu would want the income, Natália pondered how long it would take her landlady to find another roommate and hoped she would get along with whomever it turned out to be. Lying down and reaching for the blanket to provide some much-needed comfort, Natália perked up a bit at the thought of being able to fully immerse herself in her sewing, with no distractions. Having recently furnished her new dressmaking studio, Natália had already completed a light wool skirt, a satin blouse, and a summer dress for Mrs Hajdu. They were conservative, simple pieces for the older woman that allowed Natália to refresh her skills. Maintaining her job at the factory, and with little else to occupy her free time, Natália sewed late into the night on weekdays and every spare hour she had at the weekends, recording the time taken to finish each garment. Customers were sure to inquire about the turnaround time for the completion of their outfits, and Natália needed to answer with certainty.

Mrs Hajdu proved to be the ideal customer, trusting in whatever styles and fabrics Natália deemed appropriate. Being an extravert, Natália thoroughly enjoyed the consultative aspect to the venture, discussing designs, choosing the right fabrics, managing the fittings, and finally revealing the finished product. The joy of seeing Mrs Hajdu delighted with her new clothes, that were not only expertly made but flattered her plump figure, was thrilling. Another unexpected boon from the experience was the friendship that sprung from the regular discussions and fittings, a closeness that Natália had never anticipated. The maturity and wisdom offered by Mrs Hajdu, more friend now than landlady, was something that Natália treasured. With renewed confidence, Natália was energised into circulating her advertising fliers, and with a bit of luck clients would soon be queuing at her door.

***

Time sailed by and the day arrived for Julia to leave. She took no time at all to pack her few belongings, drag her bag down the stairs and drop it near the front door. Popping her head into the living room, she saw Robi and Natália seated on the sofa, chatting inconsequentially, Robi seemingly uncomfortable. Natália had asked after Lukács. Robi replied offhandedly that his friend was enjoying his new job, that the pay was better, and that he had a new girlfriend. Natália smiled, saying how pleased she was that things had worked out so well for him. Julia walked casually over to Robi to rescue him from any further probing and rested her hand on his shoulder. With relief he asked, "Ready, love?"

"You bet!" Julia replied as she stood to leave.

Turning to face Natália, the two girls remained motionless, eyes fixed on one another, unsure of what to say. Natália was the first to cry. Tears slowly spilled down her cheeks. They were tears of sorrow for a lost friend, knowing that this was the end of their friendship.

"Take care of yourself, Julia," Natália said with a slight wobble in her voice as she brushed the tears from her face with the back of her hand. The girls hugged, and as Julia stepped back, her eyes were filled with tears.

"I'm really happy, Natália. I hope you'll find happiness someday too," Julia said quietly.

Turning back to Robi, who was by this time hovering by the living room door, she grabbed his hand, dragged him into the corridor, picked up her suitcase and was out the front door in a flash.

Natália collapsed onto the sofa, wrapping her arms around herself, allowing the tears to run freely down her face as she stared absently at the flames dancing in the fireplace. The double brick construction of the house made the nights chilly throughout much of the year, and the fire was a comfort for body and soul. Feeling abandoned, and more alone than ever, Natália wondered how her life could have flipped so badly. A couple of girlfriends who had stood by her provided some company, yet parting with Julia, who had been her best friend and confidante for such a long time, felt like a piece of her heart had been severed. Perhaps her mother was right after all. Maybe her expectations and goals in life were unrealistic, and that she simply alienated everyone she cared for in the process of pursuing her selfish dreams. Her mother's smirking face was imprinted in her mind, fuelling her misery. Would her father be more sympathetic, offering a guiding light for her future? Discussing boyfriends with her father was always difficult, as his protective instincts meant that he found fault in any man, yet, despite this, Natália felt the need to seek his council. He had supported her renewed passion for dress design, delivering her sewing machine and helping with installing the furniture for her studio. He was a solid rock whom Natália could always depend upon. Wiping her nose on a handkerchief, Natália resolved to invite her father to lunch at a nearby café as soon as he could manage a trip to the city. Just the two of them. Her mother need not know.

Shaken from her reverie by the rattling of china cups, Natália glanced up to see Mrs Hajdu shuffling into the room carrying a tray of tea and cookies. Placing the tray on the table she sat beside Natália, gently patted her arm, and said, "Have some tea, dear. It'll make you feel better." Mrs Hajdu then poured the tea into a cup and passed it to Natália, before stating in a rather matter of fact way, "That girl has no morals to speak of. She's loose with her tongue and more besides. Not like you. In time you'll forget her, which is just as well. You're much better than that." Picking up her cup, she changed the subject and said cheerily, "Now, I was thinking about a new summer dress to wear to church. Any suggestions?"

Natália smiled at her kind landlady, a discerning woman who filled the maternal void in her life. Feeling less alone, she brushed away the remnants of her tears and took a sip of the hot tea, which slid soothingly down her throat, before replying, "I'm sure I can think of something. Perhaps we can pop across to the fabric store tomorrow morning and see if we can find something you like?"

***

Natália had the short-lived luxury of having the bedroom to herself for two weeks before Mrs Hajdu introduced her new lodger. Having become accustomed to the privacy and extra space, she was a little put out by having to share again. It was not her decision though, so she put her feelings to one side and focused her attention on making the new girl feel welcome.

"Rózsa Varga, this is Natália Kardos. Natália, meet Rózsa. Try to get on and don't forget, no boys in the room," Mrs Hajdu decreed in a stern voice, before promptly leaving.

Natália burst out laughing. The colour drained from Rózsa's face as she stared, open mouthed, horrified at her new landlady.

"Don't worry, she's not fierce, she's actually very soft-hearted. If you don't break the rules, she'll warm to you and even give you a little wine with dinner, if you choose to eat here sometimes. I eat here often, for convenience as much as anything. Mrs Hajdu is quite a good cook and doesn't charge that much extra for meals on top of the weekly rent. She seems to enjoy the company. Her husband died in the war, and I think she's lonely," Natália explained, trying to allay Rózsa's concerns.

Sitting on the edge of her bed Natália watched Rózsa unpack her suitcase. There wasn't much to unpack, as it happened. Rózsa grew up in a poor farming village with few possessions. She smiled shyly at Natália and said, "Sounds good to me."

The pair spent the next hour amicably chatting as Natália showed Rózsa around the boarding house, highlighting all the strict rules and bathroom etiquette. Mrs Hajdu made a pot of tea and set a plate of shortbread cookies next to the teapot on the kitchen table, then went about her business. It was a lovely invitation for the girls to relax and become acquainted. Rózsa was still rattled by her experience with her previous landlady and wanted to confide in her new roommate. Natália was warming to Rózsa, an innocent country girl, not unlike herself when she was eighteen.

Having arrived in Budapest just two months before, Rózsa despised the woman who ran the previous guesthouse where she had boarded. The landlady was unkind and bossy, forcing Rózsa to do chores around the house and even to do some of the cooking, with no discount on her rent. Rózsa was often exhausted and had little free time to herself or for making new friends. She felt used and abused, which were the exact reasons why she left home in the first place. It didn't take long for her to decide to look for somewhere else to live. After a few sleepless nights, contemplating how she would approach the subject of leaving, Rózsa finally plucked up the courage to confront her landlady and gave two weeks' notice. The woman was furious, yelling at her for being ungrateful. Rózsa was terrified but held her nerve, kept out of the woman's way as best she could, and counted the days until the deadline. She just hoped that her new landlady, Mrs Hajdu, would be more empathetic and friendly than the horrible crone from whom she was fleeing. As the time to leave drew nearer, Rózsa felt a huge weight lift from her shoulders and found that the spring in her step had returned.

Within days of arriving in Budapest, Rózsa secured a position as a kitchen hand at a nearby café called The Coffee Pot. Quickly settling into a routine, she found the work most enjoyable. The staff were welcoming and happily showed her the ropes, so that it was not long before she felt part of the team. The café was housed in an old building, the exterior a little battered from the bombings during the war. However, it was solid enough and rather quaint inside. Dark timber panelling lined the walls. Several large, rectangular mirrors with ornate, gilt frames hung on two walls, giving the illusion of a much larger space. Teardrop shaped glass and brass light fittings hung low from the ceiling, infusing the café with an air of elegance. Yet it was homely too, with chairs covered in a dusty rose-pink velvet, newspapers scattered around the tables for patrons to read free of charge, and vases of fresh cut flowers from the owner's courtyard. It was truly a pleasure to go to work each day. For once in her life, Rózsa felt competent and valued. And to make her situation even more complete, Rózsa knew she had just found a true friend in Natália. The atmosphere in her new home was more relaxed and hospitable than she was accustomed to, thanks to her new roommate's efforts to make her feel at home. Whilst she was only a few years older, Natália seemed far more mature and worldly, an effervescent and self-assured woman whom Rózsa hoped she could emulate.

Natália observed that Rózsa was shy and reserved, and instinctively took the girl under her wing. She had hoped that Rózsa worked at the factory so they could travel to work together and get to know one another better, but it was not to be. The Coffee Pot Café was in the opposite direction to the cosmetic factory, but still relatively close to home. On the upside, Rózsa said she could wrangle discounts on meals for family and friends at the café. Natália was delighted, thinking it would make a nice change to venture out again, and perhaps meet some new friends.

***

As the orange glow of the sun slowly dissipated and was replaced by a darkness that enveloped the narrow streets between the Coffee Pot Café and Mrs Hajdu's guesthouse, Rózsa flew home as quickly as she could. Gasping for breath, she opened the door and found Natália in the living room reading the paper. Rózsa flopped into a chair opposite her friend, breathing deeply to calm herself, trying to contain her excitement. Natália looked up, smiled, and asked, "What's gotten into you?"

Like a speeding bullet Rózsa replied, "I've been asked out on my first date. His name is János Vadas. He's so cute and friendly and smart and tall with dark brown eyes and—"

"Whoa, hold on, not so fast," Natália jumped in. "Who's János?"

"He's a regular customer at the café," Rózsa exclaimed, grinning widely. Her cheeks were flushed from running home and her eyes sparkled with eagerness. "János is always joking and making me laugh. And today he asked me if I'd like to go to the movies with him next Saturday night. Isn't that wonderful?"

"I suppose it is," Natália replied a little cautiously. "Do you know much about him?"

"Only that he works at the steel works as a labourer but has recently applied for a promotion. If he's successful, he'll report to one of the big bosses. He lives a few streets away from the café and calls in often for coffee, and sometimes a beer or two or a light supper. I said that I'd only consider going out with him if you came too, knowing a chaperone on my first date was proper. You will come won't you, Natália?" Rózsa pleaded, twisting her fingers through her wavy brown hair as she eyed Natália, waiting for her answer.

Sounds familiar, Natália thought, as she remembered saying the same thing to Lukács on their first date. Gosh, how long ago that now seemed. She chuckled and said, "Sure, why not. What movie are we seeing?"

"I have no idea. I didn't think to ask."

They both burst out laughing. Rózsa's excitement was infectious. Natália hadn't been to the movies in ages and thought a night out would do her good.

"Let's see what Mrs Hajdu has prepared for dinner tonight. We can discuss what dress you should wear to impress this nice boy," Natália smiled.

The girls headed towards the kitchen, contentedly breathing in the delicious aromas that streamed into the passageway. Once seated, Mrs Hajdu placed bowls of steaming tomato and capsicum pasta in front of each of the girls before serving herself. Rózsa became a little subdued during the meal, pushing her fork around the plate in contemplation, and then quietly remarked that she didn't have many clothes and certainly nothing pretty to wear on a date. Natália was expecting this, having witnessed Rózsa unpack when she arrived, noting that the few items of clothing she possessed were quite plain and made from coarse material.

"Don't worry, Rózsa. You can borrow one of my dresses. You're not much smaller than me and I'm sure I can make minor adjustments where necessary. You can borrow my makeup too. A little colour on your cheeks and lips is all that's needed to brighten your face. But shoes will be the problem. We're not the same size. You'll need something nicer to wear with dresses. The shoe factory on the other side of the city has a store that's open to the public selling 'seconds' at discounted prices, but you can hardly tell what the faults are. I'm sure we'll find something appropriate without having to spend too much. János will be completely dazzled by you, I'm sure of it," Natália reassured her friend.

"Oh, thanks, Natália. I don't know how I would manage without you," Rózsa said, and ran around the table to where Natália was sitting to hug her tightly.

"If you like, I can make you a couple of dresses of your own when you've saved up some money. I won't charge you for the labour, only the materials," Natália offered, wanting to help the younger girl.

"Really? That would be wonderful! I can't thank you enough."

"And how exactly do you intend on making any money from dressmaking if you don't charge for your services?" Mrs Hajdu chimed in; eyebrows raised.

Natália gave her landlady a lopsided smile and shrugged.

**

The girls went about their work during the following week, excitement building as the weekend loomed. During the evenings, after dinner, they deliberated over which dress would be most appropriate for the big night out, finally selecting a pale blue, lightweight wool dress with three quarter length sleeves and a full, calf length skirt. It was perfect for the late spring weather, as the nights were still cool enough to warrant something a little warm. The colour of the dress matched Rózsa's crystal blue eyes. Natália only needed to make minor adjustments to the hemline and sleeve length, which would not take much time at all. An adjustable belt cinched at the waist enhanced the fit. The neckline was cut round in the front and back, but not too low to preserve her modesty. Rózsa couldn't believe her reflection when she stood in front of the mirror. She had never owned, nor even had the opportunity to wear, anything as pretty. Tears welled up in her eyes.

"I really don't know what to say, Natália. It's beautiful. This means so much to me, thank you," Rózsa whispered through the tears, before hugging her friend.

"It's my pleasure. I'm curious now about this boy, János. He must be pretty special since you're going to so much trouble to impress him."

"Oh, he is. He really is."

***

Saturday finally arrived. As the day wore on, Rózsa's eagerness was replaced by anxiety at meeting János socially. Butterflies whirled around her stomach, and she hardly ate a thing, such was her nervousness. The entire afternoon was spent styling her hair in different ways until she settled on soft curls just above her shoulders. Her fringe was pinned to the right side of her head with an ornamental comb, adorned with pale pink roses in a similar shade to the lipstick Natália had lent her. It was soft and subtle, nothing too dramatic.

"If we want to make the 6.00pm tram, Rózsa, we need to get going now," Natália called to Rózsa from outside the bathroom door. She headed downstairs and waited patiently for the girl to materialise. When Rózsa appeared on the landing Natália was struck by how beautiful the young girl looked. It didn't take much to transform this shy, plain looking farmer's daughter into an attractive young woman, eager to impress on her first date. Draping their shawls around their shoulders, they headed out the door.

Although they arrived at the cinema ten minutes earlier than the rendezvous time, János was already there, smoking a cigarette and searching the crowd. The comedy, "A Glass of Beer" directed by Félix Máriássy, was recently released, so the box office was thick with queues. Once Rózsa spotted János, her pace quickened. Natália grabbed her arm, pulled her back, and said, "Slow down, you don't want to appear too eager."

The next moment, János looked in their direction and spotted Rózsa walking toward him.

He kissed her on the cheek. "You look gorgeous. And this must be Natália. It's lovely to finally meet you. Rózsa has told me a lot about you. Thanks for agreeing to come." He kissed Natália's hand, as was customary.

"It's good to meet you too. I couldn't possibly refuse a request from this very persistent young lady," Natália said as she looked over at Rózsa, who seemed mesmerised by János.

"I hope you don't mind, but I brought a friend of mine along. He's at the box office buying the tickets. I thought that since Rózsa wanted to bring a friend, I would too. A foursome will be more fun," János said with a twinkle in his eye. He observed that Natália straitened her back and seemed to bristle a little. Rózsa on the other hand was oblivious and chimed in, "Great idea! I'm sure Natália won't mind."

"Speak of the devil, here he is. I'd like to introduce my dear friend and work colleague, István Szabó," János said. "István, this is the lovely Rózsa I've told you about, and her friend Natália."

"I'm happy to make your acquaintance, ladies," István replied, noticing that Natália was not smiling. It was obvious that she hadn't been made aware of the blind date. Finding the situation amusing, he couldn't resist teasing her by saying, "I'm pleased to be your date tonight, Natália," then reached for her hand and planted a soft kiss on her knuckles. Remaining mute she smiled weakly, then turned to walk towards the cinema entrance. The others quickly followed. Once inside, they took their seats and settled themselves in anticipation of the new comedy. In the years that followed Stalin's death, under Khrushchev's leadership, there were marginal attempts to democratise society. Political messages were toned down in the media, as well as in film production. Félix Máriássy, a prominent film maker, excelled in this new form of film production, allowing his characters to be multi-faceted and far more entertaining.

It took Natália a while to accept that she had been hoodwinked into a blind date, but she gradually relaxed and enjoyed the movie. Once the lights went up, Natália noticed that Rózsa was holding hands with János and they were sitting shoulder to shoulder. János was leaning close to Rózsa and whispering something. It looked too cosy on a first date in Natália's estimation, and she decided that she would chastise Rózsa when they got home. Not that Rózsa was formally in her care, but rather that Natália felt like an older sister, looking out for a younger, impressionable sibling.

"The night is still young, and I'm famished, "János declared to the group as they walked outside. "How about we go across to the bar at the end of the street and indulge in a light supper and drinks? I've been there many times and it has a comfortable atmosphere with a good selection of light meals."

Rózsa and István agreed, saying they were equally hungry, whilst Natália said nothing. Taking silence as a yes, the group set off down the street towards the bar. István hung back, electing to walk alongside Natália. Turning on his charm to put her at ease, he tried to engage her in light-hearted conversation.

"I haven't laughed so much in ages. It was a good story, don't you think?" István asked.

"Yes, I suppose so," Natália replied coolly.

"I'm sorry if my presence has upset you. János was trying to make me feel better by inviting me out. I recently broke up with my girlfriend and haven't been out for ages. I've been sullen and moody and, quite frankly, very poor company. János was trying to cheer me up. It worked too. The film was very entertaining, and I got to meet not one but two beautiful young women. Life must be looking up," he said with a wide grin that reached his eyes, searching her face for some hint of softening. He hoped the little white lie about breaking up with a girlfriend sounded genuine.

Deciding there really wasn't any harm done by István's presence, and that her behaviour was churlish, Natália replied, "I'm not angry with you. It's just that I wasn't aware that anyone else was coming tonight and it caught me off guard. I've never been on a blind date. It's not something I would normally do."

"I see. Well, we're both here now, so why don't we make the most of the situation and try to have some fun."

István raised his arm, offered it to Natália, which she graciously accepted, looking up into his face and smiling warmly. István's heart skipped a beat as her emerald eyes glittered in the moonlight. Her beauty was quite breathtaking.

The venue was bustling when they arrived. Others from the cinema were already enjoying their first drink. János spotted a vacant booth towards the rear of the bar and headed there with the girls in tow whilst István muscled his way to the front of the counter and ordered the first round of drinks. It was obvious to Natália as she observed them from across the table that Rózsa was infatuated with János, and he with her. Natália spent a few minutes sizing him up while she waited for István to return with the drinks. He was certainly tall, as Rózsa had mentioned, and handsome. His eyes were dark brown pools that seemed to penetrate deep into your soul when he looked directly at you, yet they revealed a hint of mischievousness. He was much older than she'd expected, late twenties in her estimation. Was he seeking a virgin bride?

"Here we are," István announced as he placed the glasses onto the table. He handed out a couple of menus and sat down beside Natália, careful not to sit too close and upset her again. The soup of the day was kidney bean and vegetable, a nice hearty meal on a chilly evening. They all opted for the soup special with crusty bread and lashings of butter.

The night passed amicably after that. Natália lightened up and found she enjoyed the company of these two handsome men. The banter between them was jovial. It had been a while since she was in the company of men in a social setting, and she realised how much she missed their dry humour and playfulness. Discreetly, she tried to appraise István with sideways glances. He too was tall and slim, but with a receding hairline. Slight creases around his eyes and deep lines were carved below his cheeks. Natália was impressed at his impeccable attire, a charcoal grey woollen suit, crisp white shirt, and highly polished, good quality leather shoes—he was undoubtedly someone who was particular about his appearance. István's demeanour suggested that he was slightly older than János, possibly in his early thirties, and he acted in a more mature and worldly manner than Lukács and Robi ever did, which greatly appealed to Natália. As soon as that thought crossed her mind, she berated herself. The evening was for Rózsa, not for her to find a new boyfriend.

When they finally parted company and headed home, Rózsa talked incessantly until they turned the light out in their bedroom. Natália was happy for her friend, pleased the evening was a success, and she chose not to mention her earlier misgivings. Sleep, however, proved elusive for

Natália. She couldn't stop thinking about István, who spoke in a smooth and educated way, and looked directly at her with hazel eyes that were kind and respectful. He didn't try to fondle her in any way, just kissed her on the cheek and thanked her for a wonderful time. "The best night I've had in a long time," he said as they went their separate ways.

János took the tram, but István elected to walk part of the way home from the bar, finding the crisp night air helped clear his thoughts. What began as a favour to János, making up a foursome for his first date with Rózsa, became one of the most enjoyable evenings he could remember. Rózsa was a lovely, bubbly young girl, clearly besotted by János who in turn was smitten by the girl. István was happy that the night turned out well for his friend, yet his own emotions were surprisingly mixed. Whilst he had no intention of taking particular interest in the other woman, István found that he was captivated by Natália's extraordinary beauty and sincerity. Once she lightened up and accepted the blind date for what it was, a favour to both their friends, she had revealed herself to be a smart, confident, and strong-minded woman. Yet behind her glittering eyes, István sensed a reserve that intrigued him. As he walked on, Anna's image popped into his mind. Guilt washed over him for feeling so enthralled by Natália and for wondering hopefully when he might see her again.

***

The following Saturday morning, István entered the guesthouse and introduced himself to Mrs Hajdu, stating that he wanted to speak with Natália if she was home. Mrs Hajdu appraised the dashing man, smartly dressed, nodded approvingly to herself, then ushered him into the living room to take a seat while she fetched Natália. Beavering away in her workroom, Natália thought she heard István's voice, or someone that sounded like him, and found her heart racing at the prospect of seeing him again. Creeping out the back door and circling back through the kitchen, she ran up to her room, removed her apron, quickly brushed her thick locks, and hastily applied some lipstick before venturing down to meet her guest. Mrs Hajdu took one look at Natália as they met halfway down the stairs and realised nothing needed to be said. Natália beamed as she skipped past the woman, then paused before entering the living room to compose herself, before casually greeting her visitor, "Hi István, I'm surprised to see you here. Is there something amiss?"

"No, not at all. I just wondered if you'd like to join me for lunch today at The Coffee Pot. János has been raving about the food there and I thought we could sample the fare together. I trust this impromptu visit isn't inappropriate. Perhaps I should have called you first. You're probably busy," he said, chastising himself for not calling ahead.

"I don't have any particular plans today, so yes, I'd be happy to accompany you. You must know that with Rózsa working there, I'm a regular customer," she replied, smiling up at him with one of her dazzling smiles.

"Of course, how could I forget? I'll happily accept your recommendations," he said, grinning.

"Wait here a minute whilst I fetch my purse."

Natália returned to her bedroom, where she dabbed a little perfume onto her wrists, then checked herself in the mirror. Despite the hammering of her heart, she demurely walked down the stairs to join the attractive man waiting patiently in the foyer. When they walked out the door, István extended his arm to Natália and cocked his head to one side in an unremarked question. She slipped her arm through his and they walked happily down the street in the direction of the café. Natália felt a warm glow suffuse her entire body and realised how thrilled she was to be in István's company once again.

CHAPTER 7

"I know what you've been up to, István, why you've stopped coming around as regularly as you used to. I saw you leave your apartment, all dressed up. Who have you been seeing behind my back?" Anna fought hard to supress the tears that welled up in her eyes, wanting to remain in control, demanding answers. Shutting the door firmly behind István as he stepped into the living room, she folded her arms firmly across her bosom.

Anna's attack took István entirely by surprise. Standing frozen in the centre of the room, he was lost for words until rage filled him with the realisation that Anna had been spying on him. Not only could that prove dangerous for them both, but he was also outraged that she would go to such lengths to check his movements. How long had that been going on? Parking his fury, he sat down at the dining table, rubbed a hand over his face and calmly replied, "I'm not seeing another woman, Anna."

The little white lie sprung from his lips. He had, in fact, gone out with Natália twice, but it was early days yet and he wasn't sure where it was heading. He certainly enjoyed Natália's company, quick wit, and zest for life, not to mention her beautiful emerald eyes and a smile that took his breath away. Natália, on the other hand, still seemed a little reserved with him. Perhaps she was shy or just wanted to keep him guessing about her feelings. Either way, he enjoyed their time together and wanted to get to know her better.

"I received word that my stepmother has been taken ill with tuberculosis and admitted to a hospice. I've been visiting her as often as possible as the doctors doubt that she'll recover. It's the reason I've been so preoccupied lately. I'm sorry I haven't spoken of her before this."

"You never mentioned a stepmother or any other relatives. We've never really discussed your family," Anna replied quietly, shocked by the revelation of a dying relative but equally stunned at the realisation that she had never asked after his family. Mortified, she was consumed with remorse.

"I refer to Mrs Horváth as my stepmother, as she took me in after the war and cared for me as her own son when my family was evicted from our home and sent away. Thankfully, I escaped their fate and remained in Budapest due to her kindness. I regret having kept this from you, but I didn't want to worry you unnecessarily," István said, all too convincingly.

Mrs Horváth was indeed a wonderful woman who took in many homeless men after the war, cooking and washing for them, and in some ways István did feel she was like a stepmother. But she had died two years before. The explanation seemed to appease Anna, who rushed over to him, threw her arms around his neck, and apologised for her foolishness through the tears that were finally released, spilling down her cheeks. István knew that the time had come to part company. Whilst he cared for Anna, he didn't love her. It was unfair to keep stringing her along, allowing her to believe they had a future together—a presumption that was reasonable given their seventeen-month relationship. It was important to find the right moment, and to be careful not to create an enemy of her. He would find a way to gently sever their relationship. But not tonight. They ate their meal in amicable silence, after speaking briefly about this newly discovered relation. Anna was ashamed of her outburst, and inwardly chastised herself for accusing István of being unfaithful.

Telling Anna that he wanted to remain at his stepmother's bedside as the end drew near, István left early. Anna had insisted on accompanying him to the nursing home, and it took all his creativity to persuade her to let him grieve alone. Anna felt rebuffed, confused, and upset that István wouldn't allow her to comfort him during this sad time in his life, but she reluctantly acquiesced. From that day, István's visits became even less frequent, and his excuses sounded feeble even to his own ears. But he hoped that when he broke up with Anna it would not be such a shock. He just needed to find the right moment to let her down gently.

Not wanting to drag out the difficult situation longer than necessary, István finally plucked up the courage to confront Anna with the truth—a flexible truth that he hoped was also a plausible one. Rather than risk breaking the tough news to Anna in her home, which would surely send her into hysterics, the grounds of the hospital where she worked provided neutral, public territory that would confine her emotional response. She was always quick to sob at any sad event, whether in real life or at the movies. In many ways she was still a naive child with simplistic expectations in life, which was a crucial reason for their lack of compatibility. István thought that meeting during her lunch break the following Friday would give Anna the weekend to begin the healing process, and the knowledge that her flat mate would be around to provide much needed support confirmed the timing.

When Friday arrived, István was agitated for the entire morning. Rehearsing his speech, he tried to choose the right words for maximum clarity but in a soft, caring way to minimise the hurt. Changing the words over and over was inconsequential. Regardless of how he delivered the message Anna would be devastated by the breakup. Arriving at the cafeteria a few minutes early, he checked to see if Anna was already seated at one of the tables. With no sign of her he queued at the counter and bought two cheese and pickle sandwiches and two coffees. Scanning the room for a more private section, he shuffled over to a corner table with fewer people nearby, trying not to spill the coffee. As soon as he was seated, Anna entered the cafeteria. István waved her over. As she approached the table, Anna beamed at him, leaned over, and kissed him on the lips. His heart sank, but he smiled back despite feeling miserable about what he was about to do.

"This was a wonderful idea, István. We rarely have lunch together when I'm at work. I'm starving," she said cheerfully as she bit into her sandwich, oblivious to what was coming.

István glanced down at his sandwich, unable to eat with his stomach churning furiously, before he took a deep breath, pushed his plate aside and began his well-rehearsed speech, "Anna, I suggested we meet because I have something important to say that I've struggled with for some time. I've been doing a lot of soul searching these past few weeks—you've noticed how distracted I've been. The death of my stepmother helped to crystallise my thoughts and feelings, and to decide what I want from life."

Anna continued to chew for a moment but then sat back in her chair, the joy that infused her moments before was dissolving as she looked intently into her lover's eyes, calmly absorbing the words that floated across the table into her confused mind. István spoke of his apparent need for solitude. The death of his stepmother had rocked him hard and he needed time to grieve, which was the reason he was absent and preoccupied so often lately. Sorting through her meagre belongings and attending to her affairs made him reflect on his own life and contemplate the future. Marriage was not what he wanted at this stage of his life. He was not ready to take on the responsibility of a family. But he knew that Anna yearned to settle down, have children, and live happily ever after—a dream that was hers alone. She was young, pretty, a fabulous cook, a wonderful catch for any man, someone much more deserving of her than he. The decision to go their separate ways was extremely difficult, he cared for her a great deal, but ultimately, he knew it was right for them both.

As his words registered, the meaning undeniably clear, Anna couldn't fathom how István would consider his future without including her, after all she'd done for him. She'd loved him with every fibre of her being. And she believed he loved her too, often bringing her gifts; sometimes flowers, a scarf, a woollen hat with matching gloves, always wine for dinner, the light red she liked the best. He was gentle and kind and loving. Overcome with a multitude of emotions; loss, hurt, fear, rejection, anger, helplessness, her bottom lip quivered, and the tears streamed down her face, dripping onto her sandwich. Realistically, she knew deep down in her core that he was lost to her. It had been a gradual separation over many weeks that she had desperately hoped was only temporary.

"But I love you with all my heart, István. I can't imagine my life without you," sobs caught in her throat. "Please don't leave me."

"You're a very special girl, Anna. I never meant to hurt you this way. You deserve much better. I'm truly sorry, but I know it's for the best."

István left his uneaten lunch on the plate, stood, kissed her on the cheek, and said, "Goodbye, Anna. Take care of yourself."

Anna watched the man of her dreams walk out the door and dissolve into a sea of people hurrying about their business. It then dawned on her that István didn't say he loved her when he left. Anna racked her brain, trying to recall a time when István spoke of love. Did he ever love her?

She felt hollow, used, and spat out. Remaining seated, with her back to everyone, Anna sobbed her heart out.

***

Over the next few weeks, István spent as much of his free time as possible searching for a one-bedroom flat. Now that his relationship with Anna had ended, the cramped space he shared with János and Péter on a permanent basis was unbearable. The boys often left the newspaper on the kitchen table, opened at the classified section, highlighting apartments for rent boldly circled in red ink in the hope István would take the hint and move out.

With a good portion of his weekly wage saved since returning to work, István was ready to find a flat of his own. Recently promoted at the steel works on higher pay, he allowed himself to be a little fussy with the location and size of the flat. Two places had become available along Akácfa Street, a neighbourhood he liked. Before making an appointment to inspect the properties he called Natália, asking if she'd help him decide; a woman's opinion was highly valued if he wanted his flat to be homely. Natália accepted eagerly, often dreaming of finding her own place, to enjoy privacy, to have her own kitchen, to entertain friends without rules imposed by anyone. Sharing a room in a boarding house provided a good start to life in the city, but she was ready to move on and yearned for her own private oasis. Whilst this was not her potential apartment she'd be inspecting, it was a good opportunity to gauge how far her wages would stretch if she were to leave the guesthouse.

The couple agreed to meet at the front of the first apartment block. Natália fell in love with it instantly. It was an old, four-storey brick building with a central courtyard that each apartment looked onto. Wrought iron benches painted in a bottle green hue dotted the garden. Several flowering shrubs brightened up the surroundings, including lavender, lilacs, camellias, and a variety of roses. The vacant flat was on the third floor, which didn't seem to bother either of them. Few residential buildings had elevators, and everyone was accustomed to hiking up flights of stairs. Once inside, they both commented on the amount of light that streamed through the windows, creating a spacious, airy, welcoming feel. White lace curtains draped the windows. The walls were painted in an off-white tone, as were the high ceilings, which had ornate, sculptured cornices. A large Persian rug covered most of the floor space in the living room, adding warmth and comfort underfoot, and an old, navy-blue sofa stood against one wall. Natália plonked herself onto the sofa and remarked, "You must take this one, István. It's perfect. The living room is large, it has two bedrooms and some furnishings, including a wardrobe in the main bedroom. The sofa seems sturdy enough. You won't need to buy much else, perhaps just a small table and chairs for the kitchen and, of course, a bed." She blushed and looked away when she said that. "And just look at the lovely communal garden. It's a special haven in the middle of town. You could grow herbs, perhaps some vegetables. Wouldn't that be nice?" Natália grinned at him, her eyes twinkling with enthusiasm.

István cocked his eyebrow at her and replied, "I've never grown a thing in my life."

Natália ignored him as she explored the rest of the flat, rattling off all the positive attributes of the place. One would presume it was to be hers, the way she was behaving. He chuckled, loving her fervent input, but insisted they inspect the second property as a comparison. A brief look at the other rental revealed it to be inferior. The decision was unanimous. The first flat won hands down. After much haggling over the next two days, István successfully negotiated a rental fee close to his budget. With few possessions there was not much to pack, and he settled in at the end of the week.

János and Péter were extremely pleased to hear that their flatmate had found a place of his own. Finally, they could reclaim their living room. To celebrate, the boys organised farewell drinks for a few of their mutual friends, including Natália and Rózsa, on István's last night. The girls whipped up a storm; dumplings filled with pitted prunes and dusted with icing sugar, lemon crepes filled with soft curd cheese, and a platter of salami, pork sausage, cheese, and crusty bread. Natália had made a special trip to her hometown the day before, begging her father to part with some of his home cured Csabai, the much-loved spicy salami loaded with paprika, and Hurka, the pork liver sausage filled with onion and rice that she knew was one of István's favourites. Her father could never refuse his favourite child anything, and Natália had brought him a gift of his favourite pipe tobacco in exchange. Deal done.

The radio was blasting out their favourite dance music. At every opportunity, István grabbed Natália's arm and twirled her around the room, enjoying the closeness of their bodies and the smell of her hair. He had never felt so contented, with Natália lighting up his life. The gang feasted, laughed a lot, drank too much, and danced the night away. Around midnight everyone began to drift home. István chose to go home too, to his empty flat. But it was his home and he loved it.

István woke the next morning with a splitting headache and someone banging on his door. Rising gingerly, he pulled on his trousers and shuffled to the foyer, rubbing the sleep from his eyes. As he opened the door the light flooded in, blinding him, exacerbating the pain in his pounding head. Natália stood there, grinning, looking as fresh as a daisy. "Good morning sleepyhead," she said cheerily.

István just stood there, squinting at the lovely vision before him.

"Don't look so surprised. We agreed last night that I'd come over today and help you organise the kitchen," she said, pushing past him. Only then did István notice that Natália held a box filled with cleaning products.

"I didn't expect you so early," he mumbled.

"What do you mean 'early'? It's already 9.00am."

István groaned and excused himself. He staggered to the bathroom, splashed cold water onto his face to clear the fog and sharpen his wits, rinsed his mouth, which felt like cotton wool, and walked into the kitchen.

"There's coffee and jam donuts on the bench over there," Natália pointed to where she had placed his breakfast.

"You're an angel. Are you real, or am I still dreaming?"

Natália glanced at István as he bit into one of the donuts. Wearing only his pyjama bottoms it was her first opportunity to examine his naked torso, appraising his wide shoulders, his muscular chest covered in dark brown hair, and his taught abdomen—not an ounce of excess fat, only muscle.

Natália had no hesitation in helping István organise the kitchen, wiping out all the cupboards before placing the second-hand crockery that they recently purchased from a flea market into the designated cupboards. The flat was quite clean in István's estimation, yet Natália insisted they scrub all surfaces from top to bottom before arranging the few items of furniture. István loved having Natália around. She was a breath of fresh air; joyful, efficient, a perfectionist, busying herself in each room, leaving her feminine touch everywhere. Even though she was wearing an old, printed dress over-laid with a faded floral apron, rubber gloves up to her elbows and her hair tied back with a cotton scarf, tendrils of glossy auburn locks peeking out around her ears, she was the most beautiful creature he had ever laid eyes on, and her enthusiasm was infectious.

"What can I do?" he asked, treating her like the boss.

"You can pop out to buy a small table and four chairs that will be placed under the window once I wash the floor. Then you can stack the rest of those plates and the glassware inside these cupboards."

"You may as well move in, Natália. After all, it seems to be more your place than mine," István remarked mischievously.

The colour rose from her neck up to her cheeks. Natália stood staring at him with her mouth open. Until then, István had only kissed her a few times and only once on the lips. How could he possibly invite her to move in with him? Before she had another thought, István swept her into his arms and kissed her with such passion that she felt her legs turn to jelly. Natália responded with equal fervour, tongue probing his, her palms on his naked chest, enjoying the feel of him. They remained embraced for several minutes before István finally released her. Catching his breath, he said in a husky voice, "That's my way of thanking you for all your hard work today. I don't have much else to give you other than a home cooked meal tonight. Will you stay for dinner? It's the least I can do."

Natália wiped her sweaty palms on her apron, surprised at the feel-ings welling up inside, instantly filled with desire for this man and shocked at the lustful sensation spreading throughout her body. She stepped back, trying not to betray her true feelings, and peered into his questioning eyes, before quietly replying, "I'd like that very much."

István kissed her again, this time more tenderly. The heat that emanated from his firm body and the closeness of his presence made her skin tingle. Never had she felt such a strong attraction or hunger for a man.

"Brilliant," he said as he released Natália from his firm grip, smiling warmly into her upturned face.

"I'll just duck out to buy the table and chairs, and some groceries, before the shops close. Won't be long." István said, before heading to the bedroom where he quickly changed into trousers and a jumper. Once outside, his mind replayed those last few moments, elated by Natália's fervent response to his embrace.

In the meantime, Natália busied herself with scrubbing the bathtub, dusting the windowsills, and washing the lace curtains, all the while pondering what had just taken place, her heart still fluttering with joy. Their friendship had blossomed and now taken on a new dimension—one that Natália was eager to explore.

By the end of the day the flat was sparklingly clean. Satisfied that she could do no more, Natália removed her apron, and sat at the small dining table. Unaccustomed to seeing a man cook a meal, she watched with fascination as István began chopping the vegetables for the soup. Offering to help in any way, István waved her away from the stove, claiming she had worked hard enough all day and deserved a well-earned rest and a meal that she hadn't slaved over.

Just as the soup was being ladled into the bowls, Natália's stomach growled loudly. Laughing together, István placed the bowls on the table, leaned over and kissed Natália tenderly on the mouth, thanking her again for making the flat such a lovely home. Blushing from her cleavage up to her face she savoured the sweet taste of his mouth, struggling to set aside the deeper feelings they had recently revealed to one another. István was tormented by his longing to take Natália to bed that night, to caress every inch of her body and to show her how he could really love her fully, but knew that Natália was a conservative Catholic, and believed that sex was permissible only to married couples. It took all his willpower to suppress his urges.

**

Only a few months after that first blind date, István and Natália became inseparable. The loving looks they exchanged were palpable. Walking hand in hand whenever they were out, dancing close with their heads together at the nightclubs, and with István's arm around her at the movies, it was apparent to everyone who knew the couple that they were meant for each other. István was love-struck. But it took him a little while to find the nerve to ask Natália to marry him. They were deeply in love, he was as certain of this as he was of the sun rising each morning, but was Natália ready for marriage? Ten years her senior, would her parents approve? Her mother certainly wouldn't, from what Natália had said about the woman, but it was Natália's father that he was most anxious about; knowing how much her father's opinion meant to her.

Despite their short courtship, as a man in his prime, István was ready to take the next step with his beloved Natália. It was after dinner one Sunday evening. The pair cooked together three or four times a week and spent hours debating the current political situation, food rations, the conditions at the factories where they worked, and how they could influence change. István had never spoken of these issues with Anna, yet felt completely safe and comfortable talking about any topic with Natália. He even trusted her with the fact that he regularly met with a covert anti-Communist dissident group that hatched a variety of passive resistance strategies to undermine the regime. István had purchased a camera and was secretly taking photos of faulty machinery and discarded protective guards at the factory during the less busy night shifts, or of the long queues in front of the various grocery stores, along with other daily events that depicted the difficulties faced by working class Hungarians. This record of life in Budapest was destined for the West German allies that were responsible for disseminating the anti-Communist propaganda. The world would know of the atrocities and hardships endured by people who desperately yearned for the Soviets to be banished from their country. Whilst he didn't name the members of the group nor speak too specifically about their current plans, he did discuss topics in broad terms. Natália loved being confided in, having her thoughts valued, and offering opposing views or different perspectives to István's ideas. He in turn treasured her curious, questioning mind. Natália completed him as a human being in ways that no other woman ever had.

The dishes done, they retired to the living room. István turned on the radio, searching for a music channel, while Natália happily chatted about some of her new ideas for dress designs. With a Strauss waltz echoing around the walls of the room, István lifted his hand, gesturing for Natália to join him. Sweeping her into his arms they waltzed around the room, adroitly sidestepping the coffee table. István was extremely light footed and graceful on the dance floor, and it was a delight to be whirled around by his steady hands. Natália was laughing, eyes shining with happiness, when István drew her close at the end of the song and kissed her tenderly. Gazing into his eyes, István beamed at her as he stepped back and pulled something from his trouser pocket. For a moment she remained rigid, unsure what he was up to. Opening his hand, he revealed a small square, red velvet box, worn on the edges. With trembling fingers, István opened the box and presented it to Natália, while searching her face for a reaction. Natália gasped, eyes wide as saucers. At first she was astonished, then an instant later she realised the significance of the gift and was overcome with joy. Taking the box from István's hand, looking intently at the jewel it contained, she choked back the tears that surfaced, her eyes locked on István's. They both laughed through the tears that could not be supressed any longer. István knelt in front of Natália, lifted her free hand to his lips and asked her to marry him. The answer to his proposal came swiftly, without hesitation, "Yes, yes, my love." Rising to his feet, István kissed her again then steered her to the sofa where they sat beside one another. Removing the ring from its box, István slipped it onto her finger. It fitted perfectly, and she wondered how he knew. István explained that the ring was a family heirloom handed down to him by his grandmother. It had survived two world wars as well as the uprising of 1848, and was deemed to have been bestowed with magical properties. Family folklore suggested that whoever wore the ring would be protected from harm. Natália studied it closely, admiring the large oval ruby that shone brilliantly in the centre of the gold setting, flanked by three smaller rubies on either side. It was magnificent. Natália wrapped her arms around István's neck and hugged him fiercely, declaring how much she loved him.

István disappeared into the kitchen, returned with the bottle of wine he had opened for dinner, poured two glasses, handed one to Natália, raised his own glass, and declared, "To a very long and happy union, blessed with as many children as you can bear."

Natália laughed, rebuking him, "Well, we'll see about that. I may stop at three children." Looking down at the ring on her hand, she became reflective then said, "Tell me about your grandmother. I want to know all about her."

István was a teenager when his grandmother had died, but he remembered many endearing qualities about her; she was a great cook, a competent seamstress, was always elegantly dressed, could be very stern at times, but had a soft spot for him and spoiled him rotten with cakes whenever he visited her. He was the eldest grandchild and her favourite.

"The two of you would have gotten on famously, I'm sure of it." István then raised his glass again and said, "To Grandma."

"To Grandma," Natália repeated, then sipped the wine.

The rest of the evening was spent discussing wedding plans. It would need to be a simple affair with only their closest friends invited to celebrate their union. István had spent all his savings on items needed to make the apartment liveable, and so a lavish wedding was out of the question. Opting to follow the custom in such situations, István suggested they take a trip to Szarvas to meet her parents and to formally ask her father's permission to marry. Natália hadn't visited her family in months and was apprehensive, knowing her mother disapproved of her absence. In her eyes, it equated to a lack of respect shown to her elders and was reprehensible. Natália dreaded the visit and tried to talk István out of it, but he insisted on showing her family respect in the traditional way.

***

It was a bright, sunny Sunday morning as they stood on the platform, waiting for the train to arrive. Mid-Autumn, the days were pleasant if the sun was shining yet cold at night. Natália wore an elegant navy-blue woollen, double-breasted suit that she had designed and constructed herself. A highly fashionable garment that she knew would impress her mother. Keen to make the day a success, Natália was rehearsing how she would greet her mother. What excuse would be acceptable for the long period since her last visit? István had never seen Natália so nervous and tried making light of the situation to put her at ease, but soon realised he was wasting his time. Nothing he said helped settle her anxieties. He too was eager to meet her father, the man Natália idolised, and prayed that he would be accepted into the family, despite the ten-year age difference between him and Natália. Immersed in their own thoughts, they spoke very little throughout the train journey.

Natália's little sister, Éva, greeted them at the station when the pair stepped off the train. They hugged each other tightly before Natália introduced Éva to István. Éva was only ten years old, and a little embarrassed when

István kissed her cheek in greeting. The twenty-minute walk to the family home seemed an eternity as Natália's apprehension grew, not knowing how her mother would react to her news. As a distraction, Natália asked her sister to fill her in on the local gossip. Éva had always been a busybody and knew all the news about Natália's old friends. Two girls had married, and one already had a baby with another on the way. Then she mentioned a couple of people Natália couldn't remember. Natália quickly tuned out, her thoughts circling back to her mother as the house came into view, Éva still prattling on regardless.

As soon as they walked up the stairs to the front porch, Éva opened the door, ushering the visitors inside and yelled, "They're here!"

Hearing voices, her mother turned off the stove and rushed to the living room where everyone had congregated, welcoming the handsome couple.

"Mother, I'd like you to meet István. István, this is my mother, Katalin."

István kissed her hand and said, "It's wonderful to finally meet you. I've heard a great deal about you."

Natália's mother raised an eyebrow, amused at the thought of what her daughter may have said about her, but before she had a chance to respond, Natália continued with the introductions, firstly her brother Lajos junior, then her father, Lajos senior, who was hovering behind the others, sizing up the man who had stolen the heart of his favourite child.

"Welcome István," he said, shaking István's hand. "Come, sit down. What can I get you to drink?"

"I brought a bottle of wine to share over lunch but wouldn't mind starting off with a glass of beer if you have any."

"Of course. Mother, could you bring us a couple of beers?"

Katalin quickly returned with the drinks, not wanting to miss any of the conversation.

"I think I can guess why Natália has brought you here today to meet the family," the patriarch stated after swallowing a mouthful of beer, wiping the froth from his lips with the back of his hand, peering intently at his future son-in-law. Natália had recently contacted her father to forewarn him of the purpose of their visit, knowing she could confide in him, mentioning the age difference and fearing her mother's reaction to István and her engagement.

"If you truly love each other then that's all that matters," he had said.

"Yes, sir. I would like to ask your permission to marry Natália. We're very much in love and want to spend our lives together." István announced very formally, then looked over at Natália and smiled.

Éva squealed with delight and hugged her sister while Lajos junior just rolled his eyes. Natália was holding her breath during this exchange, watching her mother's expression closely. Her head snapped up. She seemed gobsmacked, completely lost for words. It was clear she wasn't expecting news of an engagement as she looked from her daughter to István and back again, shaking her head in utter disbelief. Excusing herself, she returned to the kitchen to finalise preparations for the mid-day meal, all the while muttering under her breath. Natália followed her, leant against the bench to steady herself and said, "I'm sorry I couldn't tell you our news sooner. We've been so busy working and settling István into his new apartment. Time just got away from us."

"You've not visited us in months and now you return with a future husband. You're too young to marry. Who is this man anyway? He seems much too old for you. What are you thinking?"

"Mother, he's a wonderful man, and I love him. Age has no bearing on our love," Natália replied.

Her mother huffed.

"Please be happy for me. Can't you just be glad that I found true love?"

"Of course I want you to be happy, but I'm also concerned that you might be making a big mistake. What does he do for a living? Can he support you properly in the lavish lifestyle you've grown accustomed to in Budapest?"

"You know very well I don't live a lavish lifestyle. I work hard at the factory, and I now design and make clothes for extra money, so I'm doing well. As for István, he has a good job at the steel factory, a nice apartment in a lovely street in the city, he is intelligent and kind, and he loves me, which is the most important thing. Look, this beautiful ruby ring which he presented to me on our engagement is a family heirloom handed down through the generations."

Curiosity got the better of the matriarch and she bent down to study the ring closely before remarking, "Well, his family certainly has good taste. I'll give him that. It's a beautiful ring. I need to dish up now or dinner will spoil. Help me take the plates to the table."

The rest of the day proceeded harmoniously. The meal was delicious: pork schnitzel with lentils in sour cream and onion—her father's favourite dish. István opened the wine and poured it for the adults only, Éva protesting, until her mother's stern glance hushed her up.

Natália cleared the plates when everyone had finished, automatically taking charge of the washing up, which was once one of her chores. Mother went into the larder and returned with a large chocolate cake, which looked amazing. It was obvious she had gone to a great deal of trouble to impress István, which made Natália smile inwardly. Perhaps she wasn't so hard-hearted after all. The cake was cut into generous portions and placed on delicate china plates with small forks on the side. Natália helped her mother serve the cake to the others, who were now comfortably seated in the living room. As they handed the plates around, the men were already engaged in deep conversation, her father quizzing István about everything from his political views to his religious faith to his line of work, deciding if this man could provide for his daughter and make her happy. Lajos interjected with questions about István's favourite sport, what football team he followed and a raft of other silly things that made István laugh about the interrogation he was enduring. For the latter part of the afternoon, the matriarch's icy demeanour thawed and she too grilled István, about his family, where he grew up and the circumstances in which he met her daughter.

They all appeared to be getting along just fine. Natália remained on edge, trying to assess her mother's opinion of her fiancé, a slight frown fixed on her brow. Intuitively, István sensed Natália's thoughts, then turned to the matriarch and asked if he could have a second slice of the best chocolate cake he'd ever eaten.

"Well, of course," she said.

Jumping up with the agility of a woman twenty years her junior she whisked away his plate and returned promptly with another very large slice, beaming with pride as she handed the cake to István, neglecting to ask if anyone else wanted seconds.

The afternoon had flown and as the sun dipped lower in the sky, a shaft of light slashed through the room, a sign that evening was approaching. István checked the time and said, "If we're to make the 4.30 train, Natália, we should be going."

As they got up to leave, István, the absolute gentleman, turned on his charm once more for good measure, and thanked his future mother-in-law for a wonderful meal, praising her culinary skills—especially the cake—then kissed her on the cheek. She smiled at István with a softness in her gaze and thanked him for his kind words. István then turned to Natália's father and asked, "Do I have your permission to marry your daughter, Mr Kardos?"

"I can see that the two of you are well matched. I have no doubt that you will take good care of my beautiful girl. You have my permission and my blessing to marry." The two men embraced.

"Thank you, Sir. You have my word that I will protect Natália and ensure no harm ever befalls her."

Natália hugged her siblings tightly, knowing the visits home would now become even less frequent. They said their goodbyes and headed back to the train station. Once comfortably seated in a vacant carriage, Natália finally relaxed. The pent-up stress melted away. István squeezed her hand, remarked on how he had enjoyed the day, and commented on her father's sociable manner, wit, and good humour. Natália was thrilled that the two men had gotten along so well.

"We have your father's permission to marry, and I even managed to crack a smile or two from your mother. Not a bad day's work, wouldn't you say?"

Natália leaned over and kissed him gently on the lips and said, "Thank you, my love."

***

The wedding date was set for the first Sunday of November 1955. Whilst it was to be a simple affair, there were still arrangements to be made and invitations sent. Just two weeks after receiving Lajos senior's blessing, the big day arrived. It was a cold late autumn day. The doves sheltered under the eaves of the buildings, and the yellow and red leaves spun from the trees whenever the wind whirled through the streets, carpeting the ground in a pretty tapestry of colour. The sun shone brightly in a pale blue sky. It was the perfect day for a new beginning.

Natália woke early, tired from lack of sleep, having tossed and turned all night, replaying the ceremony, rehearsing her vows, and overjoyed by thoughts of her future with István. Yet an underlying unease refused to be shrugged off whenever she contemplated the intimacy they would share. Her mother never spoke of a wife's obligation in the marriage bed. The only clue Natália had about sex came from the girls at the factory, some of whom were quite explicit about a man's anatomy, which she found terrifying.

Rózsa fussed over Natália all morning, helping her friend look her best for the special day. Natália chose her favourite bottle green dress that complimented her vibrant eyes. Her soft curls hung free, caressing her shoulders. The lipstick she chose matched the rubies of her engagement ring, and she carried a small posy of pale pink camellias, freshly picked from the courtyard garden at István's apartment. István in turn wore his best grey suit, which was cleaned and pressed for the occasion, with a single camellia pinned to the lapel of his jacket. They made a very handsome couple as they walked hand in hand to the Town Hall for their 2.00pm wedding. János borrowed István's camera and snapped a few photos to mark the occasion. Rózsa and János were delighted to act as witnesses, Rózsa dreamily wondering when János would pop the question to her.

Twenty minutes after arriving at the Town Hall for their designated appointment, Natália and István were husband and wife. Natália proudly slipped the marriage certificate into her handbag for safekeeping. She could hardly contain her elation, arm in arm with her husband, chatting all the way to the Coffee Pot Café where the guests awaited their arrival. Being such frequent patrons and friends of Rózsa, who still worked there, the owner of the café gave them a sizeable discount off the bill as a wedding gift. Apart from the witnesses, the small party included Ferenc, Albert, Tomás, Iván and their wives, Mrs Hajdu, and two other girlfriends who worked at the cosmetic factory with Natália. Regrettably, Natália's family were unable to attend the celebration. Lajos was ill with influenza, bed ridden with a high fever, preventing the family from leaving his side. Natália was disappointed that her father could not see how happy she was on this most important day when she became Mrs Szabó, but understood it was unavoidable. The only other person missing was Natália's long-lost friend, Julia. A moment of sadness washed over her as she thought of Julia, but she quickly pushed the gloom from her mind. This was the happiest day of her life—the beginning of her future with István—and nothing was going to spoil it.

As soon as the bridal party entered the café a cheer went up, and wine was poured and passed around. Ferenc stood, raised his glass, and proposed a toast, "To Mr and Mrs Szabó."

Everyone repeated the refrain and drank deeply from their glasses. Then János stood and proposed another toast, "To the bride and groom! May you have lots of healthy children to look after you in your old age."

Everyone raised their glasses again, shouting exuberantly, "Here, here!"

Platters of freshly made delicacies, ranging from chicken schnitzel, potato casserole, pork and lentil stew, a variety of cold meats, cheeses, condiments, and sourdough bread were soon brought out and placed in the centre of the table for everyone to share. Soon, the celebrations were in full swing, and continued late into the night. There were more toasts to the bride and groom, to the witnesses, and to the café owner for his generous gift— then the bawdy jokes started. Merriment filled the café. The other patrons had long gone and the jubilation from the wedding guests became rowdier. When the tipsy couple announced that it was time to leave, another cheer erupted from the guests. Ferenc and János jested about letting the couple go to consummate the marriage, eliciting guffaws from the men and tittering from the women. Natália handed her posy of flowers to Rózsa, winked at her, and said, "You're next!" Rózsa blushed while János looked uncomfortable.

Another roar burst from the crowd. With that, the newlyweds left. They made their way back to the apartment. Stumbling along the footpath, one propping the other up, they relived the events of the day, remarking how wonderful it was, with all their closest friends sharing the beginning of a long and happy life together. When they reached the front door, István insisted on carrying Natália over the threshold. It was harder than he had anticipated, and he complained heartily about how heavy she was. Natália giggled throughout the ordeal until they both collapsed onto the living room floor. Natália was the first to get up and announced that she was retiring to the bedroom. István quickly followed, having waited months for this moment. Respecting her wishes to remain a virgin until their wedding night, István was aching to caress his wife's sensuous body. Their laughter subsided as they reached the bed. Butterflies were fluttering in Natália's stomach. She was both excited and nervous about what was to come.

"Let me help you undress," István said in a husky voice.

Slowly he unzipped her dress and brushed his hands over her shoulders, forcing the dress to fall to the floor. István kissed her slender neck while unfastening her bra. Cupping Natália's firm breasts he stroked her nipples, which instantly hardened, causing Natália to whimper aloud at the wonderful new tingling sensation that spread throughout her body. István then picked her up and gently placed her on the bed while he undressed. Her eyes were like saucers as she stared at his naked body, penis fully engorged. For a moment she was horrified. How was that huge member meant to enter her? István noticed the change in her expression, then lay beside her and kissed her passionately, reassuring his sensitive wife that he would be gentle, murmuring loving words in her ear. István constrained his urge to take her quickly, wanting Natália's first sexual experience to be pleasurable. He fondled and kissed every inch of her body, starting from her ear lobes, playfully biting her neck, licking his way down her supple frame, barely touching her skin as his hand moved up the inside of her thigh to caress her moist intimate mound. Natália was trembling, moaning, and writhing to the rhythm of István's probing fingers. Before allowing her to climax he rolled on top of her, sucked her right nipple, then carefully entered her. Gasping, she winced at the initial pain when he penetrated her maidenhead, then dug her fingers into his shoulders as István rocked back and forth, trying not to come too quickly. Wrapping her legs around his body she begged him not to stop. István's thrusts quickened. Then it was over. Both drenched in sweat they lay together for several minutes before István rolled onto his back; his heart rate slowly normalising.

Natália curled up to her husband, feeling wonderfully content and the happiest she'd ever been. Fascinated by this strong, male specimen, she began to explore his body, feeling it was her right now that he was legally hers. Tracing her fingers across his chest, she kissed his nipples then fondled his wet, shrivelled penis, laughing at how something so large could shrink back to a floppy shadow of its former self. Then, without warning, Natália felt his penis rise in her hand. Stroking him, she felt the same desire flood her body again. István sensed her reaction. Spreading her thighs apart, he knelt before her, teasing her with his tongue, kneading her nipples with his thumbs. She grabbed his hair with both hands to hold him steady, ensuring he didn't stop. This time he allowed her to climax on her own. Feeling her spasm, he could not hold back any longer. He quickly slid inside her and spilled his seed. The lovemaking he'd experienced with Anna and his previous girlfriends was always gratifying. Yet somehow it was different with Natália, and he found himself enjoying her body and her reaction to their lovemaking in ways he had never experienced with other women. It was then that István realised that he was truly in love with his wife.

***

The weeks that followed were joyous for the newlyweds. Natália glowed with contentment. The realisation that sex need not be feared but was extremely enjoyable empowered her as a woman. On many occasions she initiated the intimacy with her husband, emboldened by the knowledge that they both enjoyed being united, tangled in each other's flesh.

Their first serious argument occurred only a few weeks after their wedding. István had intimated on several occasions that Natália should leave work. He could provide for them both, which would allow her more time to attend to her sewing, as well as household chores, meal preparation and socialising. Resisting his counsel, István further argued that she was always tired after work, sewed late into the night, and lacked the energy to go out with their friends, rarely even meeting up with Rózsa. Whilst she agreed that going out after work was arduous, Natália was reluctant to forgo her financial independence. She had supported herself since leaving school and could not envisage life without her own income. The conflict persisted.

One morning, almost two months to the day since her wedding, Natália rose early and ran to the bathroom, vomiting in the sink. Sweat beaded on her forehead and her hands were clammy. Thinking she must have eaten something off she decided not to mention the matter to István. The same thing occurred in the days that followed, lingering into the late morning while at work. Standing all day at her station was causing discomfort that she hadn't experienced before, and she was often fatigued. Natália suspected that she was pregnant. A visit to her doctor confirmed her suspicion. Elation, fear, apprehension, and hope churned through her mind with the realisation that she would be bringing a child into the world: a child she created with her loving István. But it was too soon to mention it to him. The doctor advised her to wait until she was further progressed with the pregnancy. Each morning for the next few weeks she would hide her morning sickness, put on a brave face, and even agreed to go out once or twice a week with friends. István was thrilled that she seemed to be back to her usual bubbly self. Then, at twelve weeks, Natália decided it was time to share the exciting news with her husband.

A man in his early thirties, István hoped that he and Natália would start a family soon, preferring to be young enough to enjoy fatherhood. The fact that they had regular sex created the opportunity. It was only a matter of time. When Natália announced one night after dinner that they needed to go shopping for a cradle, István wept with joy. That night, after their love-making, he placed an ear on Natália's belly, trying to hear a little heartbeat. They laughed and cried at the same time. Not surprisingly, the subject of Natália working whilst she was pregnant surfaced, but stubbornness won out. The money she earned would help buy the things needed for a baby. István found it difficult to argue, not wanting to cause any distress that may impact both Natália and their unborn child.

The weeks that followed were exhausting. Friends popped around to celebrate with the excited parents-to-be, the flat was reorganised to accommodate the arrival of the baby, and shopping expeditions were taken to buy the baby items needed. The second bedroom, which had been Natália's sewing studio, now doubled up as the nursery. Natália's mother even ventured out of her hometown to deliver a gift to her daughter. Skilled in all aspects of needlecraft, Natália's mother presented her with a lemon-coloured woollen baby blanket, embroidered on the edges with pink silk roses of various shades. It was a sign that her mother finally accepted her daughter's new life, and that she was clearly thrilled about becoming a grandmother. Whilst their relationship was still sometimes strained, her mother showed signs of softening, visiting her daughter more frequently and always bringing gifts of homemade casseroles, cakes, salamis, and preserves. It was a welcome relief that the baby was bringing her closer to her mother.

The shifts at the factory seemed to drag as the weeks passed. Natália's supervisor was aware of her pregnancy but didn't reduce her production quotas. Pregnancy was not an excuse for poor work performance. Natália's stubbornness in retaining her job prevented her from complaining to anyone about how difficult it had become to complete a full day at work. Swollen feet and an unrelenting ache in her lower back became unbearable.

But six months had passed, and with not much longer before her full term, Natália persisted at the factory.

Rising from the trestle table in the lunchroom at the start of her third trimester, Natália doubled over in pain. Sharp cramps knifed through her belly. She quickly sat down again, breathing deeply, trying to compose herself. One of her colleagues saw the distressed look on her face and brought her a glass of water. Despite drinking slowly and trying to keep calm, the cramps persisted. Moisture trickled down the inside of her leg. Forcing herself to stand she hobbled to the bathroom, shocked to see that the moisture was blood. Terrified, Natália asked to be taken to the nearest hospital. After waiting anxiously in the emergency department for what seemed like hours, a young intern finally appeared and ushered her into an examination cubicle. A thorough inspection confirmed her worst fears. The intern's face was ashen and his brow creased when he looked sympathetically into her eyes and advised her that the baby's heart had stopped beating. Natália screamed at him, saying that he was wrong, insisting another doctor examine her. Overcome with compassion for this beautiful woman who had just lost her baby, the intern complied and fetched an older doctor to examine his patient, knowing she would believe a more experienced doctor. After a brief introduction, the doctor placed his stethoscope on various parts of her belly but failed to locate a heartbeat. Thick blood was pooling on the bed between her legs.

Deep down she knew her baby was gone. For over a week she had felt no movement, dreading that something was wrong, willing it to be well. So much blood loss was serious. Natália knew that. The doctor spoke gently to her, explaining that the significant amount of blood loss and absence of a heartbeat meant that the baby was dead. Natália wailed, refusing to accept the truth. The attending nurse gave her a sedative to calm her down while the doctor went on to explain how he would induce contractions to birth the baby. Natália slowly slipped into oblivion only to be awakened a short while later to severe contractions that delivered her dead baby.

CHAPTER 8

After Stalin's death, the political leadership in Hungary was volatile, and in a constant state of flux. Khrushchev openly criticised Stalin's brutality and abuse of power. By shattering the mindset of terror that permeated Hungarian society, Khrushchev's softer approach led to widespread hope for greater freedoms. Mátyás Rákosi, a staunch Stalinist and subservient to Moscow, was extremely unpopular with the public and soon found himself out of favour with Khrushchev, forced to relinquish his Premiership to the reform-minded Imre Nagy. Rákosi did, however, retain his position as Party Secretary, wielding significant influence and ultimately orchestrating the removal of Nagy. This toing and froing of the leadership was a key contributor to Hungary's severe economic decline.

***

"A pity Imre Nagy lost power. The harsh brutality that we suffered at the hands of Rákosi and his cronies was tempered under Nagy's leadership. He seemed genuine in his attempts to improve the welfare of the peasants, to change the course of politics, and to improve the economy. Democratising the party and wanting party members to take a more active role in political activity was his aim. We even got a taste of freedom of speech with the Szabad Nép daily paper covering a range of anti-communist topics, including criticisms of the previous Rákosi government, some of which were written by Nagy himself. Clearly, no love lost there," Iván said as he took a sip from his second cup of coffee and swished the brown liquid in his mouth before swallowing.

"I agree. What a lost opportunity," Tomás said, shaking his head.

It was one of their regular monthly meetings, this time at Albert's home. To deflect unwanted attention from themselves, should their movements be under scrutiny, the group agreed to rotate the location. The secret police maintained their patrols through the streets, interrogating people going about their business. Most of the junior officers enjoyed the power they held and would detain civilians without cause. It was a game to them, a fear tactic. Caution continued to be the order of the day.

"Nagy's major downfall was his failure to swiftly deliver on the economic reforms he promised," Albert stated emphatically.

"He really wasn't given much of a chance to implement any changes before he was sacked, Albert. Nor was he able to garner enough support from within his own party room. Too many government ministers fear reprisals from the Soviets," Tomás said, echoing the thoughts of his companions.

"The Soviets thought he was too soft on those that dared speak out against our worsening living conditions. Nagy failed to toe the party line and was too radical in his reformist views, so we have regressed again. It's beyond disappointing to see Rákosi reinstated as General Secretary, and to have his lackey Hegedus as Prime Minister. We seem to take one small step forward and then, in no time, we're right where we started, with the brute Rákosi back at the helm," Iván chimed in.

The mood became sombre, the men nodding in agreement but not adding anything more to the discussion.

"I attended a recent meeting at the University, organised by the Petőfi Club. Are you familiar with them?" István asked, steering the conversation to the present rather than regurgitating the past.

No one piped up, so István proceeded to explain the club's purpose.

"It's predominantly a group of university students who debate a variety of social issues and who are very vocal about the injustices meted out by our current government. Interestingly, they named the club after the famous poet, Sándor Petőfi, who fought for Hungarian freedom in 1848, against the Austrian Empire. This new group also has strong connections with the Writer's Union. They've written several articles condemning the secret police and the deteriorating situation in Hungary. Their articles have spread throughout the community, including many factories, which is where I came to hear about them. I'm sure you've seen some of this material, Ferenc?" His friend nodded.

"How can these students get away with being so openly hostile towards the Communist doctrine? Aren't they afraid of being arrested?" Iván piped up.

"Apparently not," Ferenc replied.

István resumed his report, "There are now demands for trade union democracy and more consultation with management on wages and welfare. There's even talk about handing factory administration back to the workers. Can you believe it?"

"Wow! That's extraordinary. But will they succeed in these demands? I doubt it. The Soviets won't stand for it, surely? I'd put money on it," Iván said rather emphatically.

"Anyway, the meeting I recently attended was packed with lots of people from various backgrounds. There were writers, students, academics, and many others like me—ordinary factory workers—some of whom were bold enough to participate in a debate around Socialist Realism, speaking out about the sham we all know it to be. There was talk of industrial and economic reform. It was amazing. I just sat at the back, observed, and listened to the different opinions. What I found particularly riveting was a heated discussion about the confiscation of our uranium deposits by the Soviets," István said, pleased to share his newly acquired information. Rummaging through his satchel he pulled out a few pamphlets and passed them around the group.

"Here are some of the fliers that were handed out. The speakers were quite forthright and critical of the government regarding this issue. Apparently, the mineral could be sold on the open market to boost our exports and has the potential to be a key driver in advancing our economy. Why doesn't the government listen to them—to our intellectuals—is what I want to know? It's another example of a wasted opportunity to improve our country's income and, therefore, our living standards. Everyone agrees our economy is declining, yet no action is being taken by our leaders to repair the damage from past decisions," István said, his tone rising in pitch with frustration.

"I hear you, István. A very valid point. However, it's one thing to agitate for change and debate political issues in these forums that you mention, which I agree is an important step towards social transformation, yet what I'm desperate to understand is when will the Western powers come to our aid? It's all well and good to distribute anti-communist propaganda and for people like us to smuggle evidence to the West of our appalling living and working conditions, but I want real action. I can't see the Soviets backing down on any of their core ideals without external intervention," Tomás added.

There were more nods of agreement around the table, but they felt powerless to affect any meaningful change.

"Well, I plan to attend these Petőfi meetings as often as I can, to keep abreast of what the intellectuals are advocating and to see what actions are being taken. They are verbalising ideas and sentiments that the general population is too fearful to voice publicly. I'll speak with the organisers to let them know they have many allies in the community who are prepared to support them in any way. Perhaps I'll see some of you there? If not, I'll keep you informed of developments," István said.

"Be careful, István. You don't know these people. Don't be too trusting. We still need to maintain vigilance in our activities. You of all people need to be extra cautious with a baby on the way," remarked Ferenc.

"Speaking of which, I think it's time I went home to my lovely wife," István said as he rose from his chair and headed towards the door. "I'll continue my photographic log, particularly of conditions at the factory. Which reminds me—here's a roll of film from the past month, Albert, and remind your cousin to be careful. He's our only link to Radio Free Europe."

The men shook hands and staggered their departure over the next hour, as an added precaution.

***

István opened the door to his apartment, stepped inside and announced his arrival only to be met with silence. The apartment was in darkness. Thinking it odd, he wondered if he failed to recall what Natália mentioned she had planned for the evening. Was he meant to meet her somewhere? Perhaps Rózsa's for dinner? He couldn't remember a discussion at all about dinner plans. He'd been so preoccupied with the Petőfi Club's revelations and the surge of support that was mounting across the community for their controversial views that he couldn't wait to meet with his friends and fill them in on all he had learned. Consequently, he had not been as attentive to his wife as he ought to have been over the past couple of weeks. He berated himself for being self-absorbed. Lately, Natália was tired all the time. Whilst she put on a brave face for him, he could see she was struggling after a long day at work, and with the added household chores. If only she would leave her job. Such a stubborn woman, he thought, shaking his head. István decided that he would make more of an effort to help with the housework from now on and try again to convince Natália to quit her job.

Walking into the kitchen he noticed that there were no pots on the stove, no indication of a meal in the making. It appeared that Natália hadn't returned home from work. Not sure what to do, István filled the kettle and placed it on the stove to make himself a cup of tea. While he waited for the kettle to boil, he sat down at the kitchen table, wondering where Natália might be and trying to fathom what was going on, when he was surprised by a knock on the front door. When István peered outside, he was bewildered to see Rózsa standing on the doorstep, her eyes red and puffy from crying. Before he had a chance to ask why she was upset, a sinking feeling hit the pit of his stomach. Something serious must have happened to Natália. He grabbed Rózsa by the shoulders and shook her, asking what had happened to his wife.

"She's in the hospital. The baby is dead," is all she could blurt out before she burst into tears.

***

The infant was whisked away by the attending nurse as soon as the umbilical cord was cut. Natália was drenched in sweat and so weak that she collapsed back onto the pillow, semi-conscious. After a time, she sensed someone fussing over her, pulling at her nightgown. Lifting her head, the nurse smiled and spoke in a quiet, soothing voice.

"You've lost a lot of blood. It's the reason you're so weak. Now that you're awake, I can clean you up properly. Here, drink some water. The more the better."

Handing Natália a couple of pills, the nurse stood by her bed to ensure she swallowed the pills as instructed, then said reassuringly, "You'll feel much better soon."

The nurse proceeded to administer a warm sponge bath, brushed Natália's damp hair off her face, and gently dressed her in a fresh nightgown. Natália's limp form remained detached from her surroundings, her belly still swollen yet no sign of the baby.

"There, that's better. I'll fetch you something to eat. You need to build up your strength after your ordeal."

The nurse turned to walk out when Natália grabbed her arm and in a faint whisper asked, "My baby, where's my baby? I want to see my baby."

"I'm sorry, dear. The baby was taken away. No need for you to fuss. You need to concentrate on getting well."

The nurse left the room while Natália continued wailing, "I want to see my baby. Please, please. Let me see my baby."

The doctor paid Natália a visit shortly after the nurse left and checked her vital signs to ensure no further complications arose from the delivery. Professional and completely thorough, he took no notice of her sopping face. Touching his hand to get his attention, she calmly asked if she could see her baby. The doctor cast a glance at the young woman and replied methodically, devoid of emotion, "The baby was dead on arrival and was immediately taken away to be buried. It's the usual practice in these situations."

Seized by a fresh wave of grief, her bottom lip trembled, and the tears streaked freely down her face, a few drops landing on the doctor's hand. Looking into her face and seeing Natália's agonised expression, he continued in a softer tone, "Your baby was a girl. I'm sorry for your loss. All things considered you seem to be physically fine, other than the loss of blood. The tablets that we're administering will help with your recovery. Be sure to take them as prescribed and try to eat lots of spinach, meat, and fish. These are the best foods to build your strength and restore the iron in your blood."

The nurse returned to her room, briefly consulted with the doctor, then injected Natália with a sedative to help her rest. Natália buried her face in her pillow and cried herself to sleep.

A short while later, the attending nurse at the reception desk saw a man approach with a puzzled look on his face.

"I'm looking for my wife, Natália Szabó. She was brought in this afternoon to give birth. I'm her husband. Am I in the right department?"

"Let me see, ah, yes," the nurse replied, avoiding István's gaze. "Natália Szabó. She's in room three, down that corridor."

István ran down the passage and peeped into room three, where he saw his cherished wife sleeping peacefully. Hesitating for a moment before entering, he quietly pulled up a chair and sat alongside her bed, gently stroking her hair, distraught at the anguish that was clearly visible on her tear-streaked face, even in sleep. An intense pang of grief and loss squeezed his heart and for a minute he couldn't breathe. The death of their child was difficult enough to accept, yet he knew the horror of birthing their dead baby would have a profound effect on Natália, her purity and vitality irreversibly damaged. An overwhelming sadness engulfed István as he suppressed the tears bubbling to the surface, fighting his emotions to be brave and strong for his fragile wife. Twenty minutes later, Natália opened her eyes and saw her visitor. One look at István and the tears flooded her eyes.

"Our baby's dead. Our little girl. We had a daughter but she's dead," Natália blurted between sobs. Looking into István's distraught face she cried, "I'm sorry, I'm so sorry. It's all my fault. I didn't look after her properly."

"Shush, Natália, it'll be alright. I'm here now. It'll be alright."

István leaned over and hugged her tightly, cradling her in his arms until the sobs abated, unsure of what else to say. Easing her into a sitting position, he propped the pillows behind her back and handed her a glass of water, when he noticed a frown creasing her brow. Looking intently into his worried face, Natália asked, "Where were you? The nurses called the factory and home several times, but you didn't answer. I then asked them to try Rózsa, who came as soon as she could. I had to birth our dead baby. Then they took her away and wouldn't let me see her. You could have insisted we say goodbye to our little girl before they buried her, had you been here. Why didn't you come?" Natália was now hysterical, unable to constrain her grief.

"I'm so sorry, love. I would have come right away had I known. I was tied up in a committee meeting for most of the afternoon and didn't receive any message, and then went to Albert's house for a couple of hours straight after work. I didn't get home until dinnertime. Then Rózsa showed up and told me what had happened. I'm sorry I let you down."

István slumped back into his chair, buried his head in his trembling hands, and wept.

***

The child was named Julia, after Natália's long-lost friend. The couple vowed to always remember her in their prayers.

Natália continued to blame herself for the baby's death. She should have listened to István and resigned from her job weeks ago. Putting her independence and the money she earned ahead of the baby's welfare, despite feeling poorly and struggling to complete a shift at the factory, was inexcusable. She felt numb, praying for the nightmare to end. Except Natália knew that the nightmare was just beginning. Thoughts churned through her mind, wondering what went wrong and how she could have prevented her baby's death. The doctors had reassured her that no damage was done during the birth. Being young and strong she would conceive again. Stillborn babies were common, particularly with the first pregnancy, the nurses said encouragingly. István reminded her of this to comfort her, but it fell on deaf ears. Her guilt could not be assuaged. Why István claimed to still love her was a mystery. How could he possibly love a woman who couldn't nurture their baby and bring her safely into the world?

After a fortnight of sheer misery, her face constantly moist from crying, and her eyes red and puffy, the tears eventually dried up. Natália was consumed by an emptiness that could not be filled, regardless of how hard anyone tried. Performing her daily chores in a trance, the once sparkling emerald eyes were shrouded in grief. She withdrew from everyone, especially István. Nothing he did or said helped ease her pain. In no fit state to return to work, both physically and emotionally, István contacted the cosmetic factory on her behalf and told the administration that his wife would not be returning. Rózsa and a few girlfriends from the factory popped in to check on Natália every day, to provide her with much needed support. They made cakes and cups of tea, gossiped about the affairs at the factory, and helped with the cleaning, particularly the heavier jobs, scrubbing the bathroom and mopping the floors. No amount of cheer that the girls brought into her sad existence helped dissolve the constant feelings of anguish, loss, and guilt. Natália thanked her friends for their kindness, but after three weeks of fussing she asked for privacy. It was exhausting to pretend that everything was alright. Life had changed forevermore.

István had taken to sleeping on the sofa in the living room. Shift work at the factory meant clocking on and off at odd hours and he didn't want to disturb Natália while she was asleep, to allow her as much rest as possible to recover from her horrible ordeal. He also sensed that she still wanted seclusion. Being pushed away hurt him deeply, yet he respected her wishes and did all he could to comfort her in any way possible. He could only imagine how heartbreaking it was for Natália not to have heard that initial cry from her newborn baby as she entered the world. To experience such a tragic event on her own tormented István every time he gazed into his wife's sad eyes, admonishing himself for letting her down. Natália couldn't face his sympathy or the hurt and sadness emblazoned in his eyes. She felt unworthy of his love.

István was beside himself, struggling to find a way to help Natália lift out of her misery and move on with life. Julia had been buried for four weeks, yet Natália was still a shell of her former self. He brought her flowers every week and cooked their meals, unless Rózsa popped by with a casserole, and proposed that they go dancing or to the movies. No matter what he suggested, Natália remained depressed, refusing to engage with the world. In desperation he confided in Rózsa one afternoon as she was leaving their apartment. He walked her out and, once safely out of earshot, explained how distant Natália remained, and that nothing he tried was helping her recovery. Begging Rózsa for any advice to help him find the woman he married, Rózsa said she would try.

Later that week, when István was at work, Rózsa popped around. She followed Natália into the kitchen and sat at the table waiting for the kettle to boil. Taking a deep breath, she blurted out what she had practiced on her way over.

"I don't think I need to keep bringing meals anymore, Natália. It's time you resumed your responsibilities as a wife. Since you're no longer working, you have more time than me, and István for that matter, to cook and clean and do the shopping. Haven't you noticed that István's run ragged with working his shifts, doing the chores, and trying to care for you? He's exhausted and completely wrung out."

"Are you finished?" Natália replied angrily.

"Well actually, no. That husband of yours loves you more than life itself. Can't you see that by pushing him away you're destroying him? Don't forget that he was the father of your baby and he's grieving too. I'm only lecturing you because I love you, and you're crumbling before our eyes. Please, Natália, come back to us."

The tirade shocked Natália deeply. Rózsa had never rebuked her, and the words sliced across her heart like a flaming blade. Initially, Natália felt aggrieved, but upon reflection she knew Rózsa was right. Self-centred and grief stricken she hadn't once thought of István's feelings. The realisation made her even more miserable, wondering if he would ever forgive her selfishness. Over the next couple of hours, Natália poured her heart out to her friend, still blaming herself for the tragedy, unable to renounce her self-loathing. Vocalising her feelings with her dearest friend, the kind and loving Rózsa, who always looked up to Natália and was never judgemental, now listened with a maturity and compassion beyond her years. It was the first step towards lifting the bleak and hollow void that filled Natália's soul. Her body had healed and now her spirit had lightened, thanks to Rózsa.

Natália was pensive when István arrived home from work, unsure about how to apologise for the hurt she had caused him. Conversation was stilted as they ate their evening meal, their relationship still awkward. István left the kitchen when Natália cleared the plates and washed the dishes. Despite the warmth from the dishwater, Natália felt a chill creep up her spine. Shivering, she popped into the bedroom to fetch a sweater, flicked the switch of the bedside lamp, and saw István slouched on the floor beside their bed, head in his hands, weeping. Frozen on the spot, all she could do was stare for a moment before seizing the opportunity to console him. Rushing over she dropped beside him, wrapped her arms around his shoulders and hugged him tightly. She held him for several minutes, lost tears now reawakening and streaking down her face. Murmuring through her sobs she kept repeating, "I'm so sorry, I'm so sorry for everything."

Finally, they both stopped crying. No words were uttered. They remained on the floor, István's head now cradled in Natália's arms, gently smoothing the hair from his brow, surrounded by a peaceful hush for what seemed like an hour. István eventually broke the spell, inhaled deeply, sighed, sat up, and wiped his eyes with the back of his hands. Looking intently into Natália's eyes he said, in barely more than a whisper, "I'm sorry too. I'm sorry I wasn't with you when Julia was born. I'm sorry I pressured you to go out and have fun instead of resting after a long shift at work. I'm sorry I didn't insist you leave work when you fell pregnant. I'm sorry I wasn't more attentive and helpful around the house. If anyone is to blame for the loss of our child, Natália, it's me. I should have protected the two of you."

István blew his nose then went on, "But the doctor said you would heal well given time. We can try again for another baby when you're ready, but we will never forget our little Julia."

Natália stroked István's face and kissed him tenderly on the lips. At that moment a spark ignited within her. They needed each other more than ever. Pledging to be strong for her husband, as he had tried to be strong for her, Natália kissed István again, more passionately. Carefully lifting her, István placed Natália on the bed, then lay beside her. Slowly removing their clothing, exploring each other's body as if for the first time, they made love. It was a gentle but fervent lovemaking, each other's need overwhelming. István, fearful of hurting Natália, and Natália desperate to feel joined once again with her husband in the most intimate way, both physically and spiritually.

***

As time passed, István became increasingly interested in the growing political discontent amongst the intellectual community in Budapest and attended more of the Petőfi Club meetings, despite Natália's insistence that it was too dangerous to be associated with them. She begged him to consider their future if he was caught fraternising with the wrong people. István argued that the members of that club were the *right* people—those agitating for change—and that he would support their voice in any way he could, assuring Natália that he would be careful to steer clear of the secret police. "You can spot them a mile away," he reassured her. No amount of pleading would sway him. The Petőfi Club was the vehicle through which he could become involved in the necessary social changes demanded by the people of Hungary.

One afternoon in late June, István headed out to the Budapest Officer's Club, the venue for the next Petőfi Club meeting. Word on the street suggested that it would be a momentous event, an opportunity for the people to voice their objections to government officials. Ferenc and Albert had agreed to attend, yet the men decided to remain anonymous, cautious not to be seen together. As István approached the building he was amazed at the size of the crowd that was already amassing at the entrance; mostly men but many women too. He hurried along to join the queue. Scanning the crowd, he waited for the doors to open, then spotted Ferenc and Albert amongst the throng, pleased they were attending so they could discuss the outcome of the event at their next rendezvous. István anxiously waited in the warm sun as more people arrived, wondering whether there would be any trouble. The atmosphere was electric. Finally, after another half an hour, the doors opened. By the time István and his friends entered the auditorium there was standing room only. Thousands of people were forced to remain outside. István glanced around the room, hoping to find a spot that provided clear visibility of the stage, but there were too many people jammed in. Pushing his way to the back near an exit, István preferred to remain hidden and, more importantly, well placed to make a run for it, if needed. People all around them spoke excitedly about the new turn of events and opportunities to finally make demands for real change. Anticipation was building. Another thirty minutes passed before proceedings commenced.

Three party leaders attended the meeting: Sándor Nógrádi, Zoltán Vas, and Márton Horváth. Horváth was first to approach the microphone, declared the meeting open, and stating it was intended as an opportunity for constructive self-criticism. István didn't know these officials but was amazed that any turned up at all for this supposed 'self-criticism'—a new turn of events for the regime.

A well-known writer, Tibor Déry, pushed his way to the stage and began the first of a series of reproaches, against Horváth personally and then against the Party itself, "As long as we direct our criticism against individuals instead of investigating whether the mistakes spring from the very system, from the very ideology, we will achieve nothing more than to exchange evil for a lesser evil."

A huge cheer erupted from the mob. Vas called for order before another person stood before the microphone and continued, "There are many peasants, workers, students, and intellectuals in this country who consider the current inflexible leadership—and the bureaucracy with its lack of information—unacceptable. It's up to the leadership to change its line and alter its practices—not gradually, but unequivocally, immediately, and structurally."

Tibor Meray, a prominent journalist, spoke—as did many others that night—about the issue of truth. He stated that truth-telling was the primary concern for all Hungarians whether they were party members or not, and that freedom was their key objective, their most inner imperative.

Several more people got up to speak; writers, students, other journalists, all voicing their dissatisfaction with the political situation. They questioned the Communist philosophy, asking the leaders to learn from past mistakes, complaining about the current leadership—their lack of humanity, lack of information, and the pathetic daily news that was pumped out, and which everyone knew was censored. As the meeting progressed, complaints quickly turned to demands: demands for the right to receive Western broadcasts and Western newspapers and, more compellingly, demands for the removal of the current leadership. István couldn't believe what he was hearing. No one ever dared speak openly in this way in the presence of Party officials without severe consequences. His heart rate quickened. The hairs on the back of his neck rose. The atmosphere was charged. This was a true turning point. Looking around the room to see if he could spot the secret police circulating through the crowd, he was relieved that no one fit their description: the only officials were those on the stage. It was four in the morning when the last speaker stood at the podium. Geza Losonczy, a close associate of Imre Nagy, was the editor of the Magyar Nemzet newspaper. He denounced the Hungarian press for their daily attack on the previous Prime Minister, stating that he was a good Hungarian and a loyal Communist. Everyone started chanting, "Long live Imre Nagy. Long live Imre Nagy. Take him back into the party. Reinstate him as leader."

István joined the throng. It was impossible not to be swept up in the mounting fervour. The chanting grew louder for many more minutes. The meeting ended abruptly as the microphones were turned off, with the party officials hastily exiting. Not wanting to be embroiled in any skirmishes that may erupt, István decided it was time to sneak out through the back door rather than file out the front with most of the other attendees in case arrests were made. István's mind was reeling. The meeting he had just witnessed was nothing short of treason. He ran part of the way home to get as far away from the club as possible before he stopped to catch his breath. Once his heart rate steadied, István lifted the collar of his coat to protect his neck from the wind that had whipped up, shoved his hands into his coat pockets and walked briskly the rest of the way home. With no trams running at that time of the morning, it was an hour before he put the key into the lock of his front door and slumped onto the sofa from both physical and emotional exhaustion. István remained in the living room, not wanting to disturb Natália, but he couldn't sleep. The events of the past several hours churned over and over in his mind. The enormity of what he had witnessed and what he had participated in was extraordinary—yet at the same time it felt exciting and liberating.

Natália woke early and was alarmed when István was not lying beside her. She tossed off the covers and found him fast asleep on the sofa, still fully dressed. Relieved that he had not been arrested as she had feared, she smiled at her husband, kissed his forehead, then went to put the kettle on. A few minutes later Natália brought two cups of tea into the living room and waited for her husband to wake. István heard the kettle's whistle but kept his eyes closed for a few moments, reliving his experience, and arranging his thoughts to articulate the key messages he had gleaned from the meeting.

"Must you slurp so loudly?" he asked teasingly. Natália smiled, handed him his tea, and proceeded to quiz him on the events of the previous day. István tried very hard to tell all and not omit anything important. Natália listened intently, without interrupting, which was most unusual. He concluded by saying, "Change is coming. The momentum is building. I can feel it." His words left Natália feeling scared.

CHAPTER 9

Cruelty, indifference, and abuse—both physical and psychological—has lasting effects upon impressionable young minds. Seeking acceptance but constantly victimised, striving for academic excellence yet dismissed as inconsequential, and yearning for a father's love that fails to materialise, all these things cast long shadows that can rarely be stepped away from. Hurt manifests as hatred that festers gradually over time, gnawing at every sinew, stripping the humanity from one's soul, transforming the victim into a callous beast. This was Viktor Molnár's fate. Loved and fussed over by his mother until she tragically died when he was only sixteen years of age, Viktor was criticised by his father for being weak and for being mollycoddled by the woman who had devoted herself to their only child. He was a father jealous of his own son. Despite Viktor's best efforts, he could not impress his father nor win his affection.

Viktor matured into a strikingly handsome, tall man, with dark curly hair clipped short to stop the curls poking out from under his hat. He carried himself with the arrogance of a high achiever, of someone fierce and not to be challenged, confident of his place in the world. But it was not always so. When he was a young boy, he was called a sissy, and other horrible names he preferred to forget, all of which implied that he looked like a girl. The bullying in the schoolyard was relentless. As an only child, there was no one to defend him against the bigger, stronger boys who often ambushed him on his way home from school, kicking and punching until he lay inert on the ground. "Man up, son," his father would spit at him when he arrived home bruised and bleeding. Viktor felt his father's disappointment keenly. As he grew older it became clear that, as far as his father was concerned, three in the household was a crowd, and Viktor was the unwelcome intruder. His father took second place, and the more love and attention Viktor's mother lavished on her boy, the more it fuelled the animosity shown by his father to both Viktor and his mother. The brutality intensified as the years wore on. At first, there was constant criticism levelled at his mother for trivial things such as the lateness of the evening meal or the supposed shoddi-ness of the housekeeping, alongside demeaning insults about her matronly appearance, dowdy clothes, and slow intellect. The belittling morphed into slaps when she defended Viktor for the minor misdemeanours typical of a growing, curious boy, which soon spiralled into raping and beating her when he returned home from the pub in a drunken rage. Viktor cried when he saw the bruises on his mother's face, the swollen welts on her cheek, the split, blood encrusted lips and broken nose, yet felt impotent, unable to protect his mother against the towering bulk of his violent, angry father, the wrath of whom Viktor himself became victim to from the age of ten, when he had unwisely deemed himself grown up enough to defend his mother from the abuse.

Determined to put a stop to the torment her son endured day after day, Viktor's mother was resolute in making her boy strong and independent, something that would boost his self-reliance and assure his success in life. When his father disappeared to the pub each afternoon after a long day working as a civil servant at the local council chambers, she patched him up whenever he arrived home from school battered and bloodied, hugged him tightly to soothe his wounded pride, reassured him that all was well, that his father never meant to be so hard on them, then sat him down at the kitchen table with a glass of milk and freshly baked cookies; comfort food to heal all wounds. Despite his mother's attempts at depicting his father in a favourable light, Viktor knew his father was a selfish brute, and recognised the fear in his mother's eyes when his father burst through the front door in a rage. He swore to end her suffering as soon as he was old enough to fight back.

After making enquiries at the local sports club, Viktor's mother arranged for him to take boxing lessons. It was the best gift she could have given her son. The pent-up hostility towards the wretched world he inhabited was expelled with his fists, pounding the punching bag for four days a week, sweat pouring off his limbs in rivers, muscle building on muscle, strengthening the once puny frame. Viktor proved to be a natural athlete, representing his club as a middleweight contender at local competitions, and winning more bouts than he lost. The schoolyard bullies soon learned to steer clear of the champion fighter. Viktor's father too, cowered from him once his reputation in the ring grew. Yet the control and pain he wielded upon his wife continued; the only way left for Viktor's father to feel important, domineering, and masculine.

Elated by a competition that was hard won, in a fight that had favoured Viktor's older, more experienced opponent, he ran home to share the thrilling news of his success with his mother, expecting her to be at the stove, cooking up a feast, when he witnessed his father slap her hard across the face. Failing to steady herself she stumbled backwards, banged her head on the doorframe, and collapsed onto the floor with a thud. Viktor lunged at his father, grabbed his arm, wheeled him around so that their noses were mere millimetres apart, stepped back a pace, then with a quick, right hook, punched his father in the face with as much venom as he could muster, years of hatred unleashed with that one hard blow. His father crashed across the timber coffee table, splintering it into pieces, rendering it useless except as firewood. Blood splattered across his face from the broken nose. Before he could haul himself up off the floor, Victor looked down upon his father, sneered at him and, in a menacing tone that shocked him to the core, said between gritted teeth, "If you so much as touch one hair on her head ever again, I'll kill you with my bare hands."

The threat was a clear message to his father that he was no longer a match to this young boxing prodigy. From that day on their lives were irrevocably changed. Viktor swore an oath to save his mother, to help her find a new beginning away from the brute of a husband she no longer loved but constantly feared. But life is fragile and unpredictable. Safe in the knowledge that Viktor was no longer a victim but a strong, self-sufficient young warrior, feared and respected by all who knew him, his mother gained a sense of achievement and relief that her job was done. Her boy would thrive in the harsh world they inhabited. Peace crept into her heart, suffusing her mind and body. When she failed to appear the following morning, the usual buzz in the kitchen deathly quiet, Viktor tentatively poked his head into the master bedroom, puzzled that his mother would still be asleep. Kneeling by her bedside he kissed her swollen cheek. The once rosy skin was icy cold and the sparkling eyes full of love for her son remained shut. Panic welled up, constricting his throat. Shaking her shoulder vigorously and begging his mother to wake up proved fruitless. The body lying on the bed was a vacant shell. His mother was gone. Viktor then noticed an empty bottle of sleeping pills clutched in her left hand.

"Wake up, wake up," he screamed over and over.

Viktor held his mother to his chest for many minutes, sobbing, demanding she not leave him. The only person in his whole world that loved him unconditionally had abandoned him suddenly, without warning. Viktor was devastated and blamed his father for his mother's suicide. Choosing death over a tormented life with a cruel, heartless man was shocking, brave, and understandable. Viktor eventually forgave his mother for deserting him to end her suffering. The serene expression on her face as she lay lifeless on the bed let him know that her soul was at peace and gave him comfort. At the funeral, Viktor promised his mother that he would devise a plan to make his father suffer as she had suffered, to pay for the destruction of their family. Over time, the hatred towards his father festered. The boxing ring, with the coaches and like-minded youth, became a surrogate home, with the young man reluctant to spend any more time with his father than was necessary.

When he became of age to sit the entrance exam at the Police Academy, Viktor passed with flying colours. Grit, determination, sacrifice, and discipline transformed the boxer into a hardened soldier, eager to fulfil his duties to the best of his abilities. Indoctrinated into the ideology of communism, a true defender of the regime's dogma, the smart, dependable, trusted, and ruthless Viktor quickly rose through the junior ranks of the police force. Boxing and weight training remained part of his life. Maintaining his physique was not only important as a law enforcer, but he knew that women liked strong, muscular men. Women of all ages constantly flirted with him. He could seduce any woman he wanted and relished the power he held over lesser beings.

PART TWO

1956: REVOLUTION

CHAPTER 10

Mátyás Rákosi began his political career as a youth in 1918 and soon rose to a leadership position within the short-lived Hungarian Soviet Republic. Fiercely loyal to the Soviet Union, he was appointed to the position of General Secretary of the Hungarian Communist Party in 1948 and became Prime Minister in 1952, a position he relinquished to Imre Nagy just ten months later. Failing to deliver on his economic reforms and deviating from the Communist Party's core doctrines, Nagy was removed from office, and in April 1955 Rákosi was reinstated as leader.

Emulating Stalin's brutal regime, Rákosi was responsible for the imprisonment of hundreds of thousands of Hungarians, and also for thousands of deaths. Feared and despised by the populace in equal measure, he orchestrated show trials, modelled on those of Russia, where the verdict was decided well before the trials commenced. Among the most prominent victims was his former lieutenant, László Rajk. No one was safe from his thirst for control. His policies of collectivisation and mass repression devastated the country's economy and its spirit. After Stalin's death and Khrushchev's denouncement of his predecessor's ruthless policies and crimes, Rákosi's position was severely compromised. His enemies within the Party increased, and his hold on power became tenuous.

***

News of the recent Petőfi Club's debate, which had attracted thousands of citizens from all walks of life, reached Rákosi as swiftly as his response. Within the same breath as hearing about the club's activities, he initiated a draft resolution through the Central Committee condemning the club's anti-party leanings. It was crucial that their momentum be quashed and the ringleaders brought to heel. Days later, further advice was received that speakers at a Writer's Union meeting had openly criticised the Central Committees' resolution. How dare they? Rákosi was fuming. Pacing around his palatial office like a caged tiger, muttering expletives under his breath, he knew that he could not allow this group of agitators to gain traction and destabilise the government. The Soviet bosses were watching him closely: he could not fail them again. Crushing the dissident voices of these so-called intellectuals was critical to his survival.

Flinging himself into the large, black leather chair behind his writing desk, Rákosi repeatedly thumped the highly polished wood. Intelligence sources reported growing discontent and anti-establishment sentiment, not only throughout the city but in the regional centres as well. The frequency of these reports was increasing. Why the citizens felt emboldened to speak out and make demands on the government was a mystery. It was imperative that he regained control and asserted his authority. Taking a few deep breaths and exhaling slowly, his anger subsided and his thoughts focussed on how he would destroy the founders of the Petőfi Club and outlaw its existence. Prone to perspiring easily, he felt the sweat trickle down his temples. Wiping the beads of moisture from his balding head with a crisp white handkerchief, Rákosi pondered how the situation had escalated so rapidly, like a genie escaping from its bottle. It had become the newest, most dangerous thorn in his side. Well, they would not triumph. The genie would be captured and squeezed back into its bottle, with the stopper sealed tightly, suffocating the creatures within. Smiling to himself as he imagined the enemy pleading for leniency, Rákosi was shaken out of his reverie by a loud knock on the door. Taking another deep breath, he paused for a moment, wiped his brow again, then barked in his customary gruff tone, "Enter."

The door creaked open. A tall, young man stepped inside looking nervous.

"Comrade Rákosi, sorry to disturb you," his personal assistant said tentatively. He was never sure in what mood he would find his boss, and so would always placate him, just in case. He quickly broke the news of the reason for his intrusion, "Comrade Anastas Mikoyan has just arrived in Budapest and has convened a meeting with a number of party members for 11.00am this morning."

"I wasn't aware of Mikoyan's visit."

Rákosi flipped through his diary for the entire month of July, but there were no scheduled meetings at all with Mikoyan. "Why is there nothing in my diary about this? Did Mikoyan say why he was here? Did he present an agenda for the meeting?"

Rákosi's voice was becoming louder with each question. Feeling his blood pressure rising, and sensing he was being undermined yet again by his superiors, Rákosi was worried. These surprise visits never ended well.

"I wasn't forewarned of his visit, Sir, nor was I given any further advice."

Seeing that his boss was agitated, he added, "Can I fetch you a coffee or tea?"

"No. That will be all," Rákosi said as he waved his assistant away, beads of sweat resurfacing on his brow.

So, Moscow had despatched one of its Politburo affiliates to sort out this mess. My, how news travels fast, Rákosi mused. He choked down the anxiety that was welling up inside. Mental toughness had sustained Rákosi throughout his career, and he would not allow a rabble of students to destabilise his authority. Straightening his back, he gathered his wits for the barrage of questions he expected from the Russian. Mikoyan had risen through the ranks and was now a senior Soviet official highly favoured by Khrushchev—a key member of his inner circle. Rumours of unrest in Hungary were clearly deemed important for the Soviet leadership to send such a high-ranking politician to reinstate order. Jotting down the circumstances that led to this impending confrontation, together with his plan to destroy the Petőfi Club and all its known members, Rákosi's aim was to convince Mikoyan to return to Russia with the confidence that he and his team were in full control of the situation and would eradicate the growing civil unrest.

As the meeting time drew near, Rákosi made his way to the conference room with his notebook in hand. Sweating profusely, he fought to maintain a calm exterior. He could not allow Mikoyan, or his other colleagues, to sense his fear. Entering the room, he was met with a steely gaze from his Russian superior. Little did Rákosi suspect that in a few short hours his career would end abruptly, and that he would be forced to retire to Moscow on the grounds of ill-health.

***

Optimism throughout the city was increasing. News of Rákosi's departure to Moscow spread like wildfire. The removal of the despised dictator for the second time—the last of the hard-line Stalinists—was viewed as a sign that the Soviets were tempering their policies. It buoyed the populace into believing that their voices would be heard and their freedoms restored.

Meanwhile, in Poland, another of the Soviet satellite states that endured poverty and tyranny, the people took matters into their own hands. A dangerous display of courage by the citizens of Poznan, an industrial town west of Warsaw, gave rise to riots that erupted at the end of June. Despite being easily crushed by Soviet troops, it was a sign of the people's contempt for Soviet control, and an attempt at demanding much needed reforms. A leadership spill on the 19th of October ensued. Wladislaw Gomulka was installed as the new Polish leader. Having recognised the validity of the protestors' demands he successfully struck a compromise with Khrushchev and facilitated reforms to placate the citizens. News of the events in Poland fuelled the ambitions of the Hungarian intellectuals. To express their solidarity, the Hungarian Writer's Union organised a demonstration at Bem Square on the 23rd of October, to lay a wreath at the foot of the statue of József Bem, a Polish general, and a leader and hero of the 1848 Hungarian Revolution.

István and his friend Albert were enlisted, along with many others, to distribute the pamphlets for the Bem Square demonstration. Natália insisted on being involved. She too felt the pulse of the city quicken and was eager to help with distributing the pamphlets, providing her with much needed purpose. István relented, thrilled that Natália's emotional wellbeing was recovering and that she was regaining some of her old spark and zest for life since the loss of their child.

The autumn chill pinched their cheeks as they set off, Natália wrapping a scarf over her head and slipping on her woollen gloves to keep out the cold. István suggested that she doorknock in their neighbourhood whilst he would venture further into town. Before heading their separate ways, István cautioned Natália to be discreet. The pamphlets could not fall into the wrong hands. She needed to be vigilant, staying well away from the police or anyone in uniform. The last thing he wanted was Natália to be arrested, interrogated or, worse still, dragged off to oblivion. Natália laughed, stating she was a big girl and could take care of herself. Smiling into her upturned face, he kissed her lips then reminded her to be back at János' flat no later than 6.00pm, as agreed.

With his camera slung around his neck, István crisscrossed the city streets handing out the leaflets to passers-by, pausing at intervals to snap a few photos of street scenes showing people congregating in small groups reading the material.

Natália walked briskly up and down the streets of her suburb to warm herself. Chatting amicably with the people who opened their doors and happily accepting the leaflets, she encouraged them to attend the demonstration. When there was no answer to her knock, she slipped the leaflet under the door. One elderly lady invited her in for a cup of tea. It was obvious the woman lived on her own and was lonely, and Natália happily accepted the invitation, the hot tea a welcome relief from the chill outside. They chatted about the forthcoming demonstration, but the lady said she was too old for rallies, although she wished Natália all the best, hoping life would improve soon. On two different intersections, Natália came across pairs of policemen surveying the area. Quickly slipping the leaflets into her handbag she casually strolled past the unsmiling men. Avoiding eye contact to prevent drawing attention to herself, her heart pounded in her throat, she fought to maintain a calm exterior. Breathing a sigh of relief, she darted down smaller streets to avoid further contact with any officials. This covert, rebellious activity was thrilling. It was the most useful and alive she had felt in months. After about three hours, and with her stock depleted, Natália made her way to the planned rendezvous. When she entered the flat, Rózsa was in the kitchen preparing dinner, one of her famous dishes; lecsó, a tomato, onion, and capsicum stew. The mouth-watering aroma wafted through the flat.

"Dinner smells divine. I'm famished," Natália announced, shrugging off her coat and hanging it up on the coat rack.

Embracing her friends, she noticed István was already in the living room. Natália kissed him lightly on the lips in greeting and proudly declared that all her leaflets were distributed. She prattled on about her adventure, how adroitly she had sidestepped the police, the lovely old woman who invited her in for a chat and a cup of tea, and how responsive everyone seemed to be to the forthcoming demonstration. István clapped with delight, commenting on what an expert revolutionary she'd turned out to be. Natália's face glinted with mischief.

Predictably, István had stopped at a bottle shop on his way to János' and bought one of his favourite red wines, Bull's Blood, to accompany the meal. Even for such a casual get together he would always take a bottle of wine for the host. He cracked it open, poured it into the glasses that were already placed upon the table, then took a sip and swished it around his mouth before swallowing.

"Ah, but that's good," he remarked. He handed a glass to János then proposed a toast.

"To change and a brighter future."

"To change," János repeated, before sampling the wine and agreeing with István's assessment. It was indeed very good.

The girls were in the kitchen chatting, Rózsa added the final touches to the meal—a sprinkling of chopped parsley on top of each serve—before placing the bowls on the dining table, while Natália poked her head into the living room and announced that dinner was ready. They all took their seats as István topped up the glasses.

István was particularly animated about the upcoming demonstration, hoping it would be a good turnout. Péter Veres, the head of the Writers Union, was expected to deliver a speech, outlining proposed reforms that would be demanded from the government. János was not as enthusiastic about the vocal criticisms against the government, fearful of reprisals, but agreed to attend the rally, privately knowing he would avoid any conflict if the situation spun out of control. After polishing off the delicious meal, with much praise lavished upon the cook, the foursome continued to discuss the forthcoming event, whether officials would be present and, if so, what interventions were to be expected. Natália raised her concerns about getting too involved in any rebellious activity, scared they would be caught. It was one thing to discreetly distribute pamphlets amongst the community but quite another to actively demonstrate against the government. Rózsa agreed vehemently with her friend, but István would not be swayed. "Security in numbers," he said. They were expecting thousands of people to attend the demonstration and would therefore be swallowed up by the crowd.

"Mark my words. This will be an historical event. Change is in the air. I wouldn't miss it for the world," István stated ardently.

***

News of the upcoming demonstration in Bem Square spread rapidly throughout the city, not just amongst the populace but through all levels of the government. Gatherings such as this were unheard of under Rákosi. The authorities were unsure of what to expect. Some officials suspected that the vocal student movement may try to intercept the airwaves to spread their propaganda to the wider population. Rákosi's replacement, Ernő Gerő would have none of it. Despite Khrushchev's tempered policies concerning the Soviet satellite states, Gerő would not tolerate dissidence of any kind. To circumvent any trouble the Budapest Police were mobilised to act as peacekeepers on the day of the rally.

Viktor Molnár's small team of officers gathered around as he read the memo regarding the Bem Square rally and the peacekeeping directive. His team was to position itself at the National Radio Broadcasting station and apprehend any troublemakers. Viktor was only too happy to bring to heel anyone out of line, another opportunity to demonstrate his loyalty and competency to his superiors.

***

Excitement and anticipation intensified with each day until Tuesday arrived. People were whispering in shops, in cafés, on trams, in their homes, wondering what to expect; a groundswell of determined citizens eager to witness the event. On the morning of the 23rd, Natália popped down to the corner store to buy a bottle of milk. Something struck her as odd as she walked along the street, observing that the shop windows, light poles, and bus stop were plastered with fliers with a heading, "The Sixteen Points." Ripping one down from a bus shelter she hurried home to show István. Heads bent together they read the flier slowly, absorbing the extent of the reforms formulated by the university students.

The Sixteen Points

1. *We demand the immediate evacuation of all Soviet troops, in conformity with the provisions of the Peace Treaty.*
2. *We demand the election by secret ballot of all Party members from top to bottom, and of new officers for the lower, middle, and upper echelons of the Hungarian Workers Party. These officers shall convene a Party Congress as early as possible to elect a Central Committee.*
3. *A new Government must be constituted under the direction of Imre Nagy. All criminal leaders of the Stalin-Rákosi era must be immediately dismissed.*
4. *We demand a public enquiry into the criminal activities of Mihály Farkas and his accomplices. Mátyás Rákosi, who is the person most responsible for crimes of the recent past as well as for our country's ruin, must be returned to Hungary for trial before a people's tribunal.*
5. *We demand general elections by universal, secret ballot to be held throughout the country to elect a new National Assembly, with all political parties participating. We demand that the right of workers to strike be recognised.*
6. *We demand revision and re-adjustment of Hungarian-Soviet and Hungarian-Yugoslav relations in the fields of politics, economics, and cultural affairs, on a basis of complete political and economic equality, and of non-interference in the internal affairs of one by the other.*
7. *We demand the complete reorganisation of Hungary's economic life under the direction of specialists. The entire economic system, based on a system of planning, must be re-examined in the light of conditions in Hungary and in the vital interest of the Hungarian people.*

8. *Our foreign trade agreements and the exact total of reparations that can never be paid must be made public. We demand to be precisely informed of the uranium deposits in our country, on their exploitation and on the concessions to the Russians in this area. We demand that Hungary have the right to sell her uranium freely at world market prices to obtain hard currency.*

9. *We demand complete revision of the norms operating in industry and an immediate and radical adjustment of salaries in accordance with the just requirements of workers and intellectuals. We demand a minimum living wage for workers.*

10. *We demand that the system of distribution be organised on a new basis and that agricultural products be utilised in a rational manner. We demand equality of treatment for individual farms.*

11. *We demand reviews by independent tribunals of all political and economic trials as well as the release and rehabilitation of the innocent. We demand the immediate repatriation of prisoners of war (World War II) and of civilian deportees to the Soviet Union, including prisoners sentenced outside Hungary.*

12. *We demand complete recognition of freedom of opinion and of expression, of freedom of the press and of radio, as well as the creation of a daily newspaper for the MEFESZ Organisation (Hungarian Federation of University and College Students' Associations)*

13. *We demand that the statue of Stalin, symbol of Stalinist tyranny and political oppression, be removed as quickly as possible and be replaced by a monument in memory of the martyred freedom fighters of 1848-49.*

14. *We demand the replacement of emblems foreign to the Hungarian people by the old Hungarian arms of Kossuth. We demand new uniforms for the Army which conform to our national traditions. We demand that March 15th be declared a national holiday and that the October 6th be a day of national mourning on which schools will be closed.*

15. *The students of the Technological University of Budapest declare unanimously their solidarity with the workers and students*

of Warsaw and Poland in their movement towards national independence.

16. *The students of the Technological University of Budapest will organise as rapidly as possible local branches of MEFESZ, and they have decided to convene at Budapest, on Saturday October 27, a Youth Parliament at which all the nation's youth shall be represented by their delegates.*

Developed by the students of the Budapest Technological University

István reread the flier a second time, stunned by the brazenness of it. Letting it drop onto the table, he looked up into Natália's worried face and said, with a hint of reverence in his voice, "This is truly revolutionary, Natália. A turning point in our future."

Natália remained silent, frightened at the thought of what this type of seditious material would unleash.

István, Natália, János, and Rózsa had agreed to meet at The Coffee Pot Café for a late lunch before setting off together towards Bem Square. It was another cold afternoon. The dry brown and gold leaves swirled in the air as the wind ripped them from swaying branches. Joining hundreds of people already lining the streets, heading in the same direction, István commented on the buzz emanating from the crowd: it was electric. Thousands of people had already congregated at the foot of the statue by the time István's troupe arrived. People huddled together, stomping their feet to keep warm as they stood around waiting for something to happen. Finally, a man was seen pushing his way through the throng. Climbing up the plinth of the statue he elevated himself from those gathered around. Holding a megaphone to his mouth he introduced himself as the president of the Writer's Union. Péter Veres thanked everyone for venturing out on such a cold day, setting aside any fears they may have had about participating in the demonstration. He recounted the uprising in Poland a few short months earlier and the subsequent success by their leader in securing a path to reforms. The crowd cheered. Péter raised his hand, calling for silence, then continued, "Poland has paved the way for us but not without bloodshed and loss of life."

Placing a large wreath at the base of the statue he went on, "We commemorate the brave Polish citizens who gave their lives for their principals. It's time we Hungarians acted, demanding reforms from our government." More cheers emanated from the crowd.

Péter then passed the megaphone to another young man standing beside him.

"Fellow Hungarians, we, the students from the Budapest Technological University, have developed a sixteen-point manifesto that we intend to present to the government, demanding immediate effect," he declared.

A hush descended upon the crowd as they eagerly listened to the speaker, the young student annunciating each point slowly and clearly. A roar reverberated around the thousands of people gathered in the square, amazed at hearing their supressed views and demands for change spoken so boldly in the open. István put his arm around Natália, pulling her close, tears pricking his eyes, completely overcome by the magnitude of the situation. The mob was highly charged by the time the speaker had finished and started chanting, 'Russians go home.' István and Natália joined in the refrain, punching the air with their fists along with everyone else. Before the student jumped off the plinth, he bellowed, "We will broadcast our demands via the airways. To the radio station on Sándor Bródy Street."

A great mass of people turned to march towards Budapest Radio, the national broadcasting station. Others remained, milling about, wondering what would happen next. A group of men splintered from the mob and raced across the lawn to the flagpole, pulling the Hungarian flag down to head height. As they held the flag taught, one man cut out the centre Communist coat of arms and threw it onto the ground. Hoisting the transformed flag up the pole, it flapped in the breeze, a testament to a new beginning. Lifting his camera up to his face, István photographed the scene unfolding before him. Then, one of the men grabbed the Communist coat of arms while another struck a match and lit it. A cheer erupted as the symbol burned. People kept chanting, 'Russians go home,' and 'bring back Imre Nagy.' István, together with Natália and their friends, chanted along with everyone else, both stunned and elated at the audaciousness of these words and the magnitude of the declaration.

The light was fading as dusk descended upon the square, casting a yellow glow upon József Bem. The temperature dropped. The squall intensified, sending a chill through István's bones. Rózsa and János decided it was time to head home, afraid to participate any further. They looked around nervously, scared of being rounded up by the police. István chose to follow the crowd to the radio station, curious to witness the events unfold, yet he insisted Natália return home, believing it was unsafe for her to stay. He asked his friends to escort her home. Natália protested vehemently, wanting to remain with her husband, but he grabbed her by the shoulders and demanded she go home with the others. Before Natália could argue further, he kissed her hard on the mouth, turned away and disappeared into the crowd. Natália called after him, but it was no use. He was gone.

A sense of unease rippled through István as the mood of the crowd shifted from a passive audience to a mob with a heightened fanaticism. Scenes of vandalism unfolded. As he ventured closer to the radio station, he witnessed people throwing bricks through shop windows, burning Communist symbols and posters of socialist propaganda, and chanting 'freedom for the people.' The restive crowd had become angry and were demanding their voices be heard.

Outside the radio station, the crowd grew more agitated. Word spread that the students attempting to broadcast their sixteen-point plan had been detained by the secret police, while others believed that they had been killed. As the crowd numbers swelled, they surged as one, trying to force open the heavy oak door to the radio station, but it refused to budge. In frustration, the mob hurled bricks and cobblestones, smashing the windows of the building. István was shocked to see hundreds of armed men, both soldiers and the secret police, surrounding the building, holding their weapons in threatening poses. Few people noticed a dozen, heavily armed police officers entering the rear of the building. It seemed the authorities were anticipating trouble. István edged his way to the back of the crowd, observing the situation from the sidewalk, careful not to become embroiled in the violence he feared would flare up, anxiously awaiting the outcome.

Viktor ushered his men into the rear of the building and quickly scaled the stairs, taking their positions on the rooftop. Three of the officers carried bags of tear gas and placed the canisters on the ground in readiness to scare the troublemakers, trusting the mob would flee once the gas was deployed. Surveying the crowd below, Viktor noticed many agitators, spurring the mob to continue to ram the front door, smash the windows, and gain entry. He instructed his men to remain vigilant, poised to act if matters escalated.

Hiding behind a parked car, István continued to take photos of the scenes playing out in front of him, trying to avoid detection by the security forces. The standoff he witnessed intensified as it became apparent that the police and soldiers were not ordered to fire, just to hold the crowd at bay. The mob continued their efforts to breach the building, emboldened by the absence of violence, when a crackle was heard over the loudspeakers. Gradually, a hush descended upon the precinct. Everyone froze and stood staring up at the point from which the voice of First Secretary Ernő Gerő boomed across the night sky. To everyone's fury, Gerő addressed the citizens like an angry parent, reprimanding them for their behaviour and for conducting unlawful demonstrations, condemning their protests, and stating that hostile elements would not be tolerated. He spoke in a harsh, uncompromising tone that enraged the people even further. The mob booed and hissed in response, hurling rocks, and other small projectiles at the loudspeakers. István's eye caught something being thrown from the rooftop of the radio station. Canisters of tear gas rained down into the crowd, spewing the contents. People fell, writhing on the ground, scratching at their swollen eyes, coughing violent as the gas penetrated their lungs. Immediately after, gunshots were fired above the demonstrators' heads in order to disperse them. It had the desired effect, with the terrified citizens fleeing in all directions, yet within a few minutes the mob surged forward again to the front of the building. István remained rooted in his hiding place behind the car, transfixed by the escalation of tensions.

The effects of the tear gas were short lived. Seeing the mob return to continue their assault on the building, determined to gain entry, Viktor's officers fired another volley of shots, only this time, the bullets ripped straight through the unsuspecting mob. Screams and shouting followed. People scattered, fleeing for their lives, yelling at the officials to stop shooting, wailing for their fellow citizens and their loved ones dying in the street. Through all the chaos, István couldn't see from where the shots were fired. Looking around, he was appalled at the carnage in front of him, people covered in blood, some motionless on the ground. The rumbling of trucks drew his attention away from the horrific scenes. Hungarian Army reinforcements arrived to quell the riot but refused to obey the orders they had been given, instead remaining motionless and failing to shoot their fellow compatriots. And then, to everyone's amazement, the soldiers who just moments before were pointing their rifles at the demonstrators, alongside those newly arrived, ripped the red stars from their caps and joined the mob, fighting back, firing at the police. When István saw not only soldiers but civilians wielding rifles and small handguns, firing back at the enemy, he was mystified as to how these weapons had materialised.

Fury was unleashed like a ferocious storm. Men carrying iron bars smashed car windows. Police cars and trucks were torched, neighbouring buildings were vandalised, and windows shattered. Black smoke billowed into the air from the tyres that were aflame, stinging István's eyes and blinding him. Tears streaked down his cheeks as he blinked rapidly to clear his vision. Terrified of being shot, István crouched low, retreating behind more parked cars, until he felt safe to stand upright and make a run for it. As he stood, he glanced up at the top of the building and saw an officer pointing his rifle directly at him. A hail of bullets tore into the wall of a building next to him. Mortar exploded into the air, narrowly missing him. Desperate to escape the firing line and the horrific massacre as quickly as possible, he turned toward the direction of home, fleeing for his life. He veered off the main road to escape detection. As he rounded the corner, still at full pelt, István careered straight into two police officers who were running towards the radio station. One of the officers fell to the ground on impact. The other grabbed his arm. István punched him in the stomach with his free hand. It was enough for the stunned policeman to release his grip. István seized his chance and bolted, zigzagging through the smaller lanes until he was sure that he was not being chased. His shirt was soaked through from panic, horror, and exertion. Hiding behind a dumpster in an alleyway at the rear of a hotel, István stopped for a few minutes to recover his breath. Parched from the pungent smoke that filled his lungs and running for his life, sharp pains knifed through his chest. Once his heart rate recovered, he stood, and cautiously peered around the bin to check that there was no one there. Satisfied that it was safe to continue, he ran the rest of the way home.

Horrified at witnessing the Hungarian Army join the civilians in retaliation, Viktor knew it was time to retreat. Yelling at his men to follow him, he flew down the stairs and back into the broadcasting room where he found Gerő still seated behind the microphone. Without any preamble he grabbed Gerő's arm and hurriedly led him out through the back door and into the bulletproof sedan, parked with the engine running. Viktor and two of his men slid into the back seat of the car before it took off at speed.

It was well past 11pm when István put the key into the lock, pushed the door open and collapsed onto the floor, his chest heaving, struggling to breathe from inhaling the acrid smoke fumes from the burning tyres and gun fire. The choking, coughing noises emanating from the hallway alerted Natália, who was lying in bed, unable to sleep from worry. Rózsa and János had stayed with Natália for a few hours when they escorted her home. They knew she was afraid for her husband. It was getting late, and after picking at a small cheese platter Natália insisted her friends head home, then she went to bed, her ears focussed on the slightest sound. Realising István was the cause of the racket, she tossed off the covers, rushed over to her husband and checked him all over, fearing he was injured.

"I'm fine, my love. Water, I just need some water," he croaked.

Natália waited patiently as her husband spent the next few minutes downing two glasses of water, coughing between gulps. Rising from the floor, he staggered into the living room and slumped onto the sofa. He removed the camera from around his neck and placed it onto the coffee table. Natália insisted he tell her all that had happened since she left him at Bem Square. Pointing to the camera he spluttered, "It's all there. I captured all of it, including the murders of innocent Hungarians just wanting their voices heard."

Natália stared at him, completely stunned. István was too distraught to describe the entire fiasco but said that what started out as a peaceful demonstration turned into carnage, the likes of which he hadn't witnessed since the war. The shock of what he had experienced slowly wore off. István began to tremble, weeping into his hands. Natália cradled his head against her shoulder and sat silently, stroking his face, digesting the news. Disbelief, fear and then relief that István escaped harm were the emotions that swirled through her. Then a slow terror crept into her stomach, wondering what the ramifications would be. How would the regime react? What did this turn of events mean for them, for their future?

***

The radio station was breached. People flooded into the building to rescue the students trapped inside, held hostage by the secret police. They searched every room for Gerő but he was nowhere to be found. His vanishing act enraged the mob. It soon became apparent that the secret police were outnumbered. Revenge for the innocent people indiscriminately cut down only a short while ago was at the forefront of their minds. Some of the police officers were beaten to death with iron bars, their pleas for mercy not only unheeded but actively fuelling the viciousness of the attacks. Others were marched outside, hung upside down by their ankles with thick ropes tied to nearby tree branches, and burned alive. Agonised screams from the men afire echoed around the surrounding buildings. Gun shots continued to pierce the night. Humanity was forgotten as years of pent-up fear and hatred was unleashed on the Soviets and their supporters.

CHAPTER 11

L ying in bed, snuggled under the blankets, Natália's legs brushed against her husband's warm body. As the sleepy fog cleared from her mind, she breathed a sigh of relief at the solid feel of him. Recollecting the shocking events that István had described to her, fear snaked around her belly. He could have been killed. István stirred beside her, still dozing. Natália remained cocooned in bed and said a silent prayer that his life had been spared. Contemplating what the fallout would be and how order would be restored, she was forced out of her musings when the ground trembled and the building shook. Two loud blasts in quick succession frightened Natália enough to jump up and peer out the bedroom window, but she couldn't see anything unusual. The menacing sound was thunderous, rattling the panes of glass as though a fierce storm was raging, except the sky was clear. The morning sun shone through the window-pane. Shimmering beams of light flooded the room, creating a warm and cosy atmosphere, a paradox to the loud booming sounds reverberating around the buildings. István yawned and stretched like a cat before asking what was happening. Exhausted from the events of the previous day and night, haunted by the images of the slaughtered demonstrators, he wanted nothing more than to sleep and erase the horrid images from his mind. Natália returned to bed, cuddled up to István, shaking from fear and replied, "I can't see anything from our window but there's something going on. I thought I heard a bomb blast."

"What!"

Sitting up in bed István rubbed his eyes and scratched his scalp to rouse himself then said, "Let's turn on the radio and see if there's a broadcast about what's going on."

Turning the dial this way and that only produced varying pitches of crackling, teeth-grinding static without a hint of a human voice. Budapest Radio seemed to be off the air. Not surprising, given the damage that was inflicted upon the building, and whatever else might have happened to the staff and equipment after István made his hasty retreat. He lay back on the pillow, thinking the worst. Another booming sound made them both jump. Curiosity mingled with trepidation won out. The couple hastily dressed, threw on their coats, and ventured outside. István locked the apartment door behind him and the couple skipped down the three flights of stairs to the front door of their building. Stepping out cautiously, they gazed around the street, tentatively searching for the source of the clamour. Many other people were milling around too, some huddled together, seemingly feeling safer in small groups, while others gravitating towards the loud rumbling. István and Natália followed the noise, in an almost trance-like state, as though they were being led by the Pied Piper. Slowly, the surrounding streets filled with men, women and children, all gravitating towards the noise.

Unexpectedly, screams ripped through the air, carried on the wind, high-pitched shrieks above the drone of the thunder. People started running towards the epicentre of the commotion. Natália linked her arm with István's, hugging him tightly, not wanting to lose sight of him as the crowd thickened. Then, as they converged on the corner at the end of their street their worst fears were realised. A row of Soviet T34 tanks was crawling along Rákoczi Street, heading straight for their group. The tanks were so large that their bulk consumed the street, crushing anything that dared block their way. Stray dogs ran alongside, barking incessantly. The huge guns at the front of the tanks moved from left to right, firing indiscriminately into buildings and into the crowd, bullets ricocheting off walls. Large chunks of brick flew into the air before crashing to the ground in piles of rubble. The tanks forged ahead, crushing the debris into dust. The screams that burst from the horrified crowd intensified. Some people fell to the ground. It was not clear who was wounded or who was instinctively trying to dodge the bullets. People ran frantically in all directions to escape the attack, colliding with one another in their desperation to flee.

Natália froze, mouth agape, transfixed at the scene unfolding not more than five feet in front of her. An elderly woman collapsed onto the ground, blood pooling around her head as she hit the pavement, dead eyes staring up at Natália . Part of the woman's throat and scull was missing from where the bullets had torn through her, saving Natália from being hit. A scream caught in Natália's throat. A faint wheezing sound was all that escaped from her lips. István grabbed her upper arm, jerked her around, yelling to run back the way they had come, back towards their apartment. For a moment Natália just looked at her husband blankly, unable to move. Then, as more shots were fired, small pieces of mortar caught Natália's shoulder, snapping her out of her bewilderment. István started running, dragging Natália behind him. They flew on winged feet, hardly connecting with the ground, with a surreal sense of weightlessness as they fled the attack. Darting into the smaller streets, away from the main thoroughfare and the looming tanks, allowed them to slow down a little, knowing they were clear of the firing line. Once they reached their apartment block István guided Natália down to the communal laundry in the basement, the safest place to hide should their building suffer an attack.

Natália became panic-stricken, sobbing hysterically, never having seen a dead person before. The poor woman. Who would tell her family what happened? István sat with Natália for a few minutes, hugging her tightly against his chest, stroking her hair, reassuring her that she was safe. He removed her coat and undid her blouse to examine the wound on her shoulder and was relieved that it was only grazed; a bruise was forming but no blood had been spilt.

"Listen to me, love. I want you to stay here until nightfall. It's the safest place in our building until the tanks stop firing. Only when it's silent will it be safe to head up to our apartment. Do you understand?"

Natália stopped crying. Frowning up at her husband, she was about to ask what the hell he meant when István said that he wanted to go back. The wounded would need to be helped to safety. He wanted to assist in any way he could. Natália insisted that István stay at home until calm was restored, terrified that he would go out and not return home. The police were sure to be rounding up anyone suspected of fighting or collaborating with the resistance. Even if István was only taking photographs of the scenes unfolding before his eyes, the police didn't ask questions. Anyone seen at the hotspots around the city would be arrested.

"I can't just stand by and do nothing, Natália. Do as I say and stay here until dark."

Before she could argue further, István was up the stairs and running back toward the carnage.

Disbelief, anger, hatred, and fear swirled through Natália's mind as she tried to comprehend what she had just witnessed. She was violently shaking again, sitting on the laundry floor on a pile of towels. The oppressor was fighting back. They should have known. Those smart students should have known that the Communists would not let the citizens win. Who are we to stand up to the might of the Soviets with their tanks and guns and torturous prisons? The vision of the dead woman was raw in her mind. How could that old woman, a grandmother, sister, and wife possibly be a threat to the Communists? Natália cried for a long time, so deep was her despair not only for the dead woman and what was happening on the streets right now, but for what was yet to come. The harsh brutality that was the hallmark of the Communist regime would undoubtedly be intensified to ensure that order was restored and thoughts of freedom crushed. Bone-weary from the pent-up tension and racking sobs, Natália eventually curled up into a foetal position and dozed off, oblivious to the war that was being waged on the streets of Budapest. When she eventually woke, the racket had died down and the laundry was in complete darkness. Rising from the floor after what seemed like hours, Natália stretched her cramped muscles, willing the circulation to return to her numb legs. Groping her way towards the door, she opened it and dragged herself up the stairs to her apartment, where she sat in stunned silence, too scared to do anything but listen intently for sounds; of trucks passing, gun blasts and, most importantly, a key in the door announcing the safe arrival of her beloved István.

***

Corpses were strewn along the roads and footpaths, lying limp amongst the wreckage. István ran from one to another checking for a pulse. The last person he knelt before, hoping to find alive, was a small girl, about eight years of age, clutching a rag doll. Her long brown hair was swept across her bloody face. István picked her up and shook her hard, trying to bring her back to life, yelling at her to wake up. He sat on the road, clutching the dead girl to his chest, crying for the precious life that was so cruelly extinguished. Gently carrying her to the footpath, he carefully propped her body against a building where two other women were lying motionless. It was futile. Rage quickly took root in his heart, replacing the despair at not finding anyone alive that he could help. His blood was pumping fast through his veins. There must be a way to fight back, to avenge these innocent people. Realising that nothing could be done for the dead, he ran through the city in search of the tanks. It didn't take long; he just followed the path of destruction. It quickly became apparent that those tanks that had swerved down the narrow streets off the main roads had made a strategic error. They could barely move forward without scraping the sides of buildings, never mind doubling back. Their progress was slow and their attacks hindered. A tense laugh escaped István's lips at the vulnerable situation some of these killing machines now faced, no longer in command of the situation. He rounded the corner, ducking past one of the tanks, when he noticed a group of teenage boys at the end of an ally behind Corvin Cinema busily making something with a row of glass bottles. Not immediately comprehending what was happening but intrigued by their little production line, István cautiously approaching the group and asked, "Hey boys, what are you up to?"

A dark haired, grubby looking boy of about sixteen years of age jumped up, pointed a rifle at István and said, "Stay right there. Who are you? What do you want from us?"

István raised his arms high into the air, trying to stay calm, as he explained that he was one of them, a Hungarian citizen shocked at the vicious attack by the Russians, desperate to retaliate in some way. The boy noticed that István was in civilian clothing, sized him up for a couple of minutes then lowered his rifle, deciding that the man before him did not possess the demeanour of the secret police. István was also unarmed, which the boy thought unusual.

"Do you know how to fire this rifle?" he asked.

István nodded. Although the Second World War had ended more than a decade ago, he recognised the 35M Puska. One such rifle was an extension to his right arm during the war, firing multiple rounds at the enemy, day in and day out. The boy threw the rifle at him and said, "Stand guard in front of us and shoot anyone that looks Russian."

István caught the rifle and did as he was asked. The boys introduced themselves by their first names only. Too much information was dangerous. Over his shoulder he continued to question the boy, Denes, wanting to know what they were making.

"Molotov Cocktails. To kill those bastard Russian soldiers and blow up their tanks. There's a fuel pump here, which is why we chose this site. There's enough fuel to make hundreds of bombs," Denes replied in a matter-of-fact way, acting as if this was business as usual.

"Where did you learn to do that?" István asked.

"From my uncle. He made them during the war and told me exactly how to disable the tanks."

Before long, István witnessed the effectiveness of the crudely made bomb. Eight bombs in total were assembled, with pieces of torn cotton shirt stuffed inside the top of gasoline-filled bottles. The gang was ready to attack. Denes assumed the role of leader, giving orders to the others. Three of the boys remained in the alley, guarding the bulk of the arsenal, while Denes and István ran behind the tank that István had snuck past not long before, crouching low to avoid detection. The tank was winding its way down the street at a snail's pace, scraping against the buildings, rippling holes in the brickwork. István watched Denes light the fuse and throw it onto the grated ventilation grill over the engine. The boy quickly ran back to where István stood, to escape the blast. The glass bomb shattered, erupting into a ball of flame, belching thick black smoke high into the sky. The engine caught fire and abruptly stopped. In less than a minute, a squeaky, grinding sound was heard as the top hatch lifted. Two soldiers stuck their heads out, coughing violently as the smoke engulfed them. István seized the opportunity and fired at the soldiers, killing both instantly. Denes whooped loudly, slapping István on the back and yelling, "Great shot, great shot!"

The other boys from the alley heard the blast and ran over to the disabled tank, jumping into the air, shouting in triumph. István was elated, his actions justified, having avenged the little girl he failed to resuscitate earlier that day, her bloodied face still fresh in his mind. Buoyed by the team's instant success, he was itching to find more targets and rid the streets of as many Russians as he could.

The boys' cheers were interrupted by the crackle of the public address system overhead. Imre Nagy addressed the citizens calling for calm, imploring them to lay down their weapons to avoid further bloodshed, to help restore order, to stand behind the Party, and to allow the government to find the right path for the country's prosperity. István scoffed at the end of the speech. Turning to his team he said, "Nagy has no idea what we want. He's not mentioned the Russians firing indiscriminately at our citizens, hasn't mentioned the sixteen-point plan that the students demanded yesterday, and hasn't confirmed that the Stalinist hardliners that are still in government have been removed. I expected more from him, but then again, he's still a Communist, a Russian puppet. Come on lads, let's find our next tank," István commanded, blood lust coursing through his veins.

The little band of rebels, with István as their new hero, scoured the smaller streets across the city throughout the rest of the day, seeking out other tanks that were hindered by their bulk. They had seven more bombs ready to deploy, utilising the same effective tactic as the first attack. István and one of the older boys held rifles, poised to fire should they run into the enemy, whilst the others ran ahead sourcing new targets. Over the course of the day, they disabled six more tanks, killing the soldiers who tried to escape the flames. Euphoria swept through the band, egging them on, thrilled that their killing strategy was such a success.

Feeling invincible, and after an anxious few hours, fatigue crept into Denes' bones and his concentration dulled. Carelessly throwing his last bomb, it missed the ventilation grill and exploded on the right side of the tank. Black smoke instantly cloaked the tank, making it difficult for the rebels to see. The hatch opened abruptly. István heard the squeaky metal door open but could not see the soldiers. They were trapped. There was nowhere to retreat. István yelled at the boys to drop to the ground directly in front of the tank, away from the firing line. The two Russians popped up and fired in a semi-circle. István then jumped up and answered the fire with a barrage of shots aimed at the sound. The smoke began to dissipate. István's eyes were red raw from the thick smoke, tears streaming down his face, yet he could just make out the head of one soldier, took aim and fired. Without waiting another moment, he fired three more shots in quick succession to the right of the dead soldier. Silence followed. As the air cleared, it was obvious that István had instantly killed the first soldier. The other one was wounded, pressing his fingers to his neck to stop the blood draining his life away. Although he was speaking Russian, István understood that the man was pleading for his life. Lifting his rifle, he aimed and said to the soldier before taking one last shot, "For the defenceless civilians."

The soldier slumped across the top of the tank, dead. István lowered his gun, his arms trembling with shock. A close call. Too close. Stepping back, he looked around for Denes and the other lad with the rifle. Denes rose from the ground, clutched István's free hand, squeezed it and thanked him over and over. István was at first stunned to see Denes crying, this fearless freedom fighter showing fragility. Then he reminded himself that the boy was just a child, terrified in the face of death. István hugged him tightly, reassuring Denes that it was over, yet at the same time grasping the enormity of what had just occurred and that he himself had narrowly escaped death. They had won the day, but the risks were immense. Looking around, they noticed the other boy, Zoli, motionless on the ground, a few feet away from the tank. Zoli had held back when the bomb was launched at the tank and did not hear István's instructions to drop to the ground. The first round of shots ripped through his torso. He died instantly. Denes ran over to his friend, cradled his head in his arms, yelling at him to wake up. István quickly fell by Zoli's side and checked for a pulse but found none. He gaped in disbelief at the boy who only moments before was alive. He stepped aside from their fallen comrade and vomited in the gutter. Shuddering with anguish, István racked his brain, wondering how the situation could have been avoided, how he could have better protected the boys, feeling responsible for Zoli's death. Then, realising that they were exposed in the street and vulnerable to further attacks, István clutched Denes's shoulder, leant over the boy, and said quietly, "He's gone, Denes. There's nothing we can do for Zoli now. Let's take him home."

István passed his rifle to Denes, knelt, and picked up the lifeless boy. Tears flowed freely down his grimy face, leaving pale streaks as he mourned another unnecessary casualty. Taking the small side streets and alleyways to avoid encountering any trouble, it took over an hour to reach Zoli's house. The dead weight strained István's weary arms, forcing him to stop a few times along the way to rest and regain his strength. He was not looking forward to confronting the boy's mother. What could he possibly say to alleviate her pain? There were no words.

Zoli's mother opened the door to find a strange man holding her son, Denes standing beside him, a few other boys hanging back at the sidewalk. The pair were dishevelled and filthy and looked as though they had finished a shift at a coal mine, except their faces were streaked with tears, leaving pale stripes on their faces. The woman was wearing an apron, her hands covered in flour, obviously interrupted from preparing the evening meal. Wiping her hands on a tea towel, it fell to the ground at the sight of the blood that covered her son. She rushed to her boy, looked intently at his face, and knew he was gone. Zoli's lips were tinged blue, his face grey and splattered with dried blood. István, desperate to put the dead body down before he inadvertently dropped it in front of the woman, pushed past her and laid Zoli on the rug in the living room. Turning to the distraught mother who was wailing with grief, István tried consoling her.

"I'm so sorry for your loss but know that Zoli fought bravely against the Russians. If there's anything I can do to help...."

"Get out. Get out," she screamed at them. "It's your fault my only son is dead. He was just a boy, not a soldier. My little Zoli." She was sobbing over her son, chanting over and over, "my little Zoli."

István and Denes left the woman to her grief, both equally distraught about the death of their friend, Denes blaming himself for missing the target, István angry that he'd failed to protect the boy. As the evening mist crept across the city, creating an eerie chill, the darkened streets became a dangerous hindrance to the resistance. Many streetlamps were blown to pieces, blackening the night even further. The adrenaline that had powered István's team earlier in the day vanished. Grief and fatigue cut bone deep.

The band of rebels agreed to call it a day once they left Zoli's home. The mood was sombre. Zoli's death was difficult to comprehend, yet it channelled everyone's anger towards the Russians. Rather than retreat into their sorrow, they agreed to continue to fight the enemy, to honour the fallen. They arranged to re-group back at the Corvin Cinema at dawn, to continue the onslaught against the tanks. More bombs would be prepared during the night in readiness for the new day, the glass bottles to be filled with gasoline once they arrived at the fuel pump.

Despite the shock and sadness over Zoli's horrific murder, István had never felt more alive. Faced with his own brush with death he was both terrified and intoxicated. Suffering through years of oppression, imprisonment, torture, and passive resistance, smuggling photos of Hungary's declining living and working conditions across the border into Austria in the hope that the West would come to their aid, holding onto a futile optimism for a freer, democratic society and Soviet expulsion, his inability to affect real change to the social order had been nullified this day. Today, he joined the revolution. Today, he fought back, killing the enemy. But the cost was great. They would need to reassess their tactics to minimise the risks and avoid further injury or, God forbid, another death.

István made his way home through the back streets, remaining alert to avoid detection by the enemy, thoughts turning to Natália as he approached his street. How could he tell her of the day's events—that he was a murderer? After mulling over a few different scenarios, he decided she was too fragile and pure of heart to accept the truth.

The sound of the key turning in the lock drew Natália's attention from her dark thoughts. Terror and worry had consumed her since she'd returned to the apartment. Why had István stayed out so long? Was he wounded? Refusing to believe he was dead she waited anxiously, deliberating for hours about venturing out in search of him, but always returning to the reality that she was too scared. Sporadic gun shots still rang out and explosions resonated nearby. She could not do anything but sit, wait, and pray to God to keep István safe. Running to the front door, Natália clung to her husband as he stepped inside, tears flooding her eyes with sheer relief, saying that her prayers were answered and he was home unscathed. Finally, she let him go, wiping the tears with the back of her hands when the rifle István had slung over his shoulder caught her attention.

"Where did you get that?" Natália demanded, pointing at the rifle, horrified at the sight of the weapon in István's possession.

"One of the rebels gave it to me, for protection," he said.

Not exactly a lie. It was protecting him. Searching her face for a reaction he went on to describe the chaos in the streets, how he had helped several wounded people to safety, and arranged transport to the nearby hospital for others with more severe injuries. The couple had never lied to one another. It sickened him that he could not speak the truth, but he also knew it was for the best. Natália could not possibly understand how useless and devastated he felt when he was unable to save anyone. Since being released from prison, this opportunity for vengeance, the chance to drive out the oppressor, was the most meaningful thing that had happened in his life. How could he explain to his wife that killing Russian soldiers gave him a sense of accomplishment? That, up to this point, he'd felt powerless to affect real change, but now he was part of the momentum, joining other patriots in fighting for their freedoms.

"I'm proud of you, István, for your bravery and humanity," she said as she reached up, kissing him tenderly. "I'll heat up some vegetable soup for you. I presume you're starving?" Shame washed over István, but there was no help for it.

"Now that you mention it, I haven't eaten since breakfast. I'm exhausted and famished. I'd kill for some hot soup. Thanks love," he replied, then winced at the dreadful turn of phrase, Zoli's lifeless image flashing into his mind.

István left the kitchen, removed his grimy clothes that were covered in Zoli's blood, took a warm bath, scrubbed his skin raw and washed away the foul smoke from his hair. Shocked from the events of the day, culminating in a young boy's death, a mother's anguish, and his own near-death experience, he was shaken to the core. Lying in the tub, trembling, István allowed his emotions to run free, shedding pent up tears for all that was lost in Hungary that day. But he was also proud to have joined his compatriots in fighting for what they believed in. Splashing water onto his face to expunge his sorrow, he composed himself before confronting his wife, refusing to allow her to witness his grief. Feeling refreshed, he returned to the kitchen and ate heartily with Natália watching on, then collapsed into bed and slept like a baby.

***

Throughout the city, people were retaliating against the Russians, caught up in the killing frenzy, the momentum accelerating despite repeated broadcasts by the government that the Soviets were successfully annihilating the revolutionaries. Just two days after the Bem Square demonstration, another attack on civilians occurred in front of Parliament House, slaughtering seventy-five people in cold blood, and leaving hundreds wounded, many of whom were women and children. News of this spread rapidly, fuelling the people's desperation to strike back. Citizens armed themselves, blocking access to streets with burnt out vehicles, forcing tanks to double back or cross into the smaller streets where the rebels lay in ambush. The Russians were not perceived as ordinary people with families and loved ones, but as the enemy that had to be destroyed. Fighting resumed at dawn each day as soon as the Soviet tanks began their patrols. The government persisted with broadcasts, claiming that the Soviets were crushing the rebel forces—yet pockets of the city were still controlled by the citizens. Rumours that the Hungarian Army refused to take part in the fight emboldened the rebels. Ordinary Hungarians, generally passive and compliant, grasped the opportunity to drive the tyrant out of their country. A sense of freedom was in the air. Everyone on the streets of Budapest could taste it.

***

Despite Natália's ongoing protestations, for the next four days, István rose at dawn and joined his band, traversing the city in search of more tanks to destroy. He refused to sit indoors, claiming that there was still more work to do and that he felt compelled to do his part, still vague about what part he was playing. Natália half-heartedly offered to go with him but he forbade her from leaving the apartment. It was still too dangerous for her to wander the streets, even with his protection. Scared, she willingly conceded, but felt helpless, worried that István was placing himself in unnecessary danger. Spending hours on the phone to Rózsa, Mrs Hajdu and her father, she gathered information to gauge their views on which side had the upper hand. Radio Free Europe was another reliable source of information, and she listened intently each day, the broadcasters strongly encouraging the revolutionaries to persevere and drive the Russians out. Reports were mixed. It was a waiting game. Natália's nerves were frayed by the end of each day, as she sat alone in the apartment, praying that István would return home safely.

István took some comfort in Natália's ignorance of the horrors that he confronted each day. He witnessed several corpses hanging from trees, Russian soldiers or secret police officers lynched by the angry mobs. Some were torched, their bodies still smouldering. The stench that hung in the air across the city was suffocating. A putrid odour, a mixture of burning rubber, charred meat, blood, mortar, and faeces, it caught in their throats, making them heave. The men wrapped towels around their heads, covering their noses and mouths so that only their eyes were visible. This was as much to maintain anonymity as it was to suppress the vile odours. Once the last of their bombs was successfully deployed each day, usually by late afternoon, they joined other rebel groups around the city, tearing down Communist flags from major buildings, destroying statues of prominent Soviet leaders, and fortifying Hungarian strongholds. Wandering the streets of this once glorious metropolis, István lamented the devastation inflicted upon the city—yet somehow it felt like a small price to pay for freedom. Several burned out tanks littered the streets, the death toll rising on both sides with each passing day.

***

At 1.20pm on the 28th of October, a ceasefire was called. People were dubious, not trusting the vacillating government. But everyone was weary, desperate to bury their dead and, for the most part, the people complied. Random skirmishes continued in small enclaves around the city, with a few shots fired, but nothing like the intensity of the past five days. Then, at dawn on the 29th of October, the Russians announced that they would withdraw their troops from Budapest. As quickly as the tanks appeared, those still mobile were suddenly retreating. The newly formed, second iteration of the Nagy government made a public broadcast whilst István and his team were outside the Parliament building, watching the last remaining tanks double back the way they had entered the city. They couldn't believe their eyes. Imre Nagy called for peace, appeasing the revolutionaries by announcing an immediate and general ceasefire, declaring amnesty for anyone who participated in the uprising, the dissolution of the secret police and, most remarkable of all, the immediate withdrawal of Soviet troops from Budapest and negotiations to withdraw all Soviet forces from Hungary. István and his friends just stared at one another, shocked and speechless. Had they, the common workers, street kids and students, really defeated the Soviets? Were they dreaming? Imre was rallying his Hungarian patriots to safeguard order, restore calm, mobilise the factories to restart production and get the public transport operational. The atmosphere in the streets was intense. People were frozen on the spot, digesting the final words of the Prime Minister's speech:

"Stand beside the National Government in the hour of this fateful decision. Long live free, democratic, and independent Hungary."

Thousands of people in the streets cheered, chanting, 'Victory!' Strangers were hugging one another, crying with sheer relief that the fighting was over and that life would return to the way it was before Soviet rule. István embraced his new-found friends. No further words were necessary. They just smiled, saluted him, and scampered off. István ran home, fatigue supplanted by triumph at this sudden turn of events. He couldn't wait to share the news with Natália. Freedom was truly around the corner. A fresh beginning heralded by the revitalised Nagy Government.

CHAPTER 12

"Quickly Natália, pack a small bag, essentials only to tide us over for a few days," István ordered as he slammed the front door shut and drew the curtains, darkening their apartment.

"What are you doing?" Natália replied in a confused tone. "Why are we packing, where are we going? Speak to me István. You're scaring me."

"Shush, keep your voice down."

"I'm not going anywhere until you tell me what's going on," she snapped.

***

István had only recently returned to work a few days before. Heeding the newly formed government's plea to restore order and get the factories producing again, he resumed his position at the steel works. It was important to get the economy back on track. István was determined to do his part in the rebuilding of their country. Tensions were still high among the populace. With the ever-increasing shift in political power, people were sceptical that Imre Nagy could negotiate a full withdrawal of Soviet troops. Surely the Russians would not give in so easily? Caution was the order of the day. Survival instincts kicked in. People kept their heads down, trying to remain under the radar, resuming their duties and toeing the party line.

Unease seized István on his first day back at work. His boss was nowhere to be found. Some said he took early retirement. István wasn't so sure. Unaware of who he was meant to report to, he brushed aside his concerns and took it upon himself to resume his supervisory position on the factory floor. No one else seemed to be in charge, and his assumed authority went unquestioned. In fact, the place was in disarray. Only about half the workers had returned to their stations. Some were idly leaning on machinery, chatting amongst themselves. Others cheered when they saw him, slapping him on the back in a welcoming gesture, relieved that normality would be restored. István set about organising the men who had returned to work into teams, formulating the roster, and posting it on the noticeboard in the canteen. It was a difficult task with a reduced workforce. Production workflows could only be satisfactorily achieved with two shifts. The men cooperated with István's instructions, pleased with his leadership. Before the end of his first day back, István's department was a hive of activity. It was a solid structure that would not only demonstrate his commitment to the factory management committee but provide stability for the workforce under his control. István returned home from an exhausting first day with a real sense of accomplishment.

Over the next few days, more men drifted back to work. Several new managers appeared in the main office. István introduced himself and was met with a cool, unfriendly response. High quotas were quickly reintroduced despite the reduced shifts. István bristled with anger. He could only push his men so hard before fatigue and the consequential accidents recurred. He made discreet enquiries with co-workers about the whereabouts of his friend Ferenc Kertesz. No one was sure where he was, only that he hadn't returned to work as expected. Many other men at the factory also failed to report for duty. Rumours spread that they were arrested and sent to jail for conspiring with the revolutionaries. István feared for his friend.

On his way home from work at the end of his fourth day he made a detour to Ferenc's home, hoping for better news. Kati tentatively opened the door when he knocked and announced himself. This once beautiful, competent woman was like a frightened deer, shaking violently. Her eyes were round saucers, red and swollen from days of weeping. She burst into tears at the sight of István, dragging him into her apartment by the arm, demanding to know if he'd heard from Ferenc. Her husband had failed to return home from work four days ago, and she feared the worse. The children crept into the living room when they heard voices, the younger girl howling at the sight of her distressed mother. István gathered them into his arms trying to calm them down. Ushering them back to their bedroom, he tucked them into bed, quietly humming the tune of a popular nursery rhyme to distract them. Kati poured herself a small Pálinka and then sat down on the sofa. Gulping the strong liquor, she coughed, then poured another. She rarely drank hard liquor but had taken to drinking a small glass each evening of late to steady her nerves. She was relieved that István had popped by—it allowed her a few minutes of respite from the façade she maintained in front of her children. The effort to appear calm and happy was incredibly tough when inwardly she was a wreck. Not knowing how much longer she could sustain the pretence of normality before collapsing into a heap, she was utterly miserable, despairing for her absent husband. Eventually, István switched off the bedroom light, closed the door and turned his attention back to Kati.

"They're both asleep now. So, when exactly did you last see Ferenc?"

"It was not long after Nagy announced his leadership, telling everyone that they must return to work to kick start the economy. Ferenc said he would return to work on Monday. I packed his lunch box and kissed him goodbye, but he didn't return that evening. I went to the factory the next day to make enquiries, but no one had seen him. That's when I knew something terrible must have happened."

Kati began crying again. István poured her another drink, which she tossed down her throat. It seemed to have the desired effect. She focussed her eyes intently on István's face and pleaded, "Can you help find him, István?"

István poured himself a drink, swishing the liquid around his mouth before swallowing. He promised to make further enquiries about Ferenc's whereabouts, but was reluctant to go directly to the authorities, fearing that he too was on a watch list. After much debate, Kati agreed to take the children and leave Budapest. She had family several kilometres to the east of the capital, in Túrkeve, where they could hide until the political situation became clearer. Ferenc would know where to find them if he returned to an empty apartment.

Leaving Kati in such a vulnerable situation was difficult. István felt helpless and distraught, unsure how to find his friend without drawing attention to himself. Deep down he knew that Ferenc was most probably detained by the authorities. Why else would he be missing for so long without sending word of his whereabouts to his family? Those who were previously involved in political parties were the first to be arrested. So much for the declaration of amnesty for anyone deemed to be a revolutionary. Ordinary people were still disappearing without a trace, just like Ferenc. There was really nothing István could do. He had Natália to consider. Her safety and their future were his major priority. István just hoped that Kati would heed his advice and leave Budapest soon. It was pitch black outside when he hugged Kati one last time, telling her to remain strong for the sake of the children, and knowing he would probably never see her again.

Stepping out into the cold night air after exiting the apartment block, István lifted his coat collar to shield himself from the icy wind. Many streetlamps were destroyed during the recent conflict, but for now the darkness was a welcome camouflage as István slunk home, melting into the shadows, making a mental note to disassociate himself from Ferenc, Iván, Albert and Tomás until the political situation became clearer. The events of the past few days played on István's mind as he walked home, ticking off the recent changes since Nagy had ordered everyone back to work. Panic gripped him. Did the authorities know he was part of the resistance? Was it only a matter of time before he, too, disappeared? What would happen to Natália if he were arrested? It didn't bear thinking about. The risk of remaining passive was too great. Escaping to the West to make a fresh start in a democratic country was an increasingly desirable prospect.

***

Few citizens shared István's fears about reprisals against the rebels—it was mostly just the rebel forces themselves. Refusing to surrender their weapons, they were wary of trusting the Russians to uphold the ceasefire agreement. Waiting for Russia's next move was harrowing. The general populous in Budapest was still celebrating in the streets, amazed that ordinary working-class people had succeeded against the might of the Russians. Food exports were diverted to the domestic market and, for the first time in years, meat and vegetables were in plentiful supply. Trust in the Nagy Government slowly increased, strikes ended, people returned to work, the public transport system began to be repaired, shops reopened and, for a few days, life returned to a semblance of normality.

Khrushchev hesitated for days; concede defeat or crush Hungary. Conceding defeat would not only show weakness on his part but would allow his enemies in the Kremlin to challenge his leadership. The future of the entire Soviet bloc was in jeopardy, hinging on his decision regarding Hungary, and he did not want to be remembered as the Soviet leader who oversaw the dissolution of the empire. He had no choice but to regain control of the rogue state.

On the 31st of October rumours from border towns indicated that the Russian tanks were amassing and returning to Budapest, with thousands of troops flooding in from Ukraine. It could only mean one thing: invasion. The Soviets were in violation of the ceasefire, protests by the government were ignored, yet Imre Nagy still hoped he could negotiate a peaceful resolution. The Russian Ambassador, Yuri Andropov, continued to deflect questions as to why the Russian military were returning en masse, spewing lies to buy his compatriots more time. When Nagy realised he was duped, it was too late to act, and he had only one card left to play. At 8.00pm on the 1st of November, in utter desperation, Nagy declared Hungary's neutrality. In doing so he appealed to the United Nations and the great Western powers for their assistance in upholding their neutrality, thereby officially severing their servitude to the Soviet Union. Everyone waited anxiously for support, but none came. The Russian tanks continued to roll into the capital.

At 4.00am on Sunday the 4th of November, Russia opened fire on Budapest. The shelling was on a grand scale, destroying buildings and randomly killing ordinary citizens. No longer a police intervention to quell civil unrest, the Russians were waging war with callous ferocity and phenomenal amounts of weaponry. At 5.20am, Imre Nagy gave his last address to the nation, confirming the Soviet attack for the purpose of overthrowing the legal Hungarian democratic government. In his statement, he falsely represented to the people that Hungarian troops were in combat, unaware that his most senior military leaders were arrested a few hours earlier, leaving the army rudderless. Within half an hour of Nagy's final address, the little known János Kádár broadcast to the nation that a new Hungarian Revolutionary Worker-Peasant Government was formed and that it was they who requested the Soviet army to destroy the revolutionary forces and restore order in the country. Believing that Hungarian troops were retaliating against the attack, and outraged by the dissolution of the Nagy Government, the rebels from the initial uprising twelve days earlier were emboldened, rearmed themselves, and went on the offensive.

***

Bombs were blasting at regular intervals. The city was aflame and the sky glowed orange. István was compelled to join the other rebels. He found Natália sitting on the floor in their bedroom, hands tightly clasped over her ears to block out the sounds of destruction, terrified that their building would be struck. Once again, he ordered her to hide in the laundry, as the basement was undoubtedly the safest place. Knowing he was right, Natália didn't argue. When she saw the rifle slung over his shoulder, she instinctively knew he was doing more than ferrying the wounded to hospital. The rage in his eyes was fierce and he stood over her with a steely determination. Grabbing her arm, he lifted her up, and the two of them fled the apartment, Natália to the basement and István to the chaos outside.

István's compulsion was to return to the Corvin Cinema where the fuel pump had fed the production line of Molotov Cocktails during the first uprising. Picking his way through the wreckage, sidestepping the gaping holes in the roads, he was surprised by the lack of activity. There were two dozen men and boys stationed there, including his friend Denes. Although they were holding rifles, no bombs were being assembled. Enquiring as to why they had abandoned that weapon, he was told that it had quickly become apparent after the first couple of attempts that the crude bombs were no match for the newer, heavier, faster, T54 tanks. The men were at a loss to know how to fight back, their rifles useless against the tanks. Wherever the Russians suspected a volley of fire had originated from, they would retaliate with such force as to destroy anything in its path, heedless of any collateral damage. Fear and indecision pervaded the small rabble of defenders.

Trying to think how else they could strike back, István felt uneasy, as the alley was momentarily cast in darkness. István and everyone around him collectively looked up into the sky, horrified by the deafening sound of Russian fighter jets zooming overhead, masking the sun. Panic swept through the men, unsure of what to do. Within moments a jet soared over the cinema, firing a volley of bullets as it approached. István automatically ran across the road and flattened himself against the wall of the building opposite the cinema, arms raised, covering his head, trying to escape the line of fire. The cinema and the alleyway behind it were blasted, rubble flying in all directions. The fuel pump exploded, sending flames and black smoke high into the air. His quick instinct to run across the road had saved his life. Showered by debris from the blast and covered in mortar dust, he was relatively unharmed, and ran back to where the other rebels lay dead and wounded. Seven of the men lay motionless on the ground while four others were running from the scene, screaming as their clothes were engulfed in flames. Those who had minor injuries or were unscathed fled the scene.

István quickly checked each person lying motionless, looking for a pulse in the hope he could save someone. Of the seven men on the ground, only one was alive and needed medical help. A section of the cinema's wall had collapsed, knocking the man to the ground. Frantically removing the bricks, István carefully raised him to a sitting position. A quick assessment revealed his injuries were not life threatening, and that the worst he had suffered was a gash on his right temple that was oozing blood down the side of his sooty face. For once during this whole conflict, István could assist a wounded compatriot. Helping the man to stand, and placing his left arm around István's shoulders, they hobbled away from the scene in the direction of the hospital. It was a risky and slow journey, with jets continuing to fire into buildings, and tanks on every corner. Meandering through the small streets and laneways where the tanks couldn't navigate provided some cover. Once the injured man was safely in the care of the medical team, István rushed over to Üllői Avenue, where another major rebel battleground was raging, and joined in the efforts to impede the Russian advance.

***

Imre Nagy's ministers had all but abandoned him, some rumoured to have fled to Moscow, others arrested or in hiding. With the persistent silence from the U.N. and the Western Allies, Nagy was under no illusions as to the fate of his country. He was offered asylum at the Yugoslav embassy, and fled. On the 7th of November János Kádár was installed as Hungary's new leader. Arriving at Parliament House in an armoured car, escorted by two Soviet tanks, it was clear that he was Khrushchev's new puppet. A few rebel strongholds continued the fight for a few days, but it was senseless: the revolution was lost.

***

Natália continued to bombard her infuriating husband with questions as István ran to their bedroom, retrieved the remaining rolls of unprocessed film depicting the brutal images of war that he had photographed during the uprising, and threw them into the fire. He couldn't risk being in possession of such material.

"I'll explain later, Natália, but for now please just do as I ask. We must leave Budapest immediately. We need to find somewhere safe and then try to make a run for the border."

"Why aren't we safe? What were you really up to, István? Don't lie to me. You were fighting with the rebels, weren't you? I know you were."

Natália was shaking from fear and hurt. István had never lied to her before, or so she believed. What other secrets did he keep from her? The rational part of her brain kicked in when she came to a realisation and remarked, "The revolution failed. The Soviets are back in control as we expected. Perhaps we can now just all get on with our lives."

István grabbed Natália by the arms, trying to shake sense into her, "You think this war is over? Don't be so naive. There will be retributions. And I can't stay to find out what they will be."

Before Natália could raise any further objections, there was a pounding on their front door. The pair froze for an instant before István recognised the voice of his friend János, calling for him to open up. János and Rózsa rushed in and quickly closed the door behind them.

"We've had the secret police at our apartment building. They showed all the residents a list of names of people that were wanted for questioning, asking if we knew where any of them were. They didn't elaborate further although they made it clear that anyone suspected of impeding their investigations would be severely dealt with. István, your name was on the list." János blurted out without drawing breath.

"We came to warn you as soon as the police left our street. What's going on István?" Rózsa chimed in.

"Don't forget that I was imprisoned only two and a half years ago for speaking out against the regime, because of the unsafe conditions at the factory. I'm not surprised if I'm on a wanted list," István replied, wondering just how much he should disclose.

Both Natália and his close friends were aware of his time in a Gulag prison and the reason he was arrested. It was why Natália supported him in his covert activities, photographing life under the brutal Communist regime and smuggling the evidence to the West, hoping for tangible aid from the Western Allies. The authorities had a valid motive for seeking him out for questioning, suspecting him to be one of the insurgents. Yet István was not inclined to fill them in on his recent activities, joining the rebels and retaliating against the Russian brutes. Did the government know of his murderous acts? How could they? His mind was racing. Walking over to the lounge room window, he carefully parted the curtain and peered out to see if the police were about.

"I hope you weren't followed here," he said, panic rising in his voice.

Before János could reply, Natália faced István with her arms crossed firmly across her chest and said defiantly, "You're not telling us the truth István. I know you were involved with the rebels. Why else did you go out each day carrying a rifle, returning home stinking of gun powder and blood?"

István sighed heavily then slumped into the nearest chair, rubbing his forehead, deciding how to explain why he had jeopardised their safety. After a few minutes he calmly replied, "I didn't only take photographs of the death and destruction perpetrated by the Soviets on our city. I wandered the streets for hours on that first day of fighting after the Bem Square demonstration, hoping to help the wounded, trying to save anyone at all. But it was useless. Death was everywhere. Natália, there were dead children in the streets. I was consumed with rage at the pointless carnage."

Running his fingers through his hair, he sighed then continued, "Then, by chance, I found a way to retaliate. I joined others on the streets who wanted to fight back. We successfully disabled several tanks with crudely made bombs and murdered the Russian soldiers as they tried to escape.

That's the real reason why I had the rifle, Natália. I shot the bastards as they tried to save themselves from the flames."

István deliberately left out the circumstances surrounding Zoli's death. The look on everyone's face was enough to suggest he had already said enough. No one spoke. They just stared at him in disbelief. Seeing their reaction, he said defiantly, "I'm not sorry. It felt good. Cutting them down as they had so quickly extinguished the life from innocent women and children felt glorious. I'm proud of what I did. We showed the Russians that we won't accept their tyranny any longer. For a few days we felt victorious when the tanks retreated. Then, when Nagy broadcast to the populace to return to work and rebuild our Soviet-free city we truly believed we had won back our freedom and I wanted to play my part in rebuilding the country. But when I went back to work, I realised how wrong I was. We hadn't won anything. New Communist thugs were running the factory, setting ridiculously high production quotas with a reduced workforce. We were back to where we started years ago, under the brute Rákosi. My good friend Ferenc Kertesz is still missing. Many other factory workers were rumoured to be detained by the authorities, and they were arresting anyone suspected of aiding the rebels."

István approached the window again, cautiously peering out through a gap in the curtain, checking for signs of any police patrolling their complex. He turned to his friends and went on, "Then when the Russians broke the ceasefire agreement and returned with their arsenal, I had to fight back. Don't you see, Natália, I couldn't allow the Russians to win, to take control of our lives again. I can't live under this vicious regime. I want us to be free. If my name is on the 'wanted' list, then I have no option but to leave the country and escape to Austria. I can't risk being arrested again, to be thrown back into prison, or worse. This is the reason, Natália, that we need to leave Budapest immediately. We must escape to safety and freedom, a chance for a better life," he implored.

Natália stared at her husband, wide eyed, trying to digest this confession. It was so surreal. Her husband just admitted to being a murderer—her worst suspicion confirmed. How could this be happening to them? Then her mind snapped back to the present. She turned to János and asked in a harsh tone, "Were you involved too, János?" Did you kill Russian soldiers?"

Rózsa was horrified by the accusation. Everyone was now gawking at János waiting for his response.

"No. I had no thoughts of rebelling. But after hearing István's confession, I feel ashamed that I didn't join our people in fighting back. I was afraid to die. I suppose I'm just a coward." These last few words were spoken in a whisper.

"We can't wait any longer, Natália. We need to get moving before the police find us here. If you love me then you'll come with me," István said, his eyes pleading with her.

Natália slumped onto the sofa. It was too much to take in. To make such a momentous decision that would change their lives forever was unfair. But she too saw innocent civilians massacred in front of her eyes and understood the depth of István's emotions. She had married István for better or for worse, and despite everything he had confessed, he was a good man and she still loved him. Looking up at her friends with tears pricking her eyes she asked, "What about you two? Will you come with us?"

János could not meet her gaze. His eyes were downcast when he replied, "I'm not on the wanted list. Rózsa and I don't need to run."

There was no point debating the issue any further. Natália arrived at her decision, went to the bedroom, and packed a small bag. A few minutes later she walked back into the living room declaring that she was ready. The friends embraced, and as they walked out the door, János said, "Good luck and God speed."

The last image in Natália's mind as they left their apartment was of Rózsa's tear streaked face.

PART THREE

November 1956:
Escape

CHAPTER 13

As they approached the end of their street, István went ahead to check if the coast was clear around the corner, before veering left towards the East Railway Station. Rail was the quickest mode of transport to reach the Austrian border. István wanted to get out of Hungary as soon as possible. It was so dark that it was difficult to see anything at all, let alone any police lurking in ambush. Few people were out after 7.00pm and the streets were virtually deserted. The political uncertainty made everyone wary. It was safer to stay home and remain invisible to the authorities. The nightclubs and bars had shut down during the uprising, with few reopening their doors. Some buildings were so badly damaged that businesses couldn't have resumed trading even if they'd wanted to. Keeping to the smaller streets, the pair steadily made their way to the railway station. István anticipated that guards would be blocking the entrance. He coached Natália, inventing a script to explain to the authorities why they were travelling at night, should they be unlucky enough to be detained and questioned.

"Once again, Natália, where are we going and why?"

"My younger brother Lajos is getting married in Győr on Sunday. We're heading there for a few days to join the family for the celebration," she said hesitantly.

"Excellent! Maintain that coolness. You sounded very believable," István said encouragingly, trying to boost her confidence.

"We're almost there. Keep practicing in your mind and look cheerful as we approach the gates. This is, after all, a happy occasion for us," he said, winking at her.

Just as István expected, two guards were posted at the entrance to the station, rifles slung over their shoulders.

"What's with the bags?" one guard barked as they approached him.

Natália looked up at him with one of her dazzling smiles and delivered her lines clearly, without faltering. The guard just snorted and waved them through. She squeezed István's arm, pleased that her performance was convincing. Making their way to the ticket counter they purchased subway tickets to the other side of town. Győr, and more importantly Austria, was accessible from the southern railway station, Déli. Once at Déli, they would purchase tickets to Győr. István fidgeted on the platform seat as they awaited the train's arrival. He felt sweat trickling down his spine. Trying to stay outwardly calm in order to mask the terror that rose within him took all his strength. He hoped that Natália could not smell his fear. Dread of being detained, tortured, and beaten senseless again sat in his stomach like a lead weight.

Once on board the train, the pair sat quietly, Natália still stricken by the sudden turn of events. István scanned the carriage, looking for any signs of the secret police. There weren't too many people in their carriage. Those that were there kept their heads down, not making eye contact with anyone, remaining anonymous. Annoyingly, there were seven stops to Déli station. After the third stop, István saw two police officers board the train. Natália was emboldened after her previous award-winning performance, and when the officer approached asking to see their papers, she beamed at him and bid him good evening. Reaching into her purse she pulled out their documents and handed them to the unfriendly man. His demeanour didn't soften despite her charm. An older man with greying hair at the temples, he was not so easily distracted by a beautiful girl, as was the case with the junior officers at the railway station. István kept his head down. After a few minutes of scrutinising the documents, the officer handed back their papers and moved onto the next passenger. Only then did István exhale, unaware that he had been holding his breath.

There was a stronger presence of armed police officers at Déli Railway Station. Some were posted at the entrance, some at the ticket booths, and a few were casually walking around the main hall. This was not surprising as Déli was the gateway to the West. István noticed that one officer held a clipboard and was conferring with one of his comrades, making notations. It was important to avoid being detained and potentially interrogated. Dreading that the officers held a list of citizens wanted for questioning, and mindful of running out of luck, he told Natália to purchase their tickets to Győr and to wait for him on the platform while he quickly went to the toilet. Not suspecting anything unusual, Natália did as she was asked, smiling at the policemen as she walked past on her way to the ticket booth. István hid in one of the toilets for a good five minutes before casually wandering back to the main hall, looking around for signs of the police. The tension in his neck evaporated when he saw the coast was clear. Quickening his step, he headed towards the platform. He spied Natália at the far end, waving as she spotted him approaching. Thankfully, the train pulled into the station only a few minutes later. They boarded an empty carriage. Natália continued to sit in silence, angry and upset that her husband's actions had risked their lives.

The whistle sounded, announcing the train's departure. It chugged along slowly at first as it pulled away from the station, before gradually picking up speed. Natália rummaged through her bag and pulled out a large package, unwrapped it, and handed her husband a salami, pickle, and cheese roll which she had purchased at one of the station's cafeteria. Knowing it was around two hours to Győr, she'd had the foresight to buy some food for the journey. After being on tenterhooks for most of the day and evening, István found he was ravenous, and thanked Natália several times for her thoughtfulness. They both ate their rolls quietly; the only sound was the rattling of the train along the tracks.

If the truth be told, beyond her anger, Natália was relieved to be heading away from Budapest and from the dangerous situation her husband had created. She was still coming to terms with what he had confessed only a few short hours before. But he was her husband, and she would stand by him no matter what the circumstances. The fact that he had murdered soldiers still shocked her to the core, shattering her belief of the man she thought she knew completely. What else had he kept from her? Could she trust him ever again? Pushing those awful thoughts from her mind Natália reflected on her family in Szarvas. Their hasty departure meant that she was unable to contact them to say goodbye. It was not wise to let them know of their plans for fear of placing them at risk. Ignorance was the safest way. Best they remain unaware of her whereabouts. It saddened her to think she would never see her siblings again or enjoy the company and council of her cherished father. Musing to herself, Natália glanced across at István and noticed how distracted he was, acting like a caged animal seeking escape. For now, though, they were safe. They finished their meagre dinner in silence, grappling with their own fears. After a little while, weary from the whirlwind of the previous few hours, Natália slumped next to the window and dozed off.

The train slowed as it approached the first stop since leaving the city. Bicske was a small, picturesque town, noted for the historic Batthyány Castle, which dated back to the 1700s. Natália revived herself, rubbed her eyes, and asked where they were. No one alighted from the train. Four men got on and sat adjacent to where the couple sat. They appeared to be farmers, non-threatening. István peered out the window, scanning the platform and noticed two police officers boarding the train. One of them was clutching a similar clipboard to the officer at Déli station. István's heart pounded, his hands instantly slick with sweat. Furiously hatching a plan, he instructed Natália to only show the policemen her papers if requested. It was safer for him to hide in the toilet. He quickly jumped off the train, ran down to the carriage that housed the toilets, and snuck into one of the cubicles, just seconds before the train edged its way forward. With so few people on board, he hoped no one would notice the locked toilet door. With his senses heightened, he strained to hear anyone approaching his hideout. His heart thumped so loudly that he prayed it was not audible outside the cubicle. Footsteps sounded. Someone was approaching. They stopped for a minute, then a voice bellowed confirmation that the carriage was empty. The footsteps quickly retreated. István stayed as quiet as a mouse, sweat pouring down his face. He remained in the cubicle until the train stopped at the next station, the much larger town of Tatabánya. Cautiously he opened the toilet door and peered out to find the carriage empty. Luck was again on his side as he skipped through the carriages to join Natália. He reached her just in time to grab their bags from the hold above their seat, whispered to her to follow him, and together they stepped off the train before its whistle blew signalling its departure.

Natália was protesting, her nerves tight after having to explain to the policeman why she was travelling alone at such a late hour. Fortunately, the officer seemed tired and not too keen to pursue the matter, much to her relief. The couple quickly exited the station and headed into town, both desperate for the safety of a hotel room and some much-needed sleep, the trip to Győr abandoned for the time being. When they eventually checked into the nearest hotel István announced, "We need to rethink our plan of escape, Natália. There are too many policemen patrolling the train stations. It will only get worse the closer we get to the border. We can't risk being caught."

It was then that Natália fully grasped the gravity of their undertaking and the danger they faced in fleeing the country—fleeing for their lives.

***

The piercing sound of the alarm startled István from a deep slumber. Tossing for hours, sleep had eluded him until well after midnight when he finally dozed off. Unlike Natália, István had a fitful sleep, his restless mind churning through the events of the last few days, wondering what lay in store for them as they edged closer to the border. He hadn't expected such a heavy police presence so soon after the fighting had stopped. The new prime minister had obviously ordered the rebels be rounded up and dealt with quickly to quash any further resistance to the new order. Leaving Budapest in such a rush and believing the rail network was their best escape route, had left István in a quandary; how best to proceed, away from prying eyes.

It was deathly quiet. Blackness engulfed the room. Not a crack of light appeared from the window or under their door. Surely it was not already time to leave. Rubbing his eyes, which felt like sandpaper, he switched on the bedside lamp and squinted at the clock. It took a moment for his eyes to adjust and to register the time: 4.00am. Growling inwardly that he had only managed to snatch a little over three hours sleep, he yawned widely, still exhausted. Natália rolled over, totally oblivious.

"Come on, Natália, we need to get going."

István threw back the covers, rolled out of bed, hastily dressed, and walked down the corridor to the shared bathroom. Natália remained motionless. The events of the previous day were harrowing. Exhausted and emotionally spent, she had fallen asleep within minutes of snuggling under the blankets. Once settled into their room at the inn, using Natália's maiden name to register and paying cash for one night's accommodation, the argument began. István insisted that continuing their journey to the Austrian border by public transport was only increasing their risk of detection. More guards and police would be stationed along the route they had originally decided to take. It was safer to travel the rest of the way on foot through smaller towns and by back roads, in order to evade the police. Natália begged him to reconsider. The weather had become a new enemy. Snow flurries over the last couple of nights brought freezing temperatures and the ground was slippery underfoot. She would rather take her chances by rail than risk freezing to death. István disagreed. Knowing his name was on the wanted list, it was only a matter of time before they were caught. If they had any chance for freedom, they needed to stay well away from the main thoroughfares. It was settled. István refused to discuss the matter any further.

Returning to their room, István found Natália still asleep, cocooned amongst the blankets. For a few moments he watched her from the foot of the bed, her breathing slow and steady. Shame draped over him, a heavy, suffocating cloak, as he recalled their argument. But he knew his decision was right if they had any chance of escape. Moving across to Natália's side, he sat on the edge of the bed next to her, swept the long strands of silky hair away from her face and lightly brushed her cheek with his lips. He marvelled not only at her beauty as she lay serenely in their rented bed but at her courage for following him on this perilous journey. Her loyalty and love for him came before threats to her own safety. He didn't deserve such a wonderful woman by his side and vowed to somehow make it up to her if they successfully escaped to the West.

"Wake up, Natália. We need to leave before the sun rises." He shook her gently by the shoulder.

Reluctantly she opened one eye and asked, "What time is it?"

"Time for us to go, love. Come on."

Natália begrudgingly left the warmth of the bed, threw her coat about her shoulders, slipped out the door and padded down the corridor towards the bathroom.

István had settled the debt when they checked in and told the innkeeper, Mária, that they would be leaving well before breakfast was served in the dining room. Knowing this, Mária provided them with provisions for a day's journey. Bread, cheese, and a few thick slices of homemade salami had been wrapped in a tea towel and handed to István the previous night. István and Natália were not the only people who had checked into the inn seeking refuge for one night over recent days. Mária suspected they were on the run. The look in their eyes was becoming familiar—fear mixed with fatigue. A handsome young couple, Mária decided to help them on their journey, as she had so many others. She asked no questions. Many people held secrets that were best kept to themselves.

Tiptoeing down the stairs with their meagre belongings, István and Natália headed for the front door, trying not to disturb any of the other occupants at such an hour. Not even the birds were awake. As they stepped outside, the cold air stung their faces. Natália shivered and wrapped her scarf around her head, tucking the ends inside her coat. It was still dark. The snow had stopped falling, but a thick layer crunched underfoot as they commenced the day's march. The air was still, and silence was their only companion. István quickly veered off the main road, skirting the central precinct, heading northwest towards Győr. Some of the homes they passed illuminated their way, the occasional porch light splitting the blackness. It was a comfort to have a little light to help guide their way. Avoiding attention, they walked briskly until they were well beyond the outskirts of Tatabánya. Natália's thoughts occupied by worry about what their future held beyond Hungary and sadness at the prospect of never seeing her family again. István's thoughts were of capture, torture, and execution. If they were caught, what would happen to Natália? Would the police throw her in jail too? He said a quiet prayer to God to see them to safety. On they trudged.

Luck seemed to be on their side. The clouds dispersed, revealing a few patches of blue sky. Sunrise was a magical sight to behold. The golden orb pierced the ice crystals on the ground and atop the trees as it awakened the new day, creating mini rainbows everywhere. A few birds started chirping, disrupting the stillness. A peaceful calm surrounded the countryside, a far cry from the Russian air raids and artillery that had destroyed their beautiful city only a short time ago. Natália's grief for all that was lost bubbled to the surface and her throat constricted, tears threatening to blur her vision. The profound sadness was quickly replaced by anger at István's wilful actions that had placed them in such terrible danger. Despite agreeing to leave her homeland and sticking by her husband, Natália could not truly forgive István. Not yet.

***

Four hours had passed since István and Natália set out on foot. Resigned to their situation, Natália was determined not to complain. Instead, she marvelled at the beauty that surrounded them in the open countryside. Having been a city dweller for the last few years, she rarely took notice of the natural world anymore, until now, as a fugitive. Stopping for a few moments she closed her eyes and faced the sun. Whilst it was still early, the sun emitted a little warmth, which was uplifting. Her tummy growling with hunger, Natália strayed away from the road and walked across a cornfield towards a stand of fir trees. It was a few moments before István realised she was not beside him, so deep was his mental solitude. He crossed the field, following her lead. Broken branches were strewn on the ground. Natália had settled herself on a sturdy log and began unwrapping the parcel that Mária had given them. István obediently sat next to her, grasping her silent suggestion.

"I thought we could rest here for a few minutes. Some food will boost our energy."

"What a good idea. I'm starving," he said, grinning broadly, trying to lighten their mood. István didn't realise how hungry he was until they stopped. He took the breather as an opportunity to check his map.

"Given the pace we've managed to set ourselves, I think we should be able to get close to Nagyigmánd by nightfall. That's if we don't stop too often," he said, glancing sidelong at Natália to gauge her reaction.

"OK. That sounds good," she replied, without further comment.

They munched on their breakfast. Conversation was still limited and the tension between them palpable. Conscious of the distance to be covered before nightfall, István soon decided it was time to move on. Shoving the last piece of bread into his mouth, he stood to survey the area. A small stream cut through the paddock about two hundred metres from where they sat. Taking the flask from their knapsack he made a beeline for the stream. The water was icy cold as he dipped his hand in to fill the flask. Drinking deeply to wash down his breakfast, he refilled the flask and returned to their log, urging Natália to drink. The cold water trickled slowly down her throat. It was clean and sweet, but the freezing water made her gasp and splutter. Freshly energised, Natália packed the remainder of the food away in her bag, stood, and said sharply, "Let's get going then."

After another trip to the stream to top up the flask, István joined Natália, who was already back on the road, walking with renewed strength. By this time many farmers were in the fields tending to their livestock. Chores for these peasants were a constant, working from sunup to sundown. There were fruit trees to prune, cows to be milked, and wood to be chopped for the hungry winter hearth—the list was endless. Occasionally one of the farmers would wave at them or stop for a chat. Only a few words were exchanged. István was suspicious of everyone. There was no knowing where the government spies lurked. It was best to keep to yourself, to remain ordinary, unidentifiable. To break the tedium and maintain a steady pace, István created a game, taking turns in thinking of all the things that awaited them in Austria. No food rations, good jobs, fashionable clothes, delicious chocolate, big houses with lots of rooms, American movies. They laughed at some of the more outlandish ideas, thawing the ice between them. It felt good to laugh. It was a long time since they'd had any fun. For a while, some of the tension in István's shoulders eased, and Natália's anger cooled.

After resting for twenty minutes at midday and devouring the remainder of their food parcel, they set out again with a fresh spring in their step. The sun was higher in the sky, radiating more warmth on their backs as they trudged along. Travelling on dirt roads, the snow quickly turned to slush as the sun's rays melted the crystals, slowing their pace. It was concerning. The last thing either of them wanted was to be stranded in the middle of nowhere at nightfall. Not wanting to alarm Natália, István checked his map again, searching for an alternative place to stop for the night. There wasn't another town close by, and István resigned himself to the fact that they may need to seek shelter in someone's barn. He only hoped the farmers were as friendly and accommodating as the last innkeeper. István suggested this option to Natália, who frowned at the prospect, when their conversation was interrupted by a raucous noise behind them. Turning around to see the source of the commotion, István spied a horse drawn cart in the distance, driven by two men who were singing loudly, the words indistinguishable. István pulled Natália off the road, waited for the cart to reach them, then waved to the men to stop.

"Hey there! We've been travelling all day and could use a lift. Which way are you headed?" he asked.

"Nagyigmánd. We've got to deliver this milk to town before dark," one wiry old man said through a toothless grin. "Why, where are you going?"

"Thankfully, the same place. Will you give us a lift in the back of the cart?"

"Sure, hop on," the old man replied.

Natália grabbed István's arm, pulling him aside and whispered, "I'm not going with them. Can't you see they're drunk?"

"We don't have much choice. We can reach Nagyigmánd tonight if we travel with them. Besides, they seem OK. They're just a bit merry."

"Well, are you coming with us or not?" the driver barked.

"Yes, yes. Thank you," István replied as he dragged Natália to the rear of the cart and hoisted her in amongst the milk cans. Clambering in, he fell beside Natália with a thud and yelled out, "We're in, ready to go."

The whip cracked and the horse lurched forward, straining with the additional weight it was forced to drag along. The men were oblivious and resumed singing, a tune István instantly recognised as an old folk song, about the love of their homeland. Patriotism had swept the countryside as well as the city since the uprising, people lamenting what was lost, yearning for the Hungary they once loved. István joined in on the second verse but couldn't remember the rest.

All my dreams go back

Where my sweet country is

Green woods, flowery meadows

And stands my old, old country home

I know I shall return

My wanderings will end

I'll be there again

In my beautiful country.

No faraway lands lure me

No glimmering cities

I am free of temptations.

Finally, I am home I know

Finally, finally

My wanderings are over

At last, I am here

In my sweet homeland

Tears pricked Natália's eyes as she was reminded that they were leaving, not returning to their homeland as the song suggested. Hunkering down amongst the milk cans, she lifted her coat collar up around her ears, both as extra protection from the wind that whipped up during the afternoon and to block the noise from the singers. The cart rocked from side to side, bouncing the occupants around. There would be bruises before the journey's end. For all that, the couple were relieved to rest their weary feet. Natália took the opportunity to slip her shoes off and massage the soles of her feet, trying to restore the circulation. Neither of them was accustomed to walking long distances. It was harder than expected, especially through the slushy snow. Natália was grateful for the ride, despite her reservations about the driver.

The singing finally stopped. The younger of the two milkmen turned his head and shouted across to István, asking if he'd like a swig of brandy to warm his innards. István gratefully accepted. He reached over and grabbed the bottle. Taking a large gulp, the fiery liquid slid down his throat, settling comfortably in his stomach. The liquor was obviously a home brew, with the high alcohol content taking István a little by surprise. He coughed, shook his head then took another swig before passing the bottle to his wife.

"Are you mad? Don't encourage them," she rebuked.

With the sun hiding behind the grey clouds that gathered during the afternoon, the cold penetrated through to their bones. The once warm sun was now low on the horizon, and darkness threatened to envelop the countryside. István put his arm around Natália and drew her into his body for warmth. Hanging onto the railing with his other hand to steady himself from being thrown about seemed to help a bit. They were making good progress, until the cart rounded a bend and almost ran into a flock of sheep crossing the road. The farmer stood in the middle of the road, yelling at his animals to hurry along. Pulling the reins in quickly to slow the horse, the animal skidded for a few feet before coming to an abrupt stop. István fell on top of Natália. She banged her head on one of the milk cans and yelped in pain.

"Are you alright, love?" He checked her over before she could reply and was relieved that he found no trace of blood.

Rubbing the bump on her head Natália just nodded. Another bruise to add to the collection. Her body ached as though she had completed three rounds in the boxing ring. Oh, how she longed for a hot bath. The pair hunkered down when the whip cracked again, and the horse set off. Natália clung to István more tightly. Closing her eyes, she hoped to catch a few minutes sleep, but it was in vain. The cart bounced along even more erratically than when they'd first hopped on. The horse seemed to be gathering speed. István yelled at the driver to slow down, but his pleas were ignored. The cart tilted forward towards the rear of the horse as the road descended sharply. István grabbed the railing again to steady himself when he heard a crack. The horse continued to fly down the hill, unaware of the disaster unfolding behind it. One of the front wheels of the cart smashed as it rode over a large rock near the side of the road. Unable to stay upright on three wheels the cart lurched forward, toppled over onto its side, spilling its contents. Natália screamed, then blacked out.

Groaning with pain, Natália slowly regained consciousness. At first, she thought she had fallen asleep. The remnants of a bad dream flickered at the corner of her mind. But why was she lying on the ground? Face down in the mud, she cautiously propped herself up. Her right leg throbbed. Her head felt like it had been split with an axe. It took her a few minutes to remember where she was and what had happened. Lifting her skirt, she saw that her stockings were ripped. Blood was oozing from a large gash a few centimetres below her right knee. Dirt and gravel were smeared over both legs, mingled with her blood. Her palms were badly grazed and stung like hell and were also covered in mud. She wiped her hands on the hem of her skirt trying to clean them. As her vision cleared, she looked around and saw the overturned cart in pieces, milk cans strewn all about, the liquid flowing down the road in a creamy stream. One of the milkmen lay motionless a few metres away, but there was no sign of István. Panic gripped Natália like a vice.

"István! István! Where are you?"

Rising from the ground she winced in pain as she attempted to stand, but her right leg buckled, unable to carry her weight. Falling hard onto her bottom she started to cry hysterically. Terrified of what might have happened to István she frantically screamed his name over and over. There was still no answer.

God hadn't completely abandoned them. By sheer luck, one of the milkmen was relatively unscathed. He took off after the horse and eventually caught up to it, grazing contentedly in a lush green paddock. Riding back to the scene of the accident he heard Natália's cries. Dismounting, he tied the horse to a nearby tree and ran over to her.

"Where's István? Where's my husband?" she pleaded with the man when he crouched beside her, asking if she was alright.

"I'm OK, but I can't see my husband. I'm afraid he's hurt," Natália blurted between sobs.

"Stay here. I'll find him," He replied, and took off in search of István.

Knowing his passenger could not have fallen far, the milkman soon spotted István unconscious in a ditch by the side of the road. Propping him up into a sitting position against a large boulder, the man lightly slapped

István's face, trying to wake him. Thankfully, he was still breathing, but was unresponsive. Returning to the remnants of the cart he found the basket that contained provisions for their journey, including the bottle of brandy that, remarkably, was unbroken. He picked it up, grabbed the blanket that served as a seat warmer, and ran back to Natália with the good news.

"Your husband is hurt, but alive," he said with a warm smile, hoping the news would calm her.

"Here, hold these, while I carry you over to him."

He handed her the brandy and blanket, which she obediently clutched to her chest. The milkman gently picked her up, walked the few metres to where István sat and placed her beside him. He unscrewed the bottle of brandy and waved it under István's nose, hoping the alcohol would revive him. Natália kissed her husband on the forehead. Speaking softly, her lips barely touching his temple she murmured, "Darling, it's me, Natália. Can you hear me?"

István's eyes fluttered open, two faces peering at him intently. He tried to move but yelped in pain, clutching his ribs. Dried blood streaked down the left side of his face where he had landed hard on the gravel, giving him a menacing look. The milkman handed him the bottle then said, "Here, drink some of this brandy. It will dull the pain." István obeyed, took two large gulps, sighed, and asked, "What happened? Where are we?"

Natália grabbed the bottle from him and took a big swig, before handing it back. The gold liquid caught the back of her throat, forcing a cough, yet it immediately had a calming effect on her nerves.

"No time for chitchat now. Your wife can fill you in. I need to check on my brother and then find help. Night will be upon us soon. Wrap the blanket around the pair of you and try to warm each other. Keep the brandy. You'll need it as it gets colder. I'll ride to the nearest farm and get help."

Natália watched the man leave, praying help would arrive soon. The shock of what had happened was slowly wearing off. She'd never felt more miserable. The wind had died down, but as dusk approached the temperature dropped and the chill seeped into each of her aching muscles. The pain in her leg was excruciating, as if a knife had slashed it open to the bone. Never one to drink hard liquor, she now found the brandy very soothing as it wound its way around her insides before settling in her stomach like a smouldering fire. She took another swig. Before she had a chance to explain anything István said quietly, in between rasping breaths, "It's my fault. I should have listened to you. It was unsafe to travel in that cart. I'm so sorry my love. Are you badly hurt?"

Natália huddled closer to István, pulled the blanket over their shoulders, kissed his cheek, and said, "Nothing that can't be mended. Try to rest now. Help will be here soon."

The couple sat huddled together quietly for a long time. Natália prayed silently to God and to her favourite saint, Saint Christopher, patron saint of travellers. As night approached Natália grew scared, not knowing what creatures lurked in the area, hoping they weren't prey for any wild animals. István had difficulty breathing without extreme pain but eventually dosed off, the brandy acting as a sedative. Natália fought hard to stay alert, anxious to be rescued before nightfall, but the brandy overpowered her will. Soon, she too fell asleep. Jerking herself upright at the sound of men's voices, she saw that the milkman had returned with another man in a flatbed truck.

"We've called the ambulance," the milkman exclaimed cheerily. "It'll be here as soon as possible but it will take a while as its coming from Tatabánya. This farmer has kindly agreed to shelter us in his home while we wait for the ambulance. Don't worry, it's not far."

The men carried Natália first, then István, and lastly the milkman's brother who was also injured, carefully laying them down in the rear of the truck on a bed of hay. István flinched, the pain agonizingly familiar, knowing he had broken some ribs but unsure of the extent of his injuries. His head felt like it was being pounded by a hammer—probably concussion. Closing his eyes, he braced himself for another bumpy ride, chastising himself for not listening to his sensible wife and passing up the fateful ride. They would not be crossing the border into Austria any time soon.

***

The aroma that emanated from the kitchen made their mouth water. Bacon, onion, carrots—a stew of some kind was in the making. Natália's stomach growled loudly. She was sitting beside István on a large, worn velvet sofa. Her right leg was propped up on a stool. The bleeding had stopped but the pain was unbearable, almost as bad as when she gave birth to Julia. The thought of her dead child awakened sad memories, adding to her misery. The kindly farmer's wife had gently cleaned most of the mud from her torn limbs with a warm flannel as Natália gritted her teeth in agony, though she felt much better once the woman had finished tending to her wounds. Glancing around the room, Natália saw glimpses of the home she grew up in. Handmade crocheted doilies sat atop each piece of the heavy, timber furniture. A gilt-framed picture of the Sacred Heart of Jesus hung on one wall, while another wall held a portrait of the Virgin Mary, despite the Communist doctrine outlawing Christianity. Natália smiled, comforted by the pictures, knowing God had a hand in their having survived the horrid accident. It was a cosy room with a large open fire that crackled soothingly. Slowly, the chill that penetrated every sinew in their bodies melted away.

"Don't worry, dear. There's plenty for everyone," Mrs Varga chuckled when she heard the rumbling of Natália's stomach. A few moments later she returned holding a tea towel underneath a bowl of the steaming potato and bacon soup. "Here. No need to get up. You can eat this right here," she said as she placed the tea towel on Natália's lap and handed her the bowl. After another trip to the kitchen, the woman returned with a second bowl of soup for István, and a plate of crusty bread, which was placed on the armrest of the sofa next to Natália.

"Eat up. The ambulance will be here soon."

"I don't know how to repay you for this kindness," Natália said, blowing on the soup to cool it down a little.

"There's nothing to repay, dear. Now, eat up."

CHAPTER 14

The flurry of activity in the busy hospital kept István awake. The man in the bed beside him snored all night long. It was impossible to catch more than a couple of hours sleep. Attempting to lie still and rest to allow his body to heal was useless. The strapping on his torso was deliberately tight to prohibit movement, and so the mere act of breathing caused unbearable pain—yet he bore it without morphine. The drugs shrouded his mind in a foggy haze, and he couldn't allow that. He needed to remain alert so that he could plan how to safely cross the border into Austria as soon as they were fit enough to be released from hospital. He promised himself and the good Lord that no further harm would befall his beloved Natália. She had suffered enough because of his political ideals. They had to find a better path out of the country.

The battering his body had sustained during the accident was severe. Three ribs on his left side were broken, two on his right side were cracked. If they were the same ribs that were fractured in prison, would they knit properly? He dared not ask the nurse, not wanting to confess to his time in prison for anti-communist activities, which may draw unnecessary attention to himself and Natália. As far as the hospital staff were concerned, the pair suffered a nasty accident on their way to a wedding. A deep gash above István's left eye needed eight stitches, and a mild concussion topped off his list of injuries. The mild painkillers he allowed himself to ingest went some way towards numbing the constant throbbing in his skull, but not enough to send him into a comfortable slumber. Misery and despair added to his restlessness. Dark rings circled his eyes, and his face was pale and gaunt. Not a pretty sight.

Natália visited her husband each morning for an hour, then returned at dinnertime so that they could eat their evening meal together. The hospital was segregated, with one wing for men and another for women. There were six patients in each drab room, and the lack of privacy was exacerbated by the comings and goings of nurses, doctors, and visitors. The duty nurse would fetch a wheelchair for Natália and wheel her across to István's room. She made a conscious effort each day before her visits to look presentable and mask her pain. Brushing her hair and applying lipstick and a little rouge to add colour to her tired features, she tried to look her best under the circumstances, to reassure István that she was recovering well. In truth, the accident had not only caused her physical pain, but psychological anguish. Feeling that their situation was hopeless, she was terrified about what awaited them as they continued their quest to reach freedom. At only twenty-two years of age, Natália had never experienced such anxiety. Fear had become her constant companion.

There was not much to say to each other during Natália's visits. Sometimes they just sat quietly, comforted by each other's presence. Often, István would dose off for a while. He blamed himself for what had happened and struggled to meet Natália's eyes, consumed with shame for the distress and injuries he had caused his beautiful wife. The gash in Natália's leg required extensive scraping and cleaning, and several stiches. The wound was deep and had filled with muddy gravel. The farmer's wife who had tended to them after the accident did her best to clean the gash, but there was still more work needed to remove all the grit and thus avoid infection. Unable to stand or put weight on the injured leg, the doctor said it would be a couple of weeks before she could walk without a cane for support. The torn palms of her hands were also covered in antiseptic cream and heavily bandaged. They would remain that way for at least a week, and the bandages needed to be changed daily. Although she was not in great shape herself, Natália did her best to cheer István with each visit, and to mask her pain. They were a little awkward with each other at first, but as the days passed the tension between them thawed. That was until Natália met Anna.

"I met your ex-girlfriend this afternoon, István," Natália said one evening as she was wheeled to her husband's bedside, intently scrutinising his face for a reaction.

"Anna. Surely you remember her? She's one of the nurses on my ward and was particularly curious about my surname, asking whether it was my married name. When I said that it was and told her your full name, the blood seemed to drain from her face. Anything you'd like to tell me?" Natália settled herself beside István, picked up her fork and stabbed at the potato salad, trying to remain composed.

Disquiet tinged with hurt bubbled up in her throat at István's horrified expression. The shock of Anna's name caught him completely off guard. He just stared at Natália blankly. She allowed a couple of minutes to pass, slowly chewing a second mouthful of salad, allowing him to digest this revelation before continuing her assault.

"Anna and I had a really long chat. She used quite a lot of foul words when describing how you broke it off with her after a long relationship. She said you were practically engaged to be married."

Natália's tone held a cold edge, furious to have discovered yet another one of István's secrets that he had kept from her. The look on István's face was priceless. The game was up, but not knowing exactly what Anna had told her made him nervous.

"We were never engaged to be married," he finally blurted after a lengthy pause. "Anna may have wanted that, but I never promised a future together."

"I see. Well, she clearly saw things differently. She told me quite openly that she gave you her virginity, a place to stay free of charge whenever it suited you, cooked for you often, and many other things besides. She's still very bitter, even after all this time. And she's still single. It seems you turned her off men completely. The poor thing hasn't quite recovered from the experience. You're the reason she left Budapest, to try and make a fresh start here in her hometown of Tatabánya."

"I'm sure she was overdramatising. Young girls can be like that," István said weakly.

Not wanting to pursue the conversation, he tucked into his meal, even though his appetite had deserted him at the mention of Anna's name.

"Well, she certainly seemed surprised when I told her how long we've been together. Playing in both camps, were you?" Natália remarked, with fury in her voice.

"It wasn't like that!" István snapped. "I tried breaking it off with her a few times, but she didn't seem to take the hint. I had no choice but to end the relationship abruptly. What's done is done and I can't change the fact that I didn't love her." István checked his temper, softened his tone a little then went on, "From the moment I laid eyes on you, Natália, that wonderful first date at the movies when you initially seemed annoyed at my presence, but then your emerald eyes twinkled at me by the end of the evening, I thought my heart would melt. I knew then that you were the one for me. I fell in love, a depth of feeling I've never known with any other woman, and I knew that I wanted to spend my entire life with you. I'm truly sorry I hurt Anna, but it was unavoidable."

The outburst caused his head to start throbbing again. Beads of sweat sprung up on his forehead and temples, trickling down his neck. Dabbing the moisture with his napkin he waved to a nearby nurse, asking for more painkillers, hoping the distraction would end the discussion.

"Why didn't you tell me about her? Or about any of your other girl-friends? It's as if I don't really know you at all. You lied to me about fighting with the rebels and lied to me about your past. What else haven't you told me?"

"Nothing, Natália. There's nothing to tell." István sighed, knowing Natália deserved an explanation. Putting his plate aside, he looked beseech-ingly into her hurt eyes then continued, "The reason I couldn't confide in you about fighting the Russians is that I didn't think you would understand. It was war. I killed Russian soldiers, but I just couldn't tell you what I had done, fearing how you would react and what you would think of me. As for my relationship with Anna, I didn't think it was important to tell you about her as I had already begun the separation, disentangling myself from her world before I met you. It took longer than I wanted, as there was never a right time to end it. But when you walked into my life, I knew it had to be done. I have never felt my heart fill with so much joy and love as when I met you."

No further words were spoken for several minutes, as Natália processed his speech, desperately wanting to believe him. Then she looked intently into his face and said sternly, "Trust, István. If we're to stay in this marriage, then we need to trust one another. No more lies. Promise me. No more lies."

"I promise, my love," he repeated quietly.

Natália nodded, more to herself than to István, and resumed eating. Once they finished dinner, Natália gently kissed István's forehead and, in parting, warned, "Don't be surprised if Anna pays you a visit soon."

Natália then motioned to an orderly to wheel her back to her ward, leaving István alone to ponder what might transpire now that Anna knew he was a patient, certain that she would seek him out for a reckoning.

István was anxious. Dread of seeing his ex-girlfriend mounted with each passing day. Sleep and appetite abandoned him, his mind churning over how to placate Anna when she confronted him. Each day, following the revelation that Anna worked at the hospital, Natália would look quizzically at István when she visited, enquiring with a raised eyebrow if he had seen his ex. István refused to be baited and ignored his wife's silent queries. On the fourth day, Anna finally appeared at the end of his bed. She casually picked up his medical chart, read through the reports, placed it back onto the bed rail and looked up at him. She still looked young and immature, but with a wariness in her round eyes that saddened him.

"Hello István. Looks like you've been through the wars. You look terrible," she said curtly, sounding a little pleased that he was hurt.

"It's lovely to see you, Anna. You look great. I wasn't aware you'd left Budapest. Life seems to be treating you well here in Tatabánya."

"Why would you know or care where I am? You dumped me for Natália. You didn't give me another thought once you met her. I gave myself to you completely, loved you with every fibre of my being, and you just threw me aside like a used dishcloth. Lying through your teeth every time I sensed something was wrong. I can't believe I trusted you," she spat the words at him, ignoring his compliments.

"I'm genuinely sorry I hurt you, Anna. It was never my intention. I hope that one day you can forgive me and find someone that really deserves you."

"Cheap words from a liar. You lied to me for what, months, before you broke off our relationship? I always knew there was another woman, but you just kept denying it. The fiction you concocted about the death of your stepmother was quite convincing. You had me fooled. Now I know the truth about everything, and I hope you rot in hell."

Anna's face was red with rage as she stormed out of the room. The other patients could not help but hear the tirade, siting up attentively in their beds. István felt humiliated. He looked at the men smirking at him, raised his hands in supplication and said, "Women!"

The men laughed knowingly.

***

After ten days recovering in Tatabánya hospital, István and Natália were finally discharged. Both were still convalescing from their injuries, but the doctors said there was nothing more that could be done for either of them apart from bed rest and time. István reluctantly acknowledged that they needed an extra couple of weeks to recuperate before they could attempt another border crossing. The journey into Austria was more arduous than they had expected, and it was vital that they rebuild their strength if they wanted to reach the border on the next attempt. They were also keenly aware that the longer they delayed, the tighter the borders would be held, offering little chance of a successful escape. It was a delicate balancing act. After a lengthy debate, it was agreed that the safest option was to return to Budapest and, once they regained their strength, try again for the border.

To say that their journey home to their abandoned apartment in Budapest was uncomfortable was an understatement. They risked travelling on the speedy rail network. It was a calculated gamble. The police presence at the railway stations heading in the direction of the capital city was remarkably thin. Resources were concentrated on the routes out of town towards the west. Settling into their seats in a half empty carriage, relieved to be out of hospital and heading home, each wondering what awaited them in Budapest. The train ride seemed to be deliberately bumpy as punishment for their attempted departure. Every muscle tensed with anticipation of the next painful stab as the carriage rocked back and forth. Yet Natália was secretly thrilled to see familiar towns and landmarks whizzing by as she gazed out the carriage window. Memorising as many aspects of her country as possible; woodlands, monuments, churches, museums, town squares, fountains, terracotta roof tiles, crumbling medieval castles, woman wearing brightly coloured headscarves hurrying to market, children playing in the streets despite the cold air, she was determined to suffuse the spirit of the land into her soul, to never forget this magnificent country.

Afraid of what may lie in wait for them when they returned to their apartment, they decided to by-pass their district and call in to see their trusted friend, János. An update on the political situation in the safety of their friend's home would provide much needed insight to help formulate their plans. Besides, a familiar face was a most welcome prospect after their traumatic ordeal. Climbing the stairs to the apartment was slow, both leaning heavily on the balustrade for support. István was first to reach the landing, pounding his fist on the front door. Before János had a chance to embrace either of them, István placed a hand on his friend's shoulder and said with a smile in his voice, "We're a little worse for wear, János. A fierce hug right now could be the end of me."

"Good God, what on earth happened to you?" his friend replied with a horrified expression as he glanced from István, with his sunken eyes and hollow cheeks, to Natália leaning on her walking stick, then back to István.

"Well, if you'll invite us in, we can explain. I'd kill for a hot cup of coffee."

The aroma of brewing coffee filled the apartment, comforting the weary travellers. Once the first cup was drunk, the chill in their bones evaporated. Natália kicked off her shoes and propped her sore leg up on the adjacent chair, sighing with relief. István began the tale of their pitiful attempt at fleeing Hungary with János listening intently, mouth agape. Coffee was then replaced with Pálinka. The strong and flavoursome liquor relaxed everyone even more, easing the tightness in their battered limbs. Even Natália took a small nip, which caressed her throat and settled comfortably in her belly. She was developing a taste for the alcohol that steadied her nerves and washed away her anxiety. Once their story was told, János was shocked that his friends had survived at all. It was a miracle. Shaking his head and muttering to himself about divine intervention, another round of Pálinka was poured and thrown back in one gulp.

János then took the stage and related the circumstances that had unfolded since his friends' hasty retreat, the constant patrols by the police in the days following the uprising, seeking who they referred to as 'traitorous scum'. A new round of arrests across the city saw many citizens imprisoned indefinitely, or they simply disappeared without evidence of sedition. Women were wailing in the streets, crying for lost sons, husbands, and fathers. A fresh wave of terror spread throughout Budapest. But the door knocking eventually stopped and life returned to a semblance of normality as people returned to work and acted as if nothing had happened. Whilst it was still unsafe to remain in Hungary, with spies lurking around the neighbourhoods hoping to curry favour with the authorities if they denounced someone as a traitor, the immediate danger had passed. János once again attempted to dissuade István from leaving, pointing out the perils, and suggesting they take their chances hiding out with family in Szarvas rather than risk imprisonment or death. But István would not be persuaded, despite the hope he detected in Natália's eyes.

János called Rózsa to pop over for dinner, intimating that there was a surprise awaiting her at his apartment. It was unusual for János to invite her over to his place at such short notice. Curiosity got the better of her and she agreed. After the initial shock of who the dinner guests turned out to be, Rózsa was delighted to see her best friends, albeit in poor shape. The girls hugged one another tightly for several minutes, István standing back to avoid a crushing greeting that his ribs would not bear. Tears flowed down Rózsa's cheeks from joy at seeing her friends again; friends she believed were lost to her forever. Natália too was happy to have returned safely to Budapest, happy to be reunited in the welcoming bosom of János and Rózsa, and thankful that she and István had survived their ordeal. She glanced at her ruby wedding ring, pondering the myth surrounding the jewel, that it was imbued with magical properties that protected the owner, and she felt a little less sceptical. Shaking her head at the ludicrous notion, her attention was brought back to the others as János suggested they stay for dinner.

Wiping the tears away with the back of her hand, Rózsa left the living room with Natália hobbling behind to prepare the meal. There was not much to eat at such short notice. Rózsa, in her element, sprang into action, transforming a few basic ingredients into a hearty dish. Noodles with onions, garlic and spicy sausage chopped into thick slices, topped with parsley and some grated cheese was mouth-wateringly good as István once again recounted the story of their failed escape to Austria, enthralling Rózsa with their hair-raising adventure. János continued to try and dissuade István from escaping to the West. He believed it was too perilous a journey, that the odds were stacked against them, and that they should see the accident as a sign. Too many people had died or vanished since the uprising. Good, honest, salt of the earth people. János didn't want his best friends to become another pitiful statistic. But there was no swaying István. He refused to continue living under communist oppression and didn't want his children to be exposed to such a harsh life and bleak future. Natália recognised the stubborn set of his jaw and decided not to argue with her husband. The group sipped wine and chatted amicably, until István announced that they should leave before it got too late. There were gentle hugs and kisses all round as the front door opened, the rush of cold air filling the foyer, and the two battered friends wrapped up and headed home.

Under the cover of darkness, everyone on the streets looked similar, unremarkable. No one paid them any heed as they walked up the steps of their apartment block and knocked on their next-door neighbour's door. Marika was an elderly widow with a soft spot for István. Not having children of her own, István was like a son to her. He often helped carry her groceries up the three flights of stairs or changed the light globes; small chores that were easy enough for a fit man like István to manage, but which Marika increasingly struggled with as the years went by. In return, Marika regularly called around with a hearty casserole or freshly baked cakes for the couple, particularly after their baby died. It was obvious how their loss had broken Natália's heart. It was all she could think of to help them recover from the trauma. Comfort food to feed the body and soul is what her own mother used to say many times when Marika was a girl. István was grateful for her kindness, since neither he nor Natália had relatives close by.

Although she begged István to reconsider attempting to leave the country she passionately loved, more out of fear that the young couple would not evade the authorities than a desire to keep them close to her, Marika had agreed to keep the keys to their apartment when they left Budapest and return them to the government-controlled estate agent. However, she hadn't yet been able to bring herself to do so. Marika gasped in surprised delight when she opened the door to find her favourite neighbours on the doorstep. Before he could say anything, Marika gave István a big hug, which left him mildly winded, clutching at his still tender left side. Only then did she notice they were injured. Ushering the pair into her living room, fluffing up the cushions and settling them onto her big brown sofa, Marika shuffled to the kitchen to put the kettle on.

"A nice cup of tea and walnut cookies is what's called for," Marika said loudly over her shoulder.

Natália glanced around the living room that was sparsely yet tastefully furnished, in a similar fashion to her own family home in Szarvas. For a moment the thought made her melancholy, as she reflected on her home-town and the family she would never see again. At that moment Natália decided she would risk giving her parents a call to let them know she was safe. To hear her father's voice one more time would be a huge comfort. He always had a knack of making her feel that all would be well.

Within minutes, Marika returned, carrying an antique silver tray with three cups of steaming tea rattling in the saucers, and a large plate of cookies. István loved Marika's baking, particularly anything with walnuts. Despite having eaten dinner at János' place, István instantly reached for a cookie and took a big bite before sighing with pleasure. Natália burst out laughing.

"Piggy," she said, before reaching across the table for her own home-baked delight.

"Now who's the piggy?" István retorted. They chuckled, before Marika's tone turned serious.

"Let's hear it, then. What happened to you? You both look awful." And for the third time that night, István explained their perilous journey and how they came to be sipping hot tea in Marika's home.

***

As an extra precaution, Marika and István discussed the possibility of swap-ping apartments to confuse anyone searching for him. Marika would claim not to know him, stating the apartment was rightfully hers. No accurate records were kept of tenancies, and so the story was feasible. It was settled. The following day, István would help Marika pack the essential items she would need for a couple of weeks' stay in their apartment, until he and Natália were strong enough to attempt another escape to Austria. Given that it was too late to make the switch that night, Marika suggested they stay the night in her spare room to get some much-needed rest after their arduous journey. It was a relief to have someone else take charge of the situation. They unanimously agreed on the plan. Whilst the couple drank their second cup of tea, Marika made up the spare room. After goodnight kisses and profuse thanks to Marika for her help, the couple retired to their new haven, collapsing onto the bed. The sheets held a faint perfume of lavender, a soothing fragrance that gave them a sense of peace. Within minutes they both fell into a deep slumber, the most restful sleep either of them experienced in many weeks.

Rays of sunlight fanned across the wall closest to Natália through a gap in the heavy brocade curtains, bringing the promise of another bright, sunny day. Slowly opening her eyes, Natália was disoriented for a few seconds. Quickly sitting up, she glanced down and saw István beside her, snoring through his open mouth. The fog cleared as she recalled the events of the previous day. Laying her head back down on the pillow, Natália remained motionless for a few more minutes, savouring the peace and quiet, before slipping out from under the blankets and limping down the corridor to the bathroom. On her way back to the bedroom, Natália heard Marika fussing about in the kitchen. She popped her head in and said, "Good morning, Marika. Can I help with anything?"

"No need. Everything's under control. I'm cooking a hearty breakfast, since we'll be working hard today switching apartments. I've decided to leave most of the food here for you. It's safer for me to venture out and buy groceries. You two should keep out of sight as much as possible. Once we've eaten breakfast I'll go out and buy bread, milk, some cheese, eggs, and whatever else is available. We can then take the few things I've already packed over to your apartment."

The whistling kettle finally roused István from his deep sleep. Not ready to open his eyes, he pretended to snooze for a while longer until guilt took a hold, knowing the others were up and about, taking charge of everything. Looking up at the ceiling he said a quiet prayer, asking God to watch over them and show them the way to safety, chuckling to himself at how religious he'd become of late. Natália's devoutness was rubbing off on him. He was not a faithful servant of any religion, yet it somehow felt right to ask for spiritual intercession with their precarious situation. Sitting on the edge of the bed he rubbed the sleep from his eyes, stretched his stiff muscles, and felt he was well and truly on the mend. The gash on his head was healing well, the firm scab flaking off little by little after each wash. And, more importantly, the headaches had stopped. No need for any more painkillers that numbed his mind. He could now focus clearly on their next escape. On the downside, his ribs still pained him when he bent down or turned his torso, but with heavy strapping he would cope. Once Natália was more mobile, without the need of her walking stick, they could leave Budapest. Pulling on his trousers to maintain modesty in front of Marika, István walked across to the window and opened the curtains to invite the sunshine to flood the bedroom. Closing his eyes for a few moments to let the sun's rays touch his skin and heal his bruises, he moaned with pleasure. The sounds emanating from the kitchen became louder. István sighed and finished getting dressed, knowing there was much work to do that day. After a brief toilet stop, he joined the women chatting amicably whilst preparing breakfast.

"Something smells good," István said, greeting the women as he inhaled the wonderful aroma of toast, scrambled eggs, and freshly brewed coffee. His stomach growled loudly, screaming to be fed. They all laughed. It was the happiest Natália had felt in ages. She planted a firm kiss on his lips and replied, "Good morning, husband."

István found himself harden against her sensuous body, covered only by a thin shift, her pert breasts pressing against his chest. Thankfully, that part of his anatomy was uninjured and ready for action. Natália met his gaze, felt his manhood rise, and smiled cheekily with a promise of intimacy as she pulled away from his embrace, casually brushing his raised member with the back of her hand. He quickly sat down at the table, his cheeks reddening with embarrassment. Marika, like a mother hen, was oblivious to this foreplay as she fussed over István, pouring him a cup of coffee, and placing toast, eggs, and homemade tomato chutney in front of him. Natália smiled at the scene of domesticity playing out before her. For a while she was able to dismiss her fears about the unknown future ahead of them.

"We can't thank you enough for all your generosity, and for agreeing to swap apartments. If only there was a way to repay you," Natália said.

"No need for that. Just stay safe and be happy. That's all I pray for, for the two of you."

Natália was still unable to walk far without her walking stick and István's ribs still caused him pain, so it took the three of them four trips to carry the few belongings Marika decided she needed to bunk down in István and Natália's apartment for a couple of weeks. Natália packed some clothing and toiletries from their apartment and shuffled them across to their new, temporary abode. It was mid-afternoon by the time both parties were settled. Not knowing who may have observed their movements or when future raids on their district would occur, the three agreed to keep out of sight as much as possible, and to pretend they were strangers. This upset Marika, as she'd hoped to spend more time with her favourite young people, but she knew it was necessary for everyone's protection.

Once they had parted company with Marika, Natália decided to take a leisurely hot bath, a luxury she had dreamed of for days. The bathroom cabinet housed a small bottle of lavender oil which Natália upturned, allowing four drops to spill into the water, the fragrance rising like fresh cut flowers through the steam. Inhaling the perfume, she sighed with sheer delight. Placing her toe in the water to gauge the temperature, Natália quickly slipped into the tub. She couldn't remember the last time she had luxuriated in fragrant, steaming water, encasing her like a silken blanket, lapping the length of her body, across her breasts, tickling her nipples. The heated pool caressed her sore muscles, soothed her bruises, and released some of the stiffness in her neck and shoulders. Sliding in completely to cover her head she held her breath, then sat up quickly, wiping the water from her eyes. Reaching for the shampoo on the ledge above the bath she squeezed a large amount onto her hand, scrubbed her scalp, then washed her hair thoroughly. It felt wonderful.

As the water cooled, Natália reluctantly stepped out of the tub, picked up the towel and started drying herself, completely unaware that István had entered the room and stood, naked, gazing hungrily at the beautiful creature before him. He came up behind her and cupped her breasts with both hands, pinching her nipples. Natália yelped and immediately felt the erotic sensation between her legs. István's penis was hot, pressed against her lower back, his need evident. Still kneading her breasts with his left hand, he slid his other hand down her right thigh, across her belly, and then gently caressed the slippery mound between her legs while nibbling her neck. Natália arched her back involuntarily, spreading her legs to allow István better purchase, writhing in concert with his thrusts. She begged him not to stop, her orgasm swift. The absence of intimacy over the last few horrendous weeks caused both of then to climax quickly, the need for each other intense. István grabbed a towel from the rail, roughly wiped the water from their bodies, then led his wife by the hand to the bedroom, unable to carry her as he would have preferred.

They lay still together for a while, legs entwined, Natália's head on István's shoulder, refusing to break the peaceful spell. No thought was given to hunger, dinner preparations or anything else, as the sun slowly disappeared, leaving their bedroom in darkness. They revelled in their newfound privacy, which had been absent for so long. István's appetite was centred on his voluptuous wife. Leaning over her upturned face, István kissed Natália fervently, tracing the curve of her firm breasts with his finger, stroking the round flesh of her buttocks, marvelling at her unblemished, translucent skin.

István's growling tummy broke the spell. They laughed, realising it was hours since they had eaten anything. Natália slid off the bed and limped across to the kitchen. Marika had left the biscuit tin filled with walnut cookies; God bless her. Natália placed a handful on a plate, filled a glass with water and returned to find István snoozing. She scoffed a biscuit with gusto. Pretending to be asleep, István barely opened his right eye to see what Natália was munching. The pretence vanished as he sat up, grabbed the plate, and consumed three biscuits in quick succession. They both chuckled. The biscuits eaten, their hunger temporarily abated, and István looked lovingly at his naked wife, remarking in a husky voice, "God, but you're beautiful."

He reached for her hand, beckoning Natália to lie beside him. He rolled over and made love to her once more before they both fell into a deep sleep, their bodies merged as one.

CHAPTER 15

The failed revolution mobilised the authorities into creating a new task-force to apprehend refugees leaving Hungary. Viktor was elevated to the rank of captain and charged with managing the operation in Győr. It was a large regional police department, few his age were trusted with such responsibility, and he took it as a sure sign of his worth in the eyes of his superiors. Gerő was impressed by Viktor's actions following the Ben Square debacle. A promotion was the least he could offer the young, ambitious policeman for ensuring his safe escape from the mob. The rise in rank gave Viktor even more power to control the events in his life.

***

Banging on the front door startled Jenci Molnár out of his drunken stupor. Clutching his beer in one hand he staggered over to the entry foyer and opened the door.

"Enough, already," he barked at the person standing in front of him. Once his eyes adjusted to the sunshine flooding into his apartment, Jenci squinted at the uniformed officer and mumbled an apology for his rudeness.

"Aren't you going to invite me in? Do you truly not recognise your only son?"

"Viktor, is that you?"

Viktor pushed past his father, walked into the living room, glanced around, and was disgusted by the pigsty surrounding him. Dirty clothes dumped haphazardly on the floor, empty beer bottles strewn around the room, ashtrays overflowing with cigarette butts, the stench of urine thick in the air.

"You spent years criticising my mother for being a bad housekeeper and yet here you are, living in squalor. You're pathetic."

"I'm sure you didn't come here to chastise me for my lack of cleanliness. I haven't seen you in years. What do you want?"

"So glad you asked. As it happens, I was recently promoted and need to practice my interrogation skills. I thought you would be an ideal candidate. You were always quick to throw a punch at my mother and me for no reason at all, so now it's your turn to be abused for no reason other than retribution. I promised Mother long ago that I'd avenge her untimely death. She was far too young to die. What kind of man beats his beautiful, loving wife? A coward. And that's what you are—a pathetic coward. But enough of the pleasantries. I don't have much time. Stand up and face me like a man."

Jenci refused to play Viktor's game and remained seated, staring up at the hulk of a man his son had become, as he stood looming over him. Viktor grabbed his father's right ear and yanked him up out of the chair. His father screamed in agony, then smashed his beer bottle into Viktor's shoulder, his aim for Viktor's neck thrown off by his son's stature. Viktor punched his father twice in the stomach. The older man doubled over, wheezing. He then thrust his right knee as hard as he could under his father's chin forcing his head to snap back. Quicker than lightening Viktor swerved behind his father, grabbed him in a headlock with his muscular biceps and said, "How does it feel to be a punching bag, Dad? Humiliating? Demeaning? Painful? Terrifying? Well now you know how Mother felt."

Before his father had a chance to speak, Viktor twisted his father's neck sharply to the right. A clear snap was audible. Releasing his grip, he threw his limp father aside, stepped over him, straightened his jacket, then casually walked out the door.

***

The latest bulletin received from police headquarters in Budapest demanding surveillance be stepped up to monitor activity near the borders endorsed Viktor's covert activities in his district of Győr. Citizens caught venturing close to the border were to be detained, questioned, and imprisoned, if they could not satisfactorily explain their movements or if their identity papers proved they were further than the allowable distance from their hometown. Only enemies of the state would be attempting to cross borders into other countries. Enemies of the state were no longer deemed citizens and could therefore be exterminated like all other vermin. Police were sanctioned to use whatever means available to stop anyone from leaving the country.

Viktor preferred to travel further afield, to smaller towns near the Czechoslovakian and Austrian borders. There, he could remain anonymous, just a traveller seeking shelter at various inns, drinking at bars, and finding pretty girls to bed with no strings attached as he moved from one town to another. The lifestyle suited him perfectly. Power coursed through his veins. He revelled in his freedom and authority. He worked best on his own, taking whatever actions he deemed necessary to fulfil his charter, his trusty revolver hidden under his coat in the holster strapped to his left shoulder. Initially, the team worked in pairs. His buddy was Béla, an amicable enough colleague, but a stickler for the rules. Béla insisted that anyone suspected of being a fugitive be taken to the police station for questioning. Viktor's methods, on the other hand, were swift and decisive, usually ending with a bullet to the back of the head of the pathetic creatures trying to escape. Viktor had no sympathy for traitors. As a captain, Viktor had a high enough level of authority to alter certain rules. Working alone, under cover, and assimilating with the local townspeople offered several advantages when looking to infiltrate the groups protecting the escapees. He initiated a directive that officers were to move through communities alone, gathering intelligence to be channelled through his headquarters in Győr. Teams were then directed to hotspots, lying in ambush to prevent anyone from crossing the border. Viktor chose to travel to towns where suspicion of traitors was high. He relished watching his victims squirm, making lame excuses for travelling beyond the restricted zones. The thrill of capturing, interrogating, and watching the escapees beg for mercy before he ended their pathetic lives sexually aroused him. The power he wielded over their lives was in his hands. It was an aphrodisiac that fuelled his desire to kill again.

***

The sun was slowly slipping below the horizon, casting a soft glow across the sky. Orange and gold streaks shimmered on the Danube River in the border town of Komárom, like the rough brushstrokes of a Van Gogh painting. Breathing in the crisp night air, Viktor rose from the park bench, lifted the collar of his coat to shield his neck from the cold wind that had whipped up moments before, picked up his small duffel bag, and crossed the road towards the local hotel. Patrons gradually filled the bar after a long shift at the nearby ammunitions' storage facility. It was a ritual with the workers, especially on Thursday and Friday evenings—a quick drink or three with their comrades before heading home to their whining wives and screaming children. A thick smoky haze greeted Viktor as he entered the building. Spying a vacant spot at the end of the bar he ordered a plum Pálinka. He tipped the entire shot into his mouth, slammed the glass down and ordered another. The barmaid smiled as she poured him the second glass and said, "You're not from around here. What brings you to Komárom?"

"Business. Shipping mainly. Nothing to concern your pretty head about," he said with a smile in his voice, his eyes twinkling at the young girl. She lowered her eyes and blushed, as he had expected. It was enough to give the barmaid the idea that he was a businessman. Someone with money. He was always smartly dressed in a tailored suit and good quality woollen coat. On this mission, he didn't want to appear out of place, and so he wore a standard, straight-cut grey suit, a little worn, not one of his best, but still good quality.

"I need a room for a couple of nights. Are there any vacancies?"

"We've been quite busy lately but I'm sure I can find a nice room for you. Let me check."

Before turning to leave, Viktor noted that the girl glanced at his hands, checking to see if he was wearing a wedding band. He smiled to himself. This would be an easy conquest. Viktor swallowed the second glass of Pálinka and casually glanced around the room, noting the people huddled together quietly, the men laughing raucously at someone's joke, and the family eating a meal at the far end of the dining room. He was adept at spotting unusual behaviour, a nervous reaction, the slightest hint of anxiety. When he turned back to face the bar, the girl had returned, still a little pink in the cheeks.

"Room seven has recently been cleaned. I'll show you up."

Viktor dutifully followed her. She was wearing a short red skirt with a white blouse embroidered with red and pink flowers around the neckline, a typical costume of the region. Her legs were long and shapely. Her firm derriere seductively swayed from side to side as she walked up the stairs. When they reached the room, she opened the door, turned to Viktor, and said, "My name is Katarina. If you need anything, please just ask for me."

Viktor walked into the room, dropped his bag onto the floor and replied, "Lovely to make your acquaintance, Katarina. My name is Viktor. This room will do just nicely, thank you." As Katarina turned to leave Viktor called her back, "Oh, wait. There is one extra thing you can do for me. Could I trouble you for a hot meal? I've been travelling all day and I'm famished."

"Of course. Tonight's special is pork sausages with gravy and mashed potato."

"Perfect. I'll be down in half an hour after I unpack and settle in."

"Sure, I'll place the order for you. It'll be ready in thirty minutes." Katarina's coquettish gaze rested on Viktor's face a little longer than necessary before she turned and left.

Room seven had a large window facing the street. Viktor could see the ammunitions' storage sheds in the distance, illuminated by the large security lights around the perimeter. It was a good vantage point to scan the neighbourhood. Yes, this room would suit him just fine, he decided. He unpacked his bag, hung the few items of clothing into the musty old wardrobe, then stripped and wiped himself down with a hot flannel. Feeling revived, he dressed in a fresh shirt, but the same suit, and splashed a little cologne on his cheeks. The young girls loved cologne.

When Viktor ventured down to the dining room, Katarina was busy with another patron, chatting good-naturedly and wiping down the highly polished bar. As soon as she spotted Viktor she quickly walked over and showed him to a table.

"I'll bring your meal, Viktor. What would you like to drink?"

"A carafe of the house red will be fine, thanks," he replied.

As she turned towards the kitchen his thoughts quickly reverted to his strategy for the next two days. Intelligence gathered at his office indicated that hotel bookings in Komárom had recently increased, which was unusual. Freedom of travel beyond fifty kilometres from a person's home was still restricted. The town was not a noteworthy tourist destination, not that anyone had the means for fancy holidays, particularly since the uprising. So why were the hotels so busy? Perhaps the attractive Katarina could help him solve the puzzle.

When she returned with his meal and carafe of wine, she paused at his table and said, "Is that all, Viktor?"

"I'd appreciate it if you would join me for a glass of wine, if you have the time. It's a lonely business, travelling on your own," he replied as he started pouring wine into an empty tumbler on the table.

Katarina glanced at the bar, decided the patrons could manage without her for a few minutes and said, "Why not? That would be lovely." She leant over another vacant table, took one of the wine glasses and handed it to Viktor. He filled her glass to the brim, expecting the wine to loosen her tongue.

"So, lovely Katarina, tell me about yourself. Have you lived and worked here long?"

Over the next half an hour, while Viktor ate his sausages and polished off the wine, Katarina revealed her whole life story. Viktor pretended to be interested, murmuring a few times in reply when she paused for breath, while keeping most of his attention on the rest of the room, until there were only a few occupied tables. Finally, she stopped talking and laughed, "I'm boring you, aren't I?"

"Not at all. You have a beautiful lilt to your voice. It's soothing. Could you bring me another carafe of wine?" Viktor looked directly into her eyes and smiled.

Katarina blushed again and headed towards the bar to fill the carafe. She was thrilled that this very handsome and important man was showing so much interest in her, a mere barmaid from a small town. He was obviously a respectable businessman with money. Not many strangers that passed through looked so stylish. She quickly reached for her purse from under the counter, rummaged around for the small bottle of perfume that was always on hand, and squirted a little behind each ear to freshen up.

When Katarina returned it didn't take much encouragement to convince her to share more of his wine, while Viktor probed her about the type of people who travelled through the town, making the conversation light-hearted but at the same time revealing, in ways that were lost on the girl. She was completely enchanted by this dashing man who seemed to like her company, so she was happy to answer his questions, trying to appear knowledgeable in order to impress him. Not wanting to sound too inquisitive on the first night, Viktor changed the subject after a short while. Fabricating a story about himself, a widower whose wife and baby had died during childbirth a few years before, he explained that he was a loner dedicating his life to his work for the shipping company. Katarina's eyes glistened with tears, so convincing was his well-oiled story.

"It's a solitary life, Katarina, travelling and living on your own. It's been a real comfort spending this time with you," he said, gazing longingly into her eyes. She leaned a little closer to him, touched his left hand and whispered, "My shift ends in half an hour. Wait here for me if you like. I can give you more comfort, Viktor."

Katarina then stood, leant over to collect his plate and the empty carafe, deliberately brushing his arm with her breast. He felt her firm nipple and realised she was not wearing a bra. He smiled at her and winked, causing her cheeks to flush brightly as she hurried off to the kitchen. Viktor mastered his control over the erection that started to fill his trousers, amused at the ease with which he seduced this young, clearly not so innocent beauty. She appeared demure but eager at the same time. Young, supple girls like Katarina were his preference. Rough sex with a little blood spilt or some bruising was his usual way. But not tonight. Viktor needed Katarina for the duration of his stay and didn't want to put her off. He was looking forward to having her under his body. Charm and gentleness were called for to win her over and extract the information he needed.

When Katarina returned to his table, she reached for his hand and led Viktor up the stairs to room seven. Within minutes of entering the room Katarina was naked and lying flat on her back on the bed, her legs slightly apart in open invitation. He scrutinised her taught, unblemished skin as he slowly undressed, heightening her desire. Her firm, perfectly round breasts, erect nipples, black pubic hair, and the inside of her thighs gleamingly moist and ready for him aroused Viktor instantly. She gasped when he stripped off his shirt, revealing his beautifully chiselled body. It was a reaction he was accustomed to. And then he was completely naked before her, fully erect.

"Stop teasing me, I can't wait any longer," she purred.

Raising herself up onto her knees like a cat about to pounce on an unsuspecting mouse, she reached for his penis, gently pulling him towards her. Viktor lay on top of her and thrust hard and fast. After only a few lunges he climaxed. Katarina screamed, "Don't stop, don't stop." He then bent down and sucked on her left nipple. Katarina made little guttural sounds from the back of her throat, which amused him. Her fingers dug into his shoulders, her long legs wrapped around his lower back, writhing towards him, loving his strength. His second arousal was swift. Plunging into her again, he moved slowly, controlling his desire. Caressing her breasts, gently stroking her nipples with his thumbs, he allowed her to climax before he released himself fully. He felt her shudder under him, groaning in complete gratification, Viktor triumphant in the power he held over her. They lay together for another hour, exploring each other's body, caressing, and teasing as if this was a new experience for them both. Viktor licked the sweat that trickled between her breasts, then kissed her abdomen and the inside of her right thigh. Before he reached her most intimate place Katarina eagerly spread her legs wide in anticipation of the pleasure that was seconds away. Viktor laughed at her wantonness. As he thrust his tongue inside her, Katarina yelped, grabbed Viktor's hair, holding his head between her legs to ensure he didn't stop too soon, screaming in utter ecstasy as she climaxed again. They lay silently for a few minutes, heart rates returning to a normal rhythm. Katarina was utterly dazzled by this charming, magnificent stranger. She had only slept with two local boys close to her own age, but they were nothing compared to this strong, ardent lover. Katarina reluctantly peeled herself away from Viktor, rose from the bed and got dressed. Glancing back at his beautiful body she said, "I must go. I'll see you tomorrow evening if you're planning to dine here again."

"Why would I dine anywhere else?" Viktor replied, chuckling at the inuendo.

Katarina beamed down at him. She combed her thick, glossy hair with her fingers to tidy herself before blowing Viktor a kiss and slipping out the door. Smiling at the thought of bedding the enthusiastic Katarina again, Viktor contemplated extending his stay. There was no deadline for his activities. Results were all that counted, whether here in Komárom or elsewhere. His lust satiated for now, his mind quickly switched to formulating a plan for the coming days. Conducting reconnaissance of the towns he visited and seeking the best vantage points to cross the border gave him the advantage over his unsuspecting victims. Satisfied with his plan, he dragged the blanket over his cooling body and slept.

***

The following day, after a big breakfast of eggs, bacon, and two slices of toast, washed down with two cups of strong black coffee, Viktor wandered the streets of Komárom, looking for any disused warehouses where he could conduct interrogations. Many small businesses had closed during the revolution, a convenient side effect of the uprising that suited Viktor's purposes very nicely. His thoughts were interrupted by the rumbling of his belly, the catalyst to find somewhere to eat. Earlier in the day he passed a small hotel at the opposite end of town from where he was staying. Making his way back there, he entered the bar and ordered a beer and a toasted cheese and tomato sandwich; a light lunch that wouldn't spoil his dinner with Katarina. Rather than a pretty face at the bar, Viktor found himself greeted by a stocky old man with a full, silver beard. Deep lines carved through his weathered face—a kindly face that had witnessed a tough life. Telling the same tale of his business interests to the old man, Viktor quizzed him about possible vacancies and was told that the hotel was fully booked.

"It must be unusual to be so busy at this time of year!" Viktor feigned surprise.

"Well, these are unusual times, comrade. It is a border town after all," the barman replied quietly in a conspiratorial tone.

"Yes, I know what you mean."

"See that older couple over there, against the wall?" Viktor nodded.

"Well, they arrived late last night with just a few belongings and only needing a room for one night. A small attic room was all that was left, and they took it. They paid for the room and the meal they're now eating and will be leaving shortly. Keeping to themselves, not very friendly, with a hint of fear in their eyes, you just wonder what they're up to. Curious, isn't it?"

"As you said, comrade, strange times indeed," Viktor replied.

"There have been many guests like this in the last few weeks. Some have a child or two, some are loners, others are just like that couple. I sometimes wonder what happens to them. Still, it keeps my business going so I don't ask any questions."

Viktor ordered another beer and retreated to a corner table, near the couple the bartender had referred to, trying to look as inconspicuous as possible whilst diligently observing them and the other patrons. The toasted sandwich he ordered arrived. Appearing to concentrate on scoffing his meal, Viktor focussed on the couple. They were in their late forties or early fifties, dressed in plain, well-made clothes and thick-soled, sturdy shoes. Good travelling attire. Each had a black satchel on the floor beside their chair. There was no conversation between them, both seemed intent on finishing their meal. After they had finished eating, the man abruptly stood, nodded to the woman, and they both headed for the door, before the plates were cleared. Viktor hurriedly polished off his sandwich and downed his beer. He stood a few minutes later, waved at the bartender in a sign of farewell, then proceeded to follow the couple, keeping a reasonable distance in order to avert suspicion. It soon became clear that the couple were headed toward the banks of the river. Small boats were tied to the pier. It mattered not who or why anyone wanted to hire a boat, provided they paid the asking price in coin.

Viktor hurried along, bridging the gap as he neared the river.

"Halt! You two. Police."

The couple froze then turned slowly around as Viktor approached them, flashing his identification.

"I need to check your papers."

"Yes, of course," the man replied. His wife stepped back, shielded by her husband, looking anxious. The papers were handed over. Victor noted that the man made a good effort to keep his composure. Obviously, he had a bit of spunk, but he would in no way be a match for Viktor if it came to a fight.

"So, comrade, what business do you have in Komárom?"

Viktor only half-heartedly listened to the man's feeble story about visiting his wife's sick relative as he scrutinised the documents. These people were clearly beyond their travel boundaries. He smiled to himself, thrilled to have successfully caught what his instincts told him were fugitives.

"You're aware of the curfew?"

"We needed to attend to my wife's sick aunt. She has no other relatives and is incapable of looking after herself. We had no choice but to come and look after her," the man blurted the little rehearsed speech too quickly, nerves taking control.

"You need to come with me for further questioning," Viktor spoke in an authoritative tone that caused the woman to start blabbering about her aunt.

"Quiet!" Viktor snapped. "Move, back down this street into town. I don't want to hear another word from either of you, now get going."

The disused shop was in a block of uninhabited buildings, damaged by fire. Viktor had located the derelict precinct at the edge of town earlier in the day, satisfied that the building was secluded enough not to attract attention. At the rear of the shop was a small storeroom. Some shelves were still intact, housing tins of nails of various sizes, different types of screws and a few other small building materials. The charred remains of other shelving and cupboards lay scattered around the room. He forced the couple to sit on the floor at the back of the room, facing the door. The floor was covered in ash, the walls blackened, the smell of soot still thick in the air. The woman coughed profusely, gagging from the smell. Viktor struggled to breath too. Some type of chemical must have burned on the premises, as the stench was sharply acidic.

"We have money. Please don't hurt us. We are just here to look after my aunt."

This was the typical response Viktor expected.

"Stop talking. I know you only arrived yesterday and spent the night at the hotel where you just ate your last meal. Now, why wouldn't you go directly to your aunt's place? Why waste precious money on a night's accommodation and a meal?"

The woman burst into tears. Clinging to her husband, visibly trembling, she looked up at Viktor and pleaded for mercy. Attempting to maintain composure, the fellow started babbling, but Viktor brushed his words aside and snapped, "It was a rhetorical question. I'm not interested in your pathetic excuses. I know precisely why you are here, seeking to hire a boat to cross over to the other side. The government has no use for traitors like you."

The man then stood, holding his hands up, his body partly shielding his wife, who remained on the floor. He pleaded again for mercy, offering the policeman all his money and anything else of value, his watch, his wife's rings. Viktor swiftly pulled his gun from its holster and shot him in the head, then shot the woman through the heart before either of them had a moment to realise what had happened. Viktor rummaged through the satchels that were lying beside each body, looking for anything of value. The man's wallet did in fact contain a wad of cash, but nothing else interested him. Leaning over the dead woman he examined her hands, roughly pulling off two gold rings, one with a sparkling diamond that would be worth a bit and the other an intricately fashioned thick gold band with two blue gemstones, perhaps sapphires. Taking trophies from his victims had become a habit, particularly jewellery. Whenever he felt generous, he would gift a piece to one of his lovers, if the girl performed to his satisfaction. Not wanting to linger too long in case anyone heard the gun shots, Viktor closed the store-room door and exited the building from the rear, walking casually in the direction of his hotel. He breathed in deeply to suck in the clean, fresh air, clearing his nostrils from the foul stench. The adrenalin was still pumping through his veins, and he was elated that he had successfully ferreted out and cleansed Hungary of two more traitors. Victorious once again over the pathetic creatures that were his enemies, Viktor felt his arousal. Taking control of himself he knew he would soon relieve his sexual need with the beauty waiting for him at the hotel. The thought of Katarina wet with desire for him urged Viktor to hurry back.

It was late afternoon when Viktor arrived at the hotel. Snow was falling steadily, quickly blanketing everything it touched. The thick flakes were in his hair and on the shoulders of his coat. He brushed himself down, opened the door, and walked into the cosy space of the front bar. Katarina was talking to a scruffy looking fellow but glanced up at the door to see who had entered. She beamed at Viktor as he approached her. He walked behind the counter, cupped his hand on her bottom and whispered in her ear, "There's something I need to tell you urgently, in private."

Katarina looked up at him quizzically. Obediently, she turned to walk into the cellar where the kegs of beer were stowed. Viktor guided her to the back of the room while unzipping his trousers, lifted her up, and before she had a chance to say anything ripped her panties off in one swift movement, as he kissed her neck and said huskily, "I've been thinking of you all day, wanting you."

Katarina giggled and instinctively wrapped her legs around his waist to remain steady. And then he entered her. She seemed ready for him; expectant, so slick with moisture that he slid into her effortlessly. He was not gentle this time, so great was his need to quench his sexual desire. Thrusting hard he sensed she was loving it, despite the rough stone wall scratching her skin through her flimsy blouse. He bit her neck and licked the small drop of blood that sprung to the surface of her white skin. It was over quickly, both climaxing in unison.

CHAPTER 16

The secret police continued their search for traitors, albeit more discreetly. They wore plain clothes and frequented bars, restaurants, train stations, and other public places, hoping to assimilate and overhear conversations that would lead to the arrest of anyone involved in the revolution. A softer approach was needed to ferret out the troublemakers now in hiding. The list of names of those suspected of crimes against the government was dwindling, but there was still more to be done to stamp out dissidence.

Many factory workers failed to return to their jobs after the futile uprising. It was vital that factories resumed production of goods, that farmers continued to grow crops, and that shops reopened as quickly as possible to repair the damage inflicted upon the economy by the unlawful rebellion. Although István made a brief appearance at work, taking charge, getting his production team mobilised, and winning the respect of his superiors when the country believed they were victorious after the initial conflict with the Russians, he had subsequently vanished. Initially, his boss thought that he was unwell, but as the days passed with no word to explain his absence, the management became suspicious and notified the authorities. He was now deemed a traitor, to be arrested and interrogated. Whilst István and Natália were on the run, and then subsequently hospitalised, the secret police appeared at their apartment block several times to secure his arrest. Neighbouring residents and known acquaintances were questioned, but they all claimed to have no knowledge of where he and his wife had gone. István had succeeded in eluding the authorities for now, but he knew his luck would soon run out. They needed to make their move quickly or it would be too late.

Apart from their neighbour Marika, János and Rózsa were the only other people who knew where István and Natália were holed up. János varied the route and his means of transport when visiting his friends, travelling on different trams, walking a few blocks, stopping at a café before hopping onto another tram, all to avoid being followed. János limited his visits but wanted to help his friends cement a new plan for their escape. He knew all too well that István was a wanted man and feared for his friends. Having recently returned to work himself, János overheard many co-workers talking about places where friends or loved ones had been arrested. Train stations were obvious hot spots where the police lurked. Grocery stores and delicatessens were also under surveillance, and fugitives who needed to buy supplies were often ambushed.

The trio poured over the map seeking alternative, less risky routes to the border. Natália was not as engaged in the discussions, too frightened to think about what awaited them. A small part of her wanted to return to the safety of her family home, where she would be under her father's protection. István's confession of his murderous acts and the subsequent danger he had imposed on her were difficult to ignore. But István was her husband, for better or worse, and despite all that had happened, she still loved him deeply. There was no other choice but to follow him to a new life.

The train heading west from Budapest, which they had boarded on their first escape attempt, was unanimously deemed high risk and out of the question. Their journey to the Austrian border would need to be on foot through small towns and villages, across fields and woodland. Natália sat quietly, listening to the men debate which places were to be avoided; Budakeszi, Bicske, Tatabánya, Győr, all large towns that were sure to be heavily policed. Natália felt panic rise and squeeze her chest as she grasped the distance that needed to be covered to reach their goal. She was hiding the fact that her leg was not fully recovered for such a long journey. No longer using the walking stick gave the appearance of a fully healed injury, however the pain was still severe and her muscles were weak. She wasn't sure how long she could last on foot each day before her leg crumpled under the strain. It was not something she wanted to worry István with. It would only add to his burden. Bravery and fortitude were called for, for both their sakes.

During the final planning meeting, János and István agreed on what they believed to be the least risky path, having spent several hours considering the pros and cons of the safest routes. The proposed direction that was finally decided upon was like the first, with the aim of reaching the Győr district on their third day of travel. Traversing north, skirting Győr through Komárom, Lébény, Kunszinet, and Varbalog. They could cross Budapest relatively safely using a series of short tram rides, interspersed with walking between stops, as János had proved. This would allow them to begin their journey on foot from the west side of the city, near Hűvösvölgy, heading in the direction of Győr, in the hope that the police presence was minimal in and around the villages.

Rózsa accompanied János on his final visit, wanting to spend as much time as possible with her best friend. The two girls sat in the kitchen preparing a light supper, chatting about inconsequential things, frightened to talk about the future, which was so uncertain. The men drank red wine in the living room, scrutinising the map and finalising the plan. Natália had given up arguing about the mode of transport. She was resigned to her fate, letting István make the decisions. As the afternoon morphed into evening, István popped his head into the kitchen and announced, "I'm starving! How's that platter going?"

He leant over the tray and snatched a dill cucumber, biting it in half before Natália slapped his hand and said, "Just wait. I'll bring it into the living room for all of us to share. Pour us some wine while I slice some bread. I'll be there in a minute."

When they were all seated, chatting congenially, Natália was engulfed in melancholy. Life had returned to normal for their friends. She was envious, wanting her own life to resume as before—before István foolishly involved himself in an unwinnable war against the powerful Soviets. She sighed and took another sip of wine. Who knew what the future held for her? Natália's reflective mood was interrupted when János said it was time they headed home. Rózsa's eyes filled with tears. Another sad farewell. There were hugs and kisses all round before the door closed. Very little was spoken for the rest of the evening. Natália cleaned up the supper plates and went to bed. István poured himself another glass of red and sat back down in front of the map, going over the final details before packing it away.

***

Deep in thought, contemplating the notion of escaping the harsh Communist regime, János was imagining a life of freedom—to live as he chose, not how the authorities mandated. He was a young adult when the Soviets took control of the country and vividly remembered life with his family before communism and before the war. His father was a well-respected schoolteacher, his specialty subjects being mathematics and chemistry. Their family life was unremarkable, yet they led a comfortable middle-class existence in a modest two-bedroom red brick house in the outskirts of Budapest, with a small yard at the rear where he and his younger brother played football. In spite of his father's encouragement, János was not academically inclined and left school at the age of sixteen, much to his father's frustration and anger. They sparred on many occasions over his education. But János couldn't wait to get a proper job, to get a flat of his own, and to taste the independence he craved. Socialising with his friends at the local pub a couple of times a week, watching the latest movies at the cinema, dancing the night away at various nightclubs, and looking smart to attract the fairer sex required more than the small stipend from his father for taking care of odd jobs around the house. One too many arguments with his father, and seeing the distress it caused his mother, was enough to convince János to leave. He had just turned eighteen. Knowing the grief that he caused his mother by leaving without his father's blessing, János called his mother often to let her know he was fine and keeping out of mischief. But the relationship with his father remained sour, and the two became completely estranged. Yet now, ten years on, János realised that many of his desired freedoms had been snatched from him as the communist dogma systematically replaced the once vibrant Hungarian culture. Everyone was forced to toe the party line, for fear of retribution. He was not as brave as his friend, who had found the courage to fight the Russians when the uprising began. But that didn't mean János was happy being subservient to a brutal oppressor.

The scent of smoky paprika, onions, garlic, and capsicum brought János out of his reverie. His stomach growled loudly as he breathed in the heavenly aroma from the magic being created in the kitchen. He often marvelled at how Rózsa could cook the most delicious meals on a shoe-string. Mrs Hajdu, her old landlady, had taught her well. Still pensive about the future, János rose from the sofa, gravitating to the kitchen where he stood beside Rózsa, watching her gently stir the stew. She seemed not to notice his presence, deep in her own thoughts. To avoid startling her he coughed and then remarked, "That smells divine. You're a wonder, my love."

"It's nothing really," Rózsa replied as she continued stirring the pot. "Just a vegetable pasta. I couldn't buy meat today, so we'll have to make do."

János sat down at the kitchen table. The room was quiet save for the comforting sound of the bubbling stew on the stove. His mind was racing. The hours he spent with István, analysing the map, realising that the promise of a better future was only a few days away, he couldn't help but be tempted to leave Hungary too. But how to convince Rózsa? She had never once suggested they join István and Natália. Quite the opposite. She openly criticised István for placing Natália in peril because of his dangerous ideals and was angry that it was his fault that her closest friend, someone akin to family, was lost to her forever. János dreaded what he felt he needed to say but owed it to his girlfriend to be honest. He took a deep breath, exhaled slowly, then said, "You know, I've been thinking. We could leave Hungary too, with István and Natália. We could all start a new life together."

"What!" Rózsa spun around to face János, her eyes wide like saucers. "Are you mad?"

The wooden spoon she held in her right hand was dripping sauce onto the floor. Neither of them noticed.

"Perhaps. But there's really nothing here for us. This life, our life, it's just an existence. The economy is in disarray and the cost of even the barest essentials is ridiculously overpriced—when you're lucky enough to find anything worth buying. You've just said that meat is hard to come by. We're only just managing to keep our heads above water. When was the last time you bought a new dress? Or a bottle of perfume?" János argued.

"You've recently been promoted. The extra money will help with those things. Besides, I don't need lots of dresses."

Rózsa's tone held a hint of panic that János had anticipated. Calmly, he replied, "Don't you remember what life was like before the Russian occupation? We had choices in life. Sure, I didn't always make the right choices, but I only had myself to blame and accepted the consequences. Now, everyone walks along the streets with their heads bent down, not wanting to meet anyone's eyes, not smiling, fearful of everything and everyone. Is that how you want to live for the rest of your life?"

"No, of course not, but I'm scared. There's no guarantee that we or anyone else—including István and Natália—no matter how carefully they plan their escape route, will successfully cross into Austria. And then what? Where would we end up? Captured, executed or in a new country where we don't speak the language. I don't know how you can even contemplate such a notion. István and Natália don't have a choice but to leave. His stupid idea to fight the Russians, blowing up tanks for Heaven's sake, has made him a traitor. And what thought did he give to Natália before he ruined their lives? None! He's dragged her into his mess, running for their lives. I don't have the nerve to attempt such a dangerous thing, nor do we have to."

Rózsa was on the verge of hysteria, tearful eyes wide with fury and terror. Wiping her nose on the sleeve of her jumper, she returned to her pot, hastily adding more water to the sauce that had burnt down to a thick paste. Straightening her back and calming herself, she continued, "Life's not so bad here. Our families are here, we have other friends, we go out and have fun sometimes. We can remain safe and have a good life if we stay out of trouble."

János knew there was no point in discussing the issue further, yet the idea of a better future haunted his thoughts. The days he'd spent with István, formulating an escape route, was intoxicating. What was life really like in the West? Surely it would be at least as good as it was in Hungary before the war?

***

After a week of solitude, much needed rest, and further healing, István became fidgety, wanting to get moving. The weather, whilst cold, was clear and crisp, with no hint of snow on the horizon. It was the perfect time to make a move before any severe weather fronts swept the country. János provided him with the latest intelligence from associates and by eavesdropping in pubs, determining where the latest targeted districts were for police raids. Rózsa too overheard people talking whilst she was serving tables in the café, snatching pieces of information that may be useful. Police activities in ferreting out dissidents had seemingly relaxed as concerns of home raids or missing family members had died down during the last weeks. Life was returning to normal, or so word on the street suggested. This confirmed István's view that their window of opportunity had arrived. Consulting with János and checking for any information that may warrant deferring their departure, it was agreed: the time was right. They each packed a small satchel containing what money they had, a change of clothes, basic toiletries, maps, some bread, cheese, tomatoes, and a flask of water. By taking few possessions, it not only made travel less burdensome, but gave anyone they encountered the impression of a short rather than a long journey, thereby inviting little comment. So many people were still displaced, their homes destroyed from all the bombing, that it was not unusual to see people wandering the streets with whatever possessions they could carry, searching for accommodation or shelter for the night.

The afternoon before their scheduled departure, Rózsa and János dropped over with a chicken and vegetable casserole as a surprise. Rózsa had saved several food coupons and had queued for an hour to buy a chicken for the farewell supper. Meat was still very expensive, but Rózsa wanted to provide her friends a hearty, nourishing meal for the start of their challenging journey. She made her favourite paprika chicken with capsicum and homemade noodles, served with pickled dill cucumbers. When Natália tentatively opened the front door to the sound of someone knocking, she was delighted to see Rózsa standing there holding a casserole dish. She ushered her friends inside and guided Rózsa to the kitchen, whilst János made himself at home in the living room, where he found István sipping wine.

Natália set the table whilst Rózsa reheated the casserole. The mood in the apartment was subdued, anticipation building for the departure. Rózsa wanted to liven things up, and animatedly chatted about a recent incident at the factory, keeping Natália abreast of the latest gossip. Natália was only half-heartedly paying attention, unable to shake the gloom that encased her heart. Earlier in the day, Natália had sorted out the clothes and accessories she would leave behind, gifting them to Rózsa. The articles were laid out on the bed; three dresses, four blouses, two woollen skirts, two scarves, and two pairs of shoes. Walking over to the stove she turned the heat to its lowest setting, took Rózsa's hand, and dragged her along the corridor to the bedroom. Tears welled up in her eyes as she pointed to the articles of clothing and said, "I want you to have these. I can't take them with me. You can think of me whenever you wear them. I know the shoes won't fit, but you might be able to sell them."

Natália slumped on the bed and burst into tears. Rózsa quickly sat beside her and hugged her friend tightly, crying on her shoulder. The finality of the situation was overwhelming. The moment passed. Sighing in resignation they wiped away their tears, and returned to the kitchen hand in hand, not wanting to let go.

"I'll think of you always, Natália, as my dear friend and as the big sister I never had. I'm really going to miss you."

János and István talked quietly in the living room. When Rózsa announced that dinner was served, István opened another one of his favourite wines and poured a generous portion into each glass before making a toast to his friends, thanking them for the years of friendship and wishing them good fortune and a happy life together in the years to come. They chinked their glasses then tucked into the delicious casserole, mopping up the spicy sauce with chunks of crusty bread.

"We'll really miss your fabulous cooking, Rózsa. This is the best paprikás chicken," István announced as he spooned another drumstick onto his plate. When they had eaten their fill, János stood and made a toast to István and Natália, wishing them good luck on their road to freedom then, as an afterthought, said, "Be sure to write to us as soon as you cross the border, so we know you're safe."

Very little else was said. The men polished off the bottle of wine and checked the satchels to ensure everything they needed for the journey was packed. Rózsa and Natália hugged each other tightly, not wanting to let go, tears threatening to spill down their cheeks, a final farewell crushing them.

As night darkened the streets, István declared it was time. The girls hastily cleaned up in the kitchen whilst István gathered their belongings.

He had also sorted through some of his possessions that he needed to leave behind and packed a bag of things that he knew would be willingly accepted by his friend; the last of his wine, a bottle of plum Pálinka, two pairs of woollen trousers and a checked woollen blazer. It broke his heart to part with the clothing, each item having been meticulously hand crafted by his father years before. But he couldn't take everything with him. János would make good use of the clothes.

The couple donned their scarves and coats and headed for the door. Rózsa and Natália hugged again for several minutes. Rózsa's face was streaming with tears as Natália pulled away.

"Travel safely and take care of each other," Rózsa said in between sniffles.

János and István embraced, wishing each other good luck. As he stepped aside, János blurted, "I wish I was coming with you."

Time stopped. István was completely stunned. Utterly speechless he just stood and stared at his friend. This was the first time János had voiced such a thought. Rózsa overheard the comment, her mind whirling with panic and fear.

"Go then. Don't let me stop you," she snapped before running back to the kitchen.

Natália quickly followed her, equally shocked by the pronouncement.

"Hey, I didn't say I was going," János said loudly enough for Rózsa to hear, "I just wish we could try to make a fresh start in the free world too."

He turned back to István and proceeded to relate the row he'd had with Rózsa earlier in the week, after he suggested they make a run for it too. The hours helping István plan the escape route and the discussions about what awaited them in Austria had enticed János into thinking seriously about joining his friends on their quest. But Rózsa was adamant that she was not leaving Hungary. So that was that.

Rózsa would not be consoled. Through her tears, she yelled at János to leave, and that she would not stand in the way of him seeking a better life. Her sobs, followed by her friends' soothing words, lasted quarter of an hour, precious time lost. István was becoming impatient.

"Natália, we need to go."

She hugged Rózsa one last time and whispered in her ear that János wasn't leaving, that he'd just said he wanted to in the heat of the moment, as losing his best friend was difficult for him. Natália turned toward the door, picked up her satchel, then flew down the three flights of stairs and into the night, with István in tow. Only when she stopped running did she regret the rash departure, her leg complaining about the sudden exertion. How on earth was she meant to travel on foot for four days? The tension inside her head had been building throughout the day in anticipation of their journey, and now she felt as though her head was about to split in two. The red wine hadn't helped. István caught up to her, asking if she was alright. A nod was all she could muster. They continued in silence.

***

It had been arranged that Rózsa would wait half an hour before leaving the apartment, to avoid being seen in the vicinity of her friends. János kept apologising for causing her distress whilst at the same time trying to persuade her of the merits in leaving the country. After twenty minutes, she could not listen to any more of his ramblings and left.

István had written a thank you note to his neighbour Marika. It was important Marika knew when they had left for good so that she could return to her own apartment as quickly as possible. Rózsa clutched István's note, knocked on Marika's front door, and handed her the message. Before Marika had the chance to invite Rózsa in for a cup of tea, the girl turned on her heel and left abruptly, still trembling with fear and anger. Bewildered, Marika opened the letter and read the final words from her favourite neighbour.

My dear Marika,

I'm sorry I couldn't say goodbye to you in person, however it is safest for both of us this way. After my parents were expelled from their ancestral home, many years ago now, I lost touch with them. You filled a void in my life, taking on the role of stepmother, and providing much needed love when our little Julia was taken away from us so cruelly. I know Natália came to rely on your wisdom and kindness. We will especially miss your delicious walnut cookies.

János will give you the key to our apartment once he helps settle you back into your own home. Please dispose of all the remaining contents and keep the profits. It won't amount to much, but it's a small parting gift of thanks for all you have done for us. Once we are settled into our new life, I'll write to let you know that we are safe and well. In the meantime, take care of yourself.

With love, István

János stayed behind as promised to help Marika move her things back to her own apartment. The notion of leaving Hungary had grown inside him like a persistent tumour. Yet the thought of leaving without Rózsa was a betrayal of her love. He thought he loved Rózsa. She was such a sweet girl, devoted and caring, but why hadn't he asked her to marry him? János was sure Rózsa would accept his proposal. She'd hinted about marriage several times. Yet he baulked at the permanency of marriage. Settling down and having a family was not something he desired, not now. He preferred his independence. Since helping István hatch an escape plan, he had warmed to the idea of migrating to another country with better opportunities and the freedom he desired. If only Rózsa would reconsider. Like his friends, he couldn't waste too much time thinking about fleeing, as the situation was becoming increasingly perilous. After leaving Marika's apartment he chose to return home the long way, not only to leave a false trail in case he was being watched, but to afford himself solitude, debating about what he should do, hoping to reach a decision before he arrived home.

***

Not two days had passed since Marika had received the note from István when there was a knock on her door. Hovering in her foyer, she hoped for the person to announce themselves before she dared opened the door, but hearing nothing, she pretended not to be home. The knocking was replaced by a relentless banging, the noise reverberating around Marika's small apartment.

"It's the police. Open up. I know you're in there," a gruff voice barked.

Marika slowly opened the front door. As soon as a thin crack of sunlight flashed into the living room, two men pushed their way in. Marika stumbled and fell to the floor.

"Who are you? What do you want?" Marika said as she got up with as much composure as she could muster, straightening her dress and reclaiming her dignity.

"Where is he? Your neighbour, István Szabó? He was spotted here two days ago," one of the smartly attired, severe looking men snapped at her. The other man, dressed in a brown, neatly pressed suit, searched each room for the fugitive. Marika could hear wardrobe doors banging and large items being tossed around.

"He's not here. I haven't seen István for weeks," Marika replied.

"You're lying," he snapped back as he struck Marika across the face with the back of his hand. She fell back onto the floor, her ear ringing, holding her head to stop the room from spinning.

It didn't take long before the second man, clearly subservient, returned, shaking his head, "Sir, he's not here. But I found this razor in the bathroom."

"I knew you were lying, you old crone," the policeman said quietly through clenched teeth.

"Please, I don't know where he is," Marika reiterated, yet with less conviction in her voice.

"You're coming with us to police headquarters. We have ways of getting to the truth."

The younger officer grabbed her right arm, forcibly hauled her up to a standing position, marched her down the steps, then roughly shoved her into the rear of the black sedan parked in front of the building. As they drove away, she said a silent prayer, asking Saint Christopher to watch over the lovely young couple that she had grown to love as her own children. Her apartment door was left ajar, and Marika vanished, never to be seen again, like so many other citizens under the Kádár Government.

CHAPTER 17

Rózsa was practiced at feigning sleep. Whenever she had a row with János, she would go to bed with her back turned away from him, blankets drawn up to her chin, stock-still. She had only recently moved in with him. For several months, she had been staying over two or three times a week when she cooked dinner at his place rather than stepping out into the cold, eerie night to head back home.

János' flatmate, Péter, had moved out. His girlfriend had fallen pregnant and before the bump was too obvious, he decided to marry her and move back to his hometown on the outskirts of Debrecen. Not everyone was told of the pregnancy. Suspicion mounted when Péter announced his plan to marry a girl he'd only been dating for a few months. An abrupt decision like that usually meant only one thing. The wedding was a small, intimate affair with a handful of their closest friends invited to celebrate with drinks at a local bar. Rózsa couldn't help but feel envious of Péter's situation, the notion of motherhood constantly tugging at her heartstrings.

The vacancy in János' apartment sparked their decision to live together permanently, to combine their incomes and save for all the things they yearned for in life—János dreamed of owning a motorbike, and Rózsa was desperate to start a family and create a nursery filled with everything a new baby needed. Her strict parents were stern and sombre, and devoid of outward affection, which was the antithesis of Rózsa's view of parenting. She would suffuse her babies with all the love in her heart, providing every opportunity for them to thrive and be happy.

With the decision made, Rózsa had given two weeks' notice to her landlady, Mrs Hajdu. She was a little sad to leave the boarding house. Mrs Hajdu treated her like a daughter and was happy to impart words of wisdom to her inexperienced lodger whenever Rózsa grappled with the travails of life. She had also taught her to cook delicious meals on a tight budget. But this next, huge step in her life was exciting. To Rózsa, living together with her long-time boyfriend was the same as marriage, and she desperately hoped that János would see it the same way and agree to officially tie the knot. Still unmarried, her parents were kept in the dark about her living arrangements. Rózsa could hear her mother's disapproving voice. Raised in a strict Catholic household, she was indoctrinated in the Church's values, including celibacy before marriage. Good Christian girls did not bed a man out of wedlock. To do so not only shamed the girl but the entire family. It didn't matter to Rózsa; her family was far away and didn't need to know how she lived. Her love for János was boundless and she knew he felt the same way. Or so she had believed until the past few days. How could he contemplate leaving Hungary and, more importantly, leaving her? Life without János was incomprehensible. Rózsa was completely bereft.

Keenly listening for the door to open, signalling János' return, she was filled with terror, pondering the question, would he really abandon her? His recent preoccupation with helping István plan his escape had been the catalyst for the arguments about joining their friends. But tonight, he had stated all too vehemently that he too wanted to go to Austria. Clearly, he had not abandoned the idea, despite her protests. Rózsa felt wretched. The loss of her best friends was difficult enough to bear, but the loss of her beloved János was unfathomable. Constantly weeping for the outcome she thought was inevitable was exhausting. She was emotionally spent from all the pent-up anxiety and dread, and finally drifted off to sleep, despite the discomfort of her sodden pillow.

When János finally returned home from helping Marika the apartment was deathly quiet, so he knew Rózsa had gone to bed, still upset with him. The turmoil whizzing through his mind during the time it took him to weave his way back through the smaller streets from Marika's place was agonising. He deliberately chose the long way home, needing the time to sort through the conflicting emotions. Dreading facing Rózsa's teary, hurt-filled eyes, he had called into a bar and downed three beers, while debating the merits of staying or leaving. Could he really break off his relationship with Rózsa? Could he desert this wonderful woman and leave her here in Budapest on her own? He felt like a cad: selfish, uncaring, heartless, and callous. Yet excitement simmered within him. A chance for a new life in a new country with freedoms that he could only dream about—freedoms now lost forever in Hungary. The time he'd spent with István, pouring over maps, seeking intelligence about police hideouts, mulling over the safest ways to traverse the city, had filled him with hope. He hadn't felt so energised in years. But there was no time for procrastination. If he was to act, he needed to flee tonight, just as his friends had. Crossing the border would become more difficult as the days passed. Although he had tried convincing Rózsa of the fabulous opportunities that awaited them in the free world, she would not be moved. He could not persuade gentle, fragile Rózsa to come away with him.

Sighing, he sagged into one of the dining chairs, eyeing off the Pálinka that István had given him as a parting gift. Pouring a generous amount into a tumbler, János downed the strong alcohol in one gulp, then wiped his mouth with the back of his hand. Courage seeped through his veins and the conviction of his choice to leave Hungary solidified. He poured another large measure, swishing the liquid around in the glass before swallowing it. Justifying a decision is easier when you want something badly enough—particularly after the amount of alcohol he had consumed that night.

Rummaging through the kitchen drawers he found a small writing pad and pen, usually used for the occasional letters Rózsa wrote to her family, reassuring her parents that she was settled and happy. Sitting at the kitchen table for what seemed like hours he tried to compose a letter that was not too brutal, choosing comforting words that would ease Rózsa's anguish when she realised he had chosen freedom over a life with her. He was no poet and quite hopeless at writing anything, never mind something as important as a letter explaining why he was leaving his partner after two wonderful years together. He wanted the note to express his love for Rózsa and at the same time his deep yearning for freedom, for a more fulfilled life. After two false starts and another large swig of Pálinka, he re-read the final draft before folding the letter in half and propping it up against the brandy bottle.

My lovely Rózsa,

I cannot begin to tell you the happiness I felt when you came into my life. I was a wayward soul that was saved when you took me under your wing, a poor soul that found a home beside you. I have been very fortunate in having someone so caring and loving, someone who taught me so much about relationships, practicalities in life, and surviving this harsh world that we face in Hungary. For that, and far more, Rózsa, I'm truly grateful.

The revolution gave many of us hope for a better future, for a life that some of us remember before communism, where people could choose their own path, enjoy a good standard of living, be free to express themselves without terror of punishment and not cower from one another in the streets. I cannot spend the rest of my days living this way. I hope you can understand that someday.

Rózsa, you deserve much more than I can possibly give you. I have agonised over leaving you but know that my decision is right for both of us, even though it will hurt you now, and I'm very sorry for that. I have taken very little of the money we have jointly saved, just enough to get me to the border. The rest I leave for you, along with the apartment. You are safe here. You love your job and your friends at work, and I know in time you'll find someone else, someone more worthy of you. I hope you have a happy and fulfilled life.

You will always have a special place in my heart.
János

Tiptoeing into the bedroom, János rummaged through his wardrobe as quietly as possible, gathering a few items of clothing to take on the journey. The woollen blazer that István had given him as a parting gift was hastily pulled over his jumper—he refused to leave such a good quality item behind. He shoved some other clothes and essential toiletries for a short journey into a small bag and left the apartment as quietly as he had arrived, not wanting to disturb Rózsa and confront her pleading, sorrowful eyes.

***

The bedroom was still in darkness when Rózsa opened her eyes. The heavy velvet curtain was often a welcome barrier against the outside world when she allowed herself a few extra minutes to snooze before the new day beckoned. Rolling over to snuggle up against János, she was alarmed when he was not there. The sheet on his side of the bed was not crumpled, a sign he had not slept beside her all night. He should have arrived home hours ago. Flinging off the covers, she ran from the kitchen to the living room to the bathroom. There was no sign of him. Trying to remember what shift he was working that week she returned to the kitchen to make a cup of tea, when she spied a note propped up against a half empty brandy bottle on the table. János had been home after all. Rózsa froze, staring at the neatly folded paper. Before reaching for it she instinctively knew what it contained. Tears swam in her frightened eyes, her hands shaking. She steadied herself by leaning against the table, breathing deeply to calm her nerves as her throat constricted. Collapsing onto one of the dining chairs she gingerly opened the note and heard János' voice flow from the words on the page. Rózsa blinked hard to clear her vision and traced her fingers across each word as she slowly re-read the letter, fully comprehending now that her worst fear was realised. János was lost to her forever. The depth of her despair was immense. She had not only lost her best friend, someone she called sister, but also the love of her life. Rózsa succumbed to her grief, sobbing until her chest ached and the tears were spent.

***

Train travel across Budapest was not a problem for János. He was not on the wanted list. He carried his identification papers and willingly showed them to the authorities when asked. János had dutifully returned to work when the factory reopened after the revolution and was not suspected of any rebellious activity. Because of this he could travel freely around the city and knew he could easily catch up to his friends who needed to walk part of the way, slowing their progress. It alarmed him to see a heavy police presence

225

at all the stations and around the city. He knew there were even more plain clothed police patrolling the streets and hoped István and Natália would reach the outskirts of the city unmolested. The days spent helping István plot their escape route had now taken on an even greater significance. He knew the exact place for a rendezvous.

CHAPTER 18

Skirting the city was relatively uneventful. István and Natália walked part of the way, hopping on and off the trams to break up the journey and make it more difficult for anyone who may have been inclined to follow them. The police presence had become noticeably reduced during the evenings in recent weeks. Perhaps they had become complacent. Perhaps the weather had got the better of them. The winter chill at night consumed the flesh and pierced the soul, and the heavy woollen coats and black leather gloves, which were standard issue for the police, did little to shield them from the freezing temperatures once the sun's rays were hidden below the horizon. The cold night air deterred travellers and the police alike. Or so Natália hoped.

István and Natália barely spoke to one another once they left their apartment, partly through fear of drawing attention to themselves but also because they were each caught up in their own emotional turmoil. The streets were quiet. Those that chose to venture out at night went about their business with true purpose, heads bent, walking briskly, as though being pursued by a dark force. As the night wore on and the cold became increasingly bitter, István rushed to the tram stop, ensuring they caught the last scheduled tram to their final rail destination, Hűvösvölgy. Natália did her best to keep up with him, always a few paces behind, her muscles still unaccustomed to walking any great distance. A few people were already huddled together at the stop, stamping their feet to maintain the circula-tion in their legs. István and Natália boarded the tram, choosing a bench towards the back, away from the door. Passengers sat apart from each other, their secrets their own. Scarves were drawn tightly around the women's heads, their coat collars turned up around their ears for added warmth, while the men wore hats with the brim pulled down to cover as much of their face as possible.

Natália leant against the window of the tram, gazing out, oblivious to the passengers boarding and alighting. She silently absorbed every-thing she saw as they trundled along, knowing she would never again see the old buildings and familiar streets of the wonderful city of Budapest. It had only been three years since Natália uprooted her life from Szarvas and relocated to the capital, seeking fun and excitement. The city had more than lived up to her expectations, with its vibrant café scene, grand boulevards, job opportunities, and new friendships—not to mention her cherished husband. Part of her yearned to stay. The relationship with her mother had always been strained but she loved her nonetheless and would miss her. But it was her father that she mourned for the most. To never see him again or seek his guidance and wisdom was heart breaking. They had often spoken about travelling the world, kindred adventurous spirits. Yet her current adventure was not what she had dreamed of. Natália felt downhearted, sadness her persistent companion. Choking back a sob that was wedged in her throat, she felt completely alone, despite her husband sitting beside her. She glanced across at him, his head absorbed in the map, tracing the route with his finger. Folding the map and returning it to the haven of his coat pocket he looked over at Natália and smiled. The apparent calm he exuded reassured her that all was well thus far. She smiled back before peering out of the window again, saying a silent farewell to the city she had grown to love.

Much to István's relief, the tram reached the end of the line at Hűvösvölgy quicker than expected. Only a handful of people had boarded the tram along the route, and even fewer continued to the end of the line. He glanced up whenever someone boarded, fearing it may be a policeman, but no one took any notice of them. Everyone kept to themselves, vacant expressions on their faces, dark clothing blending into the carriage like a magic curtain of invisibility. István breathed a sigh of relief at each stop. No officials to contend with. With few possessions to weigh them down, István and Natália quickly disembarked at the rear exit. The station was brightly lit. They hurriedly moved away from the lights, avoiding the main street, blending into the landscape.

Every town and village in the country had a least one church that was always open, particularly since the failed revolution. The numbers of homeless had grown. Churches offered shelter from the harsh winters. Many of the larger ones ran soup kitchens, providing a hot meal to anyone who turned up on their doorstep at midday. Vegetable soup with a couple of slices of crusty bread was a mainstay, but occasionally a hearty stew with rice and a few shreds of slow-cooked meat was offered, depending on the generosity of the local farmers. The Catholic Church of Our Lady at Nagykovácsi was the shelter that István decided would protect them on their first night, allowing them a few hours' sleep before they embarked on the next leg of their journey. The church was an eight-kilometre hike from the tram stop by the most direct route but steering clear of the main road to remain hidden from prying eyes meant the trek would take at least two to three hours.

There was very little light to guide them once they came to the open fields. The sky was clear and the soft orb of the moon cast a gentle glow, illuminating their path enough to guide them. Natália felt anxious, and conscious of her weakened leg, so she clung tightly to István's arm for support. Occasionally, a glimmer of light emanated from a farmhouse window. István would creep as close as possible to the building, remaining very quiet to avoid disturbing the occupants, then check his compass in the light that spilled out through the window before signalling the way forward. Occasionally a dog barked, heralding their presence. Instinctively, they would crouch down, keeping below the windowsills, and scurry away to put as much distance as possible between themselves and the dog, before the occupants poked their heads outside wondering what was amiss. It was a steadfast but cautious trek. At the halfway point, Natália asked for a few minutes respite to catch her breath. Her injured leg was tiring. Not wanting to worry István about the throbbing pain that had flared up, she asked for the flask, slowly drinking some of the water, before handing it back. István took a quick gulp, then returned the flask to his satchel, and they continued at the same determined pace. Dew had settled on the ground, adding to the chill that encased them. Moisture from the long grasses whipped around their legs, soaking through their shoes and clothing as they trudged along. Despite the discomfort, Natália refused to complain, not wanting to appear weak or defeated at such an early stage in their journey.

The Church of Our Lady's spire was visible from a distance. Sparse street lighting illuminated the town with a golden glimmer that ruptured the blackness of the night. Natália was instantly buoyed when they saw the town at the base of the valley, knowing safety and comfort was within reach. They hastened their pace, hearts pumping with renewed strength. As the town drew nearer István stopped to survey the landscape. There were no visible sentries. The farm animals were silent. Peace surrounded them. He could not sense any danger in the deserted streets but chose to guide Natália swiftly to the church in any event. Using the spire to guide their way, they quickly came upon the front steps of the church. The wrought iron gate stood ajar. Natália released the grip on her husband's arm and skipped up the stairs like a young girl. Relief filled her when the solid timber door gave way as she pushed it open a fraction and squeezed her way in. The interior was dim. A few candles dotted around the stone walls burned low in their sconces. It took a moment for her eyes to adjust. The pungent smell of incense hung in the air, the type that was used during Benediction. Some churches continued to conduct services despite being persecuted as was the case in Natália's hometown of Szarvas. Natália's gaze was soon transfixed by the elaborately carved golden pillars that surrounded the altar. It was a stunning sight, the pillars shining as brightly as the midday sun, the light ricocheting off their surfaces from the surrounding candles. The Stations of the Cross were intricately carved in a dark timber, depicting Christ's journey to his death. After a few minutes, absorbing the comforting interior of their temporary sanctuary, she knelt at one of the pews at the rear of the church and said a pray of thanks for their safe delivery to Nagykovácsi. The anxiety that had gripped her for the last few days seemed to melt away once she was cocooned in this humble house of God.

When István entered the church, he noticed a few other people huddled in alcoves at the rear, away from the light, wrapped in blankets. There was a small bundle of grey woollen blankets to the left of the front entrance at the base of a statue of the Virgin Mary. He made the sign of the cross at the statue, picked up two blankets, then looked around for Natália. He spied his wife praying in one of the rear pews, walked over, knelt beside her, and draped one of the blankets across her shoulders. She beamed up at him and said, "We survived the first part of our journey without incident. God is watching over us."

István put his arm around her and hugged her tightly to his chest, kissing the top of her head. "Let's find a quiet corner away from the door, where we can bunk down and get a few hours' sleep. We need to rest and restore our strength for the morning."

As they stood up, looking around for a suitable spot to hunker down, someone approached them, also draped in one of the blankets. Natália stepped back, fearful of what this person wanted with them.

"What took you so long? I've been waiting for hours," János asked, removing the blanket from his head and grinning broadly. The recognition and surprise on the faces of his dear friends was priceless. He laughed out loud and was quickly shushed by a couple huddled near to where they were standing.

"János, is it really you?" Natália exclaimed in a hushed tone as she gave him a big hug. Stepping back from him her eyes darted around the church searching for her best friend. János ushered them to a space away from the others and sat down. His smile evaporated when he realised that Natália was looking for Rózsa.

"Where is she? Where's Rózsa?" Natália asked timidly, fearing some mishap had befallen her friend.

"Rózsa has been against this from the start, Natália. You know that. A new life in a foreign country is not what she wants. I begged her to come many times, but she can be very stubborn, as you well know," he said with a slight smile in his voice. "It's just the three of us. I hope you don't mind me tagging along?"

"I can't believe you abandoned Rózsa. I thought the two of you were made for each other, perhaps even marrying soon. How could you leave her?" The pitch of her voice was rising. An older woman got up and told the trio to either stop talking or get out. People were trying to sleep.

"This is not the time nor the place for all these questions, Natália," István whispered, then clapped his hand on János' shoulder, saying, "I'm really glad to see you, János. I'm relieved to have your company, to have another pair of eyes checking the map we spent so much time deliberating over."

"What am I then?"

"The love of my life, Natália, but maps are not your forte." István replied. "Now, I think we should all try to get some sleep. We have a big day ahead of us."

István walked back to the statue of the Virgin Mary and picked up another two blankets, which he placed on the floor in the corner where János had led them. The blankets were a poor substitute for a mattress, but they helped to shield them from the cold stone tiles. They used their packs as makeshift pillows, but the whole arrangement was a poor substitute for the comfort of a proper bed and Natália fidgeted most of the night. Someone in the church was snoring loudly. She wanted to scream at them to shut up. The cold slowly seeped through the blankets they had spread out on the flagstones and she began to shiver. Careful not to disturb István, she snuggled up and curled herself into his body for warmth. István's body usually exuded heat during the night regardless of the weather. The closeness of her husband helped somewhat, but it was still impossible to get comfortable on such a hard surface. Each bone that contacted the hard floor complained bitterly. But she was so tired from the journey, trudging across fields, careful not to misstep. It was a relief to take the weight off her aching leg. Gradually, the tension in her body eased, and she felt safe in the presence of God. Exhaustion finally conquered her discomfort.

***

There were butterflies everywhere. Butterflies coloured orange with black stripes and white dots on the edges of their wings; smaller chocolate brown butterflies with white markings that looked like the keys on a piano; and delicate powder blue ones—her favourites. Brushing her hands through the lavender bushes, scattering the butterflies in all directions. Natália laughs as she runs through her grandmother's garden, attempting to catch one of the beauties, the sun on her upturned face, her grandmother calling out for her to come and drink tea and eat cake. Yummy cakes made from the apples and peaches grown on the property. Tea and cake, their weekend treat. She is her grandmother's favourite. Everyone knows, but she doesn't care. She is laughing. The butterflies are just out of her reach. Black clouds suddenly sweep across the sky, masking the sun, and dark shadows encase the garden. Running towards her grandmother she becomes agitated, unable to recall what her grandmother looks like. Distressed, Natália awakens to find tears streaming down her face. Sitting up, it takes a few moments to register where she is. A dream. It was only a dream. Yet the grief lingers, because she struggles to bring her grandmother's face to mind, and she would never again enjoy tea and cake with the woman who treasured her, while her own mother was so cruel. Wiping her face with the sleeve of her dress, she settled back down under the blanket, snuggling up against István, closing her eyes in the hope of a little more rest before they must face the challenges of the new day.

No sooner had she dozed off again than István got up to relieve himself. He was unable to move without disturbing her and apologised as he got up. Luckily, the church presbytery had a toilet, so there was no need to venture outside where his piss was sure to freeze mid-stream. Once inside the rest room, István noted his shirt was damp with sweat. He quickly removed it, so that he could use the small sink to cleanse himself of the pungent smell of fear. He too had slept fitfully. Running and running from an unknown terror, he was grabbed from behind and thrown into a damp, crumbling cell, where dark, hooded men had punched and kicked him. There was blood on the floor. His blood. The stench of his urine filling his nostrils, which were caked with blood. It was hard to breath. The cell looked familiar. He was back where he started. István splashed more cold water onto his face to shake the vision from his mind. Clear thoughts were needed to tackle the new day. He sat on the toilet longer than necessary, contemplating what lay ahead, knowing he needed to be strong for Natália, praying for safe passage. He washed his hands, put his shirt back on, and quietly went back to the others, tiptoeing through the church, careful not to disturb anyone.

When István returned to his makeshift bed, he and Natália sat huddled together for another hour before István decided that they might as well get going. Sleep had evaded them both for most of the night, and it was unlikely to come now, as daybreak approached. Natália still couldn't believe that János had abandoned the loving, caring Rózsa, and her heart ached at the thought that she was unable to comfort her friend. János, on the other hand, was out like a light, completely oblivious to the world around him. The cathedral provided a spiritual comfort that Natália was reluctant to leave, and yet the physical pain from the cold, hard floor could not be ignored. Every bone in her body was screaming at her to get up and get moving. It was not long before dawn. István promised that they would find an inn at the next village where they could eat a proper home cooked meal, sleep in a cosy bed, and catch up on some much-needed rest. He reached over to where János was sleeping soundly and shook him by the shoulder.

"Wake up, János. We need to get going."

A bleary-eyed János reluctantly stirred, then replied, "What, already? I've barely slept a wink."

"You've been out for hours, János. Come on, we're going."

Whilst János continued to grumble, Natália pulled out a bread stick and the cheese she carried in her knapsack and divided it into three portions, making sure that István got the biggest share. The trio ate quickly, then folded up the blankets and returned them to the statue for the next round of evacuees. Natália hurried over to the toilet before anyone else appeared to have the need, whilst István and János reviewed the map, checking their bearings to ensure they were on track for the next stage of the journey. Washing her hands, Natália stole a glance at herself in the small oval mirror above the sink. Dark rings circled her haunted eyes and tears surfaced as panic gripped her chest, for fear of what lay ahead. Maintaining a brave façade for István's sake was hard, and she allowed herself a few moments of release, weeping in the privacy of the small room. She still couldn't face the prospect of leaving Hungary permanently. It was one thing to dream of travelling to faraway places, but it was a completely different proposition to never set foot in her country ever again. Where would they end up? What kind of life awaited them? Washing away the grime and tears with ice-cold water rejuvenated her body and spirit, readying her for the new day.

As she was leaving the presbytery, Natália saw a priest bent over some papers in a small office. Heavily embroidered vestments hung on a hook on one wall, and two gold chalices flanked a large, bejewelled silver crucifix on the shelf behind the priest; familiar items that made her feel closer to God. She hesitated at the doorway, bade him good morning and was about to leave when he beckoned her to enter. Noticing the exhaustion on her face and the dishevelled clothing he surmised why she was sheltering in his church. He had seen so many people like her and was sad for her plight, and equally sad for the destruction inflicted upon the country by the Russians. It was a risk to allow people to shelter in the house of God and to provide food for those in need, and he feared retribution would only be a matter of time, but the old priest took his chances whilst he could still offer solace to his flock. Gesturing for Natália to take a seat he asked if she wanted him to hear her confession. She looked into his gentle eyes and nodded. The priest listened, allowing her to pour her heart out before absolving her of her sins. Not that he felt she had sinned. It seemed to be her husband's actions that tore her from her family and her country, following the man she loved to an unknown future.

Before she got up to leave, Natália asked the priest for a special favour, "Father, there's no certainty that we will evade the police and successfully cross the border. I'm terrified of being captured. Who knows what will become of us then? We've heard terrible rumours in Budapest of people suspected of treason being executed. I'm really scared, Father. Will you pray for us?"

"Of course, my child. I will keep you in my prayers, asking God to watch over you and see you to safety." Then the priest made the sign of the cross above Natália's head as he murmured, "In the name of the Father and of the Son and of the Holy Ghost, Amen."

"Amen," Natália repeated.

Stepping out of the church into the half-light of the coming dawn, a slight breeze touched Natália's cheeks. The sky was clear and there was no sign of snow. It would be a good day for travelling. A weight had lifted from her heart, her mood lighter since confessing to the priest. It had been a long while since she had attended Mass and confessed her sins. It was an uplifting experience that gave her renewed determination for what lie ahead. Glancing around, she saw the two men standing under a streetlamp waiting for her. Looking over at János, rage crept up her throat. She was furious with him for deserting Rózsa. How could he be so selfish? Did Rózsa mean nothing to him? This was not the man she thought she knew, and she was incensed that he was accompanying them, making her feel like an accomplice in his abandonment of her friend.

When István saw her standing on the top step of the church he waved to her, said something to János, then the two of them set out confidently in front, commencing the day's march. Natália hung back, observing János' behaviour. He certainly didn't appear to be grieving for the loss of his lover, or even to be mildly subdued about his change of circumstance. The opposite was true. He was laughing at something that István had said, slapping him on the back in jest, acting as if he was on the holiday of a lifetime.

CHAPTER 19

Győr Police Headquarters was a hive of activity. The main incident room was dominated by a large map of western Hungary, which took up most of the far wall next to Viktor's office. Coloured stickers dotted the map, highlighting towns and villages where successful arrests occurred in their region. Blue for known places, red for new zones. A few officers huddled together, scrutinising the map, conferring with one another, noting where the new hot spots had recently surfaced. Intelligence gathered by the police during their scouting trips was collated in this room. Two junior officers dedicated their time to typing up the reports as the information flowed through to them. The reports were then collated in date order and handed to Attila, Viktor's right-hand man, a trusted lieutenant who had followed Viktor to Győr. Puffing on his fourth cigarette of the morning, Attila read through the reports for completeness and accuracy. He knew full well that his boss did not tolerate errors of any kind. Sloppy work led to a drop in rank or being handed the worst assignments, if not to being expelled altogether, depending on the severity of the error. Attila composed a summary of the reports; where the arrests occurred, along with the age, gender, and number of people interrogated and subsequently deemed to be guilty of attempting to flee the country. Information relating to increases in 'tourism', hotel occupancies higher than normal, places such as churches where the numbers of people sleeping rough had increased, the number of train tickets sold at each station, and the destinations to which the passengers were travelling. Some of the traitors were brought back to Győr for further questioning. However, more often, they were dealt with immediately after being detained. The reports indicated that in many instances the accused turned to flee when asked to show their papers. The officers had no choice but to shoot, the guilt evident. The assassinations were aligned with police protocol. There was no elaboration needed in Attila's summary. This week's results consisted of three males and one female in the cells awaiting further interrogation, and twenty-four fugitives killed.

The sights and sounds of the incident room impressed Viktor as he pushed open the left-hand side of the double doors. Typewriters pinged and officers conversed. There were more red stickers plastered across the map, and thick cigarette smoke drifted throughout the air like an early morning fog—a sure sign of productivity. As he walked through the room, he greeted his team with his usual, authoritarian gruffness.

"What's the latest on the ground?"

Attila stubbed out his cigarette in the overflowing ashtray on his desk, collected the reports, and followed Viktor into his office.

"Another successful week, sir," Attila replied as he placed the reports in the centre of the large wooden desk, with his signed summary on top. He quoted the number of people captured, knowing it would please his boss.

"Excellent! I can add a few more traitors to the report. My trip to Komárom proved very rewarding indeed, and on more than one front, if you get my meaning," Viktor laughed as he shook his heavy coat off and hung it on the rack. "I chose to stay longer than expected, such was my success in rounding up our enemies."

"Congratulations, sir. I'll leave this week's results with you, but thought I'd mention that we have four detainees in the cells awaiting further questioning."

"Good! That will be all for now, Attila." Attila closed the door quietly behind him, knowing the captain preferred not to be disturbed when reading the reports.

Viktor lit a cigarette, took a long drag, and scanned the report on top of the files that were meticulously prepared according to his instructions, and placed in the centre of his desk for review. The report summarised the towns where the most arrests occurred and clearly mapped the routes taken by the escapees. The files were collated in date order, oldest on top, and grouped together for each town. Attila had stepped up since joining him in Győr, becoming an integral part of the team. Making Attila responsible for supervising the junior officers allowed Viktor to undertake the more rewarding task of ferreting out the unsuspecting victims. Viktor came to rely on Attila heavily, finding him eager to please and willing to take on as much responsibility as Viktor was prepared to give him.

The reconnaissance that had expanded across a wider arc both east and west of Győr had revealed several new towns where the refugees could be ambushed. Some of the newer hotspots where refugees were apprehended included Tata, Lébény, Moson-Magyaróvár, Kapuvár, Csorna, and even as far southwest as Nagykanizsa. The team's coordination had improved considerably under Viktor's command, resulting in a steady rise in arrest rates. Pride oozed from Viktor's pores as his superiors praised him for his excellent achievements. Another promotion was imminent. Viktor smiled inwardly, gratified with the pace at which he was forging his career.

Placing the summarised report aside, he opened the files. Flipping through them, he selected the ones that caught his interest, reading those first. More interested in the details of each report rather than Attila's carefully crafted summary, he was mentally transported to the towns, and could vividly imagine the scenes playing out, like attending the theatre. Immersed in one of the files relating to a young family of four who were caught on the train heading to Csorna without the required documents, his concentration was broken when there was a light tap on his door. One of the junior officers entered his office without being invited in, closing the door behind her. Viktor sighed, annoyed at the interruption, and looked up to see who had the audacity to barge into his office unannounced.

"I was worried about you, Viktor. You were meant to return two days ago. Not a word from you. Is everything all right?"

Margi spoke in a hushed tone to avoid being overheard. The office walls were paper thin, lacking privacy for intimate conversations. It was a poor attempt at concealing their affair, which was common knowledge in the station. They had been seeing each other, not that discreetly since Viktor assumed his new post in Győr.

"Of course, Margi. The trip was a greater success than I had anticipated, which required me to stay longer to finalise matters. Nothing for you to be concerned about."

Thinking it was appropriate to sound a little conciliatory he added, "I did miss you though, honey. The nights were particularly lonely, and I ached to have you. Come back at five when the team has finished for the day. I have a small gift for you. Oh, and could you fetch me a coffee? Thanks, Margi."

Margi smiled longingly at her lover, ran her tongue over her lips, blew him a kiss, then turned on her heel and left. Despite the newness of the relationship, she was smitten with Viktor. A handsome, powerful, and well-respected officer, he was exactly the type of man Margi wanted to marry. Viktor, on the other hand, was already tiring of Margi's whining. She was too needy and possessive, wanting a more permanent arrangement. But he enjoyed the sex for now. Margi was always ready for him, willing to experiment and keen to please him, despite the bruises. Even so, a transfer to another police station, preferably on the other side of the country, was on the cards for her. Viktor made a mental note to review positions vacant in outlying police stations to rid himself of her when the timing suited him.

Margi returned with Viktor's coffee, placed it on his desk, and brushed his hand with her fingers.

"See you at five, my love," she purred, before leaving his office.

Viktor blew on the hot drink and sipped tentatively a few times before it cooled down. Thoughts of Margi drifted from his mind as he refocussed on the reports in front of him. His team had done well in pinpointing the various escape routes, ambushing several people, and thwarting their plans to flee Hungary. Their prize was the booty confiscated from their victims. The wealthier women usually carried jewellery and other small family heirlooms, items that could easily be sold on the black market. These treasures, together with the cash that filled the victims' wallets, provided well-earned bonuses, supplementing the meagre police wages. It was a strong incentive for the officers to increase their success rate.

The light in Viktor's office faded as the late afternoon sun was shrouded by the gathering clouds. It was time to check on the prisoners. Women were generally weaker than men and gave up their secrets more readily, particularly if they thought they had a chance of being released. Flicking through the reports he located the file on the woman. Edit Beres was in her mid-thirties and had been apprehended in the small village of Csorna. Her husband, Péter, was a professor of economics at the Corvinus University in Budapest. Viktor recalled that Imre Nagy, the recently disgraced prime minister, had been a lecturer at that same university, an institution reputed to be in favour of democratisation. It was an interesting coincidence, he thought. Striding into the main office, Viktor selected one of the more junior male officers and asked to be taken to the woman's cell. As they made their way down the corridor, Viktor explained the young officer's duty should the prisoner not cooperate. The cadet nodded, smiling happily.

***

The concrete floor was like a slab of ice. The thin, ragged blanket had been carefully folded to create a bit of padding, separating Edit's tired limbs from the unforgiving surface. It hardly made a difference to the chill that penetrated every inch of her body. Her back ached terribly, but the pain was nothing compared to the fear she held for her husband. The police were cruel, consumed by their power. Edit knew her husband would be beaten into confessing. He was weak—an intellectual, not a soldier. The interrogators would not stop torturing him until they heard the truth of why they were travelling so far from their home in Budapest. Would he sacrifice himself to save her? Dark thoughts of what was to become of them tormented Edit. Her body trembled violently. She felt sick. They hadn't eaten since the previous morning, so there was nothing in her stomach but bile. If only she could sit in the same cell as Péter. To be beside him and face their captors together would give her strength. Edit hugged her knees, trying to stop herself from shivering, when she heard someone approach her cell door. The key turned slowly in the lock. Edit looked up, frightened by the two stern looking officers who confronted her.

"Edit Beres? Wife of Péter Beres?" Viktor addressed the woman cowering on the floor in the furthest corner of the small cell. He instantly summed her up as being upper middle class. Although she was somewhat dishevelled, she was smartly dressed in a good quality overcoat, black leather gloves and low heeled, highly polished black leather shoes. Despite the fearful look in her eyes, she was rather pretty.

"Yes," Edit replied.

"I have a proposition for you. You see this nice young officer? He's a virgin and needs to be broken in. I thought you could assist him in this endeavour. Being a married woman of experience, you'll know what to do." Viktor's statement was very businesslike, quite matter of fact.

Edit looked blankly at Viktor, shocked by this pronouncement. She turned her gaze to the young officer who was smiling broadly at her. She pressed her back hard against the wall and wrapped her arms around herself in a protective pose.

"Of course, if you cooperate with our enquiries, we will reconsider this and perhaps even let you visit your husband."

"What have you done to Péter?" Rage flashed in the woman's frightened eyes.

Viktor found her sudden passion rather attractive, but replied coolly, "We haven't done anything to him. Yet. With your cooperation we may show some leniency in sentencing. Now, what were you doing in Csorna?"

"As we explained to the other officer, we were on our way to Sopron University. My husband was meant to conduct a lecture there. He's an economics professor."

Edit blurted out the rehearsed line too quickly. A sure sign of nerves. It was the same script that the couple had continued to spout since being arrested. Viktor raised his voice and spoke with more authority.

"Yes, yes, of course he is. But what evidence do you have of this lecture? None was provided."

Edit started crying, babbling incoherently, "My husband, he has the papers, I know he has the papers."

"You're lying. Tell me why you were so far from home, heading towards the Austrian border with so few possessions?"

Edit whimpered over and over, "Sopron University, we were going to the university."

Viktor ignored Edit's whimpering and spoke over the top of her.

"We checked out your story, and no one at Sopron University could corroborate your claims. No one knows anything about a lecture your husband was to give. How do you explain that?"

Edit stared at Viktor, her eyes wide with horror, tears spilling over onto her pale cheeks. Weakly, she stated over and over, "Péter has the documents."

"You've left us no choice." Viktor turned to his comrade and said, "Tibor, please demonstrate to the prisoner the consequences of lying to the authorities."

Tibor walked to the centre of the cell. He casually removed his jacket, folded it neatly and laid it on the floor. Unbuckling his belt, he ripped it from his waistband and threw it on the floor beside his jacket. Within seconds, his trousers and underpants were around his ankles. He sidestepped the bundle and stood tall and fully erect in front of Edit. Her eyes were wide as saucers. Her back to the wall, there was no escape.

"Please, please, you must believe me. My husband is a professor. We were going to Sopron."

Edit sobbed and lashed out at her attacker with her fists. Tibor pushed her roughly to the ground, lifted her skirt up to her waist, prised her legs apart and deftly tore her panties away. He slapped her across the face with his large open palm to shut her up and then plunged deep inside her, thrusting hard. Edit tried to fight the beast, but Tibor easily pinned her down. He was twice her size and strength. And then it was over. Like a robot, Tibor stood, walked over to his clothes, dressed, and calmly walked back to the doorway, where he stood silently behind Viktor.

"Perhaps tomorrow you will consider telling us the truth. If not, then Tibor here will be getting some more practice in his manly duties. In the meantime, we will see what your husband has to say about how easily you spread your legs for this handsome officer. Maybe then he will tell us the truth."

Viktor left, the screams emanating from Edit's cell reverberating down the corridor. As he approached his office, Viktor felt amorous. It wasn't the first time he had enjoyed watching one of his junior officers attempting to extract a confession in this way.

***

The dutiful Margi was diligently typing away on a report when Viktor returned to the incident room. She abruptly stopped at the sight of her lover and followed him into his office like a loyal puppy. Everyone else had left for the day and discretion was no longer necessary. Before she had a chance to say anything Viktor grabbed her, slammed her down on his desk, and unzipped his fly while pushing her skirt up. He was pleasantly surprised to find that her panties were missing. He laughed, a gruff purr emanating from the back of his throat, and kissed her roughly on the mouth, his tongue probing hers. Margi spread her legs wide in anticipation of his hard thrusts. She wrapped her legs around his hips, trying to climax before he was spent.

Viktor's lovemaking was mechanical. Margi felt that he was insensitive to her wants and needs and feared that he had other lovers. But she was at a loss to know how to stop him from straying to other women. She thought that she might win him over by passively going along with some of his rougher antics; tying her wrists to the bedhead so she couldn't defend herself when he slapped her, causing deep red welts to flare up on her unblemished skin, taking her roughly from behind, biting her breasts. Although he did seem satisfied by her compliance, she knew deep down in her soul that he didn't love her. Never once did he use the word love in any context. The subject of marriage was taboo, as it only made Viktor angry, so she just did what she could to make him happy and to keep him coming back for more. Margi was desperately in love with Viktor and would do anything to keep him by her side.

"I missed you, Margi, and couldn't wait until tonight," Viktor said huskily as he pulled away from her, zipped up his fly, walked around to the other side of his desk, and sat down. The fact remained that he was sexually aroused from the incident in Edit's cell and couldn't wait to gratify his hunger. Opening the desk draw, he pulled out a small box wrapped in gold paper. Margi slid off the desk, straightened her clothing, and sat opposite Viktor in anticipation of the promised gift.

"A little something I picked up for you in Komárom. I hope you like it." He pushed the box towards her.

Margi beamed at him. Carefully unwrapping the gift, she opened the box, clapped her hand over her mouth in surprise and said, "Oh Viktor. It's beautiful."

Margi lifted the delicate gold pendant from the red velvet pad that held the chain in place and held it up to the light. A brilliant, round, blue sapphire was mounted in the centre of the medallion. It was one of the nicest presents she had received from him, and she wondered if this was a turning point in their relationship. She leant across the desk and gave

Viktor a passionate kiss, then handed the necklace back to him, walked over, sat on his lap, and said, "Can you help me fasten the clasp?"

That should keep her contented for a while he thought as he smiled back, placing the necklace around her slender neck, and kissing the spot where the chain caressed her skin. Margi turned around and kissed Viktor again while unzipping his trousers. Sliding off his lap, she knelt in front of him and took his member in her mouth, sucking until he climaxed.

Later that night, as Viktor polished off a bottle of red wine in his apartment, his thoughts wandered to his time in Komárom. He had successfully apprehended four couples, all of whom he had found guilty of treason. It intrigued him that some of these people tried to escape the inevitable, whilst others passively accepted their fate. The last woman he shot was an old hag in her late sixties. It was her necklace that he had given to Margi, prised from the old woman's neck as she lay dying. But then the image of Katarina, naked on his hotel bed, intruded into his thoughts. She was such an exuberant lover, knocking on his bedroom door each night when her shift ended, staying until dawn, when they made love again as the sun pierced the flimsy curtain of his room, faintly lighting her pearl-like skin. God, she was beautiful. She begged him to allow her to return with him to Győr as she tickled his nipples with her tongue on their last morning together. But of course, that was impossible. Viktor would not put it past Margi to conduct surveillance on him if she thought he was seeing another woman. Besides, Viktor was not committed to any woman, despite Margi's fantasies about their relationship. Katarina would serve her purpose during his visits to Komárom. Viktor convincingly fabricated a story when he checked out of the hotel, claiming that his boss at the shipping company required him to attend meetings in Komárom more frequently, due to an increase in trade. His secretary would call ahead and book a room at the hotel for his scheduled visits. Katarina was not very happy, but was unable to change his mind. Whilst the story was a lie, Viktor had every intention of returning to Komárom. It was still a flashpoint for fugitives, and he had not yet tired of bedding the voluptuous Katarina.

The next morning, Viktor commandeered Tibor and paid a visit to Péter Beres. The meeting was brief, and no evidence materialised of a lecture he was meant to conduct in Sopron. Viktor took great pleasure in describing how Tibor had attempted to extract the truth from Edit and couldn't help himself from baiting the prisoner by remarking, "She seemed to enjoy spreading her legs during the interrogation."

"You bastard! How could you? Edit, Edit, Edit," Péter screamed her name over and over, yelling at Viktor to let her go.

"Péter Beres, I find you guilty of treason against the Hungarian government. You will be executed by nightfall," Viktor announced sternly and turned to leave.

"What about Edit? She's innocent. What will become of her? Please, please, let her go. She has done nothing wrong," Péter begged, desperate to save his young wife.

Viktor ignored him and left the cell with Tibor in tow. As they walked back to the incident room, Viktor gave Tibor free rein to continue 'interrogating' Edit for as long as he pleased, provided she was executed by the end of the week.

"Happy to do my duty, sir," Tibor replied.

***

Despite resuming his normal duties at the station since returning from Komárom, barking orders at his subordinates, interrogating prisoners, overseeing executions, and issuing regular reports to his superiors in Budapest, Viktor was surprised to find that images of Katarina constantly interrupted his thoughts. For the past few nights, he had woken before dawn, covered in sweat, the last glimmer of a dream of their erotic lovemaking permeating his consciousness, his penis engorged and throbbing. No other woman had ever had that effect on him. It was startling. Taking control of himself, he buried himself deeper into his work. But it was hopeless. The more he tried to cleanse her from his mind, the greater his lust for her. It was an addiction that needed feeding. Margi became a poor substitute and sensed his preoccupation. The persistent questions and the way she threw herself at him at every opportunity repelled him. Nothing she did pleased him any longer. Viktor's decision to rid himself of Margi came when she threw a tantrum in his office, demanding he explain his indifference and the coldness towards her despite her every effort to satisfy him. The officers in the incident room froze, frightened of the boss's reaction. Typewriters stopped their clatter and discussions ceased. Every face was fixed on Viktor's office door, expecting a burst of rage. But there was only a deathly silence. Then, a few hushed words were spoken, difficult to make out. The door opened and Margi was ushered out, tears streaming down her cheeks, completely humiliated. Not one of her colleagues met her eyes, their heads suddenly bent over paperwork, busying themselves in their tasks, too scared to react. With a nod from Viktor, Attila escorted her out of the building. The time had arrived for Viktor to contact his colleague in Debrecen, in the eastern part of the country, a long way from Győr. Initial enquiries the previous week had indicated that it would be easy to find the junior officer a position. The time had now come to arrange a transfer for Margi. Viktor was surprised by the weight that seemed to lift from his shoulders once he placed the phone back on the receiver. He had allowed the affair to continue far too long—a mistake he would not repeat.

Viktor's next scheduled trip was to Kapuvár, west of Győr, one of the newest transit towns for refugees. It was in the opposite direction to where his new lover awaited his return. Mulling over his options to continue the excellent success of thwarting fugitives whilst at the same time spending time with the young barmaid in Komárom, Viktor arrived at his decision. Calling Attila into his office, the man obediently entered and awaited his instructions.

"There's been a slight change of plan, Attila. Instead of travelling to Kapuvár, I want you to take charge of the mission there. It will be a good opportunity for you to demonstrate your leadership skills. Take two officers, whoever you believe is up to the task."

"Thank you, Captain, for giving me this opportunity. I won't let you down."

"Be sure that you don't. We have an excellent track record that needs to be maintained. I'm counting on you. And, before you go, book me a week's accommodation at the same hotel I stayed at in Komárom. I've decided there's more to accomplish. I'll be heading there tomorrow afternoon."

"Yes, sir, right away, Captain."

Viktor smiled. Soon he'd be caressing the enthusiastic, impish Katarina.

CHAPTER 20

István hadn't planned on stopping in Komárom, hoping instead to seek shelter in a barn in the surrounding countryside. But Natália looked exhausted, her face was ashen, and he had promised that after their uncomfortable night on the cold stone floor in the Church of Our Lady, they would spend the next night at an inn with a hot bath and a hearty meal. So, they walked to the next place on their route, in the hope that Komárom would be a big enough town to have at least one guesthouse.

Natália lagged behind the men. Her injured leg throbbed and her lower back felt as though she'd been stabbed with a dull knife. But she fought on, knowing that a soft bed beckoned. The first hotel they came to was fully booked, which alarmed the trio, and caused Natália's eyes to fill with tears. Seeing the young woman's distress, the kindly proprietor directed them to the Komárom's other hotel, at the opposite end of town, close to the river, suggesting that as it was much larger there was a good chance of vacancies. Natália thanked the innkeeper, the overwhelming relief evident on her tired face.

Trudging across town, they reached the riverside hotel fifteen minutes later. The foyer was large, and the dark wood panelling that lined the walls provided a warm welcome. János closed the front door, shutting out the freezing cold air. Natália feared the worst, not knowing where they would go if they were turned away again. The thought of wandering around aimlessly in the bitter cold night made her shudder. She gravitated to the large open fire that was blazing at the far end of the dining room. The warmth of the flames seeped through her clothes, melting the icicles that stubbornly stuck to the fabric of her coat. Glancing back towards the counter, István waved her over. He had secured a room for the night, much to everyone's relief. It was a small loft on the top floor with one double bed. It would have to do. Besides, sharing a room saved money. Extra blankets provided János with some cushioning from the timber floor, so he happily agreed to sleep at the foot of the bed.

Despite arriving after the kitchen had closed, the cook took pity on the trio, who looked travel worn and weary. She was a plump, jolly lady in her late fifties, and looked as though she heartily relished the fruits of her labour. Fussing like a mother hen rounding up her chicks, she guided the travellers to a freshly set table, returned with a large basket of bread, then disappeared into the kitchen. She reheated the leftover pork and lentil stew, and within half an hour of arriving, the threesome was scraping their plates with the remnants of the crusty bread. It was a wonderful meal, just as delicious as Natália's mother's lentil stew. When the cook returned to clear their plates, the boys cheekily asked for seconds, lavishing the cook with as many compliments as possible until she returned with fresh bowls of piping hot stew, beaming with pride at the two charming men. The boys finished the carafe of wine with the second helping of stew and continued their conversation about the forthcoming day. Natália struggled to stay awake. She kissed István on the cheek, reminding him not to retire too late given their early start the following morning.

Thoughts of a relaxing bath revived Natália. To scrub herself clean after such a long journey would be blissful. Her only hope was that the bathroom was unoccupied. When she reached the landing on the top floor, Natália noticed that the bathroom door was slightly ajar, a good indication that it was free. She stepped in, inserted the plug into the tub, then turned the hot water tap on before popping back to their room to fetch her towel. Within minutes, the small tub was steaming with hot water, fresh soap resting on a ceramic soap dish. Locking the door behind her, Natália quickly undressed and slid into the bath, soaking her abused muscles, sighing with absolute pleasure as the water lapped her skin, caressing every crevice of her body like a gentle lover. Having rubbed every inch of her body with the fragrant soap she proceeded to wash her hair, immersing herself completely to rinse out the suds. She felt tinglingly clean. As the water cooled, she reluctantly stepped out of the tub, wrapped the towel around herself, collected her clothes and padded back to their room. She was sound asleep as soon as her head hit the pillow, completely unaware of the boys entering the room about an hour later.

***

It was Viktor's second night in Komárom. He sat at his usual corner table, where he could observe people as they came and went. Having devoured the delicious stew, Viktor drank a carafe of red wine while continuing to observe the patrons. He was certain that more refugees were travelling through Komárom as an escape route to Austria. It was only a matter of time before someone caught his attention.

Katarina's shift ended at 9.00pm. There were only a few patrons drinking at the bar, time having been called five minutes before. A handful of guests were finishing their meals. Katarina walked seductively over to Viktor's table, swaying her hips under her red mini skirt. Sitting opposite him, she picked up his wine glass and drank the remainder of its contents in one gulp, ran her tongue slowly over her lips to capture the ruby drops that threatened to spill down her chin, leaned closer to him, and said in a husky voice, "Let's go to bed."

Viktor was mesmerised by Katarina's large, firm breasts, inches from his face, most of the flesh exposed by the low-cut blouse. He was about to stand and lead the way up the stairs when he caught a movement at the edge of his vision. He looked past Katarina to the three people who had just entered the hotel: two men and a woman. All three were carrying small satchels. The woman's face was flushed and her shoulders slumped. He recognised the sheer exhaustion on her face as she walked into the dining room to stand by the fire. There was no mistaking that she was a weary traveller. Viktor smiled inwardly and his interest sharpened.

"You go on up, honey. I'll join you shortly," Viktor said, instantly distracted and rather dismissive of Katarina's suggestion.

Katarina felt rebuffed and looked quizzically at Viktor but decided not to question him. She dutifully rose and went up to his room. Viktor remained seated, patiently observing the new arrivals. After checking in, the three blow-ins were shown to a table in the dining room and, despite the bar being closed, were served a carafe of wine. The woman appeared agitated, rubbing her right knee, while the man sitting next to her poured the wine. Viktor couldn't help but notice that the woman, who sat facing him and looked to be in her early twenties, was strikingly beautiful. She had large, almond-shaped eyes, her thick auburn, hair spilled across her shoulders, and her lips were lusciously plump. She had a petite figure that was accentuated by the broad shoulders of her woollen jacket, an outfit of exceptional quality. Not paupers then, he mused. Refusing the wine offered, she chose to drink water. Viktor noticed a gold wedding ring on her finger, so it was probable that one of the men was her husband. After a few minutes it was obvious that the older of the two men was indeed her husband, as she lay her hand on his arm when she spoke, and he in turn placed an arm around her shoulders, whispering something in her ear. The hotel's cook, still wearing her soiled apron, arrived with their meals and all three tucked in as if they hadn't eaten in weeks. Viktor supressed a grin that threatened to disrupt his blank expression, instinctively sensing that these three people were fugitives. He sat for a while longer, observing them, but his gaze kept shifting to the woman, like a moth to a flame. And then suddenly, she looked up and stared straight at him, eyebrow raised. Natália had noticed the handsome man sitting alone, looking in their direction, but decided he was harmless enough. She was accustomed to being gawked at. Viktor quickly averted his gaze, coughed, drank some water, then got up to leave. Retiring to his room, he made a mental note to rise early the following morning and follow the suspects before ambushing them.

***

A black void enveloped Natália as she woke early the next morning, her stomach churning. István was still dead to the world, so she crept out of bed as quietly as possible. She had expected that she'd need to step over János and was surprised to find that he had already left the room. Frowning at the empty space where her friend should have been sleeping, she was distracted by her stomach heaving again, realising she was about to throw up. Closing the door quietly behind her to avoid disturbing István, she bolted down the corridor, relieved that the bathroom was vacant. After five minutes of vomiting, Natália was sure she had just expelled every mouthful of the stew she had devoured the previous night. What a waste, she thought. Looking at her reflection in the mirror, her face was pale and her hands a little clammy. She had struggled to eat breakfast for over a week without feeling ill. At first, she believed it was anxiety and fear that was the cause of her upset stomach. But now she suspected it was a pregnancy. Her symptoms had become worse and were identical to when she was pregnant with Julia. István seemed oblivious, and Natália decided to keep her secret, not sure if the news would delight or distress her husband, given their circumstances. Splashing cold water over her face helped to settle the nausea. She rinsed her mouth out several times, brushed her teeth, and rinsed again before she felt normal enough to face breakfast. She had been frequently praying since leaving Budapest, but now she made an extra plea to God as she gazed at her image in the mirror, asking for strength and protection for the new life she believed she was carrying.

The plan was to leave as early as possible, but their departure had been delayed by István refusing to wake. Too much red wine and a second helping of stew had knocked him out. The escape to Austria seemed to be an adventure for János, and his attitude had started to grate on his friends. The cautious approach to reach the border that had been agreed upon before they set out from Budapest was taking too long for János, who was becoming increasingly impatient. He hadn't been tortured in prison for months like István, beaten to within an inch of his life, expecting death to carry him away every time the prison guards decided to pay him a visit. István was set on never returning to prison. An encounter with the authorities, especially the secret police, had to be avoided—not only for his own sake but for Natália's. He would protect his beloved wife until his last breath, and so he insisted the journey continue according to what he deemed to be the safest route, regardless of the delay in reaching the border. This had become a source of disagreements. János wanted to keep moving, to take shorter breaks, and to make a dash for Austria, regardless of the danger.

An argument between the two men was audible as Natália approached the bedroom door, having tidied herself in the bathroom. The voices stopped as she entered the room. A stern glare to both her husband and their friend dispensed with the possibility of any further conflict. When they quietly made their way down the stairs to the dining room, János joined another family for breakfast. Natália sat beside her husband and questioned him, wondering who they were and why János was sitting with them.

"János thinks it's safer to travel in a larger group. We met that family last night after you went to bed. They're heading to Austria as well, no surprises there, but think they can cross much sooner than we've planned to, so of course János is keen to travel with them. That's what the argument was about just now."

"I don't suppose the young woman sitting with them, the one who seems enthralled by whatever János is saying, has anything to do with his decision to travel with them?" Natália snapped.

"Never mind them. Eat up, honey. The sun will rise soon. I'm afraid I overslept, so we can't linger," István said quietly as he sat patiently waiting for Natália to eat her breakfast. He had already managed to scoff two boiled eggs, some bread, and a thick slice of cheese.

Natália sat opposite him, staring at the food on her plate. Clenching her jaw, she breathed in deeply, slowly exhaled, ate the egg and a small piece of bread, looked up at István and said, "I'm not really that hungry."

Wrapping the remainder of the bread and cheese in a napkin, Natália suggested they take it with them to snack on during the day. Tiptoeing up the stairs to their room, so as not to disturb anyone, they hurriedly packed their satchels. It was still dark when István and Natália stepped outside, before the birds woke, heralding the new dawn. It was deathly still. Not a leaf stirred. Natália found the brisk morning air on her face refreshing. It relieved some of her queasiness. She breathed in deeply, the fresh air filling her lungs, clearing her head, preparing herself for the day ahead. István walked across the road to the nearest streetlamp to study his map, while waiting for János to join them. The next town on their route was Lébény. István hoped they would reach it by nightfall. He'd never ventured this far west of Budapest. Heartened that he had eluded the police so far, István felt confident that Lébény would not be on their radar. It was too far off the beaten track. Eager to get going, he stamped his feet on the light cover of snow that covered the ground, warming his muscles for the long march ahead. János finally materialised, with a few stragglers in tow.

***

As the faint light of dawn penetrated the sheer lace curtain draped across the sole window in the bedroom, the couple stirred. Katarina was the first to open her eyes. Looking across at her naked lover she smiled, admiring the vision before her, delighted by the magnificence of the man who had returned to her. Tracing around his left nipple with her finger, she wound her way down past his abdomen and cupped his penis in her hand, stroking it with her thumb. Viktor's arousal was immediate. Before she could say good morning, he rolled on top of her, sucked her right nipple, making her yelp. He pushed her legs apart and easily entered Katarina. They climaxed swiftly, in unison. Katarina clung to him, her fingers digging into his broad shoulders, not wanting to let go. Viktor rolled off her, reached for his watch to check the time, then swore under his breath. Their lovemaking the night before was rougher than usual. Viktor's heart rate had accelerated, power surging through him, thoughts of the arrests he would make the following day fuelling his machismo. But he had meant to rise much earlier than this.

"What's wrong, Viktor? Did I displease you?" Katarina was stunned, not having experienced Viktor's annoyance before.

Viktor ignored her, hastily dressed, combed his unruly hair into place, then ran down the stairs to the dining room where a few of the guests were breakfasting. Composing himself before he reached the bottom step, he scanned the room, looking for the three people who had checked in the previous night. There was no sign of them. Viktor berated himself for allowing his lust for Katarina to dictate his behaviour. Running out of the hotel he looked left then right, hoping to spot them. He checked the streets fanning off the main road but saw no sign of the fugitives. He was too late. The plan to rise before dawn, to ensure he kept close to the traitors, had failed miserably. Furious, he clenched his fists, nails digging into his palms, mumbling expletives to himself before resuming his normal calm demeanour as he walked briskly back to the hotel.

Returning to his room, Viktor found Katarina sitting up in bed, waiting patiently for her lover to return. Katarina was infatuated with Viktor, despite not knowing a great deal about him. She had never met anyone so sophisticated, knowledgeable, and worldly. Conversation with Viktor was limited, with Katarina doing most of the talking. There were many aspects of his life he preferred to keep private, and he would cut her off if she asked too many questions. Marriage and children were what she craved with this important businessman, and she hoped he felt the same, yet she was too scared to broach the subject for fear of rejection. Perhaps it was too soon. Perhaps he was still grieving for his dead wife and child. Katarina knew that Viktor was the man of her dreams, and she would wait as long as necessary to win his heart. Reflecting on the previous night's lovemaking and Viktor's extraordinary stamina, Katarina giggled at the thought of the beautiful children they could create together from their sexual pleasure. Despite the bites and bruises he inflicted upon her, she accepted the heightened brutishness of their lovemaking without complaint, desperate to keep him coming back to her, hoping he would eventually love her as she desperately loved him.

Katarina's expression changed when Viktor looked at her. She threw the sheet off, unveiling her lithe body, legs slightly parted. He couldn't help but admire how beautiful she was, her skin still glistening from their earlier encounter, but he shrugged the lustful thoughts from his mind. There was no time for that now. As he hastily packed his bag, he said, "Sorry, love. I've been summoned to our office in Sopron for a few days. Some urgent matters need my immediate attention."

Viktor dropped his bag by the door, went to the bed and kissed Katarina full on the mouth whilst caressing her left breast, then purred into her ear, "I'll be back as soon as I can."

Reaching into his trouser pocket he pulled out a few Forint to cover the cost of the room for the week, placed the money on the bedside table, then was out the door as quick as lightening, much to Katarina's disappointment.

Realising he could get the upper hand by travelling via the rail network, Viktor was confident he could outrun the defectors and get to the border ahead of them. But which direction would they take? Analysing his map, he decided to head toward Mosonmagyaróvár. It was the logical route to the border from Komárom. Before commencing his pursuit, Viktor contacted the officer in charge of the incident room in Győr, providing descriptions of the three escapees, with instructions to inform all officers in the neighbouring villages near Mosonmagyaróvár to keep watch and to inform him immediately if the trio was apprehended. Viktor wanted to deal with these people personally. The woman intrigued him. Her sparkling eyes were imprinted in his mind and her quizzical expression as she caught him staring seemed to unhinge him a little. He may yet thwart their escape to the West.

***

István, Natália and János had met other refugees during their journey, but had chosen to distance themselves, feeling it was safer. Natália believed travelling in a large group would only attract unwanted attention from the authorities. Clearly, since meeting Mária, János had other ideas, and convinced his friends to join her family. After a few introductions, they set off for Lébény, a party of eight. Aside from Mária's parents they travelled with her brother, Albert, and her uncle Fülöp, her mother's older brother. Natália hung back, dragging István away from the others for a private conversation. Mária seemed charmed by János' good looks and humour. She was petit and rather pretty in a childish way. How could János forget Rózsa so quickly? They had been a couple for over two years, and he was acting as if she'd never existed. This enraged Natália and increased the feelings of betrayal on behalf of her friend, left behind in Budapest. Yet, against her better judgement, not wanting to abandon her husband's best friend, she felt compelled to travel with these strangers. István too was apprehensive of travelling in a group but provided they didn't deviate from his chosen route he didn't argue.

János stuck like glue to Mária from the moment they set out at first light. Walking together side by side and sitting slightly apart from everyone else when resting, Mária was quick to laugh at his jokes, and blushed when he spoke softly to her, their heads bent in private conversation. Natália glared at János whenever he seemed to be acting too familiar with the girl, but he completely ignored her.

"You should remind János of the wonderful girlfriend he left behind, István. He's behaving inappropriately. He hardly knows this girl and look, he's acting as if they're a couple."

"It's none of our business, Natália. Leave him be."

On the outskirts of Lébény, an argument erupted. Natália was headed in the direction of the town but Mária's family decided to continue travelling through the night, rather than resting in Lébény. János wanted to join them, and it was obvious to Natália why. He was clearly smitten with Mária. The group had made great headway that day and were nearing the Austrian border; freedom was tantalisingly close. János agreed that they should continue travelling through the night and cross the border under the cover of darkness. His impatience was infuriating, and Natália angrily argued that he couldn't understand the potential danger. The closer they got to the border, the greater the police presence would be. They needed to be even more vigilant than ever if they were to avoid a confrontation with the authorities. How could János not know this? How could he be so cavalier? Natália swallowed her pride and acted like a feeble woman, using her injured leg as an excuse to rest.

"We've been travelling since five this morning. I'm exhausted. If I don't eat something soon, I'll collapse, and you'll have to carry me the rest of the way. Besides, my leg hasn't fully recovered from our accident and it's aching terribly. I really can't go on," she said imploringly, with her gaze finally resting on her husband, seeking support before driving her point home,

"And besides, we can't afford to get complacent. It's even more critical we keep our wits sharp with the police patrolling the borders. We've acted cautiously up until now. Let's be smart about this, take a break, and reassess the best path to the border over a nice hot meal."

Mária's father would not be swayed. As the head of the family, his decision was final.

"I don't want to waste any more time. We're almost there. We'll be shielded by the darkness and the oak trees lining the stream. It's safest this way."

"Well, I'm heading into town and checking into the first inn we come across," Natália said defiantly as she looked earnestly at her husband.

István knew that once she had her mind made up, it was futile to argue with his wife. He had noticed that she had become more irritable since they left Komárom. He knew that she hadn't forgiven János for leaving Rózsa, and that she couldn't bear to see him so friendly with another woman. István sighed in resignation and said, "I agree with Natália. We need to eat and rest. We'll find lodgings and make a fresh start at dawn tomorrow." Inwardly, he felt that it was safer to continue their journey alone, rather than as part of the larger group.

János shrugged his shoulders. "Well, my friends. This is where we will part company. I'm happier in a larger group, so I'll continue with Mária's family and wait for you on the other side."

Natália hugged János. A strong sense of foreboding crept up her spine as she stepped back and said, "The police won't let us cross the border too easily, János. A bigger group is more likely to be noticed. Are you sure about this?"

János looked back to where Mária was standing with her family and said, "Yes, I'm sure. I can almost taste freedom, and I want to reach it as quickly as possible."

"Please be careful, János," Natália said as she choked back tears.

The men shook hands and then embraced. István nodded to his long-time friend and said, "On the other side then, János. If we don't show up within three days, you'll know we didn't make it."

"You're the luckiest man I know, my friend. You'll make it!" János gripped István's shoulder, then turned away.

Natália and István watched their friend walk away, before turning towards the town centre. They walked in silence, sad and scared for their friend, and scared for themselves, unsure of how they would cross into Austria undetected. They were so close now, yet freedom felt illusive. Their thoughts soon turned to a hot meal and a warm bed, as Natália's tummy growled. It had been many hours since she ate anything. She hastened her pace as they walked down the main street, spotting an old stone building displaying a 'vacancy' sign in large bold letters. Without a word to István she made a beeline for the front entrance and was already making enquiries about a room for the night when István caught up to her. Natália grinned at him and said, "I've just booked us a room and a table in the dining room. Let's eat." It was the most cheerful he'd seen his wife in days. Her faced glowed and her eyes shone. István returned her smile before ushering her into the dining room.

***

The sun had almost set when János and his companions reached the edge of the forest on the outskirts of Lébény. The light was fading fast and shadows blanketed the countryside. It would be difficult and slow going from this point, stepping cautiously, hoping that the darkness did not disorient them. Mária's father, Péter, assumed leadership of the group, indicating the quickest route to the border and the best way to conceal themselves along the line of oak trees. Albert and Fülöp acted as scouts, to ensure the way was clear. The rest of the group waited for twenty minutes before the scouts returned. The damp earth seeped up through the soles of their boots and chilled every muscle. It was a task to stop teeth from clattering, a sound that echoed around them through the trees. Talking was kept to a minimum as the men conferred about the dangers ahead. Everyone else was commanded to stop speaking completely, to avoid detection.

Mária clung to János' arm, for both safety and comfort. The way forward was clear, so they set out, the scouts in front, János and Mária in the centre, and Péter and his wife at the rear. Try as they might to walk in silence, it was difficult not to step on dry twigs that crunched and snapped loudly underfoot. Occasionally, someone would stumble over a large branch or tree root and yelp out loud. The sound thundered into the black void of night as if shouted through a megaphone. Each time, everyone instinctively froze, ears pricked for the tiniest sound of a human reaction. Fülöp's raised arm was the signal for everyone to halt. When he was confident the coast was clear, he lowered his arm and the procession resumed. The tension was palpable. János prayed silently to Saint Christopher, to the Virgin Mary, to Jesus, and to any other figure that sprung to mind as they scrambled through the dense woodland. The breeze had picked up and the wind was icy. The slightest sound carried across a huge distance intensifying the danger.

It felt as if they had been tiptoeing through the forest for hours. They forged on; their progress slower than expected. As the trees thinned, they came upon a wide stream, partly iced over. It glistened in the moonlight, eerily beautiful. Péter claimed that the village of Jánossomorja was close. In daylight, the outskirts would be visible from where they stood. This buoyed the group. Péter, Albert and Fülöp conferred again, and determined that the way forward was across the stream. But how to cross safely? It was difficult to determine the thickness of the ice and to judge whether it would withstand the weight of six adults. It was agreed that the largest man, Fülöp, who was also a strong swimmer, would cross first. It would soon become apparent if the ice was going to give way. If he fell into the water, he could swim back to the bank. Péter combed the forest floor for a large branch. Finding one twice as thick as his thumb, he stripped off the smaller branches and leaves and handed it over to Fülöp with the following instruction, "Prod the ice in front of you before taking each step. You'll feel it crack if it's too thin."

Fülöp gauged the weight of the branch in his hands, stepped onto the riverbank, and tapped the ice a few times in front of where he was standing, searching for the thickest part. The others gathered around and watched anxiously. Nothing happened. Cautiously, one foot was placed on the ice. It felt stable. Fülöp then placed one foot in front of the other very confidently, not detecting any instability. Once he was halfway across, he took a gamble and ran the rest of the way without incident. When he reached the opposite bank, Fülöp waved to the party on the other side, encouraging them to follow his path. Mária was overjoyed, but János, sensing she was about to squeal, quickly clapped a hand over her mouth to stifle any sounds. Elation amongst the family was soon replaced with shock, confusion and then horror as the sound of gunfire blasted the quiet night into oblivion. Fülöp was still holding the branch above his head when he toppled face first into the stream. The splintering crack of the ice was heard above the sound of the guns. Mária's mother shrieked as he plunged into the water, crying out to her brother. Within seconds, the stream consumed the dead man as if he had never existed. Further shots rang out, surrounding the family on the opposite bank. The women screamed. Péter yelled out for everyone to retreat into the trees. No one responded. Terror seized them, immobilising them as if their feet were concreted to the ground. János was the first to react. He grabbed Mária and threw her to the ground, lying across her body to shield her from the bullets. The gunfire stopped as suddenly as it had started. János' heart was pounding hard. He rolled off Mária, coaxing her up so that they could make a run for it. She lay listless, her vacant eyes staring up at the starry sky. It took János mere seconds to realise that she was dead.

"You're not going anywhere, chum."

János spun around and faced his executioner. He opened his mouth to plead for mercy. Before a syllable left his lips he dropped to his knees and was lifeless before he hit the ground.

CHAPTER 21

The hunt was not as successful as the boys had hoped. After a day's expedition in the countryside near Sándor's farm on the outskirts of Mosonszolnok, two rabbits and one rather small boar was all they managed to snare. Aggressive and cunning, the boar consumed most of the day, but the boys finally won out, although not without incident. There was still life in the beast when it collapsed onto the earth. Sándor bent over to tie the legs together when the boar turned its head, and with its final breath lunged at Sándor, piercing his left forearm with a tusk. After a quick examination the wound proved not to be as severe as the pain had indicated, yet it would still need treatment with antiseptic to avoid infection.

Sándor and Laci had been mates since early childhood. Neither had progressed very far with their education. The expectation that they would work for their fathers, Laci at the inn and Sándor on the family farm, dispelled any ambition for a more adventurous life. They found enough adventure in the countryside surrounding their village, hunting together as often as time permitted, enjoying the thrill of the chase, the comradery, and the responsibility of providing for their families.

The blue skies soon disappeared as the wind increased during the afternoon, whipping the clouds into a thick, ominous blanket. The dark fingers of night would soon extinguish the remaining daylight. It was time to call it a day. With their meagre bounty, it was decided that Laci would keep the rabbits and Sándor the boar. Back at the farmhouse, Laci placed the rabbits into a sack, secured them inside the pannier slung over his workhorse's back, leaving Sándor in his mother's capable, healing hands. Clicking his tongue at Poros, the horse trotted away from the farm, homeward bound. Once they reached the main track to Lébény, Laci urged Poros forward into a full gallop, hoping to reach home before darkness fully descended, which made for a hazardous journey for both horse and rider.

They were not quite halfway home when thoughts of a warm dinner captured Laci's imagination. Preoccupied with notions of a hot stew, Laci did not notice a large boar break from the stand of oak trees to his right and was completely taken by surprise when it ran straight in front of Poros. He quickly pulled on the reins but was unable to stop the horse. Poros had no choice but to collide with the boar, throwing Laci over his head, before collapsing onto the beast. The full weight of the horse pinned the boar to the ground, its squealing short lived, its life snuffed.

Laci was unsure how long he lay on the ground. Poros' whinnying eventually entered his consciousness. Cautiously, he moved himself into a sitting position, checking for any broken bones, and was relieved that he was relatively unscathed except for a pounding headache and scratches on the palms of his hands from landing heavily on the gravel. Looking around for Poros, he saw him only a few feet from where he sat, trying to get up off the boar, snorting in pain. Laci darted over to him, alarmed that he was struggling to stand, bent down, and stroked its head, speaking soothingly to calm the animal. Tears sprung into his eyes when he saw the two front legs of his horse grotesquely twisted, bones poking out through the skin. Instantly, the magnitude of the damage was clear. Laci understood what was necessary. Apologising to his faithful friend for his carelessness, through his choking sobs, he knew he needed to act quickly to spare the animal any further agony. Reaching for the rifle that was strapped to the pannier, and despite his arms shaking, he continued to speak calmly—as much for himself as for the horse. Aiming at the spot between the horse's eyes, Laci fired one shot. The snorting abruptly stopped. The rifle slipped from his grip as he dropped to his knees beside Poros, pressing his face into the horse's neck, his tears flowing freely. Poros had been his friend and had served him well since he was a young boy of ten. How could he have been so negligent? He should have been alert to the ever-present danger of wild animals lurking in the woods. Yet berating himself was not going to bring his horse back, nor get him home. It was fully dark now, save for the faint glimmer of light that filtered through the trees from the moon. The rest of his journey would be on foot. Collecting his pannier and rifle, Laci left his horse and continued homeward. It was an eerie feeling, walking amongst the majestic oaks, with not a sound to be heard except his footfalls upon the earth, twigs snapping underfoot.

Hearing water rippling over rocks, Laci gravitated towards the stream to fill his canteen, which he had neglected to refill before leaving Sándor's place. Another careless mistake. He hadn't eaten or drunk anything since noon, and he was parched. Carefully, he knelt on the edge of the bank, trying not to slip into the icy stream, then filled his canteen with the crystal-clear water. As he stood, a large shape further upstream near an overhanging tree branch caught his eye. It was difficult to discern what it might be, and so Laci walked along the bank for a closer look. At first, he suspected it to be a dead animal, perhaps a deer, but when he leaned over the edge of the bank, he was shocked to see that it was a man, floating face down, his overcoat snagged on a tree branch. Despite the poor visibility, it was obvious the man had been shot, the gaping hole in the back of his neck was unmistakable. The police presence in the area had stepped up in recent weeks. The hairs on the back of Laci's neck rose, fear filled his belly, and he instinctively knew that he needed to get the hell out of there as quickly as possible, to avoid a confrontation with the police, in case they believed that he too was a refugee. Gathering his belongings, Laci darted away from the stream, moving cautiously through the thickest part of the woodland as quietly as possible.

Sounds of merriment wafted through the trees. Men laughing and joking, a few clear words registering in Laci's brain: rings, watches, money. Stolen items from the poor unsuspecting victims.

"Did you see the look on that young guy's face before I popped him? He never saw it coming."

More laughter, clearer this time, as Laci realised the patrol was very close. Propping his pannier against a large oak, he slung his rifle over his shoulder and clambered up the tree, settling into the bushy canopy halfway up. Crouching between the branches and holding his breath, he waited silently for the danger to pass. As the voices grew louder Laci cautiously peered down, looking in the direction of the laughter, and spied four armed policemen walking about two hundred metres to the right of his refuge, heading in the direction of Jánossomorja. Laci remained in the safe arms of the oak for longer than was necessary but was too scared to move. Closing his eyes, he crossed himself, praying soundlessly for his dead horse, for God's forgiveness, and for a safe journey home. Dangling his legs from a branch, Laci waited for the cramps in his legs to ease before sliding down from his haven. The pannier was where he left it, which suggested that the patrol was not as close as he'd first thought—either that or the police hadn't noticed it, too preoccupied with their revelry.

Thankful that home was in the opposite direction from where the police were headed, Laci ran for about a kilometre, keen to create as much distance as possible between himself and the patrol. As he slowed to catch his breath, the final words he heard from the police rang through his mind. A young guy. Yet the man in the stream had whitish grey hair. Were there more people travelling with the old man? Did any survive? Would anyone need help? His conscience forced him back to the stream. The darkness grew blacker amid the ancient trees, but soon he spotted what appeared to be boulders, two side-by-side and then further along another three clumped together. A sinking feeling gripped him. As he approached, Laci knew he found the guy who was taken by surprise by his executioner. The young man lay dead beside a pretty girl who stared sightlessly up at the stars.

***

Natália's peaceful slumber was shattered by loud voices, a commotion that reverberated throughout the hotel. Rolling over onto her side and pulling the blanket up over her head she tried to doze off again. It was no use. The disturbance persisted. István was out like a light, on his back, snoring. A carafe of red wine with dinner usually had that effect on him. Shaking her husband's shoulder, she urged him to get up and see what was going on. István grudgingly propped himself up on one elbow, rubbed the sleep from his eyes and asked, "What time is it? Have we overslept?"

"It's still dark. Can't you hear the voices downstairs? Something must be wrong. You need to go down and find out what's happening."

István reached for his watch, noted that it was 11.30pm, dropped back onto his pillow and told Natália to go back to sleep. They had several hours before they needed to be up and gone. But his pesky wife persisted.

She threw off the blanket, got up and flicked on the light switch, transforming the cosy sheath of darkness into bright daylight. István growled, opened one eye, and saw Natália standing over him, hands on hips.

"Come on, István. Something's wrong," she urged her husband.

István noted the panic in her voice. Acknowledging that the racket was unusual, he pulled on his trousers, threw on his coat, instructed Natália to remain in their room until he returned, then ran down the stairs. The proprietor, his wife and some of the other guests were in a huddle in the middle of the dining room. A teenage boy of about nineteen was at the centre of the group, sitting at a small table, clearly distressed, the others talking over one another.

"Hey, what's going on?" István asked in a loud, stern voice. "People are trying to sleep."

Everyone stopped babbling and stared at the intruder. The proprietor recognised István from earlier that evening, walked over to him and replied, "There's been a shooting at the edge of the forest a few kilometres out of town. Our son, Laci, was on his way home from a hunting trip when he stopped at the stream alongside the forest. When he knelt at the bank to fill his canteen with water, he saw an old man, face down in the stream. His coat had snagged on a large branch overhanging the bank and he was just floating there."

Before the proprietor had a chance to say anything else, István hurried over to the boy, grabbed him by the shoulders and asked him if he saw anyone else. Laci stopped shaking and stared at István, wide eyed, still in shock.

"It's really important. Did you see anyone else?" István pleaded, trying to keep calm, not wanting to scare the lad.

The other guests stopped talking, surprised by the urgency in István's voice. Laci wiped his nose on his sleeve. His mother rushed over with a wet flannel, deftly wiped his face, then handed him a small glass of Pálinka, the strongest liquor in the house, urging him to drink it to calm his nerves. He gulped it down quickly, looked back at István, and relayed his story again to his new audience.

"A boar came out of nowhere and ran straight into Poros, my horse. I was thrown clear but when I came to, my poor Poros was in terrible pain, crippled from that lousy beast. I did what I had to do; God rest his soul.

Realising that I had a long journey home on foot I headed to the stream to fill my canteen when I saw the old man floating face down in the water, his coat caught on a low hanging branch. I could see that he had been shot. I've never seen a dead person before," Laci paused, overcome with memories of the gruesome scene that he had witnessed, and started crying again.

"It's alright, son. You're safe now. Tell the man the rest of the story," the innkeeper said.

Laci took a deep breath, composed himself, and then continued, "I was terrified in case the police were still around—they might have thought that I was one of the refugees. Then I heard them. The murdering bastards. Laughing and joking about what they stole. But when one of them bragged about a young guy that he killed I knew there were more victims, perhaps some needing help. About a kilometre further upstream I saw a couple of people lying on the ground, a younger man, and what looked like his girl-friend. I saw that they had been shot. The girl's eyes were staring up at me. When I glanced around there were another two men and a woman on the ground a few metres away. I didn't go over to check but guessed they were dead, too, so I just got the hell out of there."

Laci started to tremble again, the shock not yet worn off, images of the dead still raw in his mind. His mother pressed another glass of Pálinka into his hand.

"It's the police all right!" one of the guests piped up. "It's not surprising, so close to the border. Everyone knows the patrols are heavier in this area. Some of them are rogues, shooting first, not bothering to ask questions. Sometimes they rape the women before killing them. Then they steal all their possessions. It's a sport to them and there's nothing we can do about it."

"The poor souls must have been ambushed," the proprietor said reverently.

Everyone slowly drifted back to their rooms, murmuring prayers for the deceased. These were harsh times. Laci's mother whispered to him and, as he rose to leave the dining room, he looked back at István, who stood frozen on the spot, visibly upset.

The blood had drained from István's face. Dizziness swept over him, his knees like jelly. Six people. The boy counted four men and two women, the same number as János' travelling party. Spying the Pálinka on the sideboard, he staggered over and poured himself a decent nip, swallowed it, then poured another, downing it quickly to steady himself. His hands were shaking. Leaning against the sideboard for support, István felt the alcohol warming his throat, chest, and stomach. The dizziness slowly abated. Still reeling from this horrific news, István wondered how he could possibly tell Natália. No. He wouldn't. It was too distressing. Best to keep her ignorant of this revelation.

Fabricating a story in his mind to explain the disturbance that Natália had insisted he investigate, István turned towards the stairs to head back to the bedroom when he saw Natália sitting on the bottom step, head in her hands, weeping. How long had she been there? Had she heard Laci's story? The distraught look in her tear-filled eyes as she glanced up at István spoke volumes. She too believed that Laci had stumbled upon János and his companions. István slumped beside Natália, hugged her tightly, and murmured soothing words to comfort her. Eventually she stopped crying and wiped her eyes on the sleeve of her coat, taking a few deep breaths. István stood, clutched Natália's right hand and walked up the stairs to their room, towing his wife behind him. Once inside, with the door closed, Natália pressed her face against István's chest, fresh tears springing to her eyes.

"János is gone. He's dead. I know it's him," she stammered, her words muffled against István's coat.

He squeezed her tightly, trying to protect her and said, "We don't know that for sure. It could be anyone."

He didn't sound very convincing, and the sinking feeling in the pit of his stomach told him that Natália was most probably right. The thought of his best friend lying murdered in the forest for the wild boars to feast upon brought tears to his own eyes. A wave of nausea flushed through him. Releasing Natália from his embrace, István fled down the corridor to the bathroom and threw up in the sink. He stayed there, bent over for a few minutes, clutching the sides of the basin, and crying for his friend. Why did János abandon him, placing his trust in complete strangers? If only he'd stayed, he would still be alive. But it was too late. There was nothing István could do now but focus his attention on protecting his beloved Natália. As he splashed water onto his face and rinsed his mouth out his thoughts turned to their precarious situation. István and Natália were heading for the border, travelling in the same direction as János and his party. Were the police still in the forest? Had they moved on to another area? How could he find out? Should they stick to their plan? Gambling with Natália's life was out of the question. But what should they do? Perhaps they should lie low for another day. Torn between staying and moving on, István returned to their room, agitated and undecided. Natália was sitting on the bed, hunched over the map.

"I'm not going anywhere near that forest!" she announced with authority as she heard István close the door behind him.

Natália appeared composed. The tears had dried on her face and a steely resolve was noticeable in her voice. She had not previously taken much notice of István's escape route but was now fully engrossed in plotting alternative paths to the border. István was slightly taken aback, surprised by Natália's newfound assertiveness. He breathed a sigh of relief in her interest to review their next move. It gave him time to rethink their options.

"I'm not keen to go that way either."

István was a little bewildered that Natália had not suggested that they take their chances on returning to Budapest, or hiding out in Szarvas with her family, but that she was instead choosing to continue the dangerous journey to freedom, despite the recent revelation of the forest murders. His adoration for this courageous woman grew ten-fold, knowing he didn't deserve her loyalty. Allowing Natália to take charge of their situation if it made her feel better, he flopped onto the edge of the bed and peered over her shoulder as she explained, "Look here." She pointed to her suggested route. "We can skirt town and head due west, just south of Jánossomorja, to the Austrian town of Hansaghof. It's another day's journey through fields, and it will probably be slow going, but it's nowhere near any other towns. I feel it poses the least risk. But we need to go soon. I don't feel safe here anymore. Those murderous policemen may still be prowling around."

István smiled warmly at his beautiful wife, whose brows were creased and deadly serious, then leaned over and kissed her gently on the mouth, saying, "Did I tell you recently how much I love you?"

Natália just blinked at him in surprise. Refocussing on her suggestion he remarked in a serious tone, "I think that's probably the safest option. Much of the land is sparse, with only fields and a couple of farmhouses dotted about. There's no obvious place from which we could be ambushed, apart from perhaps any wooded areas, but there's nothing significant like that marked on the map. We'll just have to remain alert if we approach the woodlands. A good plan, my clever beauty."

István kissed her on the nose, his heart a little lighter at having agreed upon the revised plan.

Natália, still visibly shaken, touched István's arm, held his gaze, and with a resoluteness he rarely witnessed pronounced, "From now on István, all our decisions—regardless of how trivial—will be discussed and settled together. We're a team. Equal partners in this marriage."

István nodded and replied quietly, "Agreed."

When she released her grip on his arm, she became pensive, then remarked tentatively, "It could have been us. We could have followed János and the others into the forest and we'd be dead too."

István nodded again, having thought the same thing when he threw up in the bathroom. Looking down at her ruby ring, twisting it around her finger in contemplation, Natália said, "We've been extraordinarily lucky so far. Firstly, after the accident with the milk truck. We could have died or been injured far more seriously. We've successfully evaded the police the whole time we've been on the run, even when we were forced to return to Budapest to convalesce, and now, we have avoided death because we chose to part company with János. I'm starting to think that it's not just Saint Christopher that's been safeguarding us. The myth about this magical ring is possibly not a myth at all. Perhaps it really has shielded us from harm."

"My grandmother thought it was special, and I do too. Let's test our luck a little further and make a run for the border." István replied, kissing the top of head.

It was 2 am. Natália hastily washed, dressed, packed her satchel, and was ready to depart. István popped into the kitchen looking for some food for the journey. The staples of bread, cheese and homemade salami were always in the pantry, provisions they would have eaten at breakfast, so he was not in the least bit guilty about taking what they needed. He wrapped the supplies in a napkin, stuffed the bundle into his bag, and met Natália in the foyer.

"Ready, love?" István asked.

"Ready as I'll ever be."

Wrapping the scarf tightly over her head, she pulled on her gloves and stepped outside. Blessed again by a dry, cloudless sky, she prayed as she clutched the ruby on her left hand; for strength, courage, and protection on this last leg of the journey, for their safe crossing into Hansaghof, and for freedom. István extended his arm, linking it with Natália's, and stepping out in the direction of Hansaghof with renewed purpose.

***

News reports flooded into the police station at Mosonmagyaróvár every day of the week. The station had become a new hub of intelligence under the leadership of Viktor Molnár. The headquarters in Győr continued ferreting out refugees to the east and south of the region, whilst the Mosonmagyaróvár police stepped up surveillance closer to the border, as far north as Hegyeshalom and as far south as Acsalag. No one would escape the country if Viktor Molnár had anything to do with it.

Thoughts of Katarina were eradicated from his mind the minute Viktor arrived at the Mosonmagyaróvár police station. The brief lapse in professionalism that he had succumbed to in Komárom was behind him and would not be repeated. Viktor's hunger for success, his loyalty to the regime, and his resolve to demonstrate his worth to the Commissioner of Police in Budapest were of far greater importance than any woman. His ambition was boundless. As the most senior officer, he quickly took charge of the station, organising the staff into teams: patrols dedicated to outlying areas, incident room officers who coordinated the patrols and collated the information received from the field, and junior officers to type up the reports—a replica of his successful organisation of the officers in Győr. It was a sizeable operation, covering a wide area, and—more significantly—very close to the Austrian border. The two junior officers delegated to carry out the administrative tasks were both female. The older of the two, a brunette in her late twenties, had flirted with Viktor when she was first introduced to him, but he didn't react as she had hoped. Instead, his stern gaze was enough to rebuke her advances.

As soon as he arrived at his new headquarters, Viktor instructed the incident room supervisor to brief all the patrols that they should be on the lookout for three young adults travelling together, two men and a woman, all suspected of treason. Detailed descriptions were provided, with strict instructions that Viktor himself wished to interrogate the suspects as soon as they were apprehended. Viktor was not entirely sure why these three had crept under his skin. Perhaps it was because the woman was strikingly attractive and audacious enough to raise her eyebrow at him, questioning his gaze. There was something about her, though. A defiance that tweaked his interest.

A bundle of reports was placed on Viktor's desk a little while before he entered his office the morning after he arrived at Mosonmagyaróvár. Shrugging off his coat he sat down behind his desk, noting that a fresh cup of coffee sat beside the neatly organised files. He smiled inwardly. This local team had obviously been briefed by the acting senior officer in Győr as to Viktor's expectations and appetites. He revelled in the respect he was shown. His power and status were clear.

Sipping his coffee, he picked up the first file and read through the account of two couples travelling together. They were in their mid-fifties, well-groomed, with wads of cash and expensive jewellery hidden in the linings of their coats. It was typical of fleeing women to hide their most prized family heirlooms within their clothing. The officers were wise to this practice. A good catch then, Viktor thought. He continued reading the report and was alarmed to discover that after a brief exchange, one of the men had taken a revolver from his coat pocket, threatening the officer who had detained them. The escapees were quickly shot from behind by the officer's comrade. Ah, a good result after all, Viktor thought. He made a mental note to discuss this case with the supervising officer, to ensure all police officers travelled in pairs from now on, as a precaution. The situation could have ended very differently had the policeman been alone during the altercation. Viktor exempted himself from working with a partner. His superior intellect and physical strength were no match for the frightened people running for their lives, but he wanted minimal casualties in his teams.

Casting the file aside, Viktor swallowed the last dregs of his coffee and opened the next file. His eyes flashed with interest, engrossed in the report of an ambush that had taken place in the oak forest beside a stream a few kilometres west of Lébény. Four men and two women had been shot as they attempted to cross the stream. One couple was younger than the others. Good. Had three of the traitors been of a similar age he may have lost his prey. He continued scanning the files over the next hour, satisfied that in the past twenty-four hours alone his men had successfully thwarted the plans of fifteen defectors. But what of the three that eluded had him in Komárom? The woman's confidence and challenging gaze crept back into his mind. There was still no word of their whereabouts. Viktor walked out of his office and spoke sternly to the incident room supervisor, László Fekete. László was a veteran in the force. He had overseen the station in his hometown of Mosonmagyaróvár for over a decade, until this younger upstart from Győr pulled rank and demoted him to the position of incident room supervisor. It rankled to be demeaned in front of his men. László contacted an old colleague in Budapest, seeking validation about Viktor's rank, and was told in no uncertain terms to toe the line. Viktor Molnár was well respected by the hierarchy and was not someone to be crossed.

"Has there been any word on the three traitors I asked you about when I arrived?"

"No, sir. None of the patrols have encountered anyone fitting their description," László replied, concerned that his superior officer appeared agitated.

"Well find them!" Viktor snapped. "They can't have disappeared into thin air. They're travelling on foot. How far can they get, man? I want the area between Mosonszolnok and Acsalag scoured. I want every barn checked, every farmer interrogated, every blade of grass swept over. Find them."

The buzz of activity within the department ceased instantly. All eyes were on László Fekete. No one had ever spoken to their boss in that manner before. László bristled at being humiliated in such a way. Nevertheless, he maintained his decorum, swallowed his pride, and replied compliantly, "We will double our efforts, Sir."

And with that pronouncement László turned to the coordinator of the patrol teams. After a brief discussion about the most likely route the party would have taken from Komárom, it was decided to redirect two additional teams to continue the search. László returned to his desk, silently speculating about what these three people could have done to Viktor to cause such a witch-hunt.

A large map of the district hung on the wall behind Viktor's large timber desk. He stared at it for several minutes when he returned to his office, furious that the defectors he sought had seemingly vanished. He traced three possible routes they could have taken, then took a gamble on which one was the most likely. Unconvinced by the local team's capabilities or sense of urgency, Viktor decided to take matters into his own hands.

CHAPTER 22

The twinkling stars had faded away and the cloudless sky was short lived as dawn morphed into daylight and grey clouds gathered, masking the promise of a clear day. Natália shivered, more from the ominous change in the weather than from the cold. The air pinched her cheeks, her eyes watering from the chill, yet she was perspiring under her heavy clothing. The couple had been walking for five hours. Natália's leg had strengthened well with all the recent exercise, yet twinges of pain persisted. Not wanting to sound weak, she trudged on for a while longer, until her growling stomach forced her to suggest they stop for a short rest and a snack. István had set a steady pace, walking with purpose, willing the border to approach as fast as possible.

Since leaving Lébény, their journey had been uneventful, just as Natália had prayed. Passing a few properties, witnessing the daily chores of farmers attending to livestock, fetching water from wells, and chopping wood, created a sense of calm—a normality that seemed aeons from the danger they were fleeing. The peace in the countryside was uplifting, providing much needed reassurance that the route they had decided to take was the right one.

It was still early morning. The sun was not yet high enough in the sky to melt the thin patches of snow that glittered like diamonds where the few rays that escaped the clouds kissed the tiny flakes. Scouring the countryside, István looked for a suitable place to shelter, rest, and breakfast on the provisions that he had taken from the inn.

Despite the harsh times, where many peasants faced starvation, István was constantly amazed and grateful for the kindness he and Natália were shown by complete strangers. It was obvious that they were refugees. Yet the generosity they received in each town they passed through, an extra piece of cheese or heel of bread to see them through the day, was heart-warming. Sadness drifted into István's soul, a dark cloak of melancholy that gripped him like a vice. Sadness that they were leaving these salt-of-the-earth, hardworking Hungarians who deserved so much more than the failed promises of the ruthless Communists. Sadness that they were forced to abandon Hungary, with its crystal-clear streams and woodlands bursting with magnificent oaks, hornbeams, poplars, and willows. Sadness that he was the reason Natália would never see her family again, that she must forego her sister's wedding, that she would never meet the nieces and nephews who were yet to enter the world, that she could never give comfort to her beloved father in his old age. But it was too late to brood on what was now lost to them. Shaking his head to dispense with these gloomy thoughts István sighed and breathed in deeply, savouring the familiar smells of the countryside, before focussing on the job at hand.

There really wasn't anywhere appropriate to stop other than a barn a few hundred metres to the right of their intended route. It was a minor deviation. István pointed in its direction and moved towards the struc-ture. He was still not in the mood for chatting. Natália sensed his need for solitude and followed willingly without question. A brief respite from the miserable weather was very welcome. Within half an hour, they had settled themselves onto the straw covered ground, enjoying the unde-manding company of the lone cow and two horses that had mooed and whinnied as they entered the barn. It was cosy inside, and the instant relief from the cold wind was comforting, affording a deep sense of secu-rity that Natália hadn't felt in days. She removed her scarf, gloves, and coat, and settled back against a stack of hay bales, waiting for her husband to serve breakfast. She hadn't realised how exhausted she felt. Not just from trekking through the fields for the last few hours, but from the pent-up tension that persisted since hearing the dreadful news of János' death. Tears welled up, threatening to burst through her toughened façade whenever she thought of her dear friend. It took all her strength to stop them from spilling down her cheeks. Determined that death would not be their fate, Natália resolved to bury all thoughts of János, the shocking description of the vicious way he was killed pushed to the far recesses of her mind. Looking across at her husband, Natália watched as he busily unpacked the food. Using a hay bale as a table, István carefully placed the napkin onto the straw, then divided the bread, cheese, and salami into four portions, two for the morning and two for the afternoon. Carefully, he passed Natália her portion, then devoured his serve with such gusto that she laughed heartily.

"I thought I was the hungry one," she exclaimed, the mouthful of bread muffling her words. Within minutes István was licking his fingers. He reached for the water flask and drank deeply, washing down the dry bread-crumbs that caught in his throat.

"I didn't realise how famished I was until we stopped for a break," he replied, smiling broadly as he passed the water flask to Natália, wiping the residual moisture from his lips with the back of his hand. The morning sickness that plagued Natália each day since leaving Budapest had waned, much to her relief. The fresh bread, buttery cheese, and spicy salami were delicious. She savoured every bite, taking her time. In no hurry to leave the comfort of the barn, she sipped the water slowly, paused, then sipped some more. The flask was handed back to István, almost empty. Walking to the entrance of the barn, István checked the area for a stream or well, hoping to fill the flask before continuing their journey.

"Wait here, love. I'll fill this before we head off."

István drank the last drops from the flask before disappearing outside. The comforting smell of the farm animals, the soft bed of hay, and a satis-fied belly left Natália feeling drowsy. Closing her eyes involuntarily, she soon fell into a deep sleep. A vision of her father appeared in her mind. At first it was just his face, very serene, gazing up toward the heavens. A thin ray of white light caught the side of his face and the vision altered. He was alone, dressed in his best dark brown woollen suit that he only wore on special occasions. Kneeling in the front pew of the Catholic church in Szarvas, he looked up at the statue of Christ on the cross and prayed. His lips were moving but she couldn't hear the words, yet instinctively knew he prayed to God for her safe passage to Austria. Her father had begged her not to leave Hungary when she last spoke with him, fearful that his favourite child could be captured, imprisoned or worse. It broke her heart to leave him, knowing she would never see or hear from him again. But her place was beside her husband, the man she loved and who she promised to cherish for the rest of her life. The image of her father slowly faded. She yearned to embrace him one last time. He rose from the pew and turned to walk down the aisle toward the exit, his image fading as he stepped out into the sunshine. A lone tear escaped the corner of her right eye, trickling down her cheek.

The animals barely stirred when the farmer entered the barn.

"Well, what have we here, Dália?" he asked the cow when he saw the sleeping woman in the far corner of the barn. The horses greeted the farmer, snorting and stamping their hooves, expecting their breakfast. The cow just looked at the old man with large, limpid eyes, showing no signs of alarm.

The farmer walked to where the hay bales were stacked, knelt in front of Natália, and spoke loudly enough to wake her, "Hello, my dear. Will you be staying long?"

Natália opened her eyes and shrieked at the man crouched two feet in front of her.

"Don't be scared, young lady, I won't harm you," the farmer said in a soft, reassuring tone, stepping back a few paces to show he was no threat.

Noticing the brilliant ruby and gold wedding ring on her finger he wondered if the woman was traveling alone or with her husband. Natália tried to scuttle away from the man, but realised her back was up against the bales and that she had nowhere to go. Before the farmer had a chance to ask Natália any further questions, István returned, having heard Natália's cry, and launched himself at the poor defenceless man. After a brief scuffle and much protesting on the part of the farmer, István let him go. The men sat eyeing each other for a few minutes, regaining their breath, when the farmer said indignantly, "Who do you think you are, attacking me in my own barn?"

"I'm sorry, sir. I heard my wife scream, saw you standing in front of her and, well, it was just an instant reaction," István replied, dusting himself down as he stood.

Looking back at Natália, the farmer smiled warmly as he rose to his knees, steadying himself before standing. He was about a foot shorter than

István, with a weathered, deeply wrinkled face that made him appear much older than his forty-five years.

"I suppose I would have acted the same way if this gorgeous creature was my wife," the farmer chuckled. "What brings the two of you to my remote farm?" he asked as he brushed the hay from his overalls.

István's face went blank as he tried to think of a good reason for sheltering in the barn. The farmer noticed István's hesitation and continued, "No need to answer that. I think I know. The police have been traipsing through this region on and off for the last few weeks, looking for what they call traitors, revolutionaries that need to be brought to justice. It's a hazard of living so close to the border. I've been accused more than once of harbouring refugees, yet they never find anyone on my property. I'm a Hungarian, not a Communist. Sheltering people who have the courage to seek a better life, helping them to become invisible until the patrols pass, is the patriotic Hungarian way," the farmer proudly announced, then rubbed his chin and said, "I'd leave Hungary, too, given the chance. But sadly, my wife won't hear of it."

István relaxed a little, sizing up the man, wondering if he was being truthful.

"Come, come inside the house for a hot cup of coffee," he said as he extended his hand to Natália, helping her up. "My, but your beautiful. You're a very lucky man, mister."

Natália straightened her clothing, picking out the strands of straw that had tangled into her curls, trying to make herself look presentable. Introductions were made as they followed the cheerful man across the field towards the farmhouse. It was a modest dwelling of three or possibly four rooms, István thought. Smoke wafted out the chimney before quickly dissipating in the strong breeze. The place was inviting, homely. István noticed the farmer walked with a slight limp, favouring his right leg. He thought better than to ask what had happened, wandering vaguely if it might have been a farm accident. As they entered the kitchen, the kettle was boiling on the open hearth. It was such a welcome sight. Natália gravitated to the fire, extending her hands over the flame, turning them slowly, allowing the heat to envelop her, when a small, rotund, stern-looking woman appeared in the doorway.

"Look what I found in the barn, Erzsi," Markos exclaimed to his wife, grinning wickedly. "Fetch us all a cup of coffee and bring some of that cake you baked yesterday. These weary travellers need some fattening up."

Erzsi looked closely at her husband and scowled with a gaze that rebuked him for bringing stray wanderers into their home again. Sensing nothing untoward about the newcomers she sniffed audibly then went about her business of slicing cake and pouring coffee. Natália felt relaxed enough in the company of these country folk to tell them a little of their story. Not so much the reason they needed to flee, that was too dangerous a topic, but their hopes and dreams for a future in a democratic society. They all agreed that life was much harsher under the Communist regime. István explained the ridiculous quotas at the factory and the wanton disregard for the men's safety. News such as this from the city was a rarity for country folk such as Markos. He leant forward, hanging on every word from these city dwellers, keen to hear the latest turn of events. The most difficult aspect of the Communist doctrine, Erzsi chimed in, was the need to renounce their faith.

"I can't just turn my back on God because some Communist thug in Budapest says I must," she said defiantly, looking up at a crucifix on the wall above the kitchen door whilst crossing herself.

István agreed wholeheartedly, then reached across the table and picked up a second slice of apple cake, his eyes twinkling mischievously at Erzsi, before taking a large bite and sighing in utter delight.

"Mmm, this is the best apple cake I've ever had in my life. Sorry, love," he apologised to Natália, who laughed at her husband, agreed that it was delicious, and thanked Erzsi again for sharing their food with strangers.

István was licking the crumbs from his fingers when a young man burst into the kitchen, visibly shaken. Zoli was Markos' youngest son. Still living at home at twenty years of age, he was a much-needed farm hand, since his older brother had left home the year before to seek his fortune in Budapest. Everyone stopped speaking and all eyes turned to Zoli as he babbled incoherently, trying to catch his breath in between words.

"Slow down, Zoli. Erzsi, fetch him a glass of water. Here, take a seat son. What's wrong?" Markos asked, concern creeping into his voice.

Erzsi handed her boy the water and watched him drink half before he placed the glass on the table, steadied himself, then began to describe what he had just witnessed.

"I delivered the milk to Mrs Tóth as usual, but as I was leaving through the back door, I saw a man riding a motorbike down the path in the direction of the house. He parked the bike at the front gate, hopped off, took his helmet off, and walked to the front door. He looked important. The way he was dressed, with his long black coat and leather gloves, I could tell he was not from around here. He looked like someone from the city, perhaps an official. So, I hid at the back of the house hoping to hear why he was here. The man said something about fugitives, two men and a woman, and demanded to know if Mrs Tóth had seen the trio he described. He spoke so loudly that poor old Mrs Tóth became very upset. She denied seeing any strangers, but the man was not satisfied. He must have forced his way into the house as I heard him banging doors as he went from room to room, searching the place. Mrs Tóth explained that she was on her own, that Mr Tóth was recovering in the hospital after a recent heart attack and said that she had no knowledge of any fugitives and would not open the door to any unknown visitors given that she was on her own. The man seemed to accept what she told him and left as briskly as he'd arrived. Once the motorbike picked up speed and he headed back to the main road, I ran home to let you know. He may come here asking the same questions."

It was only when Zoli finished speaking, drew breath and relaxed a little that he registered two strangers sitting at the end of the table. He handed his empty glass to his mother and frowned at her inquiringly.

"Well done, son. There's no trio here, but just to be on the safe side we might hide our visitors here for a while."

Markos stood, motioning to István to follow him out through the back door, back to the barn. Natália's heart skipped a beat after Zoli's news. She froze in her seat, her mind racing. They had been a trio before János was killed. Was it a coincidence? She didn't believe in coincidences. When or where could they have been spotted by the police? If they were in fact on the police radar, why hadn't they already been apprehended? It didn't make sense. Then she recalled the handsome man sitting alone in the dining room in Komárom. She had caught him staring intently at her when they were eating their dinner. She had even raised her eyebrow at him questioningly, assuming he was flirting with her. Could he be the man Zoli just described? Natália suddenly felt sick.

"Come on, Natália," István called over his shoulder.

Snapping back to the present, Natália quickly got up and ran after the men, terrified that they were being pursued by the authorities. Once inside the barn, Markos told István to gather all their belongings and wait by the horses. He then proceeded to lead the cow from her pen, murmuring soothing words to calm the animal. Pulling a rake off the rack on the wall, Markos swept aside the hay on the floor, revealing a trap door, which he heaved open.

"You can hide in here until it's safe to leave. There's a ladder that leads down into a small storage cellar." Looking at Natália's ashen face, Markos continued, "I promise there are no rats down there. It's perfectly safe. Keep very still and very quiet until I return to let you out."

The couple did as Markos instructed, placing their trust in the stranger. It was clear he had done this before. Once the couple descended the stairs, Markos replaced the trap door, swept the hay over it, and then led the cow back into her pen. Walking over to where the hay bales were stacked, he picked up a bale and scattered it around the pen, leaving half in front of the cow. Dália stood on top of the concealed door, contentedly munching on the fresh hay as if nothing unusual had happened. Natália and István sat in a corner of their hiding place, István's arm around Natália's shoulders. She was trembling with fear, too scared to let István know her thoughts about the man from the hotel.

By the time Markos returned to the house, Erzsi had washed and put away the cake plates and coffee cups, leaving no trace of the visitors. The household resumed their daily chores: Zoli chopping wood for the hearth, Erzsi making bread, and Markos fixing a small leak in the roof. Not fifteen minutes had elapsed since Zoli returned home from Mrs Tóth's house, then there was the faint buzzing sound of a motorbike headed their way. Erzsi heard the bike pull up and the engine cut before a pounding on their front door reverberated throughout the house. She put down her rolling pin, walked to the front of the house and opened the door, wiping her hands on her well-worn apron.

"May I help you?" she asked politely.

The young man standing before her was very handsome, with dark, curly hair that was a little unruly after removing the motorbike helmet. He was dressed in a good quality black woollen coat, with black leather gloves, the exact description of the man Zoli had spoken of. His eyes held a steely glint that made Erzsi shiver involuntarily. The stranger flashed a badge at her and tucked it back into the inside pocket of his coat before she had a chance to read it, assuming a peasant such as her would be illiterate.

"I'm on official police business. I'm searching for three fugitives who are suspected of passing through this region. Two men and a woman, all in their mid to late twenties. They are smartly dressed, perhaps a little dishevelled from travelling. The woman has shoulder length, wavy brown hair and is wearing a wedding ring. She is obviously married to one of the men. Both men have dark hair, but one has a receding hairline and is older than his friend. Have you seen any outsiders fitting this description?"

Before Erzsi had thought of a suitable reply, a voice boomed out, "Hey, Erzsi! Do we have visitors?" Markos climbed down the ladder, making his way to the front of the house, where he saw a tall, well-built man standing at the door, looking rather menacing. Markos clutched his hammer for reassurance in case there was trouble.

"Viktor Molnár, Captain of the Győr Police Headquarters, here on an official police matter. I was just asking your wife if you'd seen any strangers pass this way," Viktor stated brusquely.

Markos was about to reply when Viktor turned back to Erzsi and asked, "Well? Have you seen them or not?"

"No sir. But then we don't get out much these days, what with all the never-ending chores and with only one son left to help run the farm," Erzsi replied as calmly as she could, despite being intimidated by the man looming over her. She felt her cheeks burn and prayed to God that she sounded convincing.

"That's right, Captain," Markos chimed in. "We've not seen any strangers around here." The farmer spoke too quickly, ringing alarm bells in Viktor's head.

"Well, you won't mind if I take a look around, then," Viktor replied, as he pushed past Erzsi and commenced the search.

Nothing appeared out of place in the sitting room or the two bedrooms. Nevertheless, Viktor's intuition that was almost always spot on, egged him on further. When he entered the kitchen, he noticed bits of straw on the floor under the dining table.

"How is it that the rest of the house is spotless, yet there's straw on the floor in the kitchen?"

"Oh, that'll be Zoli, our son. He was feeding the animals in the barn a little while ago and must have brought the straw in on his clothing. He's a bit careless like that," Erzsi replied offhandedly, clicking her tongue in disapproval.

"Take me to the barn," Viktor snapped back, staring ferociously at Markos, his temper rising, sensing something amiss.

Erzsi went back to her breadmaking, appearing untroubled by the officer's gruffness, whilst inwardly her stomach was knotted with fear. Markos led Viktor out through the back door, silence a thick wedge between the men. As they entered the barn, the strong smell of animals, manure, and hay affronted Viktor. He gagged and reached for the crisp white handkerchief in his coat pocket, then covered his nose and mouth to mask the offensive odours. Viktor loathed these peasants, and everything associated with farming. They were a necessity to the nation, but one that he preferred not to associate with. However, his quest to locate the trio he had seen in Komárom had become an obsession that he refused to surrender. Markos waited by the door, watching anxiously as Viktor approached the pen where Dália happily munched the fresh hay, oblivious to the visitor. It was the smaller of the two pens and the cow filled the space with little extra room to move about. Viktor looked around, then walked over to the larger pen where the horses were snorting, detecting an alien presence. Viktor peered inside. Not satisfied with a cursory glance, he decided to take a closer look. The horses became more agitated when Viktor opened the stable gate and approached them. The male horse, two hands taller than the female, stamped his hooves and tossed his head back, ears flat and eyes wild, his whinnying intensifying. Suddenly, the horse reared up, striking Viktor on the right shoulder, forcing him to fall to the ground. Markos rushed into the pen to calm his horse, grabbed his long mane, and steered him to the furthermost corner of the pen, all the while murmuring soothing words to settle him down before he trampled the fallen officer. Markos was keenly aware of the fierce repercussions for his entire family if the officer was badly hurt.

Hearing the scuffle above ground from their basement hideout, Natália gasped. István instinctively placed a hand over her mouth to silence her, cradling her head against his chest. They were both trembling and holding their breath to keep as quiet as possible, listening intently for any sign of the trap door being forced open.

Viktor quickly jumped up, clutching his injured shoulder, and rushed out of the barn, feeling rattled and humiliated.

"That animal should be shot. It could have killed me," he roared, furious that the horse had got the better of him.

He drew his revolver from the inside pocket of his coat, strode back into the barn and raised the gun, but before he could take aim at the horse, Markos dashed forward, placing himself between Victor and the animal, arms outstretched, begging for his horse's life.

"Please, Sir, don't shoot. Please. I need him on the farm. We can't manage without our workhorses."

Viktor hesitated for a moment then slowly lowered the gun, his rage subsiding as his dignity was restored as Markos spoke subserviently, pleading for mercy from the powerful man.

"As I said before, we don't get many visitors here, and no one that's interested in the horses. They're not used to strangers."

Markos' attempt to mollify the captain seemed to be working. He added, "Can I have my wife tend to your shoulder?"

"That won't be necessary. It's just bruised," Viktor replied curtly, making light of the injury that throbbed like hell, then barked a warning at Markos, "If I discover that you've been lying to me about harbouring traitors then I will personally return and kill every living thing on this property, including you and your family."

Viktor tucked his revolver back into his coat pocket, then strode briskly to where he had parked his motorbike, fastened his helmet, and rode off. Markos waited until he could no longer hear the whine of the bike's engine before he coaxed Dália away from her feast and out of the pen. He opened the trap door, hearing Natália squeak as a shaft of light penetrated the cellar, then climbed down the steps before collapsing into a heap on the floor opposite the couple huddled in the far corner. Relief washed over him as the realisation struck at the disastrous precipice he had just managed to claw his way back from. Markos made the sign of the cross and said a silent prayer.

"That was a close call. Too close for my liking. I've never seen that police captain before. He is truly evil incarnate." Seeing that Natália was crying, he tried reassuring her, "It's alright, he's gone. You're safe now." He crossed himself again, then briefly described the events that had unfolded after the officer arrived, and the threats the man had made against his family.

"I don't think you should linger here any longer. It's best that you get on your way as soon as possible. I'll ask Erzsi to put a small food hamper together, which should see you through to the nearest town across the border. It's not far now. Wait here until I come back."

István and Natália had listened in silence to Markos' shocking account of what took place in the barn. Both were horrified at the thought of what could have befallen them had it not been for Markos' bravery. They watched the farmer leave the cellar before Natália said quietly, "Another lucky escape."

"That may be so, but who is this trio that the captain seems so determined to capture?" István asked as he scratched his head in bewilderment.

"We were a trio before János was murdered," Natália whispered.

"You think the captain was looking for us?" István asked, his voice rising incredulously.

Natália proceeded to describe the evening in Komárom and her brief non-verbal exchange with the handsome man on the other side of the dining room.

"Of course, I can't be sure. But it could be him. Where else could we three have been identified as possible fugitives?" she said.

István ran a hand over his face, trying to recount their movements of the past few days, sighed loudly, and said, "Well, we'll never really know. As Markos said, we're close to the border, so we'll just have to make a run for it."

Markos promptly returned with the promised hamper. The couple clambered out of the storeroom, packed the parcel into Natália's satchel, then strode out into the persistent gloom. The men quickly discussed the quickest route to Hansaghof, just over the border. Natália hugged Markos, kissed his cheek, and thanked him for saving their lives. She stepped aside as István shook hands with the farmer, expressing his gratitude. The farmer smiled softly and said, "Good luck and may God see you to safety."

***

Viktor took his foot off the accelerator ten minutes after leaving the farm and pulled over to the side of the dirt road. He gingerly rubbed his shoulder. His heavy clothing had prevented a more serious injury, yet the pain he felt was excruciating. The impact from the horse's hoof had the full weight of the beast behind it, and he hoped his shoulder was not fractured. He would have it seen to when he returned to Mosonmagyaróvár, but that would have to wait for now. Viktor was convinced the farmer was hiding something or someone, and he was determined to discover what it was. Reaching into the travel compartment of the bike, he grabbed the binoculars and scanned the countryside surrounding the farm. Left to right, right to left, then back again. Zooming into the farmhouse he saw the farmer leaving the house with a parcel in his hand, walking back towards the barn. He kept his focus on the man as he entered the barn, waiting for what was to come. Three adults emerged a few minutes later. Viktor relaxed a little then snickered, "Got you!" vowing to return to make good on his promise of executing the lying peasant. The couple, however, were unknown to him. He was sure the trio he was searching for must have been hiding there. Keeping the binoculars steady, he watched the woman kiss the farmer's cheek, obviously in thanks for concealing them from the authorities. Then, as chance would have it, the woman stepped back as her partner shook hands with the farmer, turning to reveal her beautiful face and wavy brown hair. The same face that had stared directly at him, eyebrow raised, in the hotel dining room in Komárom. Shifting his focus onto the man beside her, he waited until he turned his head towards his wife. Viktor recognised him as the older of the two men in Komárom.

"So, no longer a trio," he muttered under his breath. "I wonder where the other man got to?" He lingered a little longer, focussing on the barn entrance in case the other man surfaced. Realising that it was futile, Viktor returned his gaze to the couple and watched as they strode off, heading west towards the border. Viktor felt elated, triumphant that his instincts had proved accurate. He hastily returned the binoculars to the storage compartment, fired up the bike, and took off down the road for a short distance before veering left, travelling in a wide arc, circling his prey. When he estimated he was about a kilometre ahead of the fugitives, he brought the bike to a stop near a stand of trees, perhaps five kilometres from the border. Hopping off the bike he manoeuvred it beside a large tree. He removed his helmet, placed it over the handlebars, grabbed the binoculars, and slung them over his left shoulder. There was no shortage of dry twigs and branches lying about, so he gathered a few leafy branches and draped them over the bike to conceal it before he ventured a few metres along the tree line, in search of the best spot to lie low and wait in ambush. Patience was not his forte. He busied himself by checking his revolver, loading two extra bullets into the chamber, before concealing it inside his coat. As he peered through the binoculars in the direction the couple were expected to materialise, Viktor mulled over the possible strategies. Kill both then strip them of their possessions? Kill the husband and spare the wife? The feistier these women were, the greater his sexual gratification. And he knew this young brunette would be feisty. Just thinking of her fighting back as he forced himself upon her was arousing. Viktor smiled; his decision made.

Concentrating on the landscape through the lenses pressed up against his eyes, Viktor's attention was heightened when something startled a flock of swallows. They took flight en masse from the trees to the right of where he was hiding. Viktor adjusted the angle of the binoculars to the base of the trees and spied a man and a woman emerge from the shadows, their dark clothing a stark contrast to the white dusting of snow on the branches and ground before them. The thrill of the chase coursed through Viktor's veins, increasing his heart rate. Mentally applauding his ingenuity in ferreting out this pair, Viktor slowly rose from his prostrate position and darted behind a tree, waiting for the couple to close the gap between them. He reached into his coat and pulled out the gun, cocked it in readiness, then brazenly walked towards the pair, gun aimed at István.

"We meet again, madam. What, may I ask, are you doing here, so far from Komárom?" Viktor addressed Natália directly with a cheeky grin, as if they were old acquaintances. She stopped dead in her tracks, instantly recognising the man from the dining room.

"Who are you?" István demanded. "What do you want from us?"

"I'm Captain Viktor Molnár of Győr Police Headquarters. Didn't you know there's a bounty on your heads? I almost had you in Komárom, but you got lucky and escaped my grasp. That won't be happening this time."

"We've done nothing wrong," István stammered, his mind furiously groping for the shred of an idea as to how they could escape unscathed.

"Well, that's where you're wrong. I wager that the two of you are trying to escape to Austria. You almost succeeded," Viktor chuckled, rather enjoying the confrontation.

"Listen, I know we are nothing more to you than statistics for your superiors. Take me prisoner and leave my innocent wife. It's my fault she's in this situation."

Viktor sighed, shook his head, laughed, and said, "So predictable. I have no intention of letting that feisty wife of yours go."

Natália was consumed with rage at the arrogance of the brute and was compelled to act. As she stepped forward István grabbed her arm to stop her, but she shrugged off his grip. Removing the glove on her left hand she spoke in a tone imbued with loathing, "I know what you officers want. We have cash, and this ruby and gold wedding ring is very valuable." She slid the ring off her finger, held it between her thumb and forefinger and extended her hand to show Viktor.

"I'm not interested in your trinkets. You must know that it's you I've been pursing as my prize," Viktor derided her, while keeping the gun pointed at István's stomach. "You've done well to elude me thus far. But tell me, what happened to your companion? There were three of you in Komárom."

Natália was incensed by the officer's fake familiarity. Overcome with fury, something inside her snapped. She hurled the ring at Viktor's face, screaming, "You killed him, you bastard."

The ring smacked into Viktor's right eye, momentarily throwing him off balance. István seized the opportunity and launched himself at Viktor's left side, hoping to sidestep the weapon. The gun fired as the two men crashed to the ground, Viktor's right shoulder connected with the hard earth with the full weight of his attacker pinning him to the ground. He howled in agony. Unable to withstand a second forceful blow, his collarbone audibly cracked. Natália instinctively staggered backwards as the scuffle unfolded before her, seemingly in slow motion. She saw Viktor drop the gun when he fell backwards onto the wet grass and grabbed her chance. Groping between the two pair of legs, she managed to pick up the gun and hurriedly stepped away from the men, shouting, "Stop! I have the gun."

István rolled off Viktor and ran to Natália's side, not realising that his left trouser leg was soaked in blood. Natália tried standing as still as a statue, despite being terrified, the gun pointed at Viktor's chest. Viktor almost blacked out from the pain that seared through his shoulder when István tackled him to the ground, yet he had the presence of mind to remind them of his rank and the consequences of harming a senior officer. He tried to stand, but the pain shot up into his skull. Gritting his teeth to suppress the agony, he attempted to reason with Natália as she approached him, gun raised, now shaking with rage, but careful to keep a safe distance.

"Don't be foolish. You will be hunted and killed if you shoot me. Put the weapon down so we can discuss this."

Natália felt truly empowered and in control of her destiny. Maintaining her stance, she replied, "There's nothing to discuss. You're a murderer of innocent civilians and would have killed us in a heartbeat—not that I believe you have a heart. You said yourself that we're close to the border. We'll be long gone by the time your comrades find you."

Steadying her hand with an inner strength that flooded every extremity of her being she whispered, "For János."

The gunshot echoed through the trees, scattering another flock of birds in all directions. Natália felt detached from herself and her surroundings. She gazed blankly at the monster lying on the ground, his lifeless eyes staring up at her, a gaping hole in his chest oozing blood. István rushed over, wrapped his arms around her trembling frame, then carefully removed the gun from her now limp hand as she slumped into his arms. Realising that she had fainted, István lay her carefully on the ground, lightly slapping her face to bring her around, cognisant of the urgency to flee. Gradually, her eyelids fluttered open, and she peered into István's concerned face and cried.

"It's over, love. We're safe now," István said reassuringly as he stroked her face and kissed her forehead. "But we need to get out of here before anyone turns up to investigate the shooting."

Natália remained motionless, still in shock at what had just transpired. Allowing her a few moments to recover, István scrambled on all fours to

Viktor's lifeless form, searching for the ruby heirloom. The sparkling gem was easily spotted amongst the wet grass. He picked it up, wiped it on his coat, then presented it to his wife with tears in his eyes and said, "You saved our lives, Natália. With this ring, you saved our lives." István slipped the ring on her finger, hugged her tightly, and whispered, "I don't know what I'd do without you."

He stood, turned back to Natália, and asked, "By the way, when did you learn to fire a gun?"

"I didn't," she replied sheepishly, still shaken from the experience, but overwhelmed with relief that they were still alive and gratified that she had avenged János.

They picked up their satchels from the snowy ground, and István carefully tucked the gun into the waistband of his trousers just in case it was needed again. It was then that he noticed his left trouser leg was drenched in blood, the fabric plastered to his calf. The dull pain that was in the deep recesses of his mind finally surfaced. Sitting back on the ground he gingerly lifted the fabric up to his knee. Blood covered his calf and soaked the top of his sock. Natália looked over at him, wondering why he was still sitting on the ground, his face as white as a sheet. Then she saw the blood. Sucking in her breath at the sight she was again thrown into action. With the water flask in hand, she pulled her handkerchief from her coat pocket, then rushed over to check the damage. As she poured water on István's leg, carefully wiping away the blood, the wound revealed itself.

"I heard the gun go off when you lunged at him but didn't realise you were shot," panic rose in her voice.

"Neither did I. I was too intent on tackling him to the ground. How bad is it?"

"It looks like a graze. There's no entry or exit holes that I can see. There's a small piece of flesh missing, which I think is the cause of so much blood. I don't think it's too serious. Wait here while I fetch a bandage."

Without glancing at the dead officer's face, Natália unbuttoned his coat, lifted the pristine white shirt out from inside his trousers, then tore a long strip from the shirt. Satisfied that it was long enough, she ran back to István, poured more water over the wound, then carefully bandaged his leg.

"That will have to do for now. How does it feel? Can you walk?"

"I have no choice, do I?" István stood, picked up his satchel, took a few steps and said, "It's not too bad, actually. Come on, not far to go now. Let's pray we don't encounter any other officers. I don't think I can handle another altercation."

"We've survived every obstacle so far," Natália said, twirling the ruby ring with her fingers. She looped her arm through István's, offering support. They walked off together towards the stand of trees to shield them from prying eyes, heading in the direction of Hansaghof.

Once they were well away from the corpse, István stopped, faced Natália and said, "You're a complete enigma, Natália. You never cease to amaze me."

Natália just smiled, kissed István on the cheek and said, "Come on, husband, we're almost there."

EPILOGUE

Sleet struck their faces like tiny pin pricks as they trudged onwards, as fast as their legs could carry them. Strong winds further hampered their progress, pushing them back in the direction they had come from. It took all their combined strength to cut through the force of nature that seemed to conspire against them in their quest to reach safety. Was this punishment for the murderous act Natália had committed? But then the image of János lying dead in the forest with no one to bury him surely absolved her of her sin. The officer was evil, and God would forgive her.

Heads bent forward to shield their eyes from the stinging wind and icy rain, Natália prayed that they were heading in the right direction. Desperate to place as much distance between themselves and the dead officer before they were seen by anyone they took off as soon as István's leg was bandaged. Natália linked her arm through István's, providing support to her injured husband. He pretended the pain was not as severe as it truly was, but Natália knew better. His pace gradually slowed and his weight was heavy on her shoulder. The faint outline of a stand of trees loomed ahead. Natália's spirits lifted at the sight of the sanctuary. Soaked through to the skin, Natália and István made their way to the nearest oak tree, grateful for a reprieve from the wild weather. Huddled together under the massive canopy, they rested, István's leg throbbing from exertion. There was no point examining the wound. No further bandages were at hand to change the dressing. Rummaging through her satchel, Natália pulled out the remnants of the provisions that Markos had given them earlier in the day.

Food would provide much needed energy to continue fighting the elements until they reached safety. Opening the hamper, Natália's heart sank when she found the bread had become a soggy mess that disintegrated in her hands. The cheese and sausage had fared better. Munching slowly to savour every bite, they hoped the storm would wane before they needed to leave their sanctuary, aware that they couldn't linger too long given István's need of medical attention.

"Shush," Natália raised her hand to stop István speaking. "Did you hear that?" she whispered.

"What? I can't hear anything."

"Shush!"

The braying of a donkey somewhere in the distance floated on the wind, alerting Natália to civilisation nearby. She stood and peered out between the huge branches, focussing on the direction of the sound. A small greyish-brown barn appeared through the haze of rain, about half a kilometre from where they sheltered. Thrilled to have stumbled on a structure that could better protect them until the storm passed, they hastily collected their satchels, propped each other up, and limped over to it as quickly as they could. As they approached, an old man was coaxing the stubborn donkey into the barn, with little success. István grasped the situation, waved at the farmer, hobbled over, and helped by pushing the animal from behind while the man pulled the donkey by its bridle. Natália ran ahead with their satchels and plonked herself down onto the welcoming carpet of straw, away from the door. Once they were all safely inside, the man thanked István. For an instant, István just stared at the stranger, uncomprehending. Then a wave of elation swept over him when he realised it was not Hungarian but German that was spoken. Forgetting his pain, he laughed out loud, gave the old man a fierce bear hug, released the confused farmer, and turned to Natália, who was watching the spectacle with amusement. István was grinning from ear to ear, tears welling up in his eyes as he said, "He's speaking German, Natália. Do you know what that means?"

Natália clapped her hands over her mouth and squealed with joy with the realisation that their journey was at an end. The kindly old man stood patiently observing the couple, then asked what the joke was about. Natália, who had learnt basic German in her early school days managed to cobble together a few words to let the man know that they were Hungarian and in need of help to reach the nearest town. He smiled warmly at Natália, patted her wet cheek in understanding, and replied in faulting Hungarian that he would help them onto Andau once the storm abated. In the meantime, he disappeared out the door, indicating that they should stay in the barn until he returned. István collapsed beside Natália, tears of sheer joy and relief streaming down their faces with the realisation that they had successfully crossed into Austria.

Hunching over István's wounded leg, Natália unwrapped the bandage and frowned intently at the redness that had spread down his calf, when the farmer returned, his wife in tow. The older couple had brought towels and a small urn which, when the lid was lifted, filled the enclosure with the most welcome aroma, a piping hot vegetable soup with parsley dumplings. Everyone chuckled as István's stomach grumbled loudly. He licked his lips in anticipation of a much-needed hot meal. Natália thanked the couple for their generosity and kindness, then beckoned the farmer's wife to look at István's wound. Peering down at the inflamed gash she shook her head from side to side, looked up into Natália's concerned eyes, smiled encouragingly, then with hand gestures and some German words that Natália only partly grasped tried to explain that it was not fatal. Muttering something unintelligible she turned and spoke to her husband then disappeared outside. The farmer handed a towel to each of them, miming how they should dry themselves, then followed his wife back to the homestead. Natália wiped as much of the water off István's face as she could before tending to herself. She then ladled the soup into the two bowls that accompanied the urn, passed one to István, and sipped her soup tentatively so as not to burn her mouth. They both sighed contentedly as the warm liquid slipped down their throats, spreading a welcome heat that permeated all the way to their freezing fingers and toes.

The Austrians soon returned with a first aid kit in hand. The woman smiled cheerily, nodding with satisfaction when she saw the urn was nearly empty and the dumplings were all gone. Then, with the precision of an army nurse, she plonked herself down in front of István, cleaned his calf and applied an antiseptic that stung like hell. István clenched his jaw to stifle a scream as she deftly bandaged the leg with clean gauze. Standing back to admire her handiwork she said something to Natália, which the younger woman guessed meant that her husband would be fine, and that the wound was nothing to worry about.

***

The Red Cross had erected refugee shelters in several of the towns close to the Hungarian border. Thousands of people escaped into Austria after the failed revolution. István and Natália were but another two poor souls in need of help. The team at Andau were very efficient, but not without sympathy, when they spotted the dishevelled pair walk into their office, István with a slight limp. After a brief interview, he was taken to the medical clinic to have his leg examined. Whilst the bullet that tore a small piece of flesh from his calf had caused only a superficial injury, the wound looked angry and needed attention.

Unlike Natália, who could understand a little German, István was quite baffled by the language. A grey-haired, overweight, unsmiling matron entered the cubicle where István had been patiently waiting for twenty minutes. Without a word, she cleaned and redressed his leg, mumbled something incomprehensible to him, then proceeded to physically roll her patient over on the examination table, until he was face down. Before he had a chance to protest at her rough handling, she jabbed him with a huge syringe filled with penicillin. István yelped so loudly that the scream reverberated throughout the waiting room where Natália had been told to wait. She ran into the cubicle, terrified as to what might have caused him to scream out in pain, but laughed hysterically when she saw her husband rubbing his bare bottom.

"I don't know which hurts more, my leg or my bum. I'm sure there'll be a permanent hole where that needle punctured me," he complained, frowning at the matron, who just sniffed audibly before marching out of the room.

Temporary lodgings and warm clothing were arranged by the Red Cross staff while the couple completed forms and considered where they planned to emigrate. It was a lengthy process, reading through documents and learning about the countries that agreed to accept the fleeing Hungarians. Natália was in no hurry to travel anywhere. István's injury needed to heal before they embarked on another journey to their chosen destination. Convalescing in Austria for a while was a welcome respite from the weeks of fear, terror, and calamities they had encountered in their quest for freedom. Not to mention the image of the murdered police officer that still haunted Natália's dreams.

The couple remained in Andau for three days before being moved to a larger centre in Graz, where they were told final arrangements would be organised for their emigration. István pored over the many documents and brochures that were provided to assist in their decision about which of the allied countries would become their new home. Whilst Switzerland, Austria and France were all sophisticated countries that offered employment and citizenship, they seemed far too close to the Eastern Bloc Communists. István wanted to leave Europe altogether, to get as far away from communism as possible. America and Canada provided the distance he sought, but the job opportunities did not appeal to him. The final brochure was on a little-known country, Australia. An English-speaking nation which would pose challenges at first, until they grasped the language, yet there was the prospect of work at a steel-making factory, for one of the biggest companies in the country. Australia offered distance from their homeland, a democratic government, and the right type of employment for István's experience. After much consultation, Natália voiced no objections to István's decision in choosing Australia. No matter where they settled, Natália knew she would never see her family again, and was resigned to put the past behind her and to think only of the future: a future where she and her beloved husband could raise their family with the freedoms and opportunities they had sacrificed so much to attain.

Although the decision was made, there was still a process to be followed before the couple was provided with the appropriate visas and travel documents to embark on their journey to their chosen country. As the weeks passed, István became stronger, until his leg was fully healed. He managed to secure odd jobs in the town, and the wages, whilst modest, paid for the lodgings, with a little saved for their impending journey.

One evening, István returned from a hard day labouring in the timber mill to find that Natália had prepared a simple meal of pork sausages and sauerkraut. She sat pensively, watching him devour his meal, filled with trepidation at the news she needed to share. Clearing the plates from the table, she busied herself with the washing up, then took a deep breath before remarking casually, "We may need to use some of our savings once we arrive in Australia. To buy a basinet and some baby clothes."

Natália turned from the sink to face István, anxious to see his reaction. He just gawked at her, wide eyed, before replying, "Baby clothes? You're pregnant? We're having a baby?"

Natália just smiled, then nodded, the tears stinging her eyes. István jumped up from his chair, knocking it over, and hugged Natália so tightly she could hardly breath. He kissed her lips, her cheeks, her eyes, and her neck, then exclaimed over and over, "We're having a baby!" They both laughed with excitement and joy, the thought of bringing a new life into their new country was overwhelming.

"Our child will be born free, in our new homeland."

***

Little Katalin, a healthy baby girl, was born just two months after her parents set foot on Australian soil.

***

Minor skirmishes persisted across Hungary despite Soviet domination. A ceasefire was eventually declared on November 10, 1956. It is estimated that two and a half thousand Hungarians and seven hundred and twenty Soviet troops were killed during the revolution. Thousands more were wounded. Fear of reprisals resulted in a mass exodus of the citizenry, with approximately two hundred thousand Hungarians fleeing to the West. Thousands of people were arrested and imprisoned, with some being deported to Russia. Citizens felt cheated by the false promise of a Soviet withdrawal from Hungary. There was continued frustration and unrest after the failed revolution, sparking intermittent armed resistance and strikes by the workers' councils, which continued until mid-1957, causing severe disruption to the economy.

The Kádár government arrested and tried twenty-six thousand people for insurrection, imprisoning at least half of them, with an estimated 350 executed. Russia heightened its presence in Hungary with additional troops, quashing notions of further conflict. Hungarians reluctantly accepted defeat, and the ongoing presence of their oppressor.

During the height of the revolution, pleas for assistance from Western democratic allies were dashed. Rhetoric failed to convert into meaningful actions to help the revolutionaries expel the Communist tyrants. However, in early 1957, the United Nations General Assembly requested a thorough investigation into the Soviet occupation of Hungary. Over a five-month period, hundreds of refugees, and other Hungarians from a multitude of backgrounds—including ex-military, former government officials, students, writers, factory workers, and teachers—were interviewed by a special committee. Other archival evidence was also reviewed, such as newspaper articles, photos, film footage, radio transcripts, and a variety of other documents and testimonials. Neither the Hungarian nor the Soviet governments cooperated with the committee, failing to respond to requests for information. The report, entitled 'Special Committee on the Problem of Hungary' was presented to the General Assembly in June 1957. Despite the damming findings that the Kádár Government and Soviet occupation contravened the human rights of the Hungarian people, and the General Assembly's resolution condemning the repression of the Hungarian people and Soviet occupation, no action was taken to seek justice.

By 1963, most political prisoners from the 1956 revolution had been released. Whilst life under the Communist regime continued in Hungary for over three decades, the brutality of the secret police was curtailed. Cultural and economic reforms through decentralisation were introduced, largely to replace the inefficiencies of central planning. This allowed Hungarian manufacturers to introduce new technologies, improve product quality, focus on profitability, create new markets, and become a serious contributor to the international economy. This helped to bring about a seismic shift in foreign affairs, that was not without challenges, notwithstanding the mounting foreign debt.

Hungary's evolution to a Western-style democracy was one of the smoothest among the former Soviet eastern bloc countries. In 1988, further calls for reform, by both intellectuals and party officials, resulted in a change of leadership. Kádár was replaced by Imre Pozsgay, a Communist who was instrumental in furthering Hungary's thirst for democracy. The following year, parliament adopted the 'Democracy Package', which included freedom of association, freedom of the press, a new electoral law, and significant revisions to the constitution—reforms the failed revolutionaries of 1956 had demanded. The Hungarian Socialist Party adopted close to one hundred constitutional amendments, allowing multi-party parliamentary elections and direct presidential elections. The legislation was transformative, guaranteeing human and civil rights and a structure that ensured separation of powers among the judicial, legislative, and executive branches of government. The Republic of Hungary was declared on the 23rd of October 1989—the thirty-third anniversary of the revolution. The date remains a Hungarian national holiday.

The first free parliamentary election was held in May 1990. Between March 1990 and June 1991, Soviet troops evacuated Hungary. During a speech to the Hungarian Parliament in 1992, the Russian President, Boris Yeltsin, apologised for the Soviet actions in Hungary during 1956.

ACKNOWLEDGEMENTS

The bones of this story depict the events of my parents' life during the rise of anti-Communist activity in Hungary in the late 1950's, and their subsequent quest for freedom. If not for my mother's tenacity, courage, and love for my father, Fülöp, my parents would not have survived their struggle to flee Hungary after the failed revolution of 1956, and I would not exist. I would like to thank my mother for her generosity of spirit. Unlike so many others who have experienced severe hardship and war, my mother willingly delved into her painful past to share the memories of her youth and encouraged me to pursue this project.

This novel would not have been possible without the love, support, and valued council of my life-long partner and dear husband, Dr Allan O'Connor. Allan provided invaluable advice on the plot, style, and form of the manuscript. My dear friend and historical fiction aficionado, Kerry Hudson provided insight into the characters, timelines, and inconsistencies of plot that significantly shaped and improved the story, for which I am extremely grateful.

Whilst this is a work of fiction, I researched this period of Hungarian history extensively and endeavoured to ensure the accuracy of events leading to the revolution and its aftermath.

ABOUT THE AUTHOR

Suzi O'Connor was born in Wollongong on the south coast of New South Wales to immigrant parents who fled Hungary after the failed revolution of 1956. This is Suzi's debut novel, a work inspired by her mother, Katalin, and her deceased father, Fülöp. She lives with her husband, Allan, in Adelaide, South Australia.

For more information visit:
Australianauthors.store/TheAncestralRingofHope

Lightning Source UK Ltd.
Milton Keynes UK
UKHW010642090223
416681UK00006B/1459